Life on the Naughty List
or What the Elf!
Jason Wrench

Pink Sloth Books

Copyright © 2024 by Jason Wrench

All rights reserved.

No portion of this book may be reproduced in any form without written permission from the publisher or author, except as permitted by U.S. copyright law.

Cover Art by GetCovers.com

Interior text design by Jason Wrench using Atticus

Published by Pink Sloth Books (https://www.pinkslothbooks.com)

Proofreader: Jen Speck (https://www.fiverr.com/jenspeck)

This is a work of fiction. All characters, places, and events are from the author's imagination and should not be confused with fact. Any resemblance to persons, living or dead, events or places is purely coincidental.

All rights reserved. No part of this publication may be reproduced in any material form, whether by printing, photocopying, scanning, or otherwise without the written permission of the publisher, Pink Sloth Books.

Applications should be addressed in the first instance, in writing, to Pink Sloth Books. Unauthorized or restricted acts in relation to this publication may result in civil proceedings and/or criminal prosecution.

The author/illustrator have asserted their respective rights under the Copyright Designs and Patents Acts 1988 (as amended) to be identified as the author of this book and illustrator of the artwork.

No part of this book may be reproduced, scanned, or distributed in any printed or electronic form without permission. Please do not participate in or encourage piracy of copyrighted materials in violation of the authors' rights. Purchase only authorized copies.

Contents

Acknowledgments	V
Dedication	VI
Prologue	1
1. Chapter 1	7
2. Chapter 2	13
3. Chapter 3	18
4. Chapter 4	25
5. Chapter 5	31
6. Chapter 6	41
7. Chapter 7	49
8. Chapter 8	65
9. Chapter 9	79
10. Chapter 10	85
11. Chapter 11	94
12. Chapter 12	102
13. Chapter 13	110
14. Chapter 14	117
15. Chapter 15	133
16. Chapter 16	138
17. Chapter 17	147
18. Chapter 18	170

19. Chapter 19	179
20. Chapter 20	192
21. Chapter 21	200
22. Chapter 22	210
23. Chapter 23	217
24. Chapter 24	238
25. Chapter 25	250
26. Chapter 26	256
27. Chapter 27	262
28. Chapter 28	275
29. Chapter 29	282
30. Chapter 30	288
Drama Bill	298
Trademarks Acknowledgment	304
About the author	309

Acknowledgments

This work contains several references to specific artistic texts. The following are sources that were used in this story that fall into the public domain:

The Faith Healer by William Vaughn Moody © 1910

"My mistress' eyes are nothing like the sun (Sonnet 130)" by William Shakespeare © 1609

12 Days of Christmas by Frederic Austin © 1909

The Hallow Men by T. S. Eliot © 1925

Beyond Tomorrow by Adele Comandini (1940) The movie's copyright was not renewed and has fallen into the public domain.

Dedication

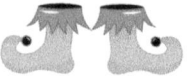

First, I want to dedicate this book to the people who get through National Novel Writing Month every November. I want to give a special shoutout to the municipal liaisons for my area, Jessica, Rebecca, and Tracy.

Second, I want to thank my writing tribe at Ninja Writers. I want to give a special shoutout to my Ninja Writer mentors, Adrienne, Deb, Juneta, Meg, Shaunta, and Zach. My writing friends give me constant feedback and encouragement all year long.

Last, I dedicate this book to all the amazing Broadway actors, producers, and backstage workers who show up every year at BroadwayCon to tell us outsiders the inside scoop of what it's like to work on the Great White Way. This book is heavily influenced by everything I've learned from them.

Prologue

Standing in the wings, I watched as the musical wound down. The last song was a quiet, almost funeral dirge with haunting orchestrations. The song ended as the cast said the last lines of the new musical based on William Vaughn Moody's play, *The Faith Healer*.

"By faith, which makes all things possible, which brings all things to pass," Michaelis said.

"Serafina," I said, leaning down into the stage manager's ear, "Isn't Bobby supposed to be on stage left right now?"

"Thanks, Erika," Serafina whispered back to me. She flipped through the giant binder containing every call for the entire show. The stage manager's prompt book was as sacred to a Broadway show as the NIV Bible to evangelicals. She found the sheet she was looking for before switching audio channels on her console and saying, "What the hell is Bobby Kenner doing on stage right? He's supposed to enter from left center stage. He has less than twenty seconds to get his ass over here."

"Come here—My baby!" said the young mother on stage.

Serafina switched channels and said in a calm, cool, and collected voice, "792...go." Serafina threw switches on the audio deck in the jump booth.

"I believe—I believe—" as the lighting on the young girl and mother dimmed.

A single spotlight shone on Rhoda, the last character on the stage, "I believe. I do believe!"

"Lights 793...go," Serafina said. The spotlight on Rhoda dimmed out completely. "Warning, lights 794 to 801 standby." I looked at the stage and waited for my personal favorite lighting moment of the show. "And...go." Several lights turned all at once causing an eerie shadowing effect that was both beautiful and haunting.

Bobby Kenner somehow made it stage left as the final light dimmed. He bent over, panting after his fast run to this side of the stage.

"Where's your head, boy?" Serafina hissed at Bobby.

"Sorry, Ms. Porcher. Won't happen again, Ms. Porcher."

"And Erika." My head swung toward Serafina. "Never interrupt someone in the jump booth." She turned and said, "Lights 802...go." She turned back to look at me, "I can multitask because I've done this forever, but *never* interrupt someone calling the show."

I knew better. *What a rookie mistake.* I nodded and mouthed, "*I'm sorry*," but I doubt she saw it.

"Lights 803...go."

The music swelled as the final lights dimmed on stage. One last spotlight from beneath the stage illuminated Michaelis.

"Rail, stand by to bring in the Main Curtain."

Michaelis lifted his hands toward the heavens as he was lowered under the stage.

"Rail...go." How Serafina called cues and kept the show running was a marvel. "Places for curtain. Places for curtain."

The backstage area was almost pitch black except for the handful of blue running lights and glow-in-the-dark tape that marked the stage to keep people out of the path of others entering and exiting. Someone squeezed in behind me before wrapping his arms around me. There was a gentle kiss at the bottom of my neck.

"You were amazing," Asher said in a low whisper.

"I may have been amazing, but you became a star tonight."

My boyfriend, Asher Fraser Alexander, played Michaelis, a con-man faith healer. We'd been working actors for years, trying to get parts in Off-Broadway and Broadway productions. We'd even gone on separate touring casts. I did my time in *Wicked* belting "Defying Gravity" while he raised the house as a Mormon missionary belting "I Believe." After a few years of pounding the pavement as Broadway babies, we finally found ourselves cast in a brand-new Broadway musical...together.

"Lights 813…go. Fly curtain…go" There was a pause as we watched the curtain rise. "Standby Chorus…go"

The chorus ran onto the stage from either side, clasped hands and took their well-earned bows. Over the next 45 seconds, the cast entered the stage and bowed as the audience roared their applause.

"Standby Mary and Matthew." Immediately an assistant stage manager tapped me on the shoulder letting me know it was time to walk on stage. "Go."

I walked onto the stage and stared at my onstage husband. I could only imagine how large my smile was. I had opened a show on Broadway. My mind raced with thousands of thoughts. I couldn't believe this was finally happening. I walked to the middle of the stage and grabbed my "husband's" hand, and we walked downstage center and bowed together. Then I applauded as he bowed, then he applauded while I bowed.

After our bows, there was a swelling of the music as the entire cast turned and extended our hands toward the backstage where Asher stood. He was radiant. I'd never seen him happier or more in his element than at that moment. He walked to the front of the stage and took a giant, dramatic bow. The place erupted. He bowed again.

Asher reached out to me and clasped my hand before clasping my "husband's" hand and led the entire company in a bow. Then he gestured to the orchestra, and we all applauded. We then took five steps backward as the creative team walked on stage. We all continued clapping.

"Take it in, Erika. Take it all in," Asher said into my ear over the audience's roar. "We're never going to have an experience like this one again. You only get one first Broadway opening of a new musical."

He was right. Sure, we'd both opened a ton of shows over the years, but this one was special. Over the next few minutes, we listened to polite speeches from the creative team, who talked about the work, how important the source material was, and how it was still relevant, given our society's political climate.

After each speech, we applauded politely. After the producer finished his speech, we took one final bow as a cast, and the orchestra began playing again as the curtain descended. When the last tassel of the curtain hit the stage, everyone started screaming, shouting, hugging, and clapping each other on the back. The backstage excitement was amazing. I couldn't believe my luck.

After a few minutes, we all made our way back to our dressing rooms. I had a small dressing room all to myself. The first time I had seen my name on the door, I had squealed in excitement. Sure, my dressing room was four floors up from the stage, but that's Broadway. People often have no idea how things work backstage. And if we do our jobs right on stage, the audience will never worry about how many steps I must climb during each show. My calves were getting a workout.

I showered quickly. I pulled out my garment bag, revealing the floor-length satin dress with empire waist and A-line silhouette. It was minimalist in design but with some light beading around the chest, just enough to make it sparkle without being intrusive.

There was a knock on my door.

"Getting dressed," I said.

"I'll meet you out front," Asher said through the door.

"Give me five…make that ten minutes."

There was another knock, and Marilyn, my dresser, and Katie, my makeup slash hair artist, came into the dressing room. Katie had me sit down as she quickly did my makeup, then put my hair in knotted faux mohawk updo. Katie transformed me from average-looking to centerfold in minutes.

When my hair and makeup were ready to go, Marilyn helped me into the dress and zipped up the back. She then held out the jewels I would wear that evening. I had a diamond necklace and teardrop diamond earrings for the occasion. A jeweler had loaned me the jewels. I grabbed my black fake-mink shawl and wrapped it over my naked shoulders when I was fully dressed. I looked like a Hollywood actress from yesteryear.

"You two are amazing," I said. "See you at the party?"

"Not me," Marilyn said. "I've been here too long today. My feet are killing me. Going to go home, have tea, and go to sleep."

"You'll see me there," Katie said excitedly. "This is my first big opening, so I wouldn't miss it for the world."

"Trust me, girly," Marilyn said. "Once you've done this a few dozen times, the parties aren't nearly as exciting. I hope the reviews are good, so we stay open for a decent run."

"From your lips to God's ears," I said with a wink.

"Go," Marilyn said with a slight smile. "Have fun tonight. You've both earned it." Marilyn looked around the cluttered dressing room. It looked like a tornado had come through since the show ended. I had been in such a hurry to get out of costume, showered, and redressed I hadn't taken the time to put anything away. "Don't worry, Erika. I'll clean up after you're gone."

"Are you sure?" I asked. I hated the idea of leaving Marilyn alone in my mess. I never wanted to be one of those stars that expected the world to clean up after her.

"This one time," Marilyn said, the corner of her mouth curved up. "Just don't do it again."

I reached out and hugged the woman, who then opened the door and waved her hand in a shooing motion. I stepped out into the hall before carefully going back downstairs. The shoes I wore during the show had a heel, but it was a sturdy, wide heel that made it pretty easy to go up and down the stairs. The six-inch heels I was wearing right now made climbing down the stairs a safety hazard. I gripped the rail and took each step one at a time.

When I finally got down to the stage level, I heard voices from the stage. I was going to ignore them until I recognized Asher's voice. I wormed my way in between the backstage cables to the edge of the set. The crew had already reset the stage to Act One for tomorrow's matinee. *Smart move*, I thought to myself.

Only the faint glow of the ghost light on stage shone, casting most of the house and stage in darkness. I followed the glow-in-the-dark tape on the floor to the door entrance I used at the top of Act One. I opened the door. In the dim shine of the ghost light, Asher was kissing our castmate, Zachary Magnus. I gasped. My hand flew to my mouth.

Asher and Zachary's heads whipped in my direction. In the low lighting, Zachary looked like a deer caught in headlights. Asher's face was calm and collected. "Erika...let me—"

I didn't wait for him to finish. I turned around, closing the fake door behind me. *Fake! Everything in my life is fake!* I had to get out of there. I started moving across the stage, the glowing floor tape passed by wholly ignored. And I fell right through the trapdoor where Michaelis was lowered at the show's end.

I screamed and it echoed around the stage. *Jamie Lee would be impressed with my vocal cords*, I thought as I plummeted into darkness.

I landed and heard a large snapping sound, almost like a tree limb falling off a tree during a winter storm. The pain hit me in waves as I let out another sound that was more caged animal than human.

"Erika!" Asher yelled. A bright shined down on me from a cell phone above. In the phone's glow, Asher and Zachary's faces filled the opening above me.

"I'm calling 911," Zachary said, panic seeping through his voice.

"Asher Fraser Alexander!" I yelled and proceeded to let out a string of obscenities that would make the most hardened sailor blush...before I passed out.

Chapter 1

Three Years Later

I lifted my head and pulled the hardback book off my face when the sound of my cell phone chirped on the end table next to me on the couch. I reached for the phone, turned it over, and looked at the screen. *Brice. Great, my agent's calling.*

"Good afternoon, Brice," I groused into the phone.

"Erika," he said, almost too chipperly into my ear. "How's my favorite client?"

"I don't know. How is Audra doing? Are we up to twenty Tonys or is it just fifteen these days?"

"Well, I have some good and bad news for you," Brice said, not taking my bait. Honestly, I was amazed he put up with me after all these years. I wasn't exactly his best, most profitable, or the most talented client. At one point, I was one of his shiniest new toys, and I had so much promise. Then one day, my world came crashing down around me. And by around me, I mean when I fell through the stage after seeing my boyfriend making out with another guy the night of the opening of my first and last show on Broadway.

That embarrassing little tumble and broken leg took me out of the show. By the time I healed, I'd already been replaced. My understudy, Darla Dabbraccio, won the Tony Award for Best Featured Actress in a Musical. Asher had been nominated, but thank God, the Tony Award voters hadn't given him a trophy. It was bad enough that my understudy had won. The Tony Awards had let *The Faith Healer's* producers substitute her name for the nomination since, technically, her name hadn't appeared above the marquee on the night the show had opened.

The most humiliating moment of my life was dragged back into the limelight as award show commentators debated whether Darla Dabbraccio deserved the nomination. The committee had hemmed and hawed, but industry insiders all agreed that the Tony Awards would let the producers do it. On the night of the award show, I was out of the city in Des Moines, Iowa, with my parents.

"Honey, it's not a big deal," my mother had said. "That award's as much yours as it is hers. I'm sure everyone knows it."

Oh, everyone knew it. The cast and crew had known Darla couldn't act her way out of a box, but that girl had mimicked me perfectly, which is why she was hired in the first place. Darla hadn't had an original idea on stage. I never wanted to see the show after the accident, but I had seen enough of her performance on YouTube to know she had even twitched her lip like I do when hitting a high note. She'd make a great impersonator for *Forbidden Broadway*. How the Tony Awards voters had given her a statue was still one of the universe's great mysteries.

"So, how is your cabaret act going?" Brice asked. From the way he said it, I knew what he thought about my cabaret act. I wasn't going to give him the satisfaction of taking the bait yet again.

I sat up on the couch. Slung my legs over the side and stood up as I went to the fridge to grab a water bottle. I know. I should be completely environmentally conscious and not use plastic bottles, but they were just easier. I screwed off the cap. My cat, Bootsy, a white short-haired Norwegian forest cat with black paws, weaved in and out of my legs. "What do you need, Bootsy?" I asked. He looked up at me and meowed, then trotted away.

"Erika…Erika, are you there? Are you listening to me?"

"Sorry, I'm here. Bootsy needed something." What's the point of having a furry overlord if you can't blame them when you need to? "What did you say?"

There was a sudden, audible sigh from the other end of the line. "I said, '*I caught some of your performance over the weekend.*'"

"You did? Why didn't you say 'hi' or come backstage?"

"I said I '*caught some of it,*' not I saw it live. You're blowing up on YouTube."

"What does that mean?"

"What am I going to do with you, Erika? You know you're hard to manage these days when you won't pay attention to your own social media presence."

"I pay attention to my social media presence," I responded. "I don't have one. See, I pay attention."

"And that, my dear Erika, is where you're wrong. Whether or not you want one, you have a social media presence."

Something about how he said the last phrase made me pause. "What do you mean, *whether or not I want one?*"

"Are you near your computer?"

"Not at the moment, but I can be."

"Get to it," Brice demanded. The tone in his voice took me back. I think we'd gone from the friendly banter phase of our afternoon conversation into the serious one.

I walked through the living room and into the guest bedroom. My computer sat atop an old-style rolltop desk I'd found when I'd gone antiquing upstate with a few of my girlfriends one weekend. I'd fallen in love with the piece and paid some local to cart the thing down to Manhattan, then hired some movers to haul it up to my apartment.

I sat down in my ergonomic chair and spun around to face the desk and monitor. I reached out, grabbed the mouse and slid it along the mouse pad to wake the computer up. While it woke, I put my cell phone down on the desk and hit the speaker. "I'm here," I said.

"Great. I just sent you an email."

I opened the email. The only thing in the email was a blue hyperlink, so I clicked on it. Immediately, a pirated video of me on stage at 54 Below from the previous weekend started playing. First, I looked good. I'd gone with a simple black cocktail dress and a pair of Manolo Blahnik's Hangisi Crystal Satin Pumps. Sure, the shoes cost me $1000, but they made my legs look fantastic. The video was a short montage of me singing some of my favorite songs. I looked good, and I sounded even better.

"What's wrong with this?" I asked. "I look amazing and sound better than ever."

"True…but wait till the end."

I kept watching. Right at the end there was a short video message. *"This video of the homophobic Erika Lynsay Saunders' man-hating cabaret act was shot last weekend. It's time to tell the cabaret spaces in New York not to book her. Join us in boycotting 54 Below."*

"What?" I gasped. "Why are they boycotting? I'm not homophobic. I thought we put that nonsense behind us?"

After I caught Asher, my ex, making out with one of our costars on opening night three years ago, I may have said a few things that I regretted later. But I was pissed. And I wasn't mad at him because of his sexual orientation. I was pissed that he made out with someone on the day our show opened. He knew how important our opening was to me...to us. I don't understand how he could think so little of me that he did that. Sure, several highly inappropriate words flew out of my mouth in the heat of the moment, but I'm not homophobic. Straight guys scared me more than any gay guys I knew. My agent is gay. My best friend is gay. I work in the gayest field imaginable. I love my gays. I, in that moment, hated Asher, so I may have called him a few choice words that he then released on the Internet while I was still laid up in the hospital. I found out about all that while I was on the mend when my gay nurse showed me the video.

"Gurl," the nurse had said, coming in one afternoon. "Your boyfriend must be pissed at you. He splayed your fight all over the Internet."

"He did what?" I had asked. Again, I'm not the most technically savvy person in the world.

"He uploaded that to YouTube."

That's right, fucking YouTube! So, here I was again, having another bout of YouTube problems because of Asher. I wasn't sure which I hated more at that moment, YouTube or Asher.

"So, what now?" I asked Brice. "Did 54 Below cancel the rest of my engagement?"

"Nope. I talked with them this morning, and they've seen a spike in tickets, so they're not planning on canceling this booking. Plus, they know you. They know you 'love the gays,' and the 'gays love you.'"

I belted my best Matron Mama Morton impersonation.

"Yes, yes, yes, go on with your bad self, *Chicago* girl. Oh wait, you turned down the role of Roxy in *Chicago* last year—"

"In Columbus, Ohio. I wasn't going to spend six weeks doing stock in Columbus. I'd rather work at Starbucks."

"If you don't get a job soon, you'll be working at Starbucks," Brice said. I could practically see him rolling his eyes as he leaned back. "How are you doing financially?"

"I'm fine. I'm pretty good with money, and living at the Manhattan Plaza helps keep my budget, despite my occasional splurge on something I shouldn't own."

"Trust me, girl. I noticed the shoes in the video," Brice said in one of his gayer moments.

"Don't hate the playa, hate the game."

"You're playing the game called poverty right now. I need you to get your head in the game and start playing the game of Broadway, *capisce*?"

"Since when are you doing a guest role on the remake of *The Sopranos*?" I asked. There was a long pause. I thought my quip was funny, but I could sense Brice's frustration through the phone. We'd had this exact conversation a dozen times over the past year. I wasn't ready to audition again. I wasn't sure if I would ever be prepared to audition again. After my last experience on Broadway, I didn't know if I'd ever be ready to take that dive into the lion's den.

I love Broadway. I love musical theater. I don't think a one-sided relationship is very healthy. And right now, Broadway was the bad boyfriend I couldn't shake. Every time I thought I'd gotten away and made a clean cut, something would happen, and I would get drawn into another audition, only to have my hopes and dreams dashed against the shore of the Hudson River.

"But really, Erika, I'm worried about you." I could tell from the change in his voice he had grown serious. "I'm going to have a problem keeping you on as a client. The senior partners keep asking why I'm keeping you on at this point."

I sighed. I knew this conversation was going to happen eventually. As much as I hated admitting it, I needed to get my act together already. "So, what do you have for me?"

"That's the spirit!"

Deep in my soul, I knew I would regret this, but I held my tongue.

"There's a new musical being mounted, and I got you an audition for later today."

"Today!" What was I going to sing? What would I wear? This was happening faster than I expected. I thought I'd at least have a few days.

Brice went on as if he hadn't heard my exclamation. "It's a musical adaptation of a movie from 1940 called *Beyond Tomorrow*."

"Never heard of it," I admitted.

"Most people probably haven't. The producers went with this property because it's considered a Christmas movie, even if it is only partially related to Christmas itself."

"Have you seen the movie?"

"Nope," Brice confessed. "I Wikipediaed what I know about it."

Great... My career hung in the balance of Wikipedia. What could go wrong? "What role am I auditioning for?"

"They wouldn't tell me. Everything right now is hush-hush." That didn't raise any red flags at all. "Everyone who is invited to audition is being asked to prepare a song, and beyond that, there's no other information provided."

"Okay. What time is my audition?"

"I have you in at 3:00 p.m. That should give you time to get yourself together."

I looked over at the clock, it was only eleven-thirty a.m., giving me a few hours to get my act together. "Where is the audition?"

"They're holding auditions at Actors' Equity. Just go on up to the sixteenth floor. You're already on the list." I'd had enough auditions at Actors' Equity over the years. I knew the routine, so I didn't bother jotting down the information. "Break a leg." As soon as he said it, I could almost see him wince on the other end of the line. "I mean figuratively, not literally. Oh geez, I think I'm talking too much."

"It's okay. I don't plan on falling through any trap doors again."

Chapter 2

After getting off the phone, I sat on my couch and made a list of everything I needed to do over the next couple of hours. Shower, pick my outfit, pick my audition song, and don't freak out. The first three were going to be easier than the last one. Thankfully, I knew who I needed to reach out to help with the last three.

I scrolled through my phonebook until I found the number I was looking for and hit the call button. There were three rings before I heard a groggy voice pick up.

"This had better be an emergency."

"It is… I have an audition."

As if he'd had a sudden jolt of coffee, my best friend Johnny immediately perked up. "When? Where? What for? What are you going to wear? How long do you have to prepare?" The rapid peppering of questions didn't leave me time to think, let alone answer any of them.

"Slow down there, tiger. As for the questions, today, Actor's Equity, new Christmas musical, I haven't a clue what I'm going to wear, and a couple of hours."

"That doesn't exactly leave us much time, then, does it?" I love how my audition suddenly became a problem for both of us. But then, that's why Johnny Braxton was my best friend. It also helped that he lived in the other tower, so he could be at my apartment as soon as he threw on some clothes.

"I'll be there in twenty."

"I'm not going anywhere. See you when you get here."

Johnny ended the phone call without saying goodbye. I honestly wasn't sure who was more excited about my audition, him or me.

Johnny Braxton was also in the business. At the ripe old age of 26, he was a veteran of a few Off-Broadway shows and had even made a Broadway debut as a replacement right before the show closed. Johnny had the perfect combination of a pop singer's voice and matinee idol good looks. Of course, I'm one of the few people who knows Johnny's real name is Steven Smith. When he had earned his Equity card, he knew his real name was way too generic, so he had created Johnny Braxton, and the man, the myth, and the legend was born...at least in his head.

Johnny had also been at the ill-fated night of *The Faith Healer* opening. I hadn't known Johnny, but he'd known Asher. Apparently, half of Broadway had *known* Asher. I was the only person who hadn't realized how much Asher had gotten around. I'd heard of love blinders before, but I had never experienced the phenomenon myself. In retrospect, there were so many red flags. I should have seen Asher's obvious deception and sleeping around, but I was in love and didn't want to see what was right in front of my face.

I pulled out a notepad and started jotting down some possible audition songs. Thankfully, my cabaret act provided me with an entire slate of possibilities. I wanted to have some ideas on paper before Johnny showed up and tried to take over my audition. He's a force of nature when he gets on a mission.

Three loud raps on my door caused me to jolt. I put the pad and pen down on the end table, walked through the apartment and opened the door.

"So, what do you have for me?" Johnny said, breezing by me and heading right into the living room.

"I made a list of audition songs. They're on the legal pad there," I said, motioning to the end table.

He picked up the list and started reading them out loud, "'I Hate Men' *Kiss Me Kate*, 'Forget About the Boy' *Thoroughly Modern Millie*, 'Gonna Wash That Man Right Out of My Hair' *South Pacific*, 'One Hundred Easy Ways (To Lose a Man)' *Wonderful Town*, 'Men! (Horrible Men!)' *Calamity Jane*, 'What Did I Ever See in Him?' *Bye, Bye Birdie*, 'Could I Leave You' *Follies*, 'Get Out and Stay Out' *9-5*...

Honey, are you trying to get the gig or are you trying to depress the creative team?"

"What?" I asked, narrowing my eyes. "These are the songs from my cabaret act."

"I should have known. I need to see the new show. But really, Erika? This is like a jilted woman's breakup playlist. Didn't you say this was a Christmas musical?" I nodded. "Then don't audition like you're gearing up for *Mack and Mabel*."

I hated to admit it, but he had a point. Ever since my breakup with Asher, I haven't exactly been the most jovial person. I sighed and asked the obvious question, "Then what do you recommend?"

"What was your go-to audition song before *the incident*?" He added extra emphasis by gesturing with air quotes.

I tilted my head and tried to think back to songs of auditions past. "'Not a Day Goes By' from *Merrily We Roll Along*."

"Nope. Too depressing."

"'Back to Before' from *Ragtime*."

"Honey, you're thirty-two, not fifty."

"'You Don't Know this Man' from *Parade*."

"Again, depressing," he drawled out the word to emphasize his dissatisfaction with my choices.

"'Woman' from *Pirate Queen*."

"Potential, but not necessarily a great audition piece. Didn't you sing 'My Most Beautiful Day' from *Tuck Everlasting* at a benefit once?"

"Yeah, but I'm not exactly twelve. I'm not the ingenue anymore, so not sure how appropriate that one is." We both sat there for a moment as we racked our brains. Finally, an idea popped into my head, "What about 'Fable' from *Light in the Piazza*?"

"Do you think you can pull it off? I mean, I'm not trying to be rude, but that's not exactly an easy piece."

"It was my go-to audition song when I first came to New York. I fell in love with *Light in the Piazza* when I was in high school. It was the first musical I saw in New York. Most of my classmates found the show boring, but the entire show transfixed me. Watching Victoria Clarke sing that song caused me fall in love with musical theater."

"I like it! And if the creative team asks you why you chose the song, you have a good story to tell."

With the audition song selected, we went into my bedroom, and Johnny rummaged through my closet until he'd put together the perfect audition ensemble. I had to agree with him. The outfit was chic and had a Christmasy element in the color combination.

"I don't want it to come right out and say, 'Deck the Halls,'" Johnny said, "but I think it has the air of Christmas without hitting you over the head with it."

I nodded in agreement. With the song and wardrobe choices out of the way, we made our way back into the living room. We sat back down on the couch. I tucked my legs under me and leaned back against the throw pillows as Bootsy jumped up and curled up in my lap.

"So, how are things with you and Amani?" I asked.

"We're still in the blissful state of love."

"You realize that's gag-worthy?"

"*Pshaw*! You wish you had what Amani and I have." As quickly as the words were out of his mouth, he blanched. "I'm so sorry. I didn't mean it like that. I can be such an insensitive buffoon."

"It's okay," I reassured him. "There's no need for self-flagellation. You're more right than you're not. I wish I had what you and Amani had. You're disgustingly cute."

"I know. I'm disgusted by our cuteness some days."

Amani Samara was a sous chef at the upscale restaurant called Evergreen Mirror. Amani had graduated from the Culinary Institute of America up in Hyde Park before moving to the city. He'd worked his way through the restaurant industry before landing the job at Evergreen Mirror. There was a three-month waitlist to get reservations. Thankfully, I had gone with Johnny a couple of times since Amani started working there, so I could attest to how excellent the food was.

"Honestly, I'm over being single. After three years of acting like a nun, I need to get myself back in the saddle and start dating again. I'm afraid I'm too rusty at this point."

"Well, get out the oil Tin Man, and let's loosen you up." A smile crept up Johnny's face. "Wow, that sounds dirtier than I intended it to sound."

"Please, I wouldn't expect anything less from you. I know how your mind works."

"That's a dangerous place to peer into. I almost feel like I should apologize."

"Apology accepted."

"As for dating, I may know someone who would be a wonderful date for someone needing to use training wheels."

"Oh really?" I questioned with a tilt of my head. "Do tell."

"His name is Ralph Seegers, and he's a publicist. And don't roll your eyes at me," Johnny said before I'd rolled them. "He's a good guy. I don't know much about him, but I've worked with him on a few projects."

"I'll think about it. But I'm not willing to commit yet."

"Okay. But as soon as you make up your mind, let me know and I'll get it arranged."

We spent the next twenty minutes talking about gossip from around the complex. By that time, it was almost 1:30, so I really needed to get into the shower and get moving if I was going to make the audition on time.

We said goodbye, then I headed off to get ready for my first major audition in almost three and a half years.

Chapter 3

I got out of the shower and immediately set about getting myself put together. I made sure my hair was pulled back and out of my face while still fashionable. I'd almost dyed it purple last week, so I was glad I hadn't made that decision. Not sure if the purple hair would go with the forest green turtleneck underneath a black knit sweater and cranberry-colored knee-length skirt. Johnny had convinced me that a hint of Christmas was good, but I didn't want to come right out and say *Santa's mistress*. I had black leggings underneath, then I slipped into a simple pair of four-inch pumps. They would be easy to walk in no matter what the weather and wouldn't detract from my outfit. The last thing I wanted was a casting agent to look at my shoes instead of me during an audition. Immediately, I heard the lyrics from Jason Robert Brown's song "Climbing Uphill" from *The Last Five Years* running through my head.

I touched up my makeup. I wanted to look put together and natural. I've seen some new girls in the business paint for the back row when they go on auditions, which is never a bright idea. Painting for the back row may look great from the mezzanine, but it makes you look like a clown in harsh fluorescent lighting to people sitting ten feet from you. I'd made that mistake on my first non-Equity audition. Thankfully, an older actor took me aside and was like, "Honey, no. You look like you're auditioning for the role of the clown in the revival of *Barnum*. Go wash your face. Just use a simple lip gloss. Nothing else." I must have looked affronted because he added, "You're clearly beautiful under all that paint, so don't hide under it."

I did as he said. In retrospect, he was unbelievably right. I ended up booking a job—a touring production of *Godspell*. After the audition, I wanted to thank him, but I never saw him again. In fact, I haven't seen my guardian angel at any audition ever. Of course, I'd end up with an old queen for a guardian angel. There's something entirely appropriate about that.

I looked at myself in my full-length mirror and did a twirl to make sure everything looked perfect. I put on my watch and no other jewelry. Again, the focus needed to be on me and not on what I'm wearing. I went into the living room and found Bootsy curled up on the couch. I made sure he had plenty of water and kibble—just in case he ate while I was out. He rarely did, but I always ensured it was there for him if he wanted it.

I grabbed my simple, black bag that held my audition music and a few other necessities before looking at myself one last time in the hallway mirror. *I look good. I'd hire me.* Of course, I didn't know what I was auditioning for, so I was ready for whatever the casting agents threw my way.

I grabbed my coat from the peg next to the front door. I opened the door and caught it with my foot while I put down my bag, slipped my jacket on and backed out into the hall.

"Watch it!" I said as I bumped into something.

"Sorry, didn't see you coming out of your apartment," a voice below me said.

I looked down. A young woman in a wheelchair smiled back at me. *Great, I just yelled at someone in a wheelchair.* "No, my bad," I immediately apologized. "I should have been watching where I was going."

"Maybe, but I was right in front of your door. You probably didn't get a chance to see me."

I looked at her and threw on my best actor smile. "No harm, no foul." I met the teenager's gaze and looked her over. She was beautiful. Flawless white skin, long raven-black hair, and a thin frame models would be jealous of.

"I'm Carissra," she said, extending her hand.

I hesitated for a moment. People in New York had never completely reverted to handshakes after the pandemic. We were all a bit cautious. But I looked at the girl and knew she wasn't trying to make me sick, so I extended my hand and said, "Erika." She shook my hand with a firm grip. "It's nice to meet you, Carissra. I haven't seen you around here before."

"No, you haven't. We're moving in next door."

I'd heard through the grapevine that my neighbor had bought a house over in Jersey, but I hadn't seen him move out. But then, I rarely saw him. He was in some late-night avant-garde circus troupe or something like that. I'd only run into him twice in the hall. For a neighbor, he'd been awesome. I never knew when he was there or away, which is precisely how I liked my neighbors. Don't get me wrong, I'm not anti-social, but the last thing I want is to hear everyone around me.

After my breakup with Asher, I'd moved out of our apartment and ended up in an apartment in Queens where the walls were paper thin. I could hear every conversation, every argument, every time someone got intimate. After the third time I'd been woken up in the middle of the night because the people above me were fighting and the people next to me were yelling at the people above us to shut up, I knew I had to get out of that place. I'd had a couple more apartments before getting lucky in the lottery and landing in the Manhattan Plaza.

The Manhattan Plaza or the Miracle on 43rd Street is a 46-story high-rise between 9th and 10th Avenues on 43rd Street. The building had opened in 1976 as Section 8 Housing, or low-income housing. The city had turned it into an apartment complex for people who worked in the performing arts. Actors, opera singers, musicians, comedians, ushers, stage managers, and anyone else who kept the entertainment business running qualified to live in the apartments. About 75 percent of the three thousand-plus people who live here are in the performing arts. And your rent adjusted as your income did. If you were in a smash Broadway show and making a ton of money, you'd pay full price. If your situation turned on a dime and your show closed, your rent was lowered.

"Are your parents in the business?" I asked casually.

"Huh?"

The girl looked at me, confused. The other 25 percent of the Manhattan Plaza residents consisted of the elderly and people in the community. From her reaction, I guessed she was in the community group.

"Well, it's been nice talking with you..." My mind drew a blank.

"Carissra."

"Sorry about that. I have an audition this afternoon and my mind is racing."

"Oh, you're an actor?"

"You'll find a lot of us around here. Most residents are in the entertainment industry in some form."

"Wow, I didn't know that."

"Didn't know what?" I heard a baritone voice behind me ask.

I spun my head and found a man in his mid to late thirties holding a couple of boxes in his arms. He had long brown hair that didn't go past his collar but was pushed back in a rocker look I'd seen gracing the pages of *Rolling Stone*.

"I asked if her parents were in the business," I said. He gave me the same clueless look she'd given me, so I added, "The entertainment business."

"Oh, no," he replied. "I'm an elementary school teacher over at Elias Howe."

I smiled and nodded. I had no idea what he was talking about. I knew there were schools in the city, but I didn't know where any of them were. I passed schools all the time walking around, but I didn't stop to pay attention to them.

"What do you teach?" I finally asked.

"I'm in special education. I primarily help students who have cognitive learning disabilities."

"Wow, hot and smart," I said. My hand flew up to my mouth when my brain processed what had flown out of my mouth.

His head bent slightly as a smirk grew across his face. "Thank you, I think."

"Wow, sometimes I can't control my mouth."

"Erika is an actor. She's heading to an audition, so her mind is in other places," Carissra said.

I smiled down at her, then back up at him, then back down at her.

"She's not my daughter. She's my niece," the man said, seeing the confusion as it etched across my face. "I became her legal guardian last year after..." He quickly glanced down at the wheelchair.

"After my parents died in a car accident that left me in this," Carissra said. She looked up at the man. "He still has a tough time talking about it. I was angry at first, but I was given this second chance to live life, even if it is from a metal chariot."

I grinned. I could tell from the look on her face that she was genuine, which is not something you see too often when you work around actors all the time.

"I'm Kirk, by the way," the guy said, extending his hand.

Again, with the handshakes. "I'm Erika," I said, extending my hand. He gripped it firmly but didn't hold it too tightly, like some guys do when trying to dominate your hand.

"Wait...Erika," he snapped his fingers a couple of times, and I could tell he was trying to remember my last name. "Erika Saunders."

"That's me...in the flesh."

"You know her?" Carissra asked.

"Yeah, I watched clips of her show on YouTube," Kirk admitted.

The hottie next door is gay. Figures. "And now I'm your neighbor. Are you a fan?"

He hesitated for a second before saying, "Not really. A friend posted a link to your video on Facebook."

"Oh really? I didn't know it was on social media."

"You've been memed and everything. You're like the poster child for women who hate men."

I took a sharp inhale.

"I'm sorry. I didn't mean to offend you. It's just...well, you know..."

"I don't really hate men. I promise I don't. I also don't hate gay people, despite my ex's rumors around town. Gays love me, so I'm sure you and I will get along great."

"Oh," he started, a confused look crossing his face. "I'm not gay."

"She thinks you're gay." Carissra shrieked with laughter. When she finally caught her breath, she said, "That's hysterical. Trust me,

Erika, he's pathetically straight. Me, I'm bisexual. I love everyone. Much easier that way."

"Well, now that I've firmly put my foot in my mouth, I really have an audition I need to get to." I turned and started walking toward the elevator. Figures, the first hot straight guy I have met in a long time, and I shove my foot right in my mouth.

"Hey, don't forget an umbrella," Kirk yelled after me.

"Got one in my bag," I said, turning around and motioning to my bag. "I was a Girl Scout. I'm always prepared."

I clicked the button and was greeted seconds later by the chiming sound as the elevator hit the floor and opened its doors. The ride to the lobby was smooth. And Kirk was right. The rain had started coming down. One joy of fall in New York City was how quickly the weather could go from summer to fall, back to summer, then to winter, all in twenty-four hours.

I slipped out of my heels and put on the tennis shoes in my bag. In the city, it's always essential to have a pair of tennis shoes in your bag because you don't want to walk around the city in heels when it's raining or snowing. Oh, and never wear open-toed sandals or heels on the streets. You'll have grime all over your toes at the end of the day. And you won't know what the grime came from. That's just nasty.

I nodded to the security guard before heading out into the rain. Fun fact about Manhattan Plaza: Samuel L. Jackson was a security guard there in the 1970s before he got his big break. I loved my apartment building because it had so much history.

Outside, I rummaged through my bag and opened my umbrella. Thankful that I always had one in the bag for just these occasions. I headed off to the Actors' Equity Building. From the Manhattan Plaza, it was maybe a ten-minute walk if the tourists weren't gawking and slowing down the sidewalks.

I crossed 9th and continued to walk down 43rd Street until I hit 7th. I stood waiting for the light to change. A few tourists were about, and one almost poked me in the eye with her umbrella. Dodging umbrellas when it was raining was a full-contact sport. I moved to the edge of the curb to get ahead of the mass of people. I was looking in the other direction when a bus turned the corner.

Suddenly, the wall of a hurricane hit me square in the chest, and I was drenched from head to toe. People behind me gasped as they watched it happen. I reached up and wiped the water from my face. I may have outwardly groaned, but the string of profanity that ran through my head would have made my mother in Iowa blush.

Chapter 4

I walked into Actors' Equity looking like a disheveled, soaked rat dragged up from the subway. I had stared at myself in the glass outside the building, so I wasn't fooling myself into thinking I looked great anymore. *Guess this is one way to get out of getting the part.* After going in, I searched for the ground-floor bathroom and did my best to make myself look at least somewhat presentable. My perfectly coiffed hair now hung limply next to my face, like the main character out of the *Grudge* movie franchise. My makeup, which had been perfect, now looked like rivers of red and black streaming down my face.

I grabbed a paper towel and wiped off any trace of makeup. Thankfully, I had lip gloss and a comb in my bag, which I pulled out. I let out an exasperated breath. I'd never re-zipped my bag after pulling out my umbrella. Everything inside was soaked. My shoes, my sheet music...I stood there in stunned silence. I didn't hear the bag as it dropped from my arms and hit the ground with a clatter as all the soggy contents scattered over the floor.

In the middle of the bathroom, I slid down right in front of the bathroom sink and cried. And I'm not talking about the single, controlled tear during an emotional scene type of crying. No, I'm talking about the full-on, uncontrolled waterworks of a madwoman. I reached into my coat pocket where my phone was and pulled it out. Thankfully, the coat had saved the phone because I sure wasn't in the position right now to buy another one...after I'd bought my new pair of expensive shoes last week. I called the only person I could think of. When a chipper voice sounded, I got out, "Mom," before I burst into another round of hysterics.

My mom let me get the latest round of crying out before she said, "Okay, dear, tell me everything." So, I did. I spent the next twenty minutes describing my mortification in every detail. "You're telling me you're sitting on a bathroom floor right now?"

"Uh-huh."

"And you have an audition you're supposed to be at?"

I glanced down at my watch. "I'm supposed to be there in like two minutes."

"Then pull yourself together and go to that audition."

"But, Mom..." As soon as the words were out of my mouth, I sounded like a petulant, whiny teenager. I might as well have thrown a stamping of my foot in for good measure.

"Erika Lynsay Saunders, your father and I did not raise a quitter. You pull yourself together and march right upstairs—"

"They have elevators—"

"Don't sass me, young woman."

"Yes, Mom," I said, feeling thoroughly chastised.

"Go!" The forcefulness in my mom's voice was exactly what I needed.

"Yes, Mom. Thanks, Mom."

"Any time, dear." She hung up the phone.

With the reinvigoration I needed from my mother, I grabbed my comb and drew it through my wet hair to at least make it look less like a bad Halloween wig right out of the bag and more Wednesday Addams-ish, albeit blonde.

I pushed myself off the floor and didn't bother looking in the mirror. If the casting team didn't like my new look, oh well. It's not like I wanted this job. I left the bathroom, walked over to the elevator bank and hit the button for the sixteenth floor. I rode in silence, putting my thoughts together. By the time I exited, I laughed and shook my head at its absurdity.

"Erika?" I heard a voice say.

One of my longest-running friends slash rivals in the business, Kathrine Kloeten, walked toward me. *Great, I so don't need this.*

"It is you," Katherine said with her genuine fake smile. "I wasn't sure at first. No one's seen you at auditions in ages."

"Was working on my cabaret act for a while, so I wasn't really auditioning very much."

"That's right, I saw the 'death to men' show a few weeks back."

"I don't remember seeing you there," I said, racking my brain to remember if I'd seen her in the audience.

"Oh, I didn't see it live." She smiled sweetly. "I saw it on YouTube."

"It's funny you should mention that. I didn't know people were trying to get the show canceled until this morning. I guess their little campaign didn't work very well. Did it?"

"Well, I'm glad to see you're here for the audition. I hope you didn't choose one of your 'I hate men' songs. I don't think that's the mood of the room today. You know...this being a holiday show audition and all."

I smiled a thin, tight smile and nodded.

"Erika Saunders?" a voice said, poking its head out of a door down the hall. *Saved by the bell*!

"Well, it was so good seeing you, Katy," I drew out the word *good* to emphasize how much I hated her and used an old nickname I knew she hated.

"Katherine," she said. "I haven't gone by Katy in almost a decade."

"Oh, that's right..." I said as if I'd genuinely forgotten. "It's hard for me to forget the good old days when you were my understudy on the national tour of *Wicked*."

That's when Katherine first started being my number one frenemy. I kept waiting for her to push me down the stairs so she could go on in my place. I only called out once during the entire tour, and that was when we were in Katherine's hometown so she could play the role in front of her parents. She never thanked me for the opportunity. She kept begrudging me that I hadn't let her play the role more often. She sat in the audience every night and gave me notes on what I could do better. At first, I guessed she was trying to be helpful. Intrusive, but helpful. Clearly, she thought she was better than me, and it galled her to no end to know that I was the one the casting agents wanted for the role and not her.

"Toodles," Katherine said with a wave of her fingers. "Break a leg in there... Oh, I don't mean literally break a leg. I hope you know that." She paused for a second to cock her head sideways and smile. "Too soon?"

"I'm over that whole incident. Have been for years," I lied. "Anyway, the audition calls." I didn't wait for a response as I strode down the hallway.

I took a deep breath, passed the woman holding the door to the audition room, and strode in as if I owned the place. The faces behind the casting table were stunned, so I figured I needed to address the situation directly.

"Sorry about this," I said, gesturing to my outfit. "I thought I was auditioning for a Christmas musical about the North Pole post-global warming." I got a chuckle from one guy at the table. "In all seriousness, I left the apartment looking like a million bucks. Now I look like a soggy MetroCard." A few more chuckles. I spent the next few minutes telling the casting table everything that had happened to me since I left my apartment. By the time I finished, I had them laughing like I was a standup comic.

Finally, when the guy who looked to be in charge caught his breath, he asked, "What did you bring to sing for us today?"

"'Fable' from *Light in the Piazza*. I thought about singing 'I Hate Men,' but I figured you'd already caught my video on YouTube." Another round of chuckles. Well, I at least read the room right. I walked over to the rehearsal pianist and handed him the soggy papers. "Sorry about this," I said.

"No worries. Sounds like you've had a day. Thankfully, I was the musical director for the first national tour back in the day. I could still play this score by heart."

"My personal miracle in a day of chaotic crazy."

I turned to the casting table and listened as the pianist started. And he wasn't joking. He was perfect. I might as well have been listening to the cast album. His fingers were so nimble as he played the intricate score on the piano. I was so enthralled with his technique that I almost missed my entrance cue. Thankfully, right before I needed to sing, he nodded in my direction.

I opened my mouth, and I sang. I sang my ever-loving songbird heart out. It was as if I willed myself to match the accompanist's skill. I pushed myself harder than I'd ever pushed myself singing

"Fable." I was so lost in the moment I forgot about the casting table completely. When the song ended, there was immediate applause. Not the usual applause I get in auditions where the table is polite, but I received genuine, appreciative applause. I took a slight bow.

"Thank you," the man in charge said.

I nodded, gathered my things and left. As soon as I was out of the room, I leaned against the wall and another round of tears came. I made it through. I don't know how I'd pulled myself together, but I had. After a few seconds, I pushed myself away from the wall and walked to the elevator bank.

"Ms. Saunders?" a voice called after me.

I turned and looked at the young redheaded guy running after me. "Yes?"

"First, let me start by saying what an honor it is to meet you."

"Thank you," I said and plastered on a genuine smile.

"Second, your audition back there was amazing."

"Again, thank you." We stood there for a few awkward moments of silence, so I cut through the tension. "And you are?"

"Sorry," the man said with a sheepish quality that made me feel warm and fuzzy inside. "I'm Eugenius Moses, but everyone calls me Eugene or just Gene."

"Well, Eugene, how can I help you?"

"We'd like to invite you for a callback tomorrow afternoon."

"What time?" I asked.

"2:00 p.m.?"

"I'll have to double-check my schedule, but that should work for me." As if I had a schedule, but he didn't need to know that.

"Amazing," he said. His cheeks flushed red, which only made him seem more boyish.

"What's your role in the show?"

"I'm the composer. Mabel Wägner is writing the book and Tyreek MacQueen is the lyricist. We were hired after a contest to work on the show for the producer."

"Well, congratulations. Welcome to the big leagues. I can't wait to hear what the three of you come up with." I have always loved working with new talent. There's something about a new team of writers that helps bring out my level of interest and excitement in a project.

"And I have to say, I saw you on the opening night of *The Faith Healer*. I was horrified when I heard what happened to you." I stiffened a bit, but thankfully the kid didn't seem to notice the change in my posture. "And I don't believe anything Asher says. What he did to you sickened me. Asher was always a jerk, but that was a new low for him."

"Ahh...Asher...I take it you dated him, too?"

"Oh, no...I'm not...I didn't. No. Oh geez, no. He was my roommate in college. I never dated him. I'm not gay. There's nothing wrong with being gay, but I'm completely straight."

Great, my straightdar is way off today. "I'm sorry. I didn't mean to insinuate that you and Asher had a fling. It's just, well, you know..."

"Trust me, I know all too well. And I think most people in the industry know, too. Despite what you may hear on social media, most people have taken your side. I wanted you to know that."

"Thanks," I said. "You do not know how much I needed to hear that. Sometimes, I've felt like I was yelling against the wind these past few years."

"Well, I need to get back in there," Eugene said. "We need to make a few phone calls and let the other people we want to see tomorrow know about the callbacks. Have a great evening."

"You too." Eugene walked back to the audition room. For the first time in a few years, I found an extra spring in my step.

Chapter 5

It was after four when I exited back onto 46th Street. The rain poured down harder than before. I looked left, looked right, and decided it was time for a celebratory mojito. Next door to the Actors' Equity Building is my favorite Cuban restaurant and the best place to go for mojitos in Manhattan, Havana Central. I walked into the restaurant and sat down at the bar.

The bartenders were already fixing the layers of glasses with the basic mojito fixings at the bar. I waved one over when I caught his eye. He was a medium-built Latino who had short dark hair and chocolate-brown eyes. I almost melted when I stared into his eyes. When he opened his mouth and asked me what I wanted to drink, I almost said something completely inappropriate, but I stopped myself and ordered a classic mojito, a combination of fresh muddled mint, sugar, rum and soda. He poured my drink and went back to prepping for the after 5:00 rush. I swirled the mint around with the fresh piece of sugar cane sticking out of the glass.

I was the only one sitting at the bar, and the music wasn't loud, so I pulled out my phone and called Brice.

"Brice Stark."

"Brice, it's Erika."

"Ahh, yes. I was waiting for the phone call. I heard about the callback tomorrow. Congrats."

"What are you doing?" I asked.

"Wrapping up some paperwork. Why?"

"I'm at Havana Central. Come join me for a celebratory drink."

I knew Brice's office was a block away, so he could be here in minutes if he really wanted to.

"Give me ten minutes. See you soon, love." And he hung up.

I played around with my phone and looked at the menu. I hadn't realized I'd skipped lunch because of my hasty preparation for the audition. I wanted something light now to make sure I wasn't drinking on an empty stomach, so I ordered a shrimp sofrito empanada. Havana Central is known for two things, mojitos and empanadas. I'd found myself here many nights before I worked on Broadway and after. It was just off the beaten path enough from Times Square that many tourists looked right past it, so many people in the theater community came here for early or late dinners, depending on how they preferred to eat. Personally, I don't like to perform on a full stomach. And if I'm dancing, food slows me down and makes me sluggish. I stick to a strict diet during the week when I'm performing. On a show day, I have a decent breakfast ranging from eggs and toast to granola with yogurt and fresh fruit. If I have a matinee, I may forgo a larger breakfast and have a smoothie from one of the many smoothie places. I would love to say that I grow my wheatgrass and cut it every morning for a shot, but no one will believe that lie. I prefer to let the professionals handle things like cooking. My skills are not domestic, I know that. I can't cook, I hate to clean, and don't let me near an ironing board unless you want a hole in your shirt.

"Look at you, celebrating with an empanada," Brice said as he approached. I stood and hugged him as he kissed me on my cheeks.

Brice was 28, drop-dead gorgeous, had short brown hair, a closely shaved beard, and Caribbean Ocean blue eyes. His suit was tailored to fit his perfectly trim athletic body. And the navy blue suit only made his eyes pop even more. Of course, I knew the suit had been made for him by a tailor he used down in SoHo. Brice was not a labels kind of guy. When you make the kind of money he does, you forgo labels and have people make your clothing. Brice's parents, Julia and Robin, were the driving force behind the Stark Agency. The elder Starks had been around the business for a few decades, but Brice had always been her agent. In fact, Erika had been Brice's first client.

"So, tell me about the show," Brice said as he stripped off his black wool coat and slung it over the back of an empty chair.

I was about to respond when the bartender saw Brice and quickly came over. Trust me, I was used to watching people hop to when Brice entered a room. He had that self-assuredness that people notice. Brice didn't need to tell you he was important; people just knew that he was. And, of course, I got to be important simply by being in his orbit when we were out in public.

Brice ordered a mango mojito before turning back to me. "Sorry about that," he said, genuinely apologizing for being interrupted by the bartender. That's the kind of guy Brice was. For an agent, he knew when he needed to have a firm hand and when he needed to use kid gloves. Us actors are tricky like that.

"Well, I do not know what the show is about," I told him.

"Still?"

I told him about the audition—the good, the bad and the ugly. He laughed when I described the fiasco. He grew somber when I admitted to breaking down and crying on the bathroom floor. Then he cheered for me when I described my performance.

"I am so proud of you. And I'm glad you chose a song that focuses on love and life and not on hating men for a change."

"I don't hate men," I said. He shot me a *'do you really think I'm buying that'* look.

"So, did they ask you to prepare anything for tomorrow?"

"Nope, they told me to show up at two."

"Who asked you to the callback?"

"Believe it or not, the composer ran after me. Told me he was a fan. Told me he was straight. Told me he didn't believe Asher. Then told me to come back tomorrow at two."

A look of confusion flashed over Brice's face. "Why did he tell you he was straight? Was he hitting on you?"

"No."

"So, you became BFFs with this guy?" Brice asked suspiciously.

"It's not like that. He was roommates with Asher in college. I may have insinuated that he'd also slept with Asher—"

"You didn't."

"I did... Thankfully, the guy took it in stride, which is when he told me he doesn't believe anything that comes out of Asher's mouth and that most of the people on Broadway were learning to do the same."

"It's about time," Brice said with a twinkle in his eye. "Just remember, I was the one who told you not to date him."

"You could have said, 'Hey Erika, don't date the man whore.'"

"I don't think he was a man whore yet. I think that happened after you started dating him."

"Ouch!"

"Erika, I didn't mean it like that," Brice quickly backpedaled. "I think living in the city started to change Asher. You were the last to see the signs."

I knew he was right. Asher had been an amazing boyfriend at first. Even when we were on tour together, he was perfectly attentive. I'd always known about the bisexual thing, and that didn't worry me for an instant because he'd also seemed so devoted to me. At some point, I just became not enough for him. It took me two years of therapy to come to that realization. I allowed him to place all the blame on me in the press. Admittedly, the video of me yelling a few choice words at him as I lay underneath the stage with a broken leg helped paint me as the villain. Still, he was the one who had betrayed me. He was the one who cheated on me. He was the one who made the poor decisions. I was the one who didn't recognize the red flags when they were waved in my face like a flag girl at a football halftime show in the South.

"So, what are you up to tonight?" I asked, trying to change the subject.

"I'm having an early dinner with the parents. Then we're going to see three clients opening a play Off-Broadway."

"Really? The agency is bringing out all the big guns tonight?"

"It's rare, but occasionally, my parents and I still see shows together. We got lucky that each of us has a client in this one, so we coordinated our schedules to make it a family affair."

"And how goes the dating life?"

"I won't ask about yours if you don't ask about mine," he said with a quirk of his lip.

"Touché." I threw my hands up in mock surrender, which was the end of that shortly lived discussion. "How goes the house hunt?"

"Still need to see a few more properties on the market. My real estate agent called. A Wall Street-type put his condo on sale. It's in a nice building near the theater district. Apparently, it's all hush-hush, so I don't know the specific location. But I'm supposed to get an early preview of the space early next week. If I like it, I may put in an offer."

"Condo board?"

"Of course, but my real estate agent doesn't think I'll have any problems with them. Apparently, the board is made up of mostly industry types, so I'd fit in nicely with the group."

"And you? Any thought about leaving the Manhattan Plaza?"

"Leave my theater commune behind? Never."

"What if you win a Tony?"

"I wouldn't be the first Tony Award winner to live in that building. Heck, the place was home to Academy, Grammy, and Emmy winners. That place has history."

"It is nice that there's a place for struggling performance artists to live and thrive while trying to make a way in this strange business." He glanced at his watch. "Well, I hate to drink and run, but I need to head on over to Sardi's, meeting up with my parents."

"You're meeting at Sardi's? Isn't that a bit cliché?"

"Of course, it's cliché. But then, what's wrong with cliché? One person's cliché is another's sense of classicism. Sardi's is like great art. It has more stories to be told than any of us will ever hear."

With that little nugget of wisdom, he grabbed the coat from the chair next to him, kissed me on the cheek, and was off to see his parents. I hadn't noticed that he'd paid my bill before he'd left. He knows I would have wrestled him to the ground if he'd asked me first, which is why he decidedly didn't ask.

I put my coat back on and grabbed my bag before heading out into the cold weather. At least the rain had stopped.

The walk back to the apartment was quick and dry. After my earlier soaking, I was looking forward to getting out of these clothes, even if they were dry now. Knowing how soaked I'd been earlier made a chill run down my spine. I entered the lobby and headed for the elevator bank.

"Hey, can you hold the door?" I heard someone yell.

I wanted to ignore the voice, but I kicked my foot out and waited for the person to join me.

"Howdy, new neighbor," a man said, walking into the elevator with a couple of pizzas.

It took me a moment to remember that I'd met him earlier that afternoon. Let's face it, I'd had a crazy afternoon. I tried to remember the guy's name, then it hit me, "Kirk...right?"

"That's me. I'm impressed you remembered."

"Guess it's that actor's mind of mine."

"How'd your audition go?"

"As well as could be expected. Well, that's a lie. It was horrible. Absolutely horrible. But I was magnificent, and they want to see me again tomorrow."

He looked at me before saying, "Sounds like you have a story to tell."

"You have no idea. It starts with me being drenched from head to toe as a bus sped by me."

His brow rose in surprise, which made me want to tell him more. Unfortunately, the elevator dinged, and story time was up. "I guess I'll have to finish telling you about my day some other time."

"Or you could come tell me now?" I looked over and caught a look of surprise that crossed his own face. "I mean, you could come over and tell Carissra and me your story. You know, Carissra, my niece. She's in the apartment, so she'd be there, too. Is it getting hot in here?"

He was kind of cute when he squirmed.

"Do you have any plans tonight?" he finally asked after I'd been staring at him for a hot minute.

"I don't know if a bottle of wine counts as *plans*. Not that I need any more alcohol. I met up with my agent for mojitos when I got the callback."

"Oh, is he your..." Kirk let the phrase hang out there between us.

"No, oh my gosh, no. Brice is gay—very, very gay. We're more like siblings than anything, except I pay him a lot to be my sibling. So, I guess we're not like siblings at all."

"Pizza?" Kirk asked, holding up the boxes. "I have meat and vegetarian."

I considered it for a moment. Part of me wanted to head into my apartment, close the door, and take a long, hot bath. Instead, I heard the words "Sure, sounds like fun," slip out of my mouth before I could stop them. "But first, I want to change. Get out of these clothes."

"No problem. We'll be waiting for you."

Kirk headed to his door as I opened mine. I pulled out the key, went inside, and made my way through the living room. After setting down my bag, I went into the bedroom and removed my clothes to throw on something more comfortable. I went with a pair of jeans, a gray sweatshirt that read *Iowa State* on it, and a pair of fuzzy house slippers. Hey, I was only going next door, and I wasn't trying to impress this guy.

On the way out of the apartment, I looked at myself once in the mirror. I didn't look half bad. I wasn't the super-hot Broadway actor from that afternoon, but I was still the gorgeous girl next door from Iowa. I grabbed my keys and headed to the adjacent apartment.

I knocked twice on the door and heard a voice from inside yell, "It's open," so I pushed and found that it had been left open enough to not latch shut.

"It's me, Erika," I said as I walked into the apartment. I'd never seen inside this specific apartment. Still, I'd been enough of the building's apartments to know all the general apartment layouts. To the right, I found an empty kitchen. There was an open hole between the kitchen and the living room area beyond the entryway wall. I could see the open pizza boxes sitting on the ledge between the two rooms, but I couldn't see the dining room area.

"We're in the living room," Kirk called to me.

I stepped further into the apartment and found Carissra and Kirk sitting at a small, circular folding table, already digging into their pizza.

"Sorry we didn't wait for you. I didn't know how long you'd be, and frankly, I was starving."

"No worries," I replied. "I would have done the same thing."

Kirk gestured toward the empty folding chair, and I sat down.

"So, Kirk told me you had a bit of an adventure this afternoon," Carissra said.

"Yes. Yes, I did."

I spent the next 25 minutes retelling my story. Admittedly, I got the story better and knew where people would laugh with each retelling. I was getting the hang of this humor thing. I'd never imagined myself a comedienne, but maybe I had some comedic chops after all.

When I finished my story, Carissra and Kirk told me more about themselves and their lives before moving in next to me. They were lucky to get into the building because it was within walking distance of Kirk's and Carissra's schools, the place was affordable, and the apartment had two rooms.

"Her parents were pretty well off," Kirk said, "But I didn't want to use any of Carissra's inheritance until she turned eighteen. I want to make sure she has enough money to go to any college or university she wants to go to. And still have enough to help her get established in a career once she has a degree."

"Uncle Kirk is kind of amazing, isn't he?" Carissra said absently.

"He sure seems like it," I admitted.

I looked around the apartment and it was quite sparse. "When are the rest of your belongings supposed to get here?" I asked.

"In two days," Kirk almost growled. "Sorry, it's a sore subject. They were supposed to unload my old apartment out in Queens, which was too small for both of us, and move us here in one day, but that isn't what happened. We're both going to sleep on the ground tonight, unfortunately."

"I have a blowup bed in my apartment you can borrow?"

"I couldn't possibly accept," Kirk said.

"You invited me over for pizza. I insist you let me return your generosity. Besides, it's just sitting in a closet right now."

"Are you sure?" Kirk questioned.

"I wouldn't offer if I wasn't sure."

"Okay, let me come get it from you. I want to make sure Carissra gets to bed at a decent hour. We both have school tomorrow."

We walked back to my apartment. "Let me get the bed out of the spare room."

He stood in the living room, taking in my place as I walked into the spare room, opened the closet and dug around until I found the box. I pulled on the plastic handle, and the box came out smoothly with only a tiny avalanche of stuff being displaced.

"You okay in there?" I heard Kirk call from the living.

"Everything's fine. Just had to move a few things."

I shoved everything back into the closet and kicked it shut with my foot before heading back out into the living room.

I handed the box to Kirk. "Thanks. This is generous of you. I hated the idea of Carissra having to sleep on the floor tonight. She's already suffered so much." The crestfallen look on his face was clearly one he hid from his niece.

"I can't imagine what she's gone through or what you're going through. But from what I can see, she adores you, and you're doing everything you can to make her happy. That's more than most people would ever do."

He smiled and nodded once before saying, "She's family. She's the only family I have left."

My heart broke for him. He was strong and yet so vulnerable.

"Anyway, I should get back. Thanks again for the use of the blowup bed. I'll get it returned when our furniture gets here."

"No worries," I said before adding in my best sinister voice, "I know where you live."

He laughed appropriately at my cheesy joke. I opened the door to see him out. "Thanks for the pizza and company tonight."

"Anytime, neighbor."

A white furball dashed between my legs and tried to make it into the hallway. Kirk bent over and scooped up the darting Bootsy with his free hand in a smooth action I'd only seen by wide receivers.

"Hey there, little guy," Kirk said.

The cat eyed the man who'd caught him, but he didn't lash out. Kirk handed Bootsy back to me. "That was some save," I said. "He generally doesn't try to get out of here. But occasionally, he tries to make a jailbreak."

"I've had pets most of my life. I know how it goes."

"Anyway, good night."

"Good night, Erika."

I shut the door, holding Bootsy firmly in my arms as I stroked his fur, and we both let out a contented sigh.

Chapter 6

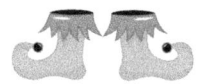

I let myself sleep in and finally dragged myself out of bed a little after 11:30 a.m. My first thought was, how did Carissra and Kirk get up so early in the morning and go to school? I remember being in high school and all the early mornings. Honestly, I don't know how I got through those long days sitting at a wooden desk staring at teachers. Now, anything before noon seems painful. Admittedly, as a theater professional, my work rarely begins in the morning unless we're rehearsing. And then, we only rehearse for six to eight weeks max, so it's not like I have month after month of early mornings.

I walked into the kitchen, started my morning slash afternoon coffee, and picked up my iPad. I opened *The New York Times* app to see what was going on in the world. I bypassed the front page and immediately pulled up the entertainment section. I scrolled through the stories until I spotted one I wanted to read. "Asher Fraser Alexander Out!" the headline said. I clicked on the hyperlink and read.

"*Asher Fraser Alexander has been fired from a romantic comedy being filmed in Upstate New York. Producers for the Hallmark Channel movie,* Tidings from a Christmas Prince, *noted that the split had been amicable while the production company stopped filming in search of a new star. Sources close to the set said the producers found a conflict of interest between Alexander and the casting agent who hired him for the project.*"

That's it? Oh, come on. I knew there had to be more to this story, so I pulled up *The New York Post* app. I flipped to their entertainment section and searched out my favorite columnist, Michelle Bouvier. Michelle was an "entertainment columnist" and not a "critic." Basically, the label let her write about shows before they ever opened. She considered herself an objective reporter, but everyone knew she was a gossip columnist focused on the entertainment industry. Sure enough, Bouvier's headline was way more salacious. "Alexander Slept His Way into the Role?" I quickly skimmed through the article and found out that the assistant to the casting agent had been fired, so the assistant contacted the producers and told them Asher had an illicit affair with the casting agent during auditions, which led to Asher being hired for the film. The producers immediately investigated and fired Asher because they didn't want their brand tainted by a sex scandal. Hallmark Christmas Movies are known for being squeaky clean, so any hint of impropriety could be a huge problem.

After reading the story, a sense of glee filled me, and I couldn't have wiped the smile off my face if I had to. Finally, Mr. Alexander appeared to be getting his comeuppance. I was auditioning for a new Broadway musical and Asher was getting fired. Maybe people would see past his matinee good looks and see the creep that existed inside. Between the article and the cup of warm coffee, I had a warm, tingly feeling inside. Maybe I shouldn't feel nearly as giddy about the story as I did, but there was something pretty satisfying about it.

After catching up on other celebrity gossip and a little actual news, I went into my bedroom, pulled out my pre-determined wardrobe for the day, and set about getting myself ready. Thankfully, I gave myself plenty of time. After revising my wardrobe twice, I settled on a sleek black pantsuit and red four-inch heels. I wanted to be more muted this time. Also, I didn't know what the callback would entail, so I wanted to make sure I could move if I needed to. I once had a callback and didn't realize until I got there that the callback would involve dancing. I'd been dressed in a miniskirt, which wasn't a smart move. There was no way I could complete the choreography in that outfit. I had tried to reschedule my audition, but that hadn't been allowed, so I ended up bowing out altogether. Ultimately, it was a good thing because I landed the second national tour of *Wicked* the next week, so it all worked out.

I left the apartment and walked the few blocks to Actors' Equity. Thankfully, there was no rain this time, so I showed up at the building completely dry. I headed up again to the sixteenth floor. This time, a woman sat outside with a clipboard. I walked over to her.

"Erika Lynsay Saunders," I said, giving her my full name, which was required for Equity purposes. There had already been an Erika Saunders at some point, so I had to use my middle name professionally to avoid confusion.

"Thank you," she said without looking up. "Here you go."

She handed me a sheet of paper. Across the top, in bold print, read, *My mistress' eyes are nothing like the sun (Sonnet 130)–William Shakespeare.*

"I think there may be a mistake," I said. "I'm here for the *Beyond Tomorrow* callback. This looks like a one-sheet for a Shakespeare audition."

From the look she gave me, I wasn't the first person who'd questioned this today. "You're in the right place. When they're ready for you, they'll call you."

Okay, then. I took the sheet over to a chair and started reading over the sonnet. Personally, I'm not a huge fan of poetry. Sure, I know it's supposed to be lovely, but I don't get it. I like things to be straight and to the point. Why do so many hidden metaphors and more profound meanings need to be buried in poetry? In college. I starred in a production of *W;t*. The long, drawn-out passages about poetry nearly bored me to tears when I learned them. I'd never heard of John Donne and had never read his work before the show or after. If someone can place so much emphasis on a comma or semicolon, then I'm not that interested.

"Erika Lynsay Saunders," a voice called, bringing me out of my haze.

I stood up and walked into the room. The table had been extended, and a few new faces sat at the table.

"Thank you, Ms. Saunders," a middle-aged woman said as I entered the room. "We're glad you join us for a callback so quickly."

"I'm happy to be here," I said. Even though I would have uttered that phrase if I hadn't been happy to be there, I was genuinely glad to be in an audition room again. As anxiety-provoking as auditioning was, there was always something purely electrifying about the experience.

"I'm Rebekka Eldridge," the woman continued. "I'm the lead producer on this project. For a little background, my late husband, Bernie, had the idea for this show years ago. Before he died, he'd been buying up real estate to build a brand-new Broadway theater. This show will be its first production." She introduced everyone at the table. To her immediate left was the show's director, Asier Zlota San Nicolás. I'd heard of San Nicolás. He's a Spanish director who had made a name for himself in London's West End. To his right was Divya Philomena Kappel, the show's choreographer. Beyond those three new faces, the other faces were the ones I'd seen the previous day, the casting agent and the creative team.

When Eldridge finished introducing everyone, I said, "It's a pleasure meeting all of you."

I stood there awkwardly for a moment, not sure what to do. Finally, San Nicolás looked up from his legal pad and said, "Let's begin." He stood up and walked around to the front of the table, then leaned against it. "Today's callback will not be *traditional*," he rolled the *l* for added emphasis. "When you got here, you were given a simple sonnet from the grand maestro of the theater himself, William Shakespeare. I will have you read the sonnet to us, but either Ms. Kappel or me will call out directions. We want to see how you respond in the moment. So, let loose, and roll with the directions."

"Okay," I said. I tried to say it with as much assuredness as I could muster, but I really had no idea what the man meant.

San Nicolás clapped his hands together once and said, "Let's begin!"

I sucked in a breath before reciting the first line, "My mistress' eyes are nothing like the sun."

"With anger," San Nicolás said.

"Coral is far more red than her lips' red," I said in a guttural voice.

"With passion!"

"And with a lyrical body movement," Kappel added.

"If snow be white, why then her breasts are dun," I said, dropping into sultry. "If hairs be wires, black wires grow on her head." I let my arms move fluidly as I received the lines. I wasn't sure if I hit passion or not, but I went for it.

"Like you're royalty."

"With the grace of a ballerina."

"I have seen roses damasked, red and white," I stood taller, trying to remember how Helen Mirren looked when she embodied Queen Elizabeth in *The Audience* on Broadway. "But no such roses see I in her cheeks."

"Like a New York Police Detective."

"Make yourself larger than life."

"And in some perfumes is there more delight," I gritted out in a farcical Bronx accent. "Than in the breath that from my mistress reeks."

"Like a mouse."

"Move like a cartoon character."

"I love to hear her speak, yet well I know," I said, getting down on all fours and squeaking in a high falsetto. "That music hath a far more pleasing sound."

"Read like a Vaudevillian."

"Move like a Follies Girl."

"I grant I never saw a goddess go," I read in my best Mae West impersonation. *She was a Follies girl, wasn't she?* "My mistress when she walks treads on the ground."

"Give me sex!"

"Move like a Pussycat Doll."

Okay, that one threw me. I paused to figure out what moving like a Pussycat Doll meant. Finally, it hit me. *I think she means to move like a pop star diva.* My Pussycat Doll may have been more Madonna with a hint of Britney Spears than the sex on a stick that is Nicole Scherzinger, but I gave it my all as I read the last two lines of the sonnet, "And yet, by heaven, I think my love as rare, as any she belied with false compare."

As the last line came out of my mouth, there was a stillness in the room. Finally, San Nicolás started clapping and said, "Bravo!" The others joined in. Kappel jumped to her feet and let out her own "Bravo!" The rest of the table stood as well and clapped. The only person who didn't seem overly impressed was the producer.

I looked her straight in the eyes and gave her my best, winning smile.

"Silence!" San Nicolás suddenly yelled. I almost laughed as the group immediately stopped applauding and sat down quickly. "Sing the *12 Days of Christmas.*"

Without waiting for a cue from me, the rehearsal pianist started playing. It took my mind a second to catch up and join in. "On the first day of Christmas, my true love gave to me…" The pianist quickly adjusted and caught back up to me. Thankfully, he was a true professional and knew how to make a singer look and sound great.

"Faster!" San Nicolás whispered seductively.

The piano sped up as I launched into the second verse, "On the second day of Christmas my true love gave to me, two turtles doves and a partridge in a pear tree."

"Higher."

The pianist modulated, so I did the same.

"On the third day of Christmas, my true love gave to me three French hens, two turtle doves and a partridge in a pear tree."

"Louder!"

And that's how it went through all twelve days. San Nicolás went back and forth among louder, faster and higher. By the time the song finished, I was belting in my falsetto at a frenzied pace. "AND A PARTRIDGE IN A PEAR TREE!" I heard myself screech the final lines. I was breathless. I wiped away a bead of sweat from my forehead.

"Thank you," San Nicolás said as he whipped a tear away from his eye. "That was beautifully brilliant. You have the power of a bear, the stamina of a racehorse, and the lyrical quality of a lark in the sunset of its life."

I smiled and did not know what to make of the compliment. *Was that a compliment?*

"Thank you. We'll let you know," the producer said from behind the table.

And just like that, I was summarily dismissed. The team didn't even wait for me to say goodbye before they started having hushed conversations behind the table. I grabbed my bag and left the room. *What was that?* I asked myself as I exited. The woman sitting outside the door didn't look up from what she was reading. I headed to the elevator bank. I was surprised to find no one else in the waiting area. *Maybe they scheduled us apart so we wouldn't know who else was auditioning?*

My feet hit the pavement, and I started walking home. Part of me wanted to head next door for mojitos again, but I refrained. My phone rang.

"Erika," I said without looking at the caller ID.

"Hey, love," Brice said.

"Well, that was different."

"How so?"

I described the audition process. He was subdued when I talked about the experience. When I finally finished telling him about a partridge in a pear tree, there was silence.

"They offered you a role," Brice said.

"What?" I asked in absolute shock. "Already?"

"Actually, the show's lawyer called during the middle of your audition."

"Huh?" I apparently was having a problem forming complete sentences.

"Yep."

"I don't even know what auditioned for."

"You have been offered the role of Michael O'Brien."

"Michael?"

"From what the lawyer told me, the source material is being reworked for a modern audience. The role you've been offered is the central character, but not necessarily the lead. Did you watch the movie?"

"No," I admitted. "I haven't had time."

"Okay. Basically, three industrialist tycoons help bring a couple together. But they die and come back as ghosts. You're the lead tycoon slash ghost."

I knew what I was doing the first thing I got home. Brice's description really didn't help me at all.

"So, what's the offer?" I asked.

"They're willing to pay higher than Equity minimums. They expect six weeks of rehearsals leading to an opening in early December. When the show opens, you'll be earning $3,123 a week. While in rehearsals, you'll be making $2,168. They also offered a guaranteed one-year contract if the show runs."

"Okay, so what's the catch?"

"None that I can see. I'll have our lawyers look over the contract once we get it, but these people sure don't know how to negotiate. They really didn't investigate the standard rates on Broadway. I wish all my clients had these kinds of dream deals."

"Where is my name placement?" I asked.

"Great question. You will not receive top billing, but your name will be above the title."

I exhaled and noticed the foggy tendrils in the cool air. I hadn't even realized I'd been holding my breath.

"So," Brice started, "what do you think?"

"I don't know what to think," I admitted. "This is all so sudden and unexpected. I'm still trying to process."

"Don't process too long. They want an answer by the end of the day."

"What?"

"Yeah, they are looking to get into rehearsals next week, so they want all the contracts signed before the weekend. This is one production team that isn't messing around."

"I don't know—"

"Erika, let me be frank with you," Brice said matter-of-factly. "You don't have anything else lined up, and no one else is banging down the door to offer you a role like this. Take it."

I took a breath in through my nose, rounded my lips, and let it out. "When do I need to come by the office and sign?"

Chapter 7

I practically skipped all the way home. The air had that crisp late October feel to it. The few trees that lined the streets on my home were already turning colors. If I really wanted to see leaves changing, I could always hike up to Central Park or take a day cruise up the Hudson River to look at leaves. When Asher and I had first coupled up, what seemed like decades ago but was only maybe six years now, we took one of those scenic cruises. We had a series of auditions that were a total bust one week, so we decided to treat ourselves.

I remember staying on deck the whole time, taking pictures while the world passed us. Asher had disappeared for a while. He'd gotten cold and had headed into the main cabin. In retrospect, I think the boat's first mate also disappeared during that same period. *Wow, I was oblivious.*

I was so lost in my memory that I bumped right into a man on the street. "I am so sorry," I said without looking at who I'd bumped into.

"Erika?"

I looked up to see who I'd run into and found a face smiling down at me, Amani Samara, Johnny's boyfriend. "Oh hey, Amani. Sorry about that. I was admiring the season."

"Which season? The garbage smell season? The rat season? Or the jackhammer season? Oh...I know, the siren season."

"Wow," I started. "Someone woke up on the wrong side of the bed today."

"Nope, I always roll off the same side of the bed. Mine. Johnny has his side, and I have mine. Some nights, we meet in the middle for playtime, but we mostly stick to our sides of the bed like an invisible demilitarized zone between us."

"Umm...okay. There's so much to unpack there. I don't know where to start." I scrunched up my nose, shrugged, and gave him an award-winning smile. "But anyway, what has you grumpy today?"

"Just anxious. We had a reviewer from *The Times* show up yesterday at Evergreen Mirror. The executive chef was in a mood, and it rubbed off on me. I haven't snapped out of it yet. Thankfully, I have the day off, so heading off to do a bit of retail therapy."

"Ohh... Retail therapy is my favorite type of therapy."

"Want to come along?" Amani offered.

"Nah, I need to make some phone calls. I was offered a role in a new Broadway musical opening this fall."

"Whoa, you should totally have led with that," Amani said before embracing me. "What can you tell me about it? Who's the star? Is it you? When can you get Johnny and me tickets?"

"Slow down there, cowboy," I said, holding out my hand and laying it gently on his chest. "Nice pec," I said absently. He shot me a questioning look, so I removed my hand quickly. "Sorry about that. I didn't mean to feel you up. Wow, that was completely inappropriate of me. I am so embarrassed."

"Don't be. Strange people want to reach out and touch me all the time...usually, they pay first, though," he said with a wink.

"Eww...I so don't need to know that." I laughed.

"Just chalk it up to my innate Jordanian sexual appeal," he said, adding an extra emphasis to his accent.

"But anyway, as for your questions, I don't have many answers yet. I'm sort of a lead...I think. It's all convoluted. I haven't seen the script."

"Wait, you accepted a role for a part you haven't seen yet?"

"It happens more often than you realize. Sometimes the creative team waits until the first rehearsal to release the script and the score. It's also quite possible that it's not finished yet. When I worked on *The Faith Healer*, about half the score was ready when we started rehearsals. Well, they had a full score. It's just most of it changed during rehearsals and the out-of-town tryout in Boston."

"Are you heading out of town with this show?"

"Nope. From what my agent said, they are mounting it right here in the city with only about six weeks of rehearsals, so it will be a whirlwind experience, I'm sure."

"Well...congratulations, nonetheless. To celebrate, I'm going to make you dinner tonight."

"Amani, I can't let you do that."

He waved his hand. "It's already done...unless you have other plans."

"No other plans. Unless you call me and a bottle of wine plans." *Didn't I use the same joke last night with Kirk?*

"I'll be over at your place at six to cook. I might bring Johnny."

I let out an exaggerated sigh. "If you have to bring my best friend, I guess I can put up with him for the evening."

"I put up with him every day. You can keep him entertained while I cook. He always tries to volunteer, and it never ends well."

"Johnny can't cook?" I asked.

"He once asked me if boiling an egg for an hour was long enough."

I barked out a laugh. In my mind's eye, I could totally see Johnny asking that question with absolute sincerity. To say that Johnny wasn't the domestic type was putting it mildly.

"Another time, we were in the grocery store. He asked the woman working in produce where the guacamoles were located. I wanted to find a counter and hide behind it."

"Oh my," was all I got out. "I'm not a cook, but even I know what avocados are."

"Precisely," Amani stood there shaking his head, clearly lost in his own memory. "Well, I'm off to buy myself something nice. And now, I have a reason to pick up a few things at the grocery store. What do you want for dinner?"

"Surprise me."

He wrinkled his brow a little as he thought about what he could cook. "I think I can come up with something you'll like."

"Amani, I've tasted nothing you've cooked that I haven't loved. You're an amazing chef. I can't wait for you to open your own restaurant."

"From your mouth to Allah's ears?"

"Well..."

"No worries, I need to get a move on, too. Also, if there's anyone else you want to invite over tonight, do so. You know me, I don't know how to cook for small groups. Chalk that up to being raised in a large Jordanian household. Growing up with my *Jaddi* and *Jaddati*, parents, and six siblings, nothing was ever small."

"And I thought growing up with two siblings and my parents made a crowded house...and we all had our own rooms."

"There's a reason I flew to America and studied up in Hyde Park for four years. I love my family. But right now, I love them on the other side of the ocean."

"Don't you miss them?"

"Of course, I do, but we talk multiple times a week with Zoom and FaceTime."

"How often do you fly home?"

"Once or twice a year. It's an eleven-hour flight on Royal Jordanian Airlines. The flight is direct from JFK into Amman, Jordan, where I grew up."

"Wow, I thought the five-hour flight to Des Moines took forever."

We hugged goodbye, and I walked into the building. The lobby was quiet. A young couple I knew lived in the other tower talked to the security guard, so I nodded and went right to the elevator bank. On the door was a taped sign that read, *Down for Maintenance*.

I let out a groan and headed to the staircase. At least I didn't have groceries with me. The metal door banged behind me, and I looked up the concrete staircase. Well, time to get my workout for the week. I climbed. Now, I'm in pretty good shape. Sure, I'm not one of those crazy Broadway stars who takes eighteen dance lessons at the Broadway Dance Center every week, but the complex has a nice gym. And I even use it when I'm feeling particularly adventurous or bored. Okay, so maybe I should have seen inside the gym a few more days in the past couple of years than I have, but I'm not entirely hopeless.

On the tenth floor, I started feeling it in my calves. I was cursing the man who invented high-rise apartments by the fifteenth floor. And let's face it, we know it was a man. No woman in her right mind would need to build a giant phallic symbol for people to live in.

By the twentieth floor, I cursed my existence and had an existential crisis of faith. Part of me wanted to lie down on the stairs and hope someone would take pity on me and call an ambulance. I passed a few people on the stairs, so I could have reached out for help and begged for mercy. But no, I was a glutton for punishment, so I pressed on.

When I rounded the 25th floor, I prayed to every deity I could think of. Whoever spared me this indignance, I would convert and become a follower right then and there. "I'll even shave my head," I groused between gasps.

"I'd recommend against that," a voice said from behind me.

I turned to yell at the voice, and Kirk stood below me with a goofy grin. His school bag was slung over his shoulder. His brown hair was in a messy mop. He had a little shine of sweat, but nothing like I imagined the cascading waterfall of sweat pouring off my body at that moment looked like. I was so startled I put my left foot down and missed a step. I lurched forward and practically threw myself at Kirk.

I screamed in terror, thinking I was about to plummet to my death and take Kirk with me, but his strong arms grabbed and steadied me.

"Easy there, tiger," he said.

When I finally got my balance back, I put weight on my left foot and grimaced.

"You, okay?"

"I think I twisted my ankle when I threw myself at you."

"Oh, so that's your version of throwing yourself at a guy?" I wanted to snap, but his lopsided grin stopped me. Besides, I was still leaning on him for support.

"No worries, I can make it up the last couple flights of stairs."

"Not on that ankle, you're not. If it's more than a simple sprain, you could do some real damage."

"Well, I can't sit here in the stairwell all night long."

"I can carry you?" I looked at him with a gaze that must have been a mix of '*are you a creep*' and '*are you for real.*' "I carry Carissra upstairs all the time. I promise I'm not some creepy guy trying to get his hands on you."

"Isn't that exactly what a creepy guy would say?"

"Maybe... But I'm not seeing any better options right now. Are you? Besides, you're not that heavy. What are you...like 130 pounds?"

I stammered, trying to say something before finally blurting out, "You don't ask a lady her weight."

He laughed. "I was just guessing. You and Carissra have roughly the same build. She's bigger than you, and I know she weighs 135 pounds. I didn't mean to offend you."

"I'm not offended," I said, letting out a sigh. "This is humiliating. Let's get it over with."

"I won't tell a soul."

With that, I threw one arm around his neck, and with his help, he lifted my legs and carried me up the next two flights of stairs. Laying in his arms, nestled next to his chest, I could feel Kirk's strength. His nerdy teacher looks and baggy clothing did an excellent job of hiding what I envisioned was a pretty solid physique. Part of me wanted to rest my free arm on his chest to cop a feel, but I stopped myself. The last thing I needed was to make a habit of grabbing men's pecs in public. The tabloids would have a field day with that one.

Before long, we stood on the landing to our floor. Kirk gently put me down.

"Just lean on me until we get you into your apartment," he said.

"Where's Carissra?" I asked, feeling the floor beneath my feet. "How is she going to get up here?"

"She's at a friend's house right now. The security guard said he'd call me when the elevators were working again. When that happens, I'll call Carissra, and she'll either come home on her own or I'll go walk with her. She's independent, but I still don't like her coming home at night by herself."

"Smart move. There's still the random act of violence or criminal mischief around here. Thankfully, this is a nice neighborhood in a nice part of town. But crime is part of living in a big city, I guess."

"Exactly."

When we got to my door, I pulled out my keys, and he helped me inside the apartment, making sure Bootsy didn't try another escape act. He helped me to the couch and made sure I propped my ankle up. He then helped me remove my shoe and sock, which was a bit on the humiliating side. He felt the ankle.

"Doesn't feel broken. Wiggle your toes for me."

"So, you're a doctor now?"

"No, but I was a camp counselor when I was in college. Those boys were always spraining or breaking things. Got pretty good at tending to the basic cuts and sprains. Your ankle," he said, gesturing to the purplish mark appearing, "is only slightly sprained from the looks of things. Staying off your foot for a couple of days with ice will get you back on your feet in no time. I wouldn't overdo it until you're 100 percent, or you could end up with a worse sprain."

I let out a sigh, and he shot me an *I'm sorry* look. I put on my best fake smile. "I know it's not your fault. And thank you, I really appreciate your help. I'm mad at myself for being stupid. With all my years of dance classes, you would think I'd be more graceful, but nope."

"Do you have an ice pack?" he asked suddenly.

"No, but I have some frozen vegetables in the freezer."

Kirk walked over to the freezer and pulled out a bag of frozen mixed vegetables. He had me put the bag of frozen peas, carrots, and cauliflower pieces on my ankle. I winced at the cold, but the ice quickly performed the soothing sensation. Bootsy jumped up on the couch and nestled in beside me.

"Well, I really should head over to my apartment. Need me to check on you later?"

"Nah, I think I can handle things."

"Great. I'm next door if you need anything."

Kirk turned to leave. "Umm, actually...I'm having some friends over for dinner. It's sort of a celebration. I would love for you and Carissra to join us if she's home already. Amani said he'll be here at 6:00 to cook, so it could be anywhere between 6:00 and 7:00, depending on what he's making."

"Sounds like fun, but you really don't need to invite me—"

"*Pshaw*. You fed me pizza last night and carried me to my apartment. It's the least I can do. Besides, Amani is cooking, not me. Trust me, I would only threaten to cook for you if I was trying to punish you for something."

He chuckled at my attempted joke.

"So, what are we celebrating? You said it was a celebration."

"I got the role."

His face lit up instantly. "I worried about your audition all day after talking about it last night. I'm happy to hear you got the role."

"Still have no idea what the show is about, but I'm guessing I'll find out eventually."

"Well, you can tell me all about it over dinner. I'll see you around 6:30?"

"Perfect!"

"Great. I'll see myself out," he said with a jerking motion of his head toward the front door. When the door closed behind him, I let out a sigh.

"That man will make a great husband one day."

I pulled out my phone. I had a slew of messages that had come in from Johnny, so I hit the call button before bothering to listen to any of them.

"It's about time you called me back," Johnny said in lieu of a greeting. "I had to find out from my boyfriend that my best friend landed a starring role in a new Broadway musical."

"I'm not in the lead. I'm a featured actor."

"Whatever. You know that means they have some stunt casting they want to put in the lead roles, so the show will really rest on your shoulders."

I rolled my eyes, but that didn't have the intended effect when Johnny wasn't here to see them roll. "If you'd slow down and let me talk, I'll tell you what happened."

"Gossip?"

"Of sorts."

"I'm all ears."

And like that, I told Johnny in minute detail everything that had transpired in the stairwell. The good, the bad, the ugly, and the hottie next door.

"I can't wait to meet this new neighbor," Johnny said with a purring sound in his voice.

"Hands off, he's straight," I blurted.

"Oh, and how do you already know this?"

"Because I may have assumed he was gay yesterday."

"You didn't?"

"I did." So, I launched into the story of the previous afternoon and how it led to dinner with Carissra and Kirk.

"Well, I will take a quick nap before you and Amani get here. Tell Amani that at least one neighbor will join us and maybe two."

The gasp on the other end of the line did its desired trick as I dropped that bombshell on Johnny.

"The hottie neighbor is coming to dinner?"

"My neighbor who helped me yesterday and today is joining us for dinner. Now, please be on your best behavior tonight. I don't want to scare him from the building."

"Would I do that?"

"In a heartbeat," I deadpanned.

"True enough. See you at 6:00."

And with that, he hung up the phone. I switched out the mixed vegetables for some green beans before downing an anti-inflammatory I kept around the house. I'm a dancer; stuff happens to us all the time. I can't be running off to the doctor every time I injure myself or have a little inflammation. Thankfully, my primary care physician and I have an understanding. If it's ever too bad, I promised I'd see her immediately.

I let myself drift off to sleep with the drugs in my system and green beans on my ankle.

The rapping sound on my door jarred me out of my sleep. A soft purring sound next to me, followed by a gentle kneading, told me that Bootsy was not happy about being roused out of his sleep. I glanced down at my watch.

"Holy Bejeezus! It's already 6:00." I stood up quickly and yelped. Once the sudden pain from my ankle subsided, I said, "I'll be right there." I looked down at the leftover green bean bag that was now de-thawed and lying on the floor. I hadn't intended to sleep for that long, but apparently, my body had decided after the trauma of walking up twenty flights of stairs, spraining my ankle, then being carried up two more flights of stairs, it was tired.

As I hobbled toward my front door, I tried to keep my weight off my ankle.

"Gurl, you look like a mess," Johnny said as he breezed past me, carrying a bag with him.

Amani came right in after him. "Don't mind him. You know how he gets when he's hungry." Then Amani looked me up and down. "On second thought, what happened to you?"

"Did Johnny tell you about the stairs incident?" Amani turned and looked at Johnny, who shrugged. "Well, do I have a story for you."

"I look forward to hearing it while I cook. Johnny said something about other guests. Do we have a number?"

"It's one or two. Depends on whether the elevators are working now."

"They came online about thirty minutes ago," Johnny informed me as he plopped down on the couch. I looked down to see Bootsy was playing with the thawed bag of green beans. He would pounce on it. Then knead it a few times, and pounce again.

"Any chance we can add green beans to the meal?" I asked. "They're already thawed."

Amani looked over to where Bootsy was still attacking the wet plastic blob. "Do I even want to know?" I hobbled into the living room and put my foot up again.

"Ah ha," Amani said, finally seeing the noticeable limp. "I didn't leave you walking like that this afternoon. What happened?"

"Well—"

"Before you answer that," Amani cut me off. "For future reference, frozen vegetables are good for ice packs only if you use them for about twenty minutes and throw them right back in the freezer. As it stands, that gooey mess down there should not be refrozen.

I'll start a broth and make a vegetable stew with them and anything else I find in your freezer, so they won't go to waste."

"Why not just heat them now?" I asked.

"The thawing process takes out some of the moisture from the vegetables, which causes them to lose their appearance, taste, and texture."

"Then you may want to include the mixed veggies bag in the freezer. I used them earlier."

"Have you ever thought about buying a regular icepack, my dear?" Johnny said casually. I threw a decorative pillow at him that had the Phantom's mask stitched into it. He caught it and hugged it to his chest.

"I would have to agree with Johnny," Amani said. "Regular icepacks work better than vegetables, and they'll stay frozen longer. Thankfully, I have one with me you can borrow." Amani pulled an icepack from the freezer bag he'd brought with him. He came over and helped me place it around my ankle. I winced a little as he molded it to the shape of my ankle a bit harder. "But really, get one of these for yourself," he said after standing up and looking down at his handiwork.

"I'll put that on my shopping list. But as to this afternoon," I started, and caught him up on everything that had happened since I'd run into him on the street.

At some point during my story, Johnny had rummaged through my cabinets and fridge, found a bottle of wine, opened it and made sure I had a glass in my hand as I completed the story. Between the wine and the drugs I'd taken earlier, I was definitely not feeling the pain nearly as much.

At 6:30, there was a knock at the door. I looked at Johnny, scrunched up my face, and pointed at my ankle pleadingly.

"Okay, drama queen," Johnny said begrudgingly. "I'll answer the door." He stood up and limped across the floor like Quasimodo, over-exaggerating how painful it was for him to do anything that resembled manual labor. "Well, hello there, sailor," he said as he opened the door to a very surprised-looking Kirk.

"You're in the right place," I yelled across the kitchen. "Ignore my manservant. He isn't house trained yet."

"I tried to train him," Amani said from the kitchen. "Trust me, I even stuck his nose in his mess, but it didn't work."

"I'm right here," Johnny said, coming back into the living room. "And you know you love me...and my messes." Johnny pulled up behind Amani in the kitchen and gave him a quick peck on the cheek. He then turned around and leaned against a kitchen counter where he could see Kirk and me.

"How's the ankle?" Kirk asked, coming to sit beside me on the couch.

"It's doing better. But that could be the medical-grade Ibuprofen or the wine speaking."

"For some reason," Kirk started, giving me a wary look, "I'm betting you're not supposed to mix those two together."

"You're probably right," I admitted as I took a sip from my wine glass. I shrugged and shot him a *what ya gonna do* look, and he smirked back. "Where's Carissra? Is she joining us?"

"She has homework to do."

"Daughter?" Johnny asked from the kitchen.

"Niece," Kirk said. "But I'm her legal guardian, so I'm basically her parent. I don't want to use the word *father* with her because she had one of those. I don't ever want to pretend or try to replace my brother."

"That's sweet of you," I said. Absently, I let my hand fall to his forearm and patted him reassuringly. When my brain caught up with my hand, I quickly withdrew it and made introductions. "Amani is the gorgeous Jordanian in the kitchen. Johnny is the hot mess next to him."

Johnny let out a dramatic guffaw.

"Just ignore him," Amani called over his shoulder. "The rest of us do." Johnny pouted and Amani leaned over and kissed him before turning back to whatever he was making on the stove.

"Well, I'm Kirk, and I live next door with my niece, Carissra."

"You may have seen her around the building. Cute teenage girl with long black hair in a wheelchair."

"I saw her this evening. She came into the lobby like Greased Lightning and headed for the elevators," Johnny said.

"I hope she didn't run anyone over," Kirk said. "Still trying to get her to be more mindful of others."

"Not at all," Johnny reassured Kirk. "She looked like a woman on a mission."

"Dinner will be ready in about five minutes," Amani said.

"What are we having?" I asked. I'd been so caught up in the conversation I hadn't paid attention to what Amani was doing in the kitchen.

"We're starting with a simple gazpacho, and for dinner, I made albondigas, or meatballs, from scratch and are serving them in tomato sauce. For the albondigas, you have your choice of pork or squid. They'll be served over a vegetarian paella Valenciana."

"And for dessert, I made him promise to make sopapillas," Johnny said.

"The Spanish kind, not the Mexican kind, mind you," Amani added.

When Amani was ready, Kirk helped me over to the table.

"Do you think your niece would want a plate?" Amani asked.

"I'm sure she would," Kirk said. "I'll take it to her afterward."

"Nonsense," Amani said. "I'll pack it up and walk it over real fast."

"You don't need to do that," Kirk pleaded. "Please, don't go out of your way."

"It's my pleasure. Besides, the food should be eaten when it's the freshest to ensure you get the full flavor experience."

Out of nowhere, Amani whipped out a to-go container, and he expertly packed up a complete to-go order. "I'll be right back," he said. Kirk tried to get up and intervene, but Johnny shook his head.

"Don't forget to throw the latch so you can get back in," I yelled after him.

"Thanks for the reminder," I heard his voice say before he entered the hall. From inside the apartment, I heard him knock on the door.

"I better text Carissra to let her know dinner is being delivered," Kirk said as he pulled out his cell phone and made quick work of the screen. His thumbs were a force to be reckoned with as they flew across the display.

A couple minutes later, Amani was back, and the four adults finally dove into our meals. The meal was terrific, and the conversation was even better. The boys grilled Kirk about everything from his hobbies to his blood type. Kirk handled their interrogation—well, Johnny's interrogation—with grace. When Johnny got a bit too personal, I caught Amani giving Johnny dirty looks that Johnny either didn't see or ignored. If I was a betting woman, I'm sure it was the latter.

When dinner ended, Kirk offered to help clean up, which Amani appreciated since I still couldn't fully put weight on my ankle without it hurting. Instead, I found myself back on the couch with my ankle up, using Amani's ice pack.

"So, I'm separating the vegetable stew into three containers. One will be in your fridge for tomorrow. The second I'm going to put in your freezer, please don't use it on your ankle, and the last I'm taking for lunch tomorrow." Amani shot Kirk a look and added, "Make that four. I'm sending lunch to school with Kirk tomorrow."

"You don't need to do—"

"Nonsense, it's my pleasure. Besides, your use of the frozen veggies on her ankle led to its creation, so you are the mastermind behind the idea."

"Yeah, I totally didn't intend on the veggies I put on Erika's ankle to be used as food. She didn't own a real icepack."

"I know. What's up with that?" Johnny chirped in.

"Please," Amani chastised. "If it wasn't for me, I doubt you'd have one either. For that matter, I don't know how you survived living in this city before we got together."

"I have some survival skills," Johnny pouted.

"Well, I must take off," Kirk said as he and Amani finished the dishes. "I wish I could stay and chat all night, but I have an early morning tomorrow. Ahh...the joys of homeroom duty."

"What time does school start?"

"The breakfast bell is at 7:45 and the first period starts at 8:15. I must be there about 7:15 to 7:30."

"Oh my!" Johnny squealed in disgust. "I haven't seen that time of the day in years."

"Not true," Amani but in. "We didn't get home until almost 8:00 a.m. last new year."

"That's so not the same," Johnny said.

I rolled my eyes and looked at Kirk. "See what I must put up with? I would walk you out, but," I said, gesturing to my ankle, "I'm a bit indisposed."

"That's understandable. Thank you, Amani, for an amazing meal. And thank you," Kirk said, turning to me, "for inviting me over and making me feel welcomed."

"You are more than welcome. Have a good day tomorrow."

"Oh and, Johnny," Kirk started. "It's been an experience meeting you." Kirk followed the statement with a raised eyebrow in Johnny's direction as he smiled. With that, Kirk left.

"I like him," Johnny said as soon as the door closed. "Does he come in my size?"

"Oi!" Amani said from the kitchen, where he was packing up the last of his supplies. "I'm right here. What am I? Chopped liver?"

"No, you're more like sweet chorizo," Johnny said with a grin.

Amani said something in Arabic. For the first time, I was glad I couldn't translate what he said.

The boys stayed at the apartment for the next hour and the three of us gossiped. We hadn't had a good girl's night in, in forever, so it was nice. Of course, half the gossip was about Kirk.

"He's totally into you," Johnny said at one point.

"We're neighbors. We're barely friends at this point," I responded.

"Mm-hmm?" Johnny questioned.

"Besides, I don't know if I'm even on the market for a relationship. I mean, sure, I want to get my date back on, but dating the neighbor is just asking for trouble. What if things sour?"

"Erika," Amani said, "If I may?" I nodded for him to continue. "You seem to have a ton of reasons not to date, but you don't have one good reason for being alone."

"Did you just go Sondheim on me?" I asked. The puzzled look on Amani's face answered the question, so I reversed tactics. "I will keep that in mind. I need to get back on the dating saddle. I don't think I should do it with the neighbor. But, I definitely need to have someone on my arm for my show's opening. I don't want to show up on the red carpet by myself. That would be just...pathetic."

"Perfect!" Johnny said. "I have the right man for you."

"Seegers again?" I asked.

"Oh, I already told you about him?" Johnny questioned.

"Yep, yesterday." I let out a sigh. "You might as well give him my number. I officially give you permission to set me up on a blind date." Outwardly, I smiled. Inwardly, I was screaming. *Erika, what are you thinking?*

Chapter 8

The rest of the week flew by in a blur. I tried to get all my major chores out of the way quickly because I knew that once rehearsals started, it would be a mad dash to the finish line. I bumped into Carissra and Kirk a few times in the hallway, but we always rushed in different directions, so we didn't get a chance to talk. I had dinner with Johnny on Sunday night because he knew his best friend was about to disappear for a while as I dove into the rehearsal process.

October ended, and November arrived. Thankfully, the weather hadn't gotten too cold yet. I could still pull off a shirt and a light jacket. When I left the building that Monday for the first day of rehearsals, the cold air of the early morning sent my body into shock. I regretted immediately having not pulled up the weather app on my phone that morning. I had thirty minutes to get to the theater where we were rehearsing, so I didn't have time to run back upstairs and make it on time, because I had to stop by Starbucks and get a venti coffee. At this early hour on a Monday morning, I needed liquid energy.

With my coffee in hand, I pulled up the address for the theater again. I hadn't stepped foot into the new Maurer Theatre. I didn't know the Maurer Theatre existed until I got the information from Brice over the weekend about where rehearsals would be located. The block where the theater was being built was off Broadway on 47th Street. An article I found in *The New York Times* had given me some of the basic backstory. Real estate mogul Bernie Eldridge had been buying up buildings for about a decade before anyone knew what was happening. Bernie wanted to create a modern performance space that was functional and profitable. He envisioned a large Broadway theater built into a taller building, similar in fashion to the Marriott Marquis. The ground floor would consist of a variety of shops. There would be the theater, and last, there would be business space for various tenants. Bernie had envisioned renting space to pay for the renovated building and keeping the theater alive at the same time. It was a lofty goal, but *The Times* made it sound like Bernie had a firm grasp on what he wanted. Unfortunately, Bernie had died, and his wife Rebekka Eldridge had taken over as the CEO of the real estate empire, the construction of the building, the construction of the theater, and mounting the first show.

I walked up to the building and found a taped sign on a glass door that read, 'Actors Enter Here.' That was it. I opened the door and looked around at the construction mess that was everywhere. About ten feet past the door was a freestanding sign that read 'Actors' with an arrow pointing to an escalator. The escalator was in place, but it wasn't moving. I was glad my ankle was better because this place was clearly not accessible yet.

When I climbed up the escalator, I found a partially finished wall and stacks of theater chairs waiting to be installed. As I exited the escalator, I could feel the squishiness of the plush carpet under my foot, so I knew it was there. Another sign led me down a hallway to a smaller, secondary theater that was in much better shape than the one I'd just seen. *So, this place has two theaters?* The Maurer Theatre didn't have the multiplex feel of New World Stages, but I was surprised that they had planned for two different theaters. Right outside the theater were a couple of long tables covered in a white tablecloth. On it were various breakfast items, coffee, tea, and water bottles. A plastic card sat on the table reading, 'Beyond Tomorrow Cast and Crew Only.' I picked up a yogurt. I'm not much of a breakfast kind of gal, but that's probably because I'm not usually awake early enough for breakfast.

With my Starbucks and yogurt in hand, I walked over to the double doors of the theater itself. Emblazoned over the door was its name, 'The Rose Theatre.' I pulled open the door and walked inside to find a few people milling around.

"Good morning, ma'am," a young Black person started, "I'm Aarya McDonald; they, them, theirs. What's your name?" They then quickly added, "I need to make sure I get you checked off my list."

"Good morning, Aarya," I said, extending my hand for a handshake. "I'm Erika Lynsay Saunders; she, her, hers."

Aarya searched the list on their clipboard before making a checkmark next to it. "Thank you," they said. "I see you already found the breakfast table, so I don't need to tell you about that. If you need anything, flag me down and let me know. For now, you can take a seat anywhere in the building. Once it's 9:30, we have a short presentation from Actors' Equity, then we'll dive feet first into the show."

I walked away and found a corner seat on the other side of the theater. As people entered the theater, I wanted a good view of them, so I took a seat in the corner of the room. I sat down and started eating my yogurt in between sips of coffee. There were a couple of other people in the room, but it was still pretty empty. One person I recognized was Jeremy McCartan, who worked at Actor's Equity. I assumed he was here representing the union. He placed several stacks of paper on the front of the stage. Through the theater community rumor mill, I'd heard McCartan and Asher had dated after we'd broken up. McCartan caught me staring at him, and I quickly looked away.

"Good morning, Erika," a chipper voice came from behind me.

I swiveled my head to find Kathrine Kloeten standing behind me. "This will be fun. You're not my understudy again, are you?" I half joked the comment, half not. Thankfully, Katherine brushed right past my snipe and tried to hug me, which was awkward.

"It's good to see you again. I'm excited to be working with you."

"I'm sure you are." *But if you try to give me notes again, I may throw you off a building*, I thought to myself.

She lowered her voice and asked, "What do you know about the show?"

"Not much," I admitted. "My agent basically let me know that I needed to get work or a new agent, so here I am. Not that I'm not thrilled to be here. I don't know anything about the show."

"My agent was approached about me auditioning," Katherine said. "I didn't want to at first, but my agent said adding more Broadway credits to my resume was a good thing, so here I am. But, I watched the movie on which the show is based."

"How did you find it?" I asked. "I tried to find it, but neither Amazon nor Netflix had it listed."

"YouTube."

"What?"

"Yep, I found the movie on YouTube. After watching the movie, I'm still not sure how any of this will work, but it seems like decent source material."

Katherine sat down in front of me so we could continue talking and people watching at the same time. Over the next twenty minutes, more and more people arrived in the room. Some faces I knew, and many I didn't recognize.

As for Katherine, she'd grown into her own since being my understudy. Something about her seemed more polished. Heck, her bubbly personality didn't even seem forced to me this time. And since we were in the show together, I didn't have to worry about her shoving me down a flight of stairs to get the role. I decided to let bygones be bygones and get to know this new, and seemingly improved, actor.

At precisely 9:30 a.m., McCartan cleared his voice. "If you do not belong to Actors' Equity, please leave the room while I talk to the union members. If you are not currently part of Actors' Equity, but this show is helping you earn your union card, you can stay." Four people got up and left the room. When the door shut, McCartan said, "On behalf of Actors' Equity, welcome to the forthcoming brand-new musical *Beyond Tomorrow*. Today, I will go over some of the basic rules and requirements. I'll also walk through the specific factors you may not have caught when you signed your contracts. I also have the paperwork here if you need to change your medical insurance or get on our insurance plan."

McCartan explained how everything within the union would work as we prepared for the opening. After another twenty minutes, he finally asked if there were questions. One woman asked about the profit-sharing within the contract, and McCartan quickly explained how that would work. Once he was satisfied that everyone knew what was expected of them and what we could expect from both the production company and Actors' Equity, he asked for any nominations to be the company's Equity Deputy. Basically, the Equity Deputy serves as the liaison between the union and the performers.

"I nominate Serafina Porcher," said Kerrie Klark. I only recognized Klark because she'd had her own scandal a couple of years back. Her ex went to prison after hitting a pedestrian one evening. Even though Klark wasn't in the car when it happened, she'd been dragged into the legal battle when someone thought going after Klark would lead to a bigger payday. The public often woefully overestimates how much we actually make working on Broadway. Sure, we may have decent salaries when working, but we have a ton of time where we're not working and making little to no money between gigs. Ultimately, the judge ruled Klark couldn't be held financially accountable for her ex since they were not legally married in the State of New York.

"Thank you for the nomination, Kerrie, but I can't accept," Porcher said. Serafina sat in the front of the theater. I hadn't even noticed her when I'd gotten there. I had a slight ping of anxiety seeing someone from *The Faith Healer*. "As the company stage manager, my views on the show and the actors' views on the show are often at odds. I think the position should be held by someone esteemed by the cast but is also one of the cast." Porcher looked around the room as everyone evaded eye contact. It was like everyone believed if Porcher couldn't make eye contact with you, she couldn't nominate you. "I nominate Maeve McKenna."

"Mrs. McKenna?" McCartan asked.

"Yes?" the older woman asked.

"Do you accept the nomination?"

"Sure," I then watched her turn to the person next to her. I couldn't hear what she said, but I have good lip-reading skills. And what I saw was, *"What did I get elected to do?"*

"Any other nominations?" McCartan asked.

"Move to close nominations," a male voice said from the other side of the auditorium. I couldn't see who said it.

"Seconded," another voice rang out.

"It's been moved and seconded to close nominations for the position of Equity Deputy. All in favor, say 'aye.'" A loud chorus of "ayes" rang out. "Nays?" McCartan paused for a moment to make sure no one wanted to speak up. "Hearing no nays, the ayes have it. Congratulations, Mrs. McKenna, on your election to the company's Equity Deputy. With that done, I have nothing else for you this morning. If there are any concerns about the show, the production team, your safety, etc…, please contact Ms. McKenna. She'll pass them on to Actors' Equity directly. Thank you for your time this morning. I wish all of you a great rehearsal period. I look forward to congratulating you all on opening night."

With that, McCartan packed away his materials. When McCartan left the theater, the lights went out and the curtain rose, showing a square set of tables and chairs. The creative team was already sitting on stage. Part of me wondered how long they had been listening to the Equity discussion in the theater.

"As I call out your name," San Nicolás, the show's director, started, "please come join us on stage. Caiden Wynter Jeanes."

A young guy wearing skinny jeans approached the stage. I knew he looked familiar, but I couldn't place my finger on it. "Who is he?" I whispered to Katherine.

"He played a teenage vampire on *Derek's Destiny* for four seasons before the show was canceled."

"Erika Lynsay Saunders," the director called.

I grabbed my coat and bag and headed toward the stage. When I got there, San Nicolás extended his hand and introduced himself to me again, as if I somehow had forgotten he was the director in the last five days. He motioned for me to join the others on stage, where I found my name on a nameplate along with my preferred pronouns. Unfortunately, my back was to the audience, so I couldn't see anyone else. Thankfully, there were only ten people in the cast's core. There was an ensemble, but we were told they were rehearsing choreography with Divya Kappel. One by one, all the main cast members walked their way to the stage.

I looked at everyone and their cardboard name tags. This approach was handy for helping me learn people's names and faces, so I was very much in favor of it. When the last name was called, "Tabatha Sharlene Thomson," San Nicolás rejoined the group, and our first day of rehearsal began in earnest.

"*Welkom, bienvenido, tere tulemast, dobrodošli, willkommen, benvenuto,* witamy, добро пожаловать, ,⬜⬜⬜⬜⬜⬜⬜and welcome."

Did he welcome us in eleven different languages? Yep. He stared at us, waiting for a reaction. Who did he think he was, the emcee from *Cabaret*? Thankfully, I wasn't the only one who sat there for a heartbeat, not reacting. Finally, Maeve McKenna started a polite golf clap, so the rest of us joined in as San Nicolás took a slight bow.

"*Buenos días, guten Morgen, buongiorno, sobh bekheir, zăoăn, ohayō, mālō tau ma'u e pongipongi ni,* and good morning."

Please don't let every phrase that comes out of his mouth come with 100 different translations. We'll be here all day to finish one sentence.

San Nicolás paused for a second before continuing, "We are gathered on the unceded land of the Lenape of the Delaware peoples. I ask you to join me in acknowledging the Lenape community, their elders both past and present, as well as future generations. The creative team, the people who work for the theater, and the cast and crew want to acknowledge that this theater was founded upon exclusions and erasures of many indigenous peoples, including those on whose land this building is located. This acknowledgment demonstrates a commitment to beginning the process of working to dismantle the ongoing legacies of White settler colonialism.

"We want to recognize that in May 1626, the Dutch West India Company representative, Peter Minuit, purchased this land from the native peoples. The exact valuation of the sixty guilders is not known to us today. But, the price bartered for the island was undervalued. Essentially, the White colonialists bought the island for useless trinkets from members of either the Canarsees, who really didn't live on Manhattan, or maybe it was bought from the Weckquaesgeeks, who lived north of the Dutch on the island itself. Either way, the settlers bought the island from a group of indigenous people who did not know what they were bartering for because of cultural differences. I want to say '*woapanacheen*' or good morning in the native Lenape tongue as a final welcome as we start this journey together."

We all sat there unsure of the appropriate reaction, so most of us bowed our heads like we were in church. Personally, I liked acknowledging the land where we stood, but I wasn't sure if the land acknowledgment was appropriate since someone from another country gave it. I want to be culturally sensitive, but sometimes, I find it hard to know what to say or not say in situations like these. Instead, I try to be reverent and nod along.

"Aarya," San Nicolás called out. I looked over and watched as the nonbinary intern jumped to attention. "Please hand out the binders."

Immediately, Aarya started handing out binders that contained copies of the script and score. When she brought me mine, the cover had my name on it along with the phrase *part formerly called* Michael O'Brien. I'd already heard from Brice that the exact name of my role hadn't been decided upon, so I wasn't too surprised that there was still a giant question mark there.

Once everyone had their binders in hand, San Nicolás clapped his hand twice to get the room to be quiet. "I want you all to open the second divider tab in the binder. You'll find the complete script for the original movie. We wanted to read the script as a group today to get us into the piece's spirit. Over the next week, this material will evolve as we mature and evolve with it."

I looked at the puzzled eyes of others around the table as I flipped open my binder. Clearly, no one was quite sure what to make of this guy. He seemed more like a new age guru than a Broadway director. Admittedly, he'd never directed anything on Broadway, but I didn't think his style was typical on the West End either.

"Let us begin," San Nicolás said. "Before any dialogue, there will be a new song called 'Christmas in New York.'"

Eugenius Moses, the composer, started playing the piano. The song was upbeat and extolled the virtues of wintery holidays in NYC. The lyricist, Tyreek MacQueen, stood next to the piano and sang the lyrics to aid Moses in the song. Immediately, I found the lyrics catchy but trite. Not horrible for a Christmas musical, but I hoped the music was tightened as we went along.

As the song ended, San Nicolás read, "Lights up on the interior of a Manhattan office building. Workers scatter around going in and out of cubicles." He then nodded toward Peeter Gaspari, who started reading, "Regarding article 47…" I followed along in my script as the first scene played out.

While Peeter read his line, I noticed that my entrance came next. I took a breath. "Put them—"

"In walks Michael carrying a handful of colorfully wrapped Christmas presents." I waited for a beat, and San Nicolás nodded toward me.

"Put them down anywhere, Martin—"

"Stop!" San Nicolás yelled. "Mabel?" he questioned, turning to the young woman in charge of rewriting the book. "Do we even have a Martin anymore?"

"No, director," Wägner replied, looking up from a notepad she had sitting in front of her. "We got rid of that character a few weeks back."

"Then why is there still a reference?" San Nicolás asked.

"Because you wanted us to read the original, unaltered script today," Wägner reminded him. "The line will be referenced to Josef the Butler instead."

"Of course, of course," San Nicolás. He turned to me. "Read the line again, and instead of referring to Martin, say Josef."

"Okay." I took a quick breath and started again, "Put them down anywhere, Josef, and run along home. We won't be needing you tonight. We're having guests. Oh, and Josef, Merry Christmas."

"Stop," San Nicolás said again. "Wouldn't Josef be in the house already?"

"They're not in the house. They're in their office right now," Wägner explained.

"That's right." We all stared at San Nicolás as he thought through something. "For simplicity and since this scene is so short, why not start in their home office. It would be easier that way, don't you think?"

"I completely agree," Wägner said. "That's what I said we should do last week," she grumbled.

It took us almost six hours to get through the script, which should have been readable in about an hour. There was constant starting and stopping. Periodically, the composer and lyricist would sing. Intermittently, San Nicolás berated the artistic team. With each stop, Wägner got more perturbed.

During one of our breaks, I walked around the part of the theater that was currently not under construction. I could tell the new theater was going to be pretty darn large, which would be nice. I hoped I'd call this place home for at least a few years.

I rounded a corner and immediately stepped back because the artistic team were huddled in an alcove. I didn't mean to spy on them, but they weren't exactly being quiet about their disapproval of what was happening in the table read-through.

"That man is on my last nerve," Wägner practically yelled.

"Mabel," Moses started. "You knew the rumors about working with him when we signed the contract. He's brilliant but obnoxious."

"He keeps trying to correct things I wanted fixed...heck, I had fixed weeks ago," Wägner groused. "This is ridiculous."

"I feel your pain," MacQueen said. "He's changed so many of my lyrics. Half the time, I want to knock him out, throw down my legal pad, and walk out, or yell, 'Here, you write it.'"

"It's not that bad," Moses responded.

"Oh really?" Wägner questioned. "I wonder if you'd be singing the same tune if he was constantly trying to rewrite your music."

"That's because he can't write music," Moses admitted. "If he could, I'm sure he'd be doing the same things to me. Instead, I get general notes like 'not very festive' or 'tone it down.' What does that mean? How does one 'tone down' a song? He's vague about what he wants."

"And he's overly explicit in my work," MacQueen responded.

"What are you listening to?" a voice said right next to my ear.

I let out a little squeal before realizing Katherine had sneaked up behind me. I didn't want to be caught, so I grabbed Katherine's arm and pulled her away from the corner wall I'd been using to eavesdrop.

As we walked away, I told her what I'd learned.

"Wow," Katherine said. "Sounds like our director is putting everyone through their paces."

"Sounds like it. But if he doesn't change, I think he'll run this show into the ground."

We rounded into the main lobby area, where cast members hung out, snacked, and drank.

"Excuse me, Ms. Saunders," a timid voice came from my right. I looked over to see the young woman playing the main romantic lead.

"Oh, hi..."

"Tabatha," she offered.

"Thanks, Tabatha. I'm horrible with names."

"I get it. Too many new faces and names."

Surprisingly, that wasn't it at all. I knew most of the cast from being in and around the Broadway community. It's just Tabatha was so...ordinary. She was almost forgettable. I wasn't quite sure why she was cast in the show. I hoped she sounded better on stage than in rehearsals. Half the time, I couldn't hear what she was saying from across the room. The poor girl was going to have to learn to project and fast. Even if the audio people turned her mic all the way up, she'd still sound like she was whispering.

"How can I help you, Tabatha?" I asked

"I wanted to let you know how much I absolutely loved your performance in the revival of *Pirate Queen* two years ago."

Katherine snickered at my side. I wasn't sure if this young thing was being humorous, evil, or dumb.

"You do realize I was turned down for that role. Right?"

The look of horror that flashed across her face looked genuine enough.

"I am so sorry. Caiden said you'd been in that show. And I so loved the production."

I glanced to where the male heartthrob, Caiden Wynter Jeanes, stood next to Peeter Gaspari, who was doubled over laughing. Peeter's face had turned beet red. I shot both a scowl.

I let out a huff before I addressed Tabatha. "Tabatha, dear, you were set up by Caiden and Peeter to get on my bad side. I don't fault you at all. I'm sure this was all Peeter's idea. He loves his practical jokes. I get it. You're young, fresh off the boat, so to speak, and naïve—"

"I'm not naïve," she said in a huff.

"Oh really?" Katherine asked. I looked at her, and she had one eyebrow cocked in a knowing glance. "When did you arrive in New York City?"

"About two weeks ago."

"And how many auditions did you have before landing this job?"

"Two..."

"As she said," Katherine noted cocking her head in my direction. "You're naïve. That's not a bad thing. It means you haven't been around this business long enough to learn who the genuine people and the creeps are. And Mr. Gaspari over there definitely falls into the creep category."

"He's kind of cute," Tabatha said.

"Yeah, but he's probably more interested in Caiden than he's interested in you."

The look of shock that crossed her face was priceless. "He's a gay?" she practically exclaimed.

I looked to my left and looked to my right before saying, "Most of the guys in here are gay."

"What?" she said, her hand shot to her mouth to cover her surprise.

"Where did you move from?" Katherine asked.

"Paducah, Kentucky?"

"Where's that?" Katherine said before she could catch herself.

"It's about two hours northeast of Nashville, Tennessee."

I tried to figure out where that would be in my head, but my geographic knowledge of that part of the world was seriously limited. The only time I'd ever been in Tennessee was a weeklong stint in Nashville with *Wicked* many years earlier.

"How large is Paducah?" I asked.

"It's huge. There are about 25,000 residents."

I ripped out a laugh. I couldn't help myself.

"You think 25,000 is huge?" Katherine asked. Clearly, our brains were on the same wavelengths. "Girl, Manhattan has 1.7 million people alone. You're looking at 8.8 million when you add in the other boroughs that make up New York City. Can you grasp how much bigger it is here?"

I felt bad for the poor girl who deflated right in front of me. She had no idea what she was in store for in the city. If she didn't toughen up quickly, this city would eat her alive and spit her out.

"I know Katherine and I are blunt," I said. "But we've both been there."

"Speak for yourself, Erika. I grew up in Brooklyn."

"Okay, I've been there. I came to the city from Des Moines, Iowa, which had a couple hundred thousand residents. I still couldn't grasp how large this city was when I first started living here. After a while, you'll start to get a sense of how large everything is. As for those guys," I said, glaring toward Caiden and Peeter, "Ignore them. They're playing games. They probably figured out quickly you were fresh off the bus—"

"I flew here," she admitted.

"Boat, bus, car, plane, it doesn't matter. You came from away, and now you're here. Don't worry. You'll become jaded like the rest of us in no time. Living in New York does that to people."

The poor thing nodded before sauntering off toward the rehearsal room.

"That was a bit harsh," Katherine said.

"I was harsh? What about you?"

"I'm from Brooklyn. That was our version of showing hospitality," she said the last word using an overexaggerated Brooklyn accent. "So, what are your thoughts about Peeter Esteban Gaspari?"

"I don't have any," I admitted. "I hear he has great comic timing, but his comic antics slip off the stage a little too often for many people."

"So, he's funny but obnoxious?"

"Pretty much." I was about to say something snarky, but I was cut off by my favorite nonbinary intern, who stood and yelled, "Break's over!"

Katherine and I turned and headed back into the theater. We sat down at our tables. This time, the producer graced us with her presence as we sat down to reread the script. We dove into the script and got about ten minutes into the piece when Maeve McKenna proudly announced, "Time."

"What do you mean 'time'?" asked the producer.

"Rebekka," McKenna said, her green eyes twinkled with mischief. "You know the union rules. We work six days a week for eight hours a day during rehearsals. We've been working for eight hours, so it's time."

The producer rolled her eyes and said something to San Nicolás. After a brief discussion, Rebekka responded, "I do believe I'm going to have to call the union on this."

"You do that," McKenna said with a smile. "They'll tell you to read the contract. But please, take up some more time to call the union office. While you do that, we'll be sitting here making overtime pay. Rules are rules."

Rebekka rolled her eyes. "Whatever. The team has work to do anyway."

And unceremoniously, like that, the day was over.

Chapter 9

The rest of the week was chaotic and crazy. I swear that no one on the creative team knew what anyone else was doing. We'd rehearse songs in the morning that were only tossed out when we got script changes in the afternoon. They hadn't bothered to change the names of the characters yet. I was still Michael O'Brien. *Do I look like a Michael O'Brien?*

I slid down the backstage wall and rested my arms on my knees. The show would hit Broadway right after Thanksgiving like the largest turkey this country has ever seen. Thankfully, the producer added an extra week to rehearsals, but that meant our scheduled opening put us right in the tourist season instead of at the beginning of the Christmas season.

"Hey, girl," Katherine said as she slumped down the wall next to me. "How are you holding up?"

"Currently, I'm holding up this wall. As precarious as this house of cards is built, it wouldn't surprise me if the whole thing caved in on top of us...literally."

"I know. They should call the show Hashtag Poo Emoji."

"It'd be better than the other names I've heard tossed around this week. I've heard of a show changing names mid-stream, but this is ridiculous. Everything is changing mid-stream. It's almost like they had no intention of opening the show."

"You don't think they're our very own *The Producers*, do you?"

"Nah, at least the show in *The Producers* became a hit. This," I gestured wildly toward the stage like a plastic blowup doll at a used car lot, "I don't know what this is."

"Take a deep breath, Erika. It will all work out."

"I wouldn't be so sure. I'm grateful this week is almost over. I really need some me-time."

"Any plans for your day off?"

"Sleep," I said. "Maybe do laundry. I hate doing laundry. I'd much rather buy new clothes."

"I've totally done that before. It's too easy to have Amazon deliver new panties than trudging down to the local laundromat some days."

I let out a sigh of agreement. "But I have a date tonight."

"With a real live boy?"

"Yes," I said with a smile.

"Please tell me he's not in the business."

"Not like we are," I admitted. "He's a publicist."

"Is this a date or a reinvention of your social media presence?"

"My social media presence isn't that bad."

"Sure thing, Ms. Queen of the I Hate Men Club."

"I don't hate men." I crossed my arms and put on my best pouty face. "I don't like specific men. And...they tend to be the men I like to date."

"Scumbags, you mean. I think the term is scumbags. You date scumbags."

"Wow, you're blunter than my therapist is."

"I thought about becoming a therapist as a day job years ago. If nothing else, it would make my Japanese parents get off my case about 'finding a real job' or 'when are you going to get married,'" she mimicked in a stereotypically Asian-sounding accent.

"George Melton, Allan Chadwick, and Michael O'Brien, you're needed by wardrobe for a fitting," a voice in the back of the theater yelled.

"I guess that's our cue," I said as I pushed myself into a standing position, using the wall to help me up. We broke into "The Ladies Who Lunch," garnering only a couple of odd looks from people around us.

I let out a quick giggle as we left backstage through a side door and into the lobby where the wardrobe had set up temporarily.

"Where have you two been hiding?" Peeter asked as we approached. One of the wardrobe people had already pulled him aside and was measuring him—and I mean all of him—from the head to the wrist to the ankle and everything in between. The seamster whipped the tape measure around like a needle ninja with sewing thread.

"Oh, there you are," a voice said off to my right. I looked over to see Aarya walking toward us. "I was standing in the back waiting for you to come my way."

"Sorry about that," Katherine said. "We knew a secret passageway that got us here faster." The poor intern gave us a blank stare. "Backstage, we were backstage. It was faster to use the side door than walk through the middle of rehearsal."

"Oh, that makes sense," Aarya said flatly.

"Who are these two?" a man's voice asked. "I thought I called for the three ghosts."

"These are the three ghosts," Aarya said, gesturing to Katherine, Peeter, and me.

"They are listed as men." The older gentleman pulled out a notebook, flipped to a page, pointed at it, and said, "See, right there. The ghosts are supposed to be George, Allan, and Michael."

"Yes, sir," Aarya said, clearly doing their best to pacify the guy. "There was a change during casting."

"And no one thought to call me?" He turned in a huff and started away as he yelled, "Lucinda!"

"What was that about?" Katherine asked, watching the man leave.

"That's Lucinda Gayle's assistant."

"The costume designer?" I asked. "I thought she retired."

"She had retired," Aarya told us. "She's come out of retirement to design the costumes for this show."

"And what was that guy's name?" Katherine asked, watching as the man still stomped away.

"Lucinda Gayle's assistant. I don't know if he has a real name," Aarya said, with no hint of humor.

I stifled a giggle, but the woman with the tape measure almost lost it at that one. Over the next twenty minutes, all three "ghosts" were measured and sent back into rehearsal. Since the three of us had most of our scenes together, we were kept on the same rehearsal track. We went from dancing, to singing, to line work as a group. Not that our group had much to work with yet. There was the opening song, which we were all part of...maybe. Apparently, there was a debate on whether we should be part of the chorus on the first song since we were needed elsewhere as soon as the song ended. So, we practiced the harmonies on the song, but were told we'd probably never sing them again once everything ironed out.

We had one number that was firmly in place. The second musical number was a jazzy ditty titled "Christmas, Nothing but a Merchant's Holiday." We were told not to get too attached to the song because it could easily be gone by noon the next day.

This show was a train wreck of epic proportions, and no one knew how to right the thing or jump off. At precisely 5:00 p.m., Maeve McKenna went around the theater to ensure no one was still working.

"The union contract says eight hours a day. So, we work only eight hours a day. If they want us for more hours, they can negotiate that with the union," McKenna said when someone tried to stop her.

Honestly, it was nice that she'd taken the Equity Deputy position, but we might as well have given her a tin star and a cowboy hat, because she sure saw herself as the sheriff around these here parts.

After rehearsal, I ran back to my apartment for a quick nap, a shower, and a costume change before my date. Of course, Bootsy had other ideas. As soon as I opened my apartment door, he bolted between my legs. Thankfully, he didn't go very far. He sped down the hall and right into Carissra and Kirk's place.

"Hello?" I called and knocked on their door. The door was open, which is how Bootsy got inside. "Anyone here? Your door was open?"

"Come on in," a voice called from within the apartment. I walked in past the kitchen on the right, then into the living room.

"He's in here, Erika," Carissra called from a semi-shut door, which I assumed would be her bedroom.

I walked over and pushed it open. Sure enough, Bootsy had gone in there, climbed into Carissra's lap, and made himself at home.

"Little Traitor!" I said as I reached down to pet Bootsy on the head. "He really likes you. And Bootsy isn't known for liking many people."

"He wanted some time with me, I guess."

"Well, I really need to get Bootsy back home and fed. I have a date tonight, so I need time to freshen up after rehearsal."

"Carissra, why is the front door standing wide open?" Kirk's voice bellowed from the kitchen.

Grabbing Bootsy up, I yelled, "Sorry, it's my fault. Bootsy jetted from my house when I got home and came over here to visit." Seeing Kirk, I lifted a not-too-happy Bootsy as proof that I wasn't a deranged thief.

"Definitely brings up a new interpretation for the phrase 'cat burglar,' doesn't it?" Kirk asked. "Oh wow, that was a totally horrific dad joke," he said when he realized how corny the joke was once it had left his lips.

"Sorry, no takebacks on that one. You aged twenty years with that one," I said with a smile.

"Do you have plans this evening? I'm making...something. And I know it will be food. Beyond that, I haven't figured out my cooking plans yet. I came back from grocery shopping, so I know the house has food."

"And furniture!" I said, finally realizing the place had gotten furnished.

"The movers got here on Tuesday evening. I already left them a one-star review on Yelp."

"As for dinner, I wish I could," I said genuinely. "I'm seeing a show then having dinner tonight."

"She has a date, Kirk," Carissra said, rolling into the room to join us. "She needs to get home to change, and little Bootsy there was trying to slow her down."

"That he was," I said.

I looked at Kirk for a second, who looked sullen before he shot me a winning smile. "I hope you have a great time. What's the show?"

"I'm seeing *The Hallow Men*," I said, but the way I said it sounded more like a question than a definitive answer.

"That's the new musical based on the T.S. Elliott poem," Kirk informed me.

"Wow, you know more than I do."

"I went through my T.S. Elliott phase when I was younger. It's a show I hope to see at some point."

"Well, I'll let you know if it works or not."

"Carissra, isn't that one Broadway musical singer in *The Hallow Men*?"

"He's thinking of Ali Stoker," Carissra said. "But there are a couple of disabled persons within the cast."

"Gosh, I remember seeing Ali when she did *Oklahoma* at Circle in the Square. Wow, she totally deserved that Tony Award," I said.

"Do you know her?" Carissra asked.

"It's not like that, I'm sure," Kirk said. "I doubt all Broadway stars know each other."

"Of course, Kirk is right. I don't know all the people starring in shows on Broadway, but I know a lot of them. Heck, I'm sure you've already run over a few of them in this building," I joked. "But to answer your question, I do know Ali. We're not friends, but the Broadway community is pretty small."

"Well, I hope the show lives up to the hype, and you have fun on your...date," Kirk said.

"Thanks. Well, Bootsy and I had better get home. It takes a little bit of time and a lot of makeup to get ready for a night at the theater."

"I'm sure you don't need that much makeup to look amazing," Kirk said. "Well, I should probably think about what we're having for dinner." He turned and headed back to the kitchen as he finished unpacking the groceries. I left the apartment, kicking the door closed as I headed next door to my apartment.

Chapter 10

I walked into the coffee shop around the corner from the Al Hirschfeld theater where *The Hallow Men* was playing with a couple minutes to spare. I ordered a flat white with almond milk and found a corner table where I could watch the comings and goings of the store patrons.

For the tenth time, I checked my watch. Mr. Seegers was now eleven minutes late. I don't like late people. I get it. We're all late occasionally. But some people are perpetually late, and they drive me crazy—especially at the theater. I'm sorry, the curtain goes up at 8:00 p.m. on most shows. If you're there at 8:05, you should not expect to be seated until Act II. The flood of latecomers after the opening number is distracting for everyone. If I ran the world, I'd have television monitors set up in the lobby and let people watch the show from that vantage point until Act II. Sadly, I don't run the world.

At 7:20, the tinkling sound of the bells above the front door alerted me to someone new. A tallish guy with a rich tan walked in. Even if I hadn't already seen a picture of Ralph Seegers, I would have known this was him. He wore a midnight blue suit that had a shine to it. His shirt was almost the same shade but was covered in chromis damsel blue polka dots. The shirt was unbuttoned at the collar, showing his hairless chest, which I was pretty sure he had professionally waxed. His face had a five o'clock shadow, but not the type of shadow that happens because people have been working all day. No, it was more the five o'clock shadow that men who manscape regularly cultivate. His dark-brown hair was highlighted by lighter shades on top, so I guessed his colorist was as expensive as his suit.

He scanned the room, found me, and threw on a thousand-watt smile before walking over. I threw on my own fake smile and stood to greet him.

"Erika?" he questioned as if he didn't already know the answer.

"That's me," I said, reaching out my hand to shake his. Instead of shaking my hand, he brought me in for a hug and kissed my cheek.

"Ralph Seegers," he said when he finally broke away. "It's nice to meet you. Johnny has told me great things about you."

"Likewise."

"Let me get a coffee, and I'll be back to join you." Without waiting for a response, he took off his suit jacket and laid it over the back of the chair.

He walked away, and let's say that watching him walk away was just as enjoyable as watching him from the front. His suit pants left very little to the imagination. I could tell he was one guy who loved doing squats at the gym...and it showed. As if he could tell I was watching him walk away, he glanced back and smiled. I wanted to divert my eyes, but I'd already been caught, so I grinned.

My phone vibrated on the table, so I picked it up and looked. There was a message waiting.

Johnny: *So, what do you think of Ralph? I told you he was hot.*

I quickly shot back a text.

Erika: *He finally got here. And yes, he's nice to look at. Hopefully, his personality matches.*

Johnny: *Well, can't wait to hear how things go. Have fun. And don't do anything I wouldn't do.*

Erika: *That leaves my options wide open.*

I finished sending the text when Ralph pulled back the chair and sat down at the table.

"I'm sorry I was late. I was brought on to a new project this afternoon, and I was trying to get up and running."

"Anything I would have heard of?" I asked.

"Maybe. There's a new Broadway theater set to open next month—"

"Let me guess, the Maurer Theatre?" The quick wrinkle of his forehead showed me he hadn't expected me to know about it yet. The crease on his forehead also showed me he wasn't using Botox...yet.

"I'm surprised you've heard of the Maurer Theatre. It's flying under the radar right now."

"The new show opening the Maurer..."

"Yes?"

"I'm in that musical."

"Really? I hadn't heard that yet. But then, the only person the producer has told me about is the lead, Caiden Wynter Jeanes. Rebekka went on and on about him when we met. She wanted to make sure that I knew Jeanes was a teen heartthrob making his Broadway debut. Honestly, I hadn't heard of him, so I watched a few old episodes of *Derek's Destiny* on YouTube."

"I'm surprised Rebekka didn't bring you Caiden's entire DVD collection," I said with a smile.

"Yeah, she sure seems to be putting a lot into his stock as a draw for a younger audience." Ralph took a drink of his coffee before he continued. "What can you tell me about the show?"

I snorted out a quick laugh that was very un-lady-like. When I got myself under control, I said, "I'll let you know once I do." He narrowed his eyes in confusion. So, I provided a few more details. Over the next ten minutes, I laid out everything that had happened in the rehearsals.

"Well...wow... I can tell you Rebekka made it sound like things were moving along much better than that."

"I think we have something, but I really have no idea what it is yet. Honestly, I don't think anyone knows what we have yet."

"Well, you better hurry up and find out. The show opens in five weeks."

"Tell me about it," I said. I then took a sip of my flat white, which had grown lukewarm. After putting down my cup, I looked at my watch—we had twenty minutes to curtain. "Shall we head on over?"

Ralph looked at his watch. "Wow, you're right. We really should make our way to the theater."

Ralph stood up and donned his coat. I put on my coat. Ralph didn't offer to help me. Not that I need help to put on my jacket, but it's still nice when a guy offers. We left the coffee shop, headed around the corner, and made our way to the will-call line. We chitchatted about nothing in particular. Before long, we had our tickets in-hand and made it past security into the theater with about five minutes to spare before curtain.

The usher handed us our *Playbills* and showed us to the sixth row of the theater. Our seats were on the aisle. Ralph took the aisle seat and I sat next to him. Almost immediately, Ralph saw someone he knew a couple of aisles over, so he went over to say hello. I spent the time flipping through the *Playbill*. One of the first pages that caught my attention was a reprint of the T.S. Elliot poem, "The Hallow Men." I hate admitting that I'd never read it before, but I hadn't heard of it until this show came about. After reading the poem, I wasn't sure what to expect from the show. The lights flashed, so I put the *Playbill* under my chair as Ralph came back to his seat.

"Sorry about that," he whispered. "That's one of the co-producers on the show. Just wanted to check in with him quickly."

The orchestra started playing before I could say anything as the theater lights dimmed.

"This is the way the world ends. Not with a bang but with a whimper," the lead actor sang as the lights faded to black.

I wasted two hours and thirty minutes of my life that I'll never get back. *What the heck was that?* The timid applause from the audience suggested I wasn't the only one who was utterly lost. The actors took their bows, and they looked defeated, like the closing notice for the musical had already been posted.

Once the curtain came down, we waded our way through the streams of people flowing out of the theater. Thankfully, the ushers opened the side doors, which made getting the masses of people inside the theater outside much faster.

"So, what did you think?" Ralph asked me.

Is this a trick question? "You're the publicist. What do you think?" *Good job, divert the question.*

"I think it will be a smash hit and run for years," he said with all seriousness without skipping a beat.

I stopped in the middle of the sidewalk, spun around, almost bumping into an older woman, and, before I could think, said, "Are you delusional? I mean, did we watch the same train wreck in there? The show had no plot. The music sounded like something I'd expect to hear in my niece's kindergarten class. And I don't have a niece. The choreography, albeit good, did nothing to further the story. If anything, it felt like someone wrote on the script 'insert dance here,' and that's exactly what the choreographer did. Shall I go on?"

"Whoa there, tiger," Ralph said, putting his arms up in mock surrender. "I wanted to see your reaction. And you're right about everything you said. Don't forget the costumes, which I swear came from the Salvation Army's secondhand store."

"And who was the person who designed the lighting? The stage was either over-saturated with light or so dark you couldn't see anything. It was like a trained monkey sat in the back and randomly flipped switches."

"You're definitely opinionated."

I looked up into his blue eyes, which perfectly matched the color of his suit. I expected to see a hint of mockery, but I didn't see any there. "Yes, I'm opinionated. This is my career. This show is their career," I said, pointing to the stage door queue where a handful of people had lined up for autographs. "When a show like this gets mounted, it's bad for everyone. Sure, it makes for great internet fodder, but a lot of actors are going to be unemployed soon. I never wish for a show to close because I know what it means to everyone involved."

The corner of his lip quirked up. "It's rare to find someone so passionate about their vocation. I want to hear more of your passion over dinner. Shall we go?" he asked, offering his arm. I looped my arm in his and let him lead me.

"Where are we heading?" I asked. I hadn't bothered to ask Johnny where we'd be going to dinner after the show, so I was open to whatever surprise Ralph threw at me.

"I was thinking somewhere not too touristy that was good but quiet. How about Serafina's? It's the restaurant in the Time Hotel. The menu is eclectic, but it's a nice ambiance."

"Sounds perfect."

We crossed the street at 8th Avenue and continued northward until 49th Street. I'd never been in The Time before. Still, I remember hearing about it years ago on a Discovery Channel episode about hotels in New York City. As we entered, it was clear that the old version of The Time had been revamped with a high-end, sleek design. There were only a handful of couples in the restaurant, so we were seated almost immediately.

We spent a few minutes perusing the menu. Ultimately, I went with the red snapper served with root vegetables. Ralph had a rack of lamb with mixed grilled vegetables and purple mashed potatoes.

We talked about our lives and where we were from. One thing about living in Manhattan, most people seem to be originally from somewhere other than Manhattan. Only crazy people from across the world wanted to live in the city's heart. Our meals arrived, and they were cooked to perfection.

"I have a question for you," I said hesitantly. "As someone who's working on publicity for *The Hallow Men*, how do you polish this turd for the press?"

He poked a piece of lamb into his mouth and chewed. When he was done chewing, he said, "First, we hope the Internet doesn't crucify the show. It is still in previews, and we hope the team can fix this thing before it officially opens. If the internet trolls come for us, we do our best to deflect. I'll say something like, 'They're still completing the artistic vision for the show' or 'Reviewing a show in previews is like reviewing a cook by only looking at the ingredients.' The goal is to spin the show. Good, bad, or train wreck, my job is to put a positive light on everything."

"You saw that monstrosity tonight. How do you save it?"

His face fell. "Honestly, I don't know. It's hard for me to know what we'll be up against until I see what people say online or in the tabloids. I have a couple of interns who scour the Internet looking for any content about the shows we represent. I'm thankful for those interns because watching social media is almost 24/7 job these days. And every time I turn around, there's a new website, blog, or TikTok channel vying for my attention. I can't be everywhere at once, so having a team that does this for me frees me up to work on the big guns like *The New York Times*, *The Washington Post*, or *Variety*."

"Interesting... I don't think I could be in your world very long without yelling at my computer monitor."

"Oh, trust me," he started, "there's a lot of that, too. I had a colleague who put his fist through a wall many years ago. He'd had enough of one of the Broadway gossip columnists who made it her personal goal to sink the show."

"Let me guess, Michelle Bouvier?"

"I take it you've had your dealings with Ms. Bouvier?"

"Me, personally? No. Thankfully, I've never had a run-in with her. But I've had a lot of friends raked over the open fire by that hatchet job over the years."

"Yeah, Ms. Bouvier is the type of reporter you always want to be leery of. They hold more power than many Broadway producers. I've spent a good deal of my adult life cleaning up after her. She's like a one-woman stampede when she decides she wants to take someone down a few notches."

I sighed, glad that I wasn't the one who had to deal with the press like that regularly. As an actor, I know dealing with the press is part of life, but dealing with them is the ultimate double-edged sword. On one side, the press can help you build word of mouth for your show. I've seen many little Off-Off-Broadway shows garner the attention of the press only to be transferred to Broadway and turned into Tony Award-winning mega-hits. On the other side, they can cut you down without a moment's hesitation, and poof, there goes the show. Sometimes, the drama reported by the press is completely legitimate. Still, other times, it feels like the reporter is out to get you or the show.

The server came by the table and took away our dishes before asking if we wanted dessert. Both Ralph and I passed on the dessert. After dinner, Ralph walked me all the way to my apartment. He was everything I look for in a guy. He's tall. He's gorgeous. He's articulate. He understands the world I live and work in. And he's conscientious of others, even if he was late.

Standing outside the Manhattan Plaza, he said, "This has been a charming evening. Admittedly, I wish we'd seen a different show, but the company and conversation were enjoyable."

"I agree completely."

He hesitated before saying, "Well, you should get inside where it's warm. I have an early morning tomorrow. After seeing the show tonight, I know I have a long Sunday ahead of me."

"Thank you for a perfectly amazing evening."

I reached out to give him a hug goodbye. He enveloped me in his strong arms. My face pressed against his chest. I could practically feel his muscles under my cheek. I slightly twisted my head and he stared down at me. Before long, his soft lips were pressed against mine. It was a completely swoon-worthy moment. If this had been a movie, my leg would have lifted off the ground behind me as I floated on air in his embrace. Instead, someone on the other side of the street yelled, "Get a room!"

That caused both of us to separate and start laughing. "Well, I guess I better be going," Ralph said. "I hope to see you again."

"Likewise." We said goodbye, and he watched as I walked into the building. The warm embrace of the lobby was a nice contrast to the bitter cold of the November evening. I said hello to the security guard and made my way to the elevator bank. I was about to push the button when I remembered I'd forgotten to pick up cat food for Bootsy. I quickly hurried my way out of the building when my phone vibrated.

Ralph: *Already missing you. Had a great time tonight.*

Erika: *I can't wait to see you again. Let's get coffee sometime this week.*

I hit send and walked the half block to the nearest Duane Reade. I entered the drug store and headed toward the pet food section. I bypassed only a handful of people in the store. I picked out seven cans of Bootsy's favorite brand when I heard a loud voice on the aisle over.

"I'm sorry, honey. You know how things are here in the city. I wish I could make it home tonight, but I missed the last train to Westchester."

I recognized that voice. I'd just been on a date with that voice. Hugging the cat food tins to my chest, I tiptoed to the end of the aisle and poked my head down the next aisle to find Ralph on the phone. While he was talking, I noticed something that hadn't been there while we were on our date, a wedding ring. I gasped and pulled my head back as Ralph's head turned in my direction. *I hope he didn't see me. Please don't let him have seen me.* I crept away from the aisle.

"Tell the kids I'm sorry I won't make it to church tomorrow. The show isn't doing very well, so I'm going to be in the office all day. I'll be home Sunday night, I promise... Love you too... Good night."

I made my way to the back corner of the floor and stood there for twenty minutes. I put the cat food on the ground and texted Johnny.

Erika: *Ralph Seegers is married. Did you know that?*

Johnny: *What? I thought he was single. How do you know he's married?*

Erika: *I caught him on the phone with his wife and saw that he'd put on a wedding ring, which most definitely was not there on our date!*

Johnny: S*orry! I didn't know. Let's talk revenge scenarios tomorrow.*

When I finally hoped the coast was clear, I made my way to the front counter and paid for the cat food.

Chapter 11

Before heading to bed, I put fresh food and water out for Bootsy so he wouldn't get me up in the morning. I learned a long time ago that an empty Bootsy dish meant an annoyed Bootsy who would do everything in his power to annoy me until I finally broke down and fed him.

The sun woke me the following morning around 10:00 a.m. I was not in the mood to be awake yet, so I rolled over and pulled the covers over my head, blocking out the light. I finally rolled out of bed an hour later and made coffee. I put on my slippers and looked out on my tiny balcony to find that a light layer of early morning snow hung around in the shaded areas.

"Hmm... I didn't know we were expecting snow overnight," I said. "Bootsy?" I called.

I heard a *meow* from my couch. I looked over and found a white furball nestled in a blanket. Technically, the blanket was a throw blanket, but Bootsy preferred it for his personal nesting place at night. At first, I tried chastising him every time he yanked it from the back of the couch, but I quickly realized that the battle was long over, and I wouldn't be winning it any time soon.

I walked over and rummaged through my cabinet, deciding what brand of coffee I wanted. Did I want something flavored, or did I want something bold? Being forced to make any kinds of decisions before noon and without caffeine should simply be illegal. I pulled the regular, bold coffee and put it in my coffee pot. When I went in for my annual physical this year, my doctor asked me how many cups of coffee I drink a day. Without thinking, I had responded, "Does a pot count as one or two cups?"

Once I poured the first cup, I went over to the couch and unplugged my iPhone from where I'd left it in its charging cradle. I flipped through emails. I had some new pages to learn for the show. Nothing too radical, but I figured I'd wait to run lines that evening. I then checked out my social media, email messages and texts.

Johnny: *Again, So, so, so sorry Seegers was married. Again, didn't know.*

I shot Johnny back a quick text, reassuring him that it wasn't his fault. I knew Johnny well enough to know that he would sit and stir until I reassured him that I didn't blame him for Ralph's infidelity.

Ralph: *Had a good time last night. Hope to see you again soon. Want to take you up on that offer for coffee. - R*

"Are you kidding me?" I mumbled at my phone. *Blocked!*

Bootsy looked over at me as if asking the human to "simmer down now. One of us is sleeping." And yes, I totally know that I anthropomorphize my cat. In my mind, he's a little furry human who happens to be mute. Some of my best conversations happen with Bootsy.

After I'd finished coffee number one of the morning, I searched my fridge for food. I opened the fridge door. I had condiments, milk, and wine...the breakfast of champion cat ladies everywhere. There was a box of pizza pockets in the freezer that had been there since the world began. I dusted the freezer burn off the box, opened it, and popped one into the microwave.

While the frozen pizza pocket was cooking, I poured myself coffee number two of the morning. I figured that I'd be ready to shower by the time I got to coffee number four. By coffee number six, I'd be ready to leave the apartment and do laundry.

Ding! The bell on the microwave dinged. I reached in and touched the pizza pocket, and immediately regretted that decision. I ripped my finger back out of the microwave. I didn't think I'd kept my hand on it long enough to burn myself badly, but I ran my hand under cold water, just in case. After drying my hands on a dishtowel, I ripped off a paper towel, folded it in half and grabbed my pizza pocket. I was at least smart enough to know that sticking my tongue in the pizza pocket was not a smart move. I blew on its edge and took a small bite to taste it. It had a kind of pepperoni pizza gooey center. Part of me almost felt bad that I was eating the pizza pocket when I had access to New York-style pizza within feet of the building's entrance, but that would require me to actually leave the comfort of my home. Instead, I ate the perversion of authentic pizza. It was, surprisingly, not bad tasting. Sure, it didn't have the extra layer of grease coating the top of the pizza like I get out on the street, but it was edible.

After I'd finished my brunch, I had cup of coffee number four and decided it was time to shower, so I crawled back into bed and took a short nap instead. I wasn't feeling in the most productive mood.

I hauled myself out of bed an hour later. I might as well have been a petulant child having a fit on the ground, pounding my fists and feet, yelling, "I don't wanna go to school!"

With complete reluctance, I dragged myself back into the kitchen and drank two more cups of now-lukewarm coffee. Hey, beggars can't be choosers. And at that moment, I wasn't in the mood to heat the coffee in the microwave or make a new pot. Of course, Bootsy eyed me from his perch on the couch. He was clearly still annoyed that I was making so much noise.

With more coffee in my system, I was ready to face the world. Well, face the laundry facilities in the building. I ran through the shower quickly, and threw on some leggings and an oversized sweatshirt I'd kept from a boyfriend years ago. What can I say? I loved the sweatshirt more than I loved him. I gathered up the laundry I had to do—along with my iPad—and headed down to the basement.

Laundry on a Sunday is always a busy place. Plus, it is the best place to find out about building gossip. Want to find out who's having an affair with whom? Do laundry on Sunday. Want to find out which tenant got a gig on a new show? Do laundry on a Sunday. Want to know who is leaving the building because now they're fancy after having landed a role in a major TV series or movie? Yep, do laundry on a Sunday. I walked in and was glad to find the room only half full. Even better, not all the machines were full, so I quickly took over two machines and separated my darks from my lights. I put in some detergent along with my quarters and waited for the laundry to finish its final spin cycle.

While I waited for my laundry to finish, I read my iPad. I checked out *The Times* to see if there were any stories I should hear about. Nothing really popped, so I checked out *The Post* to see if they had any salacious gossip I needed to know about, still nothing that urgent. I finally opened the new pages I'd been emailed from Aarya and set about reading. Most of the changes were minor and didn't impact my part of the show, which made me happy. I really didn't want to spend my day off learning new lines.

"Hey, stranger." I looked up from my iPad to see Kirk holding a laundry basket. "How was your date last night?"

"How did you…" I said, catching myself. "I forgot I saw you when Bootsy escaped."

"How is the little guy today?"

"He stared at me all morning wondering why I had to make noise and disturb his sleep."

"I hate to admit it, but some days I do the same thing when someone wakes me up."

He found a couple of empty washing machines and loaded his clothes into them.

"What did you end up making last night for dinner? I left before you made your decision."

"A full-on gourmet meal with all the sides."

"Yeah, that doesn't sound fishy at all," I said, narrowing my eyes.

"We ordered Chinese."

I cracked out a laugh. When I recovered my breath, I asked, "What about all those groceries you bought?"

"They're for food during the week. After doing all that shopping, I couldn't bring myself to cook any of it."

"I notice you avoided my question. How was the date?"

"Abysmal," I admitted. "Well, the date part was amazing. The show is horrible. I wouldn't want to force my ex-boyfriend to watch it."

"It's that bad, huh?"

"It's that bad and then some. I've seen a bunch of trash at the theater over the years, but this was a new level of 'what the heck are they thinking.' I even said to Ralph—"

"Ralph?"

"The jerk I saw the show with. But we'll circle back to that little disaster number. Anyway, I said I felt bad for the people working on the show because a lot of those people will be unemployed soon."

Once Kirk had finished unloading his laundry into the shiny metal washing machines, he plopped in the requisite number of quarters and came to sit next to me on the row of empty chairs. I ran down a laundry list of everything wrong with the show after making sure no one in the room was working on the show. I had made that mistake once. I'd been doing laundry and was talking to Johnny when I started mouthing off about how bad a show was. I was brutally honest and hadn't seen the poor girl who was in the show until she burst into tears and ran from the laundry. I hadn't seen that poor girl again. I always wondered if I scared her back to whatever flyover state she'd come from, hoping to make it big on Broadway.

"So, what about Ralph?" Kirk asked.

"He was perfect. He was gorgeous, he said all the right things, he kissed me good night, and I felt like it was a complete princess moment."

"Princess moment."

"You know Anne Hathaway in *The Princess Diaries*. In the movie, Anne has this line that goes something like, 'You know, in the old movies, whenever a girl would get seriously kissed, her foot would just kind of...pop.' And the next thing she knew, she'd be standing on one leg as her knee bent and foot sailed into the air. You know, the foot-popping kiss."

"I don't think I've ever seen that movie, so I'll take your word for it," Kirk said with amusement and skepticism.

"It's a real thing! I swear. Girls are taught about the foot-popping kiss as kids. We want the foot-popping kiss. And there I was, in full foot-pop mode, and I wanted to swoon. If he'd asked me to run off with him to Paris, I would have done so in a heartbeat."

"So, how did you go from foot-popping, which I'm still not sure is real, to thinking he's a jerk in less than twelve hours?"

"Oh, I went from foot-popping to jerk mode in under twenty minutes." I told him how I forgot Bootsy's food, so I went to Duane Reade only to find the jerk talking to his wife on the phone after he'd slipped on his wedding ring."

"Could have been his twin? I mean, if it was one of those old movies, wouldn't the guy have had some explanation for why he'd done what he'd done?"

"Nope. Not unless the twins are walking around New York wearing the same suit. So, no. Not a twin. Just one royal jerk."

"Ouch," Kirk said, shaking his head. "Sorry to hear that happened to you. Sadly, there are a ton of jerks out there in the world."

"That there are. I'm glad I found out he was a jerk before we'd had a second date or before we'd gotten serious."

I looked over at my washing machines and it was time to put them in the dryer. "Be right back." I grabbed one of the rolling carts that helped transfer the clean, wet clothes into the dryer. I looked through what I was laundering. I threw a couple of dryer sheets in the dryer and plunked down more quarters to get the clothes dried.

"What were you doing before I got down here?" Kirk asked. "I didn't mean to monopolize your time."

"Not a problem. I was looking at some new lines the creative team sent out. Thankfully, most of the changes aren't to me, so I don't have much to work on."

"I'm always amazed at how you actors memorize those lines. The high school play I was in was a disaster. I forgot all my lines, and when they started coming out of my mouth suddenly, they all came out in the wrong order." I giggled at the mental image of a young Kirk trying to act when the gobbledygook flowed from his mouth. "That was my first and last time on a stage."

"I'm lucky. I have an amazing memory for learning lines. Some actors put a lot of effort into learning lines. I'm not one of them. Sure, I must rehearse and practice. And I've had a few stage managers yell at me to stop changing the lines. But then, I wouldn't need to change the lines if the writers wrote them right in the first place."

"I'm sure writers love hearing that."

"Of course not, but some of them desperately need to hear it."

"Do you regularly work with playwrights?"

"Depends on the show. I've worked with some playwrights who are in rehearsal every day telling us exactly how the line should be said. Frankly, I want the director to banish those authors from the theater. Theater is collaborative. At some point, the playwright, the composer, the lyricist, or, in the world of musical theater, the book writer, must give up their baby and let the actors and directors do their jobs. If you're too close to the material, you won't see the giant, glaring mistakes in the show."

"How so?"

"I think some directors who are involved in writing the show can get so invested in the show that they don't want to see the problems. The classic example was *Spiderman: Turn Off the Dark.*"

"I heard about that one. Wasn't that show dangerous?"

"Dangerous? No. Were mistakes made on the stage that led to safety problems that should have been caught before actors were harmed? Yes. I think Julie Taymor, who is a brilliant director, got so caught up in making this weird Shakespearean version of Spiderman that she really did not see the giant fiasco that was right in front of her."

"It couldn't have been that bad. Was it?"

"Oh, it was that bad, and then some. I don't think I do the level of horribleness enough justice in an explanation. It was that bad. Again, a director who was so caught up in writing the show that she didn't see the problems. But anyway, what about you? Why teaching?"

"I was always the kid who wanted to be a teacher. When other kids played army, I wanted to play school. I used to get extra worksheets and bring them home and play teacher with the younger kids on my block."

"You didn't!"

"I did. Hey, there were some bright five-year-olds when I was in the second grade. By the time they got to school themselves, they were head and shoulders above their peers."

"How did you pick which grade you wanted to teach?"

"The grade kind of picked me. I have a general degree in elementary education, then got my master's in special education. I read that the school districts were not fully serving kids with learning disabilities or behavioral problems, so I decided I wanted to be *that guy*. I didn't want to work with the brightest and best students. I wanted to work with those who were struggling. I wanted to help them 'become the best they could be,' to steal from the Army."

"I thought about teaching elementary English for a hot second, but I don't really like kids."

"Well, then, it's a good thing you decided against teaching. There tend to be kids in elementary schools."

"Exactly." The buzzing sound of my drier finishing snapped me back to reality. "Time to fold," I said as I rose off the chair and headed toward the dryer. "Just as an FYI," I said, leaning in close enough to Kirk to smell his cologne, "I take my stuff back to the apartment to fold. I don't know when the last time those folding tables were cleaned. Personally, I wouldn't trust them unless you bring a box of disinfectant wipes to clean them off first."

"Thanks for the tip. And if you ever need help running your lines or something, I'm next door."

"I may take you up on that offer."

Chapter 12

I stood at the front of the stage, getting ready to belt the eleven o'clock number. I looked up at the monitor hanging from the mezzanine. The conductor's arms were flying as the tempo for the song grew faster. *Beep!* Her arms grew more chaotic and became a blur on the screen. I kept staring at the monitor, waiting for my cue. *Beep!* Finally, there was a pause in her movement. She looked straight into the camera mounted above her station so I could see when she held out her hand to me, which seemed to come right out of the monitor, beckoning me to sing. There was a moment when, I swear, she could see me through the monitor. She gave me a downbeat. *Beep!* I opened my mouth. Nothing came out. The conductor had a look of confusion cross her face. She led the orchestra back around to my cue and she gestured toward me again, giving me my cue. I tried to force something out. *BEEP!* The sound of a foghorn burst forth from me. My arms flew to my open mouth, but covering my mouth with my hands couldn't make the sound stop. *BEEP!* A new sensation rolled over my body. It was as if a ghost was standing on my chest, trying to give me CPR. I wanted to panic, but it's hard to hyperventilate when a foghorn is roaring from your chest. I closed my eyes, wishing it would all disappear. *BEEP! BEEP! BEEP!*

My eyes flew open. A mound of white furry butt greeted me. A tail swished frantically in front of me as Bootsy slowly kneaded my left breast. *What the...? BEEP! BEEP! BEEP!* I slowly shook the brain fog out of my head as I nuzzled Bootsy off my chest, rolled over, and turned off my alarm clock. It was 6:30 a.m. Part of me just wanted to roll back over and sleep for another hour, but I had to get out of bed and head downstairs to the gym or I'd skip it again.

One would think all the crazy running around and dancing on stage would keep a Broadway actor in great shape. And it helps. But you need to be in pretty good shape if you're going to sustain yourself eight shows a week during a long run of a Broadway musical. I threw my legs over the edge of my bed and grabbed the workout clothes I'd laid out on the dresser the night before. I put on my sports bra, which immediately squished my breasts firmly against my body. I then threw a tank top on which read, *Divalicious*! in a bright red font. I slipped into a pair of black running leggings, socks, and a pair of tennis shoes. I pulled my hair back into a ponytail, then pulled the ponytail through the back of a baseball cap emblazoned with the *Wicked* logo. With my hat in place, I was ready to work out. Well, ready to head downstairs.

Bootsy was already curled back up next to my pillow, probably enjoying the warmth from my body that had seeped into the bed while I slept. I grabbed my AirPods, iPhone, and keys and headed out of the apartment. I walked over to the elevator and pushed the button for the floor where the gym was located.

After I had finished laundry the previous afternoon, I'd lounged around the rest of the day doing a whole lot of nothing. I had wanted to have a chill evening without too much going on. Between six days of rehearsals and my disastrous date, I had wanted to lie on the couch, watch some Netflix, and veg out, so I had.

The elevator door opened, and someone else headed down to the gym nodded at me as I entered. She was wearing a similar outfit, but her ballcap was from the most recent revival of *Company*. *What is her name?* She was slightly older, and I knew she'd been in the latest revival, but I couldn't remember what her name was off the top of my head. I really should get to know the people in my building better. Then again, this was New York City. We do a lot of nodding our heads to sort-of-strangers as we go throughout our daily lives when we're not busy avoiding eye contact with people on the street.

After a couple more stops and a few more early risers joined us, our little group of morning gym-goers stepped out into the hallway before heading to the glass enclosure that was the building gym. For a Monday morning, the gym was already active. Thankfully, no one was on my favorite treadmill, so I went over and snagged it before doing a few light stretches. When I was ready, I hopped onto the treadmill and started moving at a nice slow jog. I ran the lines I'd learned the previous evening in my head. Once I was good to go with the lines, I put my AirPods in and pulled up my Broadway Mega Mix, which I'd created. The list of songs were all the ones that were upbeat and fun to run to.

Forty-five minutes later, I pulled myself off the machine and wiped it off quickly because no one wants to get on a machine coated in someone else's sweaty mess. I did a few more stretches to ensure I wouldn't get sore. Then, I headed back upstairs to the apartment. Before heading into the shower, I pulled out a protein shake from my fridge. I learned a long time ago that I am horrible at taking care of myself first thing in the morning, so a friend of mine from college who's a dietician recommended protein shakes. I'd picked up some new pumpkin spice-flavored ones when I went grocery shopping a couple of weeks ago. But I grabbed the coffee-flavored protein shake because it had the same amount of caffeine as a cup of coffee.

I sat down at my small dining room table and looked through the news. Not too much was going on, so by the time I'd finished my protein shake, it was already 8:10, so I needed to get my butt in gear if I was going to make it to rehearsal by 9:00.

I showered quickly and then threw on a cream-colored cashmere sweater and a pair of black jeans. I said goodbye to Bootsy and headed out into the cold November morning. And it was downright chilly. I pulled my coat up around my throat as high as possible as I traipsed out into the morning air. Thankfully, most tourists aren't blocking the sidewalks around the theater district early on a Monday morning, so I could make it to the theater in under ten minutes with no problem. One thing you learn about New Yorkers living in the city is we have two speeds, fast and get the heck out of my way—I have somewhere to be like ten minutes ago. Most New Yorkers avoid the places where tourists congregate because tourists gawk a lot and saunter down the sidewalk like they're out for a Sunday stroll. I always joke there should be two different sidewalk lanes, one for tourists and one for people who live here.

The construction people were already streaming into the Maurer Theatre. Since I was early, I peeked into the main theater to see how things were progressing. The seats in the back part of the theater were already being installed, but there was still a ton of work that needed to be accomplished before the space was ready for audiences. I strolled into the orchestra level to see what it would look like. The interior was sleek and modern. Personally, I prefer the sense of history one gets when stepping foot into the older Broadway theaters. I continued walking down the center aisle until I emerged from the overhang of the flying circle, which was the level just above the orchestra. I looked up and could see both the flying circle and the mezzanine levels from that vantage point.

"Hey! This is a hardhat-only area, lady," a voice yelled from somewhere in the theater. The acoustics of the hall made it difficult to see where the voice came from.

"Sorry," I yelled back into the void. "I wanted to see how things looked." I didn't wait for a response. I headed out of the space and made my way to the Rose Theater, the small black-box theater we used as the rehearsal space.

I walked into the Rose Theater and found several cast members already sitting around the table at the front of the room. *Guess we're going to run the new script.* I walked up and said hello to a handful of people. I found my name tag. Someone had already put out bottles of water on the table for all of us, which I was going to appreciate as the morning progressed. I looked at the names on either side of me and found that Katherine would be on my left and Peeter would be on my right. *I guess they wanted to keep the ghosts together.*

"Good morning," Katherine said, sitting down next to me. "How was your Sunday?"

"Sunday was nice and relaxing. You?"

"Uneventful, like I wanted it to be." Katherine looked around to make sure no one was within earshot before she asked, "How was the date?" Apparently, the facial expression I made instinctually answered the question. "That bad, huh?"

"The date was great. The finding out he was married part kind of killed the evening."

"Doh!" Katherine said in her best Homer Simpson impersonation. "How'd you find out?"

I quickly told her the story. She guffawed at the right moment.

"Oh wow," Katherine said. "That's horrible. Men!"

"Men, indeed," I groused. "Sometimes, I think it would be easier to be a lesbian or asexual."

"Well, don't give up yet," Katherine said. "You know, I have a friend—"

"No more blind dates," I said, crossing my arms in a big x in front of my body.

"He's a hot lawyer," Katherine said in response. She pulled out her phone and flipped through a few images. "Take a look." She handed me the phone. I had to admit, he was hot.

"And he's single?"

"Very."

"And we're sure that he's single?"

Katherine chuckled. "I can guarantee you he's single. He's shy. And his law firm has him working crazy hours, so he really doesn't have time to get out and socialize."

"Let me think about it," I said.

"Don't think about it too long. I'm sure a hottie like him will eventually be snatched up."

"Ahh...heck, why not?"

"Awesome," Katherine sung in her falsetto, which garnered a few looks from people around the table. "Are you free any night this week?"

"Basically, I have rehearsals and vocal lessons. That's about it," I told her, wondering why I'd agreed to go on another blind date.

"Perfect! I'll text him at our first break."

There was a clearing of a throat. I pivoted my attention to Rebekka Eldridge, who now stood at the front of the table.

"Good morning, team," she said. "I know the first week was wonky as we all got our sea legs. After thinking about the show and where it was headed this weekend, I had a brilliant spark of inspiration." Something about how she said the last part made me queasy inside. "The show wasn't...festive enough. It needs more Christmas spirit. Suppose you go back and watch the original movie. In that case, it's only really considered a Christmas movie because of the first part of the movie. We need to rethink everything and make it considerably more joyful. I want this show to be the ultimate holiday musical."

San Nicolás quickly burst into applause. The rest of the table joined in with polite applause.

Eldridge waited for the applause to wane before she continued. "After discussing the show with the artistic team over dinner," she started. I looked over at the artistic team, and their stone-cold faces told me everything I needed to know. Clearly, the creative team looked blindsided. "I've heightened the holiday spirit of the show. I went through the scripts and did my best to make them jollier." Eldridge said, looking around the room for the intern. "Aarya, please pass out the new scripts."

Aarya appeared with a box of binders and started handing out the updated scripts. Part of me wanted to complain since I'd spent time yesterday memorizing the new lines I'd been given, but I kept my mouth shut. Aarya came over and they handed me the new binder. My name was printed on the top of the binder. The title had changed from *Beyond Tomorrow* to *The Naughty List*. I opened the binder and looked at the cast. I can only imagine what my face looked like when I read that my character's name had changed. I was no longer Michael O'Brien. I was now listed as Tinsel Hollicane. We were now listed as The Elves. Katherine's character was now called Icelyn Candywine, and Peeter's character was Blitz Nightwish.

"As you can see," Eldridge started. "I've updated the three tycoons and made them North Pole elves living in New York City." She said this with such excitement. She clearly thought everyone else would be as enthusiastic about these changes as she was. Instead, the room sat there in stunned silence, unsure what they were supposed to do with the new information. She gave a broad smile and sat down.

San Nicolás stood to address the group. "I know these changes are complex and add new dimensions to your characters, but I think these changes will be beneficial for ensuring the long-term success of the show."

I looked around the table and watched as everyone nodded. From what I could see, most people didn't agree with the sentiment, but everyone was at least willing to see where this would take us.

"This morning," San Nicolás started again, "we will read through the new script. We'll also be looking for places where we think we can enhance the holiday vibes of the show, so don't be surprised when we have more rewrites as the week goes on." He turned his head and looked at the composer, lyricist, and book writer. "Our joyful team here," he said, gesturing to the three, "have their work cut out for them this week. They'll be updating the script and coming up with new musical numbers all week long, so be prepared for lots of changes."

We sat there quietly until Peeter said what everyone was thinking. "What the f—"

"None of that," Eldridge snapped. "We want to keep in the festive spirit of the show. Think like elves would think. Instead of using *dirty* words, say something like...I don't know... *what the fudge?*"

"Is she *fudging* kidding me?" Peeter asked under his breath.

San Nicolás looked at the group and could tell they needed a moment, so he said politely, "Let's take a break. When we get back, we'll start working our way through the new script."

As people got up from the table, I leaned back and sat there in stunned silence.

"Well, it looks like I need to update my vocabulary," Peeter said. He paused for a second, clearly in deep thought. If I tried hard enough, I could almost see the steam coming from his ears. "Son of a nutcracker," he said. "Or maybe, Mother Frosty the Snowman...or maybe Not Today Santa."

I turned my head and looked at him. "What are you doing?"

"Well, the producer doesn't want us to use *bad* words, so I'm festivizing my vocabulary."

"Festivizing?" Katherine and I said in unison.

"Let's face it, this show is turning into a real elf-ing mess," Peeter grumbled.

"Go elf yourself," Katherine responded before bursting into a giggle fit.

"What the elf is wrong with you two?" I asked. I couldn't help myself.

"Well, Kiss My Artificial Tree," Katherine said, using a southern twang that reminded me of Flo from the nineteen-seventies television show *Alice*.

"Holly Fudge," Peeter said, "You two are a bunch of ice-holes."

"Go stuff yourself in a stocking," I responded. "Or better yet, eat coal."

The three of us burst into a fit of giggles, which caught Eldridge's unwanted attention, so we smiled and left the stage to take our break elsewhere.

I went to the bathroom quickly before heading back into the theater. Most of the cast had trickled back in when I got back inside. One person was visibly not there, Eldridge.

Once the last cast member was in her chair, San Nicolás addressed the group. "I know Eldridge's announcement this morning was a bit of a shock for all of us."

"Wait...you didn't know about these changes?" Maeve McKenna asked.

"Umm..." San Nicolás said hesitantly. "Although Rebekka and I had discussed the need to think through the lighter Christmas elements of the show, we had not discussed her artistic vision."

"What the elf!" Peeter whispered. It took all my control not to burst out laughing.

Chapter 13

The rest of Monday was uneventful. We played a few theater games as the creative team struggled to update the script based on the new requirements from Eldridge. We rehearsed a few of the songs in the afternoon that the creatives hoped could be salvaged. Since we were supposed to start truly blocking the show later that week, I felt horrible for the bind Eldridge had put everyone in. But hey, I was still getting paid, even if I did spend thirty minutes pretending I was on a bobsled racing down a hill.

During rehearsals, I got a text from Brice and Johnny telling me that my favorite reporter, Michelle Bouvier from *The Post*, had authored a tell-all book about *The Faith Healer*. She'd titled the book *Blinded by Faith*. I ran by The Drama Book Shop to pick up a copy on the way home. Part of me wanted to wear a giant hat, huge sunglasses, and a scarf to make myself look inconspicuous as I walked into the store. Right in front of the door was the display with the new book. The book's tagline made me want to throw up, "Blinded by Faith: What Happens Backstage Can Kill You."

"Geeze, Louise. That's not hyperbolic," I said out loud.

"Can I help you?" a twenty-something store clerk said, looking up from where she'd been straightening out books.

"Sorry, I was talking to myself."

"Oh my God, you're Erika Lynsay Saunders!"

I beamed my best smile. "That's me."

"Would you mind autographing my copy of your book?"

"My book?" I questioned without thinking. From the look of shock on her face, I could tell that I was missing something. I narrowed my eyes. "I've never written a book."

"Oh...I'm sorry, I figured you authorized the book." My eyes must have grown three sizes—like the Grinch's heart. "Umm...well, it's a tell-all story that places you as the hero."

"It what?" I asked. The poor saleswoman looked at me blandly. "I didn't know this book existed until an hour ago." The words were out of my mouth before I could stop them.

"Oh, wow," the saleswoman said. "Do you need to sit down?" I'm not sure what I looked like, but she must have observed the look of unease that washed over me. "There are chairs in the back. Why don't you take the book and look through it? I'll bring you a bottle of water."

I snagged a copy of the book from the shelf, then let the woman escort me to a chair in the back part of the store where all the play scripts were housed. As I opened the book in my lap, I said something appreciative to the salesclerk. I looked at the book for a second like it was a live snake going to strike, but I finally calmed my nerves and flipped open the book to the first chapter.

"*I was lucky enough to be in the audience to watch Erika Lynsay Saunders as Mary Beeler in the original production of* The Faith Healer, *the musicalized version of William Vaughn Moody's turn of the twentieth century play.*"

I pulled out my phone and texted Brice.

Did you know about this?

I then texted Johnny.

No one warned me this was coming out.

I continued reading the book. "*Saunders' voice that night reminded me of a blend of the vocal quality of Kelli O'Hara, the power of Bernadette Peters, and the charisma of Sutton Foster.*"

Wow, can I put that on a business card? I don't think my mother could have written this any better. I continued to read the first chapter, which had a lot of details about the opening night. Someone or multiple someones from the cast and crew had given Bouvier a ton of backstage gossip. I almost teared up as she described them wheeling my body out of the theater, having passed out after falling through the stage. She made it all sound so...dramatic.

A buzzing sensation next to my leg caused me to jump. I pulled out the phone. *Brice.*

"Did you know about this?" I asked without saying hello.

"I'd heard rumors about a book coming out about *The Faith Healer*, but I assumed it would be a coffee table-type book."

"Have you read it yet?" I asked.

"I read the first chapter online. You come off smelling like a singing version of Mother Teresa. It's almost as if we wrote a press release telling your side of the story."

"Can you please keep your voice down?" said a woman who was browsing plays on the other side of the room.

"Sorry," I said.

"Where are you?" Brice asked.

"The Drama Book Shop. I came in to buy a copy. The clerk wanted me to autograph the book. She thought I'd had it written."

"I need to get my team together and figure out how we can spin it. I'm going to go out and buy a copy. Well, you know, I will send an intern out to procure a copy. I'll have the interns break the book up, read different sections, and report back in the morning."

I stifled a laugh. I couldn't believe that Brice wouldn't be bothered to read the book, but he would make sure his interns gave book reports in the morning. I listened to Brice as he chatted away, coming up with new plans about how he could use this book to further my career. I said, "uh-huh," "wow," and "great idea" every couple of minutes as he prattled on. Finally, I said, "I need to get home, Brice. Call me tomorrow."

"Will do," and he hung up the phone.

I spent the next ten minutes flipping through the book to see what was inside. Toward the end of the book, I found another passage with my name.

"I sat in stunned silence in Radio City Music Hall as they called out Darla Dabbraccio's name for Best Actress in a Musical. I looked around me and saw a bunch of us from the media world with our jaws dropped open. How could the Tony Award voters give that woman an award? She hadn't earned it, not really. Everything from the tone of her voice to how she raised her arms in big numbers were imitations of Saunders' version of the role. If anything, Dabbraccio should have gotten an award for best mimicry or the most likable puppet on Broadway. The woman who deserved that award hadn't been seen on Broadway since her accident."

I couldn't have written this better if I had written it myself. I stood. There was a lighter feeling in me as I walked out of the back room and into the front part of the store. I found the young salesclerk and said, "I'd like to buy this book. Oh, and I'd be happy to autograph your copy," I added with a wink. "In fact, if you want me to, I'll autograph any copies you have."

"Really?" the clerk said. "Let me get my manager."

They set me up in the back room with a couple of boxes of books, and I signed them all. I also promised that my autograph in the book would be their exclusive. As a reward, they gave me the copy of the book I'd been reading, plus two more. I beamed as I stepped out in the cold evening air. I was floating on air. Nothing could get me down. And I ran smack dab into a man drinking a slushie. *Who drinks a slushie when it's cold outside?* I looked down as the blue, syrupy, icy concoction ran down my cream-colored cashmere sweater.

"Watch where you're going, lady," the man yelled at me.

He didn't apologize. He didn't stop to make sure I was okay. As he walked away, he complained about dumb blondes. He didn't bother to pick up his empty cup, which laid right at my feet. I tried to wipe slushie off my sweater and onto the street. When the bulk of the mess was either soaked into my sweater or laid on the ground, I turned to walk away.

"Aren't you going to throw the cup away?" a voice asked. I swiveled my head around, about to bite someone's head off, and found a homeless teenage girl sitting in a doorway of a closed shop. "I mean, don't litter. It's bad for the environment."

I wanted to clap back, but I stooped, grabbed the empty cup, and walked away. Thankfully, there was a trashcan in the middle of the block, so I deposited the cup there. Somehow, my plastic-wrapped bag stuck in my purse hadn't been affected by the blue. I shook my head and walked home. I passed a window and thought I looked like I'd been in a brawl with a Smurf—and the Smurf won.

The rest of my trek home wasn't as exciting. I got a couple of odd stares from people standing in the lobby. Admittedly, one of them held a copy of *Blinded by Faith*, so it's possible the stare wasn't because I was covered in blue.

As soon as I was in my apartment, I stripped off my clothes and placed the sticky mess in a plastic bag so it wouldn't make all my dirty clothes tacky. I quickly showered, then threw on some pajama pants and a sweatshirt before curling up on the couch with Bootsy and my new book. The book was a tell-all, and I was the only one who came out ahead. Bouvier went after Asher and Zachary Magnus. The two had been having secret rendezvous behind the scenes since the first day of rehearsals.

I sat in shock to learn how long the affair had been going on. I also learned about the fallout from my accident. No one ever told me about the backstage drama. At one point, the director quit over his objections to Darla Dabbraccio being cast in my role. Unbeknownst to me, Dabbraccio had been having an affair with one of the producers, which is how she got the understudy job in the first place.

"*After Saunders' accident, the producers turned to the only person who knew the role, Darla Dabbraccio. Unfortunately, Dabbraccio didn't know the first thing about acting or the role. Instead of watching Saunders during rehearsals or previews, she'd been using her dressing room for other things.*"

"Eww..." I said out loud. "I could have gone my whole life without knowing that."

The book then went into a whole chapter about how much Dabbraccio had relied on the stage manager for all her lines because Dabbraccio hadn't known any of them. Somehow, they had muddled through that first show as Dabbraccio had recited the lines exactly like the stage manager gave them. The stage manager and the producer had then forced Dabbraccio to sit down with a bootleg copy of the show filmed during previews and watch my performance repeatedly. Eventually, the woman acted and sounded like me. *Well, that sure explains a lot.*

I finally finished the book around 1:00 a.m. As I drifted to sleep, I smiled, thinking about all the people I wanted to send copies to.

I skipped the gym the following day but got myself ready in record time before heading out to work. I opened the door and backed out of my apartment, keeping one eye on Bootsy to make sure he didn't dart out.

"*Ooff,*" I said as I backed into someone. "Sorry about—"

"No biggie," Carissra said, looking up at me. "You just hit the side of the wheelchair. I'm glad I didn't run over your foot."

"I need to stop running into you like this," I joked. I glanced down at my watch. "Shouldn't you already be at school?"

"Normally, I would have left about thirty minutes earlier. But with the ice out there today, I've been waiting for the van."

"Van?"

"I have a number I can call that sends a van to pick me up when I need it. I hate using it. The guy who usually shows up gives me the creeps. He's not handsy or anything, but he smells weird and looks at me strangely."

"Sadly, there are a ton of creeps in this world."

Carissra started wheeling toward the elevator and I joined her. "So, how is school going?" I asked, trying to make small talk.

"It's going. I'm pretty much ahead of most people in my class, so it's easy for me."

"That's always good."

"How's the show going?" I must have rolled my eyes a bit too exaggeratedly because Carissra cocked her head and asked, "That bad?"

I let out a brief huff, not sure how to respond to that question. The elevator's ding caught our attention and the doors slid open. The elevator was empty, so I let Carissra get herself situated before joining her.

When the doors closed, I said, "It's not that the show is bad. Right now, the show is rudderless." I spent the short ride down to the lobby giving Carissra the short version of what had transpired the day before.

"So, really? You're not allowed to cuss at all?"

"I know. We had fun coming up with alternatives, though," and I rattled off some of our ideas.

"Wow. All I can think of now are sexual innuendos related to candy canes."

"Carissra!" I said, my eyes turning the size of saucers.

"What?" she said, looking up at me. "I'm a bisexual teenager, not a nun."

I shook my head. "What am I going to do with you?"

The doors to the elevator slid open, Carissra wheeled out, and I followed. "Well, I'm off to school. Don't go sitting on Santa's lap today!"

My jaw dropped, and she rolled out the door, snickering. I followed. Outside, I pulled up my coat against the sleet that slicked the sidewalk. I watched from a distance as a guy in his forties helped Carissra into the van. I wanted to make sure he didn't do anything inappropriate. Thankfully, he didn't. He gave off weird guy vibes, but he was completely professional. As the van drove away from the curb, I walked toward the theater.

Next to the Maurer Theatre, there was a fun theater-themed coffee shop called Hello, Coffee! The logo for the shop looked like the one used for the 2017 revival of *Hello, Dolly!* starring Bette Midler. They were already playing Christmas music, which I thought was a bit early since we still had three weeks to Thanksgiving. When it was my turn, a gorgeous barista in his early twenties stared at me with sky-blue eyes.

"Good morning," he said. "What can we steep for you this morning?"

"Uh…" I stammered, trying to get my tongue to work properly. I stared at the menu as if I was still trying to think of something. I finally spat out, "What's good for a throat?

"We have a cooling throat tea a lot of singers really enjoy. It's a blend of sweet licorice, anise, and fresh raspberry leaves."

"Sounds delightful," I said.

"Size?"

"Large," I mumbled as I noticed how large the man's hands were. "I like large…drinks," I said, catching myself. He turned around to get my tea, and he had a perfectly sculpted butt under his jeans. "Whoa," I said aloud, but thankfully no one heard me. *I'd like to jingle his bells.*

Chapter 14

Tea in hand, I entered the theater, then climbed up the escalator, which was still not moving. I wondered if they'd get the blasted thing working before the first day of previews. Thankfully, I didn't have to worry about those details. I had to worry about whether we'd have a show to put up.

I walked into the rehearsal theater. The tables were set up again on the stage. I smiled at Eugenius Moses, the composer, and he lifted one corner of his lips in a cordial greeting. From the looks of the bags under his young eyes, I didn't think he'd slept.

I crossed the stage and found my seat. Sure enough, there's a brand-new notebook with a brand-new script inside. There were a few new sheets of music, too. I glanced around the table and saw a sea of weary faces on the creative team. From the looks on everyone's faces, the entire team was on-hand last night to work through the producer's new vision. At precisely 9:00 a.m., Divya Philomena Kappel, the choreographer, sauntered into the theater. She made a grand entrance up the stage. The level of drama she exuded reminded me of Glenn Close in the last scene of *Sunset Boulevard*.

"If you will please settle down," Kappel said, in her thick Spanish accent. "Asier is taking a meeting with the producer, so he asked me to rehearse you this morning. And by rehearse, he wants us to go through the new materials. Since I am not really needed until it is time for you to move your bodies, I will sit back and let Maestro Moses take over." She looked over at Eugene, who clearly didn't know this was coming.

Eugene stood up and turned to face us. "Well, as you, umm...well know. We were thrown a bit of a curveball yesterday. Umm...Mabel,

Tyreek, and I stayed up all night trying to make the producer's vision a reality."

Kishor Khatri, who was dressed in a tan suit, looked at Eugene and asked, "Is this your show or her show?"

"Well, umm—"

"We're hired to create the show the producer pays us to," Tyreek said, cutting Eugene off. "I get it. This isn't the process any of you expected, but it's the one we have. I'm going to ask that you work with us. Trust me, we're working as hard as we can."

Mabel looked at Tyreek and added, "We all have a job to do. Our job is to write a show. Your job is to put that show on. We wished we had a fully developed show on day one, but that's not how it turned out. I suspect it's not the last curveball we'll be thrown—to pick up on Eugene's baseball metaphor."

"Err...thanks, guys," Eugene said, clearly getting his bearings again. "Our goal is to walk you through the current vision of the show. We're hoping that when San Nicolás gets back from his meeting, we'll have a better idea of...well, we'll know if the show is going forward as is or if more major rewrites are coming down the pipeline." Eugene looked at everyone expectantly. No one asked questions or appeared to have any qualms with the group's process that morning. "Great, let's open our scripts to page one. We might as well sing the first song. We haven't changed anything on it at all, but the dialogue after the song differs from the steel barons...ghosts...I mean, now elves. Geez, I need some sleep," he mumbled as he sat down at the piano.

He started playing the now-familiar tune, and the cast joined in. We read through each scene, then Eugene and Tyreek would sing the song that would happen. If there wasn't a song yet, Eugene or Tyreek would explain the general direction of the score. A couple of times, one of them would tell us what would happen next, and the group would groan. Either Eugene or Tyreek would be like, "Okay, maybe that was a bad idea."

There were a few giant plot holes in the script and Mable would tell us she's working it out. By the time noon got there, we'd finished the first run-through of the new material, and I had to admit, it didn't totally suck. Sure, with each passing day, our new musical looked less and less like the movie it was supposedly based on, but that's show business.

"Hey, how are things going in your world?" Katherine asked, sidling up next to me.

"Things are going well. The show looks less and less like a disaster. I think we've passed *Carrie* terrain and are heading toward the NBC *Grinch* musical."

"Ouch! The reworks aren't that bad."

"True, but there is still a lot of room for improvement. At this rate, we'll have a show bad enough to ruin anyone's Christmas," I groused.

"Tell me how you really feel, Mrs. Grinch," Katherine joked as she narrowed her eyes at me.

"I know. It's not that bad. Just out of it is all. A lot of weird things are happening, and I'm still trying to make sense out of it all."

"Let me guess, *Blinded by Faith*?"

"You've heard?"

"I heard it was published. What type of hatchet job did Michelle Bouvier do to you?"

"That's it," I stammered, "She was nice. Very nice. It was like she went out of her way to make me sound like the golden child of Broadway. She practically makes me seem like some musical theater saint."

"And this is a bad thing, how?" Before I could respond, she then asked, "Wanna go to lunch and talk about it?"

"Sure."

We grabbed our coats and purses before heading out into the cold. Kappel yelled after us to be back in an hour as we left. Technically, we weren't supposed to have that long at lunch, but if the director-stand-in tells us to take a long lunch, that's precisely what we planned to do.

We went around the corner to a diner that was always fast and cheap. We were seated at a booth in the back, away from staring eyes and prying ears. Between being seated, getting menus, ordering, and receiving our food, I told Katherine everything that had happened after I left rehearsal yesterday.

"You really had no idea this book was coming out?" Katherine asked between bites of her grilled chicken and roasted asparagus.

"Not a clue. I didn't know a book about the show was being written. No one contacted me or asked if I wanted to say anything on or off the record."

"And Brice didn't know either?"

"He said he knew a book was coming out about the show, but he figured it was a coffee table-type book."

"I could see how he thought that, but don't those usually come out while the show is still running? The only people who buy those books are theater geeks and tourists who saw the show on Broadway and want the book as a memento."

"Hey, I own a few of those books. My favorite one is the *Avenue Q* book with the orange furry cover."

"As I said," Katherine said, pointing at me with her fork, "theater geeks."

She had me there, so I laughed and shrugged slightly. I had been a high school theater nerd through and through. I had wanted to be on Broadway since I watched a touring production of *The Phantom of the Opera* as a child. The tour was okay, but I fell in love with the whole idea of musical theater after seeing that show.

"What are you doing tonight?" Katherine asked.

I snapped my attention back to her. My mind had wandered. "Say again?"

"I asked, '*What are you doing tonight?*' You really are in a funk today, aren't you?"

"Yes, to the funk. And I don't know what I'm doing tonight. Why?"

"Well, I talked to my friend Darrin Becker, the hottie lawyer, and he said he could squeeze in a dinner date between 8:00 and 10:00 if you could meet him at a restaurant near his office."

"I can tell he's really into this whole dating thing." My voice dripped with sarcasm.

"It's not like that. I promise, Erika. It's just," she paused to put the right words together for a second, "he's a bit different. It's like I said, he's a little shy. But he has a smoking hot bod."

"And how have you seen his body?" I asked.

"Okay, full disclosure. His parents are friends with my parents. We grew up together. And I may have seen his body once, twice, or a dozen times over the years. We shared the same rental property every summer. I would play out in the ocean, and he would read under an umbrella, avoiding the sun."

"So, you're setting me up with a nerd. Better than my last date, but that's easy."

"Yes, he's a total nerd, but he's a great guy. And he has a killer six-pack. He's one of those guys who doesn't have to do anything to stay fit or look hot. He wakes up, throws on clothes, and goes about his life. But he has one of those male model bodies. You know the type. No matter what the guy wears, it fits him like a glove and looks like he stepped out of a catalog."

"I may have dated a couple of guys like that. Admittedly, the last one who could pull that off was Asher. As much as I hate admitting it, he could wear anything and look like a fashion model gracing the cover of *GQ*."

"Maybe so, but from what you've told me about Asher's recent problems, this Michelle Bouvier character at *The Post* has an ax to grind with Asher."

"Or Bouvier had the unfortunate experience of holding a conversation with Asher," I grumbled. I had to check myself. I may not like Asher, and he was many unflattering things, but he wasn't a completely horrible person. "I don't think anyone deserves to be beaten up in the press unless they've done something horrible. And no matter how much I think being a prick should be punishable by death, it's not. And whether I want to admit it, there's still a place deep inside my body that cares about him."

"Those are called your ovaries, dear. You want to borrow his sperm and make babies," Katherine joked.

"Don't ever say that again. Not even as a joke. The idea of having any part of Asher worming its way into my body is enough to make me go get my tubes tied tomorrow."

"Ahhh...come on. He's not that unattractive. The two of you would have such adorably cute babies."

I knew she was joking and trying to get under my skin. But the thought of having anything to do with Asher made me physically ill. I never really dealt with Asher's betrayal. Sure, I've talked to my shrink about Asher, but I haven't seen him or talked to him since *the incident*.

"Okay," I finally blurted out. "I'll go on a date with the hot lawyer. But if he ends up being married or engaged, I may go Lorena Bobbitt on him."

"Who?"

"I sometimes forget how young you actually are," I joked.

"Huh?" Katherine asked, clearly not following my brain's thought train.

"Lorena Bobbitt chopped off her husband's...*candy cane* and threw it into a field."

"When was this?" Katherine asked as she gasped in disbelief.

"It happened in the early to mid-1990s."

"Ahh...pre-millennium news. Kind of surprised more women didn't join her movement over the years."

I considered it for a second, and realized I don't think I'd heard about another woman chopping off her husband's candy cane since Bobbitt.

Katherine texted the lawyer. A couple minutes later, she texted me the location and time. I'd heard of the restaurant but knew little about it. I glanced down at my watch, and it was almost time for us to be back in the theater.

"We really need to pay up and hurry out of here. We don't want to be late for whatever grand new idea Eldridge has come up with last night."

"Maybe she'll decide that the whole show will take place in Whoville," Katherine said as she giggled at her own joke.

"I'm sure there's a copyright infringement in there somewhere. But I'm sure she could stage the whole show on Mars. We could call it *Christmas on Mars*. We could all be aliens instead of elves."

"Don't you dare give her that idea," Katherine said in all seriousness. "You know as well as I do, Eldridge might like the idea. And honestly, I don't want to play green again."

"Me neither. Playing Elphaba was fun for a time, but I swear I still have nightmares. I'm still painted green, hitting the C# five to eight times a week. After a show, I go to my dressing room to shower, but the green won't come off. I scrub and scrub. But the more I try to wash the green makeup off my body, the greener I become."

"If I was a shrink, I'm sure I would have a field day with that dream. You're like an analyst's fantasy."

I shot her a dirty look and wrinkled my brow. "You don't stay in show business too long before you develop enough neuroses to need a whole team of shrinks."

"Preach, girl."

We got our check, paid, and walked back to the theater. We talked more about Katherine's schoolgirl crush on Mr. Darrin Becker, esquire. She told me they never dated because he didn't talk enough for her.

"I'm sorry, but I need a guy who can uphold his end of the conversation," Katherine said. "He doesn't need to *out-talk* me, but he needs to converse in more than monosyllabic responses."

"And why am I letting you set me up on a blind date again?" I asked.

Katherine shrugged and said, "Because you're that desperate."

"I'm really not that desperate," I fought back.

"Oh really? Should I call Mr. Married Man for you?"

"Okay, so maybe I am that desperate," I said with a little more humility. "If nothing else, it will be a good meal."

We got back to the theater and the rest of the afternoon went by in a flash. San Nicolás reported that Eldridge was on board with the new direction the creative team was taking. Eugene audibly sighed in relief when he heard the good news. Part of me wondered what it would take to get the three younger people to stand up and leave the show. I didn't want them to, but I had to wonder how much they could take.

The rest of the afternoon was spent going over the new script with San Nicolás now that he was back and could see and hear everything. The show sounded like it had a clear narrative arc, which was a definite positive improvement.

After work, I walked home and ran into Kirk on the streets. He was juggling a bunch of recycled bags filled with groceries.

"Hey, stranger," I said as I approached him.

"Oh," he said, spinning his head to see who was talking. "Hey, Erika, how are you doing?" he asked. His dimples flared.

"I'm doing well. The show's moving along, so this was an overall good day." I took stock of how awkward he was walking with all the bags, so I offered to help.

"No thanks, I got 'em," Kirk said.

"I didn't think you were one of *those* guys," I said, narrowing my eyes at him.

"What's that supposed to mean?" Kirk asked.

"Well, you clearly need help, but won't ask a woman for help."

"I'm not *that* guy. I really don't need help." He almost tripped over a crack in the sidewalk as he said that.

"Mmm-hmmm," I started. "Want to rephrase your answer?"

"Fine. Would you please help me, Erika?"

"Gladly," I said and grabbed a couple of bags. My body language may have gloated, but I kept my tongue in check, which is more than I can say for myself on a typical day.

We chitchatted about nothing, and I told him about the book. He was surprised to find out a book had been written about me without my knowledge.

"Well, the book is about the show. I happened to be a large part of that show." He nodded and encouraged me to go on with my story. We talked all the way into the building and up the elevator. He let himself into his apartment, and I handed him the two bags I'd been carrying.

"Would you like to join Carissra and me for dinner?" Kirk asked.

"I wish I could, but I have a date tonight."

"Another one?" Kirk asked.

"Excuse me?" My body tensed, and I was ready to throw down...metaphorically.

"Nothing bad," he said, quickly backpedaling. "I remember how much the last jerk had hurt you when you found out he was married."

"Well, my friend who set me up on this blind date has assured me he's single, so that's a check plus in my book." On that note, I made a big gesture of looking down at my watch and telling Kirk that I needed to head home. "Gotta get ready for my date."

"I sincerely hope this date is beyond your wildest dreams," Kirk said. "I think the universe owes you."

"Thanks. I'll see you around," I said, pulling the door closed behind me. I walked next door to my blue-painted door and let myself inside.

The warm water cascaded over me as I stepped into the shower. I wanted to wash my worries and fears away, but there wasn't enough water in the Hudson River to do that these days. I picked up my loofa, squeezed a dollop of my favorite British Rose bath gel on it, and began the slow, methodical process of exfoliating my whole body. I scrubbed everything until it was nice and foamy without being crazy rough and causing my skin to pinken because of abrasion. I then used a nice tea tree shampoo and conditioner before using a seaweed and aloe face cleanser I'd picked up the last time I'd been home in Iowa. My mother had begged me to go to the mall with her and my sisters, so I had. Who'd have guessed that I'd find a product there that I fell in love with? Thankfully, the shop had a small web presence, and I could order more any time I needed. I probably could have had my mother pick it up for me and ship it, but I didn't want to bother her with something like that. She had enough on her plate without catering to my facial cleanliness.

Once I rinsed off, I stepped out of the shower onto the plush shower mat, which absorbed any extra moisture. I reached over and grabbed a towel from the hanger and patted myself dry. I looked into the bedroom. Bootsy was lying on the front part of the bed, cleaning himself.

After brushing my teeth, I set about applying makeup. Now, I'd learned a long time ago how amazing makeup is. It can completely transform someone, but you must be careful because a little goes a long way when you're sitting across a table from someone. You need more if you're going to be on a television screen, and you'll need a lot more to make sure someone in the back row of the 1926 seats of the Gershwin Theatre, where *Wicked* has called home for forever and a day. I rubbed an excellent moisturizer onto my skin before applying a primer. I waited for a second for the primer to set before starting on my foundation. I still preferred to use my fingers when evening out my foundation, though I know a lot of women both on and off the stage that use foam wedges or brushes to lay it down. Foundation in place, I placed a little concealer under my eyes and over a couple of spots on my face that I wanted to hide. Post concealer, I pounded my face with powder to get the base to set and dry. I added highlights quickly to my nose and cheekbones to make them pop. Then it was all about the eyes. I'd chosen a blue sweater that hung low enough to show a little cleavage without giving the girls completely away, so I went with a simple black eyeliner, followed by cranberry eye shadow, and ended with a smoky mascara. I then lined my lip with a shade of cranberry before applying the lipstick to ensure I had nice, plump-looking lips. The cranberry color was still in the red family, so I liked it. Once I was happy with everything, I used a setting spray and waited for a minute before getting dressed. I took extra care to make sure my face didn't touch the front part of the sweater. The last thing I needed was to turn my clothing into the Shroud of Turin.

I looked at my clock. *7:15, I'm still on target.* I picked up the phone and ordered an Uber, then I shimmied into my black pants and pulled on my black leather Laura Chelsea boots. I went into the kitchen and made sure Bootsy had fresh food before sitting down and reading a couple of text messages. Nothing important, so I figured I'd respond to them at a later point. For now, my goal was to go out and have a great date.

I transferred my essential belongings into a small black clutch that was considerably smaller than the regular, bulky purse I used when running around the city. I wanted to make sure I had my wallet, cash, credit cards, phone battery backup, charging cable, keys, and iPhone. I put on a black leather coat I had hanging next to the front door. I looked back to make sure Bootsy wasn't about to try a runner, but he was more interested in the food I'd placed on the ground for him to care about what I was up to.

After opening the door, I closed it behind me and headed to the elevator. There was a couple in the elevator holding hands. I recognized one from a children's television show, but I couldn't remember his name or the show's name. I knew his husband worked as a substitute pianist all over town. When someone needed a day off or went on vacation, they'd call him up. He'd show up and hang out in the pit to see how the show ran. If he was lucky, he sat in the pit twice before taking over. Mostly, he sat through the show once before taking over conducting the orchestra while playing a score he'd just learned. The technical skills substitutes have on Broadway amazes me. Their ability to sightread music with little to no rehearsal in front of a live audience was beyond impressive.

The elevator opened in the lobby right when I got a message from the Uber app letting me know my driver had arrived, along with the make and model of the car and my driver's name. I stepped out of the black town car, walked over, and opened the door closest to the street before saying hello. He nodded and took off driving. We arrived at il Buco Alimentari & Vineria, located at Fifty-three Great Jones Street between Broadway and Lafayette Streets. The car pulled up to the curb, and I got out, double-checking to make sure I had everything I entered the car with.

"Thanks for the ride," I said.

"Have a good evening," the driver responded in broken English.

I looked around and found the tall Black man I was meeting for dinner standing to the side of the front door. His thumbs were moving at lightning speed over the face of his phone. I took a minute to take him in. He was as fine as Katherine had told me. He was probably 6'3" and looked like a cross between Tyson Beckford and Wentworth Miller. He finally looked up from his phone and caught me staring at him. What I had not expected were green eyes the shade of an emerald.

"Hi, I'm Darrin Becker. You must be Erika?" he asked as he extended his hand.

I lifted my hand into his. Cradling it gently, he shook my hand. "I'm Erika Saunders. It's nice to meet you, Darrin."

"Shall we?" he said, gesturing to the restaurant's door.

We walked into the restaurant, and the maître d' immediately said hello to Darrin, grabbed a couple of menus, and showed us to a back corner table where we were quasi-alone. The Italian restaurant was tiny and used all the space it had. Thankfully, the place was only half full, or I doubt we would have been able to hear each other.

"So, what's good?" I asked, picking up the menu.

"Everything's good," Darrin said in response. His nose was buried in his menu, and he didn't look up at me once.

The server soon approached, and Darrin took over almost immediately. "We will start with the fresh-baked bread and an olive oil tasting." He then looked at me. "I hope you're not one of those girls who avoids carbs or is allergic to olive oil. If you are, we're in the wrong place."

"Nope," I responded lightly. "I love me a good carb."

He looked at me with a quizzical look as he cocked his head. He then turned back to the server. "I'm going to have the spit-roasted Long Island duck. Erika?"

I hadn't looked at the menu fully, so I glanced down and ordered the first thing on the menu. "How about the cavatelli with a side of the cast-iron roasted cauliflower?"

"Great choice," Darrin said. "We'll also take a bottle of Château des Rontets."

"Great pairing choice," the server said before leaving the table.

"I hope you like red wine," Darrin said. "It's a red wine from Beaujolais, France. Made from gamay grapes by Côte de Besset. They only have the 2016 vintage on the menu, but I prefer the 2019. That's not to say that the 2016 isn't a great blend of fruit, but it lacks something that the 2019 year had."

"Wow, you know your wine," I cut in.

"I know enough about wine to differentiate small nuances, but not enough to explain the complexities involved. In essence, I won't join the Court of Master Sommeliers any time soon. I guess it's a good thing I'm a lawyer." He then chuckled at his own joke. I forced my lips into a smile.

"What type of law?" I asked, trying to break into the conversation he appeared to be having all by himself.

"I practice corporate law, primarily. I handle a range of contract negotiations, mostly in the entertainment industry, but I can handle almost any type of contract." He told me about every type of contract he worked on...in great detail.

By the time the freshly baked bread and different olive oils appeared, I was hoping the combination would stop Darrin from talking, but nope. He kept talking as if I was a student in a law class. He talked about the intricacies of different legal cases and settlements. I did my best to smile and nod my head, looking for a way out of this disastrous date. I will say that, in retrospect, his choice of wine and food was top-notch. Too bad his conversational skills weren't at the same level.

I ate the whole time, primarily out of boredom. He kept droning on, and I kept shoveling food into my mouth to keep myself entertained. At one point, I stopped listening and watched his lips move. He had gorgeous lips, and I could think of a few things I'd rather do with those lips than listen to them talk.

"What do you think, Erika?"

The question pulled me out of the internal monologue in my head. I smiled and said, "Uh-huh."

He tilted his head to the side like a dog does when trying to hear better before asking, "What type of dessert would you like?"

Only then did I notice the server standing next to our table. Wow, I really had ventured into la-la land. "What would you recommend?"

"Personally, I think all their desserts here are amazing. The olive oil cake is a unique experience if you haven't had it. And, of course, you can never go wrong with gelato. I always love the vanilla bean panna cotta. It comes with aged balsamic on the side."

"I guess I'll try the panna cotta then," I said, looking at the server who jotted it down.

"Espresso?" the server asked.

"Yes," both Darrin and I said simultaneously.

The server turned and left. Darrin's lips started moving again. This time I was extolled on the virtues of balsamic vinegar and all the different types he'd tried during his travels across Europe. I couldn't figure out if the man had zero social skills, was completely into hearing his own voice, or was as bored as I was on this date.

"Excuse me," a woman said as she approached the table. "I hate being a bother, but would you mind signing my book?" She whipped out a copy of *Blinded by Faith* and a pen.

I smiled at finally having something to do over dinner besides listening to Darrin drone on and on about whatever topic caught his fancy at any moment. "Who should I make it out to?"

"Margaret Johnson." She handed me the book and a pen as she beamed. "I want you to know, I never believed those rumors about you on the Internet. I always assumed you were the wronged party in all this."

"Thanks, Margaret. It's nice that the truth about everything is getting out there," I said. I took a second to think about what to write. I ultimately penned, "*Thanks for believing in me and the healing power of faith. - Erika Lynsay Saunders*"

I handed the book back to her. Mrs. Johnson beamed as she walked to the other side of the room to a table where four women sat. I watched as she showed everyone at her table the book.

"I take it you're famous?" Darrin asked.

"I'm Broadway famous," I admitted.

"What's that mean?"

"People who love musical theater will know who I am. People who only watch television and movies do not know I exist. Sure, I've done a couple of episodes of *Law and Order*. Who hasn't? But I'm known primarily in the musical theater and cabaret world."

"I see," he said, steepling his hands under his chin. "I have a few clients on Broadway. Nothing lately, but the firm works with a wide range of clients."

The server showed up with our desserts and espressos. I gently dug into the panna cotta with my spoon. To get the full effect, I dipped the underside of my spoon in the balsamic before scooping up the panna cotta. I put the silky concoction in my mouth and was wowed by the burst of flavors. "Oh my gosh, this is amazing."

"I'm glad you like it. If you'd like to taste the olive oil cake, I'd be happy to share it with you."

"Just a small bite." He used a leftover fork on the table and cut off a small corner and gave me the fork. I bit into the piece of cake. I wasn't sure what an olive oil cake would taste like, but this wasn't it. Sure, I could taste the olive oil. It had a slightly fruitier taste than the olive oils we'd tried with our bread, but it was coupled with a hint of almond and sugar. "Wow, that is pretty amazing too."

"I would agree. That's why I ordered it," Darrin said without irony in his voice. We sat in silence for the first time as we ate our desserts. When I spooned the last bite of my panna cotta into my mouth, Darrin said, "Well, I hate ending our dinner short, but I do have to get back to the office."

"I completely understand. You have work to do and clients to bill," I joked.

"Yes, I do. It's good that you understand," Darrin said, completely missing any humor in my statement.

He flagged the server and got the check. He paid for the meal, saying it was the least he could do since I had come to him for our date. I opened the app and got an Uber sent to the restaurant for my journey home. Darrin walked out with me and offered to stay until Uber showed up.

"I'm good," I said. "I'll stand right outside the restaurant until Uber gets here."

"Well," Darrin said, extending his hand. "It was nice to meet you."

I offered my hand, saying, "Likewise."

"Let me be perfectly frank," Darrin said. "I don't think we're a match."

"Whoa," I blurted out. "Where did that come from?"

"Well, you clearly had your mind on other things this evening and did not participate in our conversation. Personally, I would recommend you try to engage more with future dating partners. I also found it rude that you let your fans interrupt our dinner for an autograph. Do you have any feedback for me? Since it's blatantly clear we're not a match, I might as well get feedback."

Maybe that's because you never shut up. "Well, I would start by not talking about the law so much. You didn't once try to bring me into the conversation."

"Hmm…that's not how I saw it. But it's always good to see how things are perceived from the opposition's standpoint."

"Okay," I stammered out of my mouth.

"As for you, I would recommend several things. First, I would wear a less revealing sweater on the first date. Second, I think your makeup was heavy-handed. In the future, I would advise going for more *girl next door* instead of a *starlet on the prowl* at night. Frankly, I couldn't imagine taking you to meet my parents dressed like that. Third, you should work on your conversational skills. I gave you ample opportunity to join in my conversation, but you missed all the cues. Fourth, I would have advised against the dessert. You could have said something like, 'Why don't we share,' which would have brought you closer to my sphere while we ate. I'm sure I'll have some more ideas once I process them. I'll forward them to Katherine, and she can get them to you."

I stared at him. He expected me to say something. I stood there, gobsmacked. I had several ideas for him, and the first one would be where he could shove his advice.

"As such, I do not see any future with you. I wish you the best. Please tell Katherine I did at least try this time." With that, Darrin turned and hurried down the street, leaving me aghast.

I stood there watching Darrin flee as the Uber pulled up. The driver smiled at me, and I slid into the back seat. I immediately pulled out my phone and texted Johnny.

Erika: *You won't believe what just happened.*

Johnny: *Do tell.*

Erika: *My apartment. 25 minutes.*

Chapter 15

I had just enough time to get into my apartment and throw on some pajama bottoms and a sweatshirt when I heard the knock on my door. I walked over and opened it.

"Gurl," Johnny drawled. "I come bearing alcohol. From your texts, I could tell it was wine-o'clock."

"Thanks," I said, holding the door open for Johnny. Bootsy made a quick dash for the door, but I got it shut before he could escape. Seeing that he was defeated again by his human adversary, Bootsy made his way back to the couch and curled up in a ball.

I walked into the kitchen and pulled out the wine opener and a couple of glasses. Johnny had the corkscrew out in no time and poured me a glass.

"So, spill it. What happened?"

I spent the next thirty or so minutes going over the date in every detail, from the initial handshake to watching Darrin flee.

"Wow, the gall of that guy! I can't imagine what that was like."

"Exactly!" I said with frustration. "No wonder I'm single. The guys in this town are gay, married, or crazy."

"Just remember, good things come to those who wait," Johnny reassured me.

"I remember your dating life. You didn't exactly wait that much," I said, lifting the corner of my mouth in a smile.

"Hey, tell me about it. I had to kiss a ton of frogs before I met Amani. Eventually, you kiss enough frogs—or lawyers—and one is bound to turn into a prince."

"Or you end up with a bad case of warts. With my luck, I'm going to kiss one of those Amazonian rainforest frogs that secretes a deadly toxin."

"Come on, Erika. You're getting back into the dating saddle. You're going to hit a few rocky patches before you get into the swing of things. As of right now, your batting average isn't great, but it can only get better. Look at that, I made a sports metaphor."

"I know you're right, but it's tiresome after a while. After Asher, I couldn't deal with a lot of stuff. And now that I finally think I'm ready to date again, the men I find are totally damaged goods."

"Give yourself time. I'm sure the right guy is out there for you. Just be open to finding him. When the time is right, he'll step into your life, and you'll be amazed that it took that long."

We spent the next hour talking about everything going on in our lives. By the time Johnny left, I was tipsy. From the wine at the restaurant to the half bottle I drank with Johnny, I was pretty much gone. I made my way into my bedroom and collapsed on the bed.

The alarm woke me the following day at 6:30 a.m. Part of me wanted to throw the blasted thing across the room, but I knew I needed to get up and get my act together. I threw on my workout clothes and headed down to the gym. By the time I finished my morning jog, I was a bit more together. I went back to my apartment and ran through the shower before throwing on my clothes, drinking a protein drink, and leaving for the day.

I made it to the theater at 8:59. I wasn't the last one there, but I was darn close. The last person strolled in right at 9:00 a.m. on the dot. Unfortunately, the last one who strolled into the theater was Rebekka Eldridge. *Oh great, what new, fantastical idea has she come up with now?*

"Good morning!" Eldridge said with a giant smile. "I hear things have been progressing amazingly this week, so I'm just an audience member. Pretend like I'm not here."

"Can we pretend like she disappeared forever?" Peeter whispered next to me, which caused me to stifle a chuckle.

"Okay," San Nicolás said. "Let's run the show from the top. Eugene and Tyreek have been working on a few new songs. When we get to those parts, I'll stop and have them play. Let's begin."

Eugene started the intro to the opening number, and we all joined in. The whole show was running around three hours at that point, but there were several starts and stops, so it wasn't too surprising that things were slower than they should be. When we finished, Eldridge clapped enthusiastically.

"Let's break for an early lunch," San Nicolás said. "We'll see you back in one hour."

Katherine caught up to me as I tried to leave the theater. I had hoped to avoid her, but I knew that was highly unlikely.

"So, how did it go last night?"

"It was an interesting experience," I said, attempting to sound noncommittal.

"Uh-oh, what happened?"

I sighed and said, "If you really want to know, I'll tell you all about it over lunch."

We walked to a nearby Mediterranean restaurant. Since we were early, the place hadn't filled with lunchtime crowds yet. We headed to a private table in the corner next to the window. We ordered, and I spent the next fifteen minutes painstakingly describing the date.

"He didn't?" Kathrine gasped when I told her about his critique session. "I can't believe he did that. He was always so nice. I'm dumbfounded."

"Yeah, he's not what I would call much of a people person, from what I can tell."

"I thought he was awkward. Now, I'm wondering if there's something else going on there."

"Who knows," I admitted. "Thankfully, that is one experience I'm not going to have again." I turned my attention to Katherine and asked, "What about you? What's going on in your dating life?"

Katherine perked up and talked about several guys she'd been casually dating. Unlike me, Katherine had no problem amassing a large number of guys to date. I'm sure I could date as much as she does, but I don't feel the need to date. I'm looking for quality at this point in my life, not quantity.

After lunch, we headed back to the theater. We hadn't stepped into the building when Aarya approached us with a clipboard. "The elves are all meeting in room Flying Circle C."

From previous experience, I knew that the room she was directing us to was on the third floor, so we headed to the escalator, ready to climb. To my surprise, the escalator worked. I hesitantly took one step on it, and it started going right up.

"Wow, this place is feeling like a real theater," I said.

"Who knows, maybe we'll have a musical ready to go before opening night," Kathrine quipped back.

We made our way to the room and found Peeter was already in there with Eugene and Tyreek.

"Nice of you ladies to join us," Peeter said, looking down at his watch.

"Technically, we still have thirty seconds to spare," Katherine clapped back.

"Okay, let's get this show on the road," Eugene said, clearly wanting to avoid any more tension in the room. "As you know, we have been reworking the script with Mable to update the 'festiveness' of the whole show. We did our best to keep a lot of the original material while updating it to reflect the fact that you are now elves and not industrial tycoons."

We spent the next two hours going over the new material. Thankfully, several songs we'd learned a couple of weeks ago would stick around. They had to rework the lyrics because we were now Santa's little helpers and not multi-millionaires playing with people's lives.

Peeter quietly said to Katherine and me during one of our breaks, "I'm not sure if this is an upgrade or a downgrade yet."

"I know the feeling," I admitted. "Every time we think we have some kind of grip on what this show is, everything gets changed."

"Exactly," Kathrine said. "I don't see how we open in four weeks."

The rest of the afternoon was a bit of a blur. Before we went home for the evening, San Nicolás brought the entire cast into the theater for a quick pep talk.

"I am amazed at how things are progressing. At this speed, we will have an amazing show in absolute shipshape in no time. Give yourselves a round of applause for all your hard work." He started clapping enthusiastically, so the cast joined in. We may not have been the loudest clappers in the world, but we were at least genuine. "I have some good news for everyone. After talking with the lovely people at Macy's, we've been invited to preview our opening number at the Thanksgiving Day Parade." I don't know if he expected us to be thrilled or scared, but the room was silent. "Don't worry, I have no fear that we'll have the opening number ready to go in the next couple of weeks. It's going to be a magnificent time."

After San Nicolás' grand announcement, he released us for the day. I headed straight home. I was still a little hungover from the previous night's drinking, so I wanted to take a bath, have dinner, cuddle with Bootsy and go to sleep, which is precisely what I did.

Chapter 16

The next morning, I rolled out of bed, ran on the treadmill, got ready, and was outside the theater with ten minutes to spare. I was prepared for a brand-new day of adventures and whatever else life threw my way. A guy in an orange vest and a white hardhat blocked me from getting into the building. The construction crew was placing the theater's name above the main entrance, *Maurer Theatre*. The whole building was called the Eldridge Plaza, named after Rebekka's late husband, Bernie.

"I sure hope they do this quickly," a voice said behind me. "My job is to make sure we stick to the union regulations."

I glanced behind me. Maeve McKenna was decked out in a black pantsuit, oversized black wide-brimmed hat, a fur coat, and a pair of sunglasses that covered half her head. She looked like a caricature of Hollywood actresses of yesteryear.

"Good morning, Maeve," I said.

"Good morning, dear," she responded. "Do you know how long this is going to take?"

I shrugged and said, "I just got here."

The woman let out a slight harumph sound. She stared at the construction worker in the orange vest. "Excuse me, young man, how long with this take? We have a show to put on."

"Sorry, Ma'am. This will take as long as it takes." He looked up at the people working on the side of the building above the door. "Shouldn't be more than five minutes, I'd guess."

Maeve let out a short puff, the steam exited her mouth in the cold air.

"Maeve," I yelled over the noise of the crane, drawing her attention away from the poor construction worker. "Do you know why they're calling it the 'Maurer Theatre?' I can't figure out why."

"Young people and their lack of theater history," she mumbled loud enough for a city block to hear. "Erika," she said, drawing out my name like it almost pained her to say it, "Michael Maurer directed the 1986 musical *Into the Light* about the Shroud of Turin."

"A musical about the Shroud of Turin?" I started to laugh, but she wasn't smiling. "You're serious."

"As a heart attack," Maeve said in her maudlin tone. "I saw it at the friends and family preview. I was understudying a witch in *The Scottish Play* at the time. Our play was next door." She leaned her head to the side and gazed upward as if looking back in time. "The musical wasn't horrible, but it wasn't good either. How any investor put up money for that turkey is still beyond me."

More of the cast and creative team were huddled around us now as they moved the crane away from the front of the building. Once it was clear the theater name wouldn't crash into the ground below, the construction worker signaled that it was safe to enter. We all proceeded to the escalators and made our way up to our rehearsal space.

We all quickly found our seats. New binders sat on the table in front of us.

"Asier," Maeve said, speaking to the director. She was the only person I'd seen call him by his first name. "When are we going to stop getting new materials? It's getting old. Every day we mark up the script or score only to have them replaced the next day. This is no way to rehearse."

"Señora McKenna, I think this will be the last major set of changes. Going forward, I only envision *minor* changes. We'll be switching out pages instead of giving you a completely new script and score daily from here on out."

Maeve didn't look too convinced. She took off her glasses, looked at San Nicolás and raised a single manicured eyebrow. "In my day, we would never have this many changes. It would have been impossible. The score had to be hand-copied, and the scripts had to be typed out using carbon paper, which meant a bank of typists would have had to stay up all night making these kinds of changes."

"Yes, the artistic process was definitely more constrained *way* back then," San Nicolás replied with a thin-lipped smile. I could tell he wasn't exactly happy with Maeve's complaints. Still, he moved away from her, leaving her looking slightly aghast. She quickly found her seat.

San Nicolás walked to his spot in the room's front. "I have some unfortunate news. Ryan Devan Butcher had an accident last night and broke his leg. He thought it would be fun to join the," San Nicolás stared at a piece of paper sitting on the table before him, then looked back up, "Polar Bear Club in Central Park. Is this some kind of fraternity?" San Nicolás asked, looking around the room for an answer.

"Um...sir," Caiden Wynter Jeanes said, raising his hand as if he was in school. "The Polar Bear Club is when a group of guys, who are often drunk, decide to go jump in a frozen river or lake."

"The real polar bears would never be drunk, and they don't jump into the pond at Central Park," Peeter said to the right of me. "The real Polar Bear club runs out of Coney Island, and they swim in the Atlantic Ocean."

"Do I even want to know why you know this?" I asked.

"I did it on a dare in college," Peeter said. "Me, my hairless body, and a neon green Speedo took the plunge."

"Bad mental picture, bad mental picture, bad mental picture," Katherine said next to me. "I won't be able to scrub that image out of my brain."

"You're jealous you didn't get to see the real thing," Peeter joked.

"I can promise you that is not the case. I am curious. How did you look in the Speedo when you went from being an outty to being an innie as your manhood tried to burrow inside your body?"

"Talk about shrinkage," I added.

"Shhh..." Maeve said, placing her finger against her lips and glaring in our direction.

"As I was saying," San Nicolás shot daggers in our direction, "Ryan Devan Butcher apparently did something while becoming a polar bear and broke his leg. The creative team found out last night when Mrs. Eldridge called to let us know about the unfortunate accident. Thankfully, Eldridge made a few phone calls and helped us recast the role." San Nicolás gazed at his watch. "They should be here any time now."

Rebekka came into the theater as if on cue, her entourage streaming in behind her. I had never really paid attention to the six people who followed her everywhere. I wondered what each one did exactly.

"Good morning, cast," Rebekka said as she walked down the center aisle like Mama Rose at the beginning of *Gypsy*. I almost expected her to scream, "Sing out, Louise!" Instead, she came on stage, leaving her minions in the darkened seats of the theater. She kissed San Nicolás on both of his cheeks in greeting before turning to the cast. "I have horrible news. Ryan Devan Butcher was injured last night in a horrific accident. Thankfully, his doctors think he'll survive and make a full recovery."

Drama queen much?

"Unfortunately, this means I had to recast his role last night. I couldn't put it off because we're already behind schedule." She glanced at Maeve, "Don't worry, Ms. McKenna, I already cleared it with Equity." McKenna arched an eyebrow but looked resigned to the change. Eldridge continued, "Today, it is my honor to welcome the newest member of our little family, Asher Fraser Alexander."

She gestured off stage, and one of her minions stood up and slowly walked up on stage. There were gasps of shock, and many heads in the room swiveled in my direction to see my reaction. I clenched my jaw. *Don't make a scene. Keep it together, keep it together, keep it together. Smile.* I forced my lips into some semblance of a smile.

"Are you okay?" I heard Katherine ask quietly.

"I will be," I said through clenched, smiling teeth.

I stared at Asher as he got on stage and found my face. His eyes grew into giant saucers and looked like a moose in headlights. *At least, he didn't know about this either.* I kept my face as neutral as possible. His jaw dropped, a look of terror flashed over his face.

"You can sit over there, Mr. Alexander," Rebekka said, gesturing to a seat opposite me at the table. The seat that idiot Butcher should be sitting.

Asher never was that good of an actor. He didn't try to hide his shock. I at least hid my emotions.

"Well," Rebekka said once Asher was seated. "Let's run the show. San Nicolás, the stage is yours."

Rebekka climbed down from the stage and walked down to where her minions were seated. The room quieted down as he turned to Eugene, who was again behind the practice piano. Eugene started playing the overture, and we quickly broke into the first song of Act One. I was glad that I had the work to focus on, but every time Asher had to do something, it reminded me that he was there. I tried not to cringe every time he opened his mouth, but it was hard.

We finished the last song of the show, "Christmas Wedding," and San Nicolás, along with the other creatives in the room, broke into applause.

No one paid any attention to Rebekka until her clunky heel was heard climbing the stairs to the stage. "Definitely an improvement, but I have a list of notes. Shall we go over them?" She asked it as a question, but anyone could tell her 'notes' were going to be commandments. I'd heard of tyrannical producers, but she wanted to make sure the show was done her way. I almost wondered why she bothered having a director since she clearly wanted to direct.

"Take twenty minutes," San Nicolás said. He let out an audible sigh and turned to Rebekka. The creative team joined them, and the group huddled and got to work on whatever magical revision Rebekka had come up with this time.

I didn't chance a glance across the table. I scurried out of the theater and ran to the women's room. I stared at myself in the mirror. "You can do this, Erika. You're a big girl now. Asher is your past. Just be professional. Act professional." I tried not to hyperventilate. I looked down at the sink, turned on the faucet, splashed some cold water on my face, then grabbed a paper towel to blot my face dry. I was wrapping up when the door to the restroom opened.

"Erika," I heard Asher say behind me. "We need to talk."

I spun around, took three steps forward, and slapped him. It was almost comical. His reaction was virtually overkill, like it was a stage slap that he had to sell to the mezzanine. His hand shot up to the cheek. He'd been caught off guard.

"Overacting much?" I gritted out.

"I guess I kind of deserve that."

"What do you want?" I asked in my best ice queen voice.

He put up his arms in mock surrender. "I just want to talk."

"Then talk."

"Can we go somewhere else?"

"You're the one who followed me in here."

"Well, you didn't exactly leave me much choice. You ran from the theater and headed in here to hide."

"I was not hiding." Even as I said the words, I knew neither of us believed them. "Whatever. You have me. Talk."

He sighed and dropped his shoulders. "I'm sorry." He wasn't putting on a show for a change. "I was a right bas—"

"Stop! Warning. You're not allowed to cuss here. It's one of Eldridge's rules of festivity."

"You're kidding me?"

"Christmas bells, I wish I was. See, right there, I've internalized it. But yes, you were a downright pile of deer droppings who gave himself a permanent spot on Santa's naughty list. And as far as I'm concerned, you can go suck on the North Pole until you choke on it."

"Well, that was...colorful, yet creative."

"You get used to it after a while. We've created a whole lexicon of ways to cuss without getting on Eldridge's bad side."

"She's a piece of work, isn't she?"

"You have no idea. She shows up once or twice a week, and chaos ensues. Anytime I see her, I expect the worse." I looked at him and said, "Back to your apology. I expect groveling."

"I'm sorry. I never said that after your accident. And well, I never had the guts to approach you after it happened. Not even on the day when you came to move out of our apartment. I didn't know how to tell you."

"Tell me what?"

He paused before saying, "I was never bi. I was always gay. You were my beard for years. I always assumed that no one would ever figure it out if we were together. Being bi was cool and sexy. It made one look edgy. Being gay was blasé. It was like a bad stereotype."

"Well, you could have at least told me before I had to find you making out with Zach on stage."

"That's what I'm saying. I am so sorry for that."

"Sorry for what, exactly? I knew you were bi. You'd been in a relationship with guys before we dated. That didn't bother me. What bothered me was that you cheated on me behind my back!" I heard my voice rising.

A sudden knock on the door broke my attention. Kerrie Klark, one of the other cast members, poked her head into the room. "I really hate to bother...whatever this is. But a few of us out here need to use this bathroom for something beyond fighting." She pushed open the door, and a small line had formed behind her. I grabbed Asher by the arm and dragged him from the women's restroom to an alcove, away from prying eyes and ears.

"I never intended to hurt you. I never intended to hurt anyone. You probably don't know, but Zach never talked to me after that."

"Okay," I said in a tone that clearly said, "and I should care about this why?"

"I may have told him we had an open relationship. He thought you knew about the two of us and that you were okay with it."

"Oh, for Frosty's sake! Are you elf-ing kidding me? Was there anyone you weren't lying to?

"You're right. I was lying to everyone. Worst of all, I was lying to myself."

At that moment, I saw Asher for what he was...a broken child who was now trying to grow up. "The part that hurt the most was that I lost not only my lover...I lost my best friend. You really hurt me."

"I know I did. Trust me, I know I did. Years of therapy later, I'm able to admit how I handled everything wrong. I was mad it all got out. I shouldn't have started those rumors about you hating bisexual and gay men."

"I always knew that was you," I said, some of my anger coming back into my voice.

"I was childish. I hoped I could drive the attention away from me back to you. It never worked. I watched as your gay following grew. I was considered a pariah in the gay community for a long time. I was that little gay boy who broke Erika Saunders."

"Really?"

"Oh yeah. The gays really stuck up for you. And when you started your cabaret act, everyone talked about it. The world knew that your show was because of me. And they sided with you."

"Well, the gays and me have always been thick as thieves."

"That's why I told Michelle Bouvier everything that had happened...off the record."

"What?" That was one revelation I had most definitely not expected.

"Yep. I had heard she was writing a tell-all book about the show, so I had my agent get her number. I called her directly. At first, she had thought I was trying to pressure her to stop writing the book. I did the exact opposite. I told her everything."

"But you made yourself the villain of the whole thing?" still in utter shock.

"It was true, though. I was the villain."

I guess he really has grown up. "So why now? Why this show?"

"Well, you may have heard about a little scandal on a movie set..." he asked, his voice trailing off.

"That was another article by Bouvier, from what I remember."

"Yep, Michelle and I have definitely become bosom buddies this last year," he said with a sigh.

"You leaked the story about your affair with the casting agent?" I asked a bit incredulously.

"No, and sadly, I didn't sleep with anyone involved in casting. It was totally made-up drama. I wanted out of the shoot because the set was toxic."

"How so?"

"The director and his husband kept pushing for a ménage à trois, but I brushed off their advances. I called up Michelle and asked for advice on starting a rumor that would be scandalous enough to get me fired but not so serious that it would destroy my career. As you can see, it worked. Everyone on the set got that it was a lie because the casting team was all women. Still, Hallmark doesn't want to put any movies in their lineup associated with scandal, so I was quietly asked to leave the project."

"Wow," was all I could muster. Part of me was saddened by all of this because it was clearly another incident of Asher getting his way through deceit, but part of me understood why he did it.

"Can you ever forgive me?" he asked.

I looked into his eyes and he was crying. Asher was expressing a genuine emotion, something I was surprised that he had the capability of doing. "I...forgive you." The words were out of my mouth before I'd even registered them in my brain. It wasn't like a magical weight was suddenly lifted off my shoulders. But forgiving him was easier than hating him. Besides, I was stuck working with him either way.

"Excuse me," Aarya suddenly said, walking up to us. "Everyone's in the theater waiting for you two to return."

"Oh geez! Sorry, we totally lost track of time," I said.

"It's totally my fault," Asher started. "I cornered Erika."

"I don't care," Aarya said. "Your business is your business. Just get your elf-y butts back in the theater before Eldridge blows the North Pole."

We hurried through the halls and into the theater. The rest of the cast was all on stage. Their attention was split between watching the creative team, who was still engaged in a heated conversation, and the other half were staring at Asher and me. I'm sure they wanted to see if I'd clawed Asher's eyes out. I pasted on a smile.

Out of nowhere, San Nicolás threw a clipboard to the ground and started strewing a series of Spanish words that I'm sure translated roughly to "I hate you. I hate you. Go elf yourself, you...you candy cane sucker."

Chapter 17

The rest of the week was a blur of activity. From new script pages to song rewrites to finally getting into the blocking and choreography, the cast and crew were exhausted after their six days of rehearsal. Thankfully, the show was starting to look like an actual show for the first time. This was great since we were supposed to finally get access to the big theater on Monday. After a couple of delays, Rebekka squeezed every worker she could to ensure everything on the stage would be ready to work with the following Monday.

On Thursday, the set designer explained how everything would work. The biggest pieces of the set were supposed to be delivered on Saturday and Sunday, so we'd be able to rehearse on the actual stage early the following week. The set designer was this little old woman who was maybe 4'5", but she had enormous energy, and had at least six Tony Awards for her work on various plays and musicals. She worked with a design team in Jersey who built the set in a giant warehouse. It would be dismantled there and then brought to Broadway on semi-trucks over the weekend. Her on-site construction team would then systematically put the set back together inside the theater.

"If you see a man in a hard hat, stay out of his way," the designer told us. "Do not interrupt. Do not go take a peek to see what it looks like when they are working. You will get access to the stage when it is safe, not one second sooner."

The Maurer Theatre's stage was on the second floor of the building, so large elevators at the back of the building would lift everything from the ground level to the stage level where it would be reassembled. And despite the set designer's warning, I poked my head in on Saturday to see how things were going. There were miles and miles of cables and giant crates. Set pieces littered the auditorium in hundreds of pieces waiting to be reassembled. How they would get all of it rebuilt in two days was beyond me.

On Friday, we showed up and were whisked away to a recording studio, where we heard the orchestrations for the opening number. We recorded a modified version of the opening that we would perform the next Thursday at the Macy's Thanksgiving Day Parade. As if we weren't stressing enough about getting the show opened in time, now we had to split rehearsal between the stage show and the televised number. My head was swimming in choreography because it was the same song, same choreography, but very different staging. I've done promotional songs for shows before, which were often different from what was performed on stage. But trying to learn both versions simultaneously was driving all of us crazy. Thankfully, the recording engineers spent all night on Friday working on the cut of the song for Macy's, so we had the exact version we'd be lip-syncing to on Thursday.

The televised Broadway numbers shown during the parade are always lip-synced, as are all the performance numbers. Nothing is left to chance with the televised musical numbers at the parade.

Carissra, Kirk, Johnny, and I had pizza on Saturday night, and I explained the whole process to them.

"So, why do you lip-sync? I thought the whole point of Broadway was that it was live?" Kirk asked.

"There are a ton of reasons why. First, the weather is unpredictable. We could be out there in the rain, snow, or sun. Unless we shot from within a theater, there's no way to prepare for all the contingencies related to weather."

"I guess that makes sense," Kirk said, stuffing a piece of cheesy bread into his mouth.

"Besides," Johnny added, "if the weather is freezing, the cold can be terrible on someone's vocal cords."

"How so?" Carissra asked.

"It's basic anatomy, my dear." Johnny picked up two breadsticks. "These are like your vocal cords. They wobble when they're all nice like this, and you can get the most out of your cheesy goodness.

Your vocal cords prefer a hot, moist climate...like a rainforest. They function better when they are warm and lubricated," he added extra emphasis to the words *moist* and *lubricated*, which got a giggle out of Carissra and a side-eye glance from Kirk.

"Okay, but I don't see what this has to do with singing," Carissra said.

"Getting there, little one," Johnny said with a roll of his eyes. "Now, imagine these cheesy breads were frozen. They won't wobble anymore. When the weather is dry and cold, your larynx is tighter, and it's harder to sing."

"It's not just harder," I admitted. "It can lead to damage if you're not careful. If we were standing still, like we were in a choir, we could be trained to take shorter, more shallow breaths while singing outside. But many of the songs performed at the parade need people to have great breath control and power while exerting themselves physically. Sure, you could belt out a song once, but you could strain your instrument and find yourself unable to sing the rest of the week."

"And, even worse," Johnny adds, "the television producers want a good show. The musical producers don't want their stars out of work the next week because they've lost their voices."

"That's not to say that no one ever sings live on the broadcast, but it's a logistical nightmare if they do," I admitted. "So, there you go, several reasons singing live at Herald Square on 35th in the cold is just never a bright idea."

We wrapped up our dinner shortly after that discussion, and I collapsed in bed with Bootsy snuggled at my side shortly thereafter. Sunday, I slept well past noon before getting up, doing laundry, and learning some new line changes I needed to have ready the next morning.

By the time Monday rolled around, I was feeling somewhat recovered. Still, my body was exhausted after rehearsing. When I got to the theater that morning, it was a hubbub of action. We started by walking through all the sets. Serafina Porcher and San Nicolás walked us through how every set piece would move. We had to learn where sightlines would be on the stage. We needed to know where our marks were to avoid running into set pieces that either flew in from above or in from one of the wings.

We then walked through the show. Basically, we talked through the songs and dialogue, so the design team and backstage crew could figure out where and how things needed to move. This wasn't even a technical rehearsal, they were giving us additional time on the stage to get used to the set pieces. Some were fully finished. Some still needed to be touched up. But even if the pieces weren't ready for an audience, it was nice to be on a stage.

After our walk-through, San Nicolás called for a break. When we came back, we ran through the production from the top. Someone had hauled in a rehearsal piano and placed it below the stage, where we could see Eugene while he played.

The run-through was a disaster, which everyone expected. Sets flew in at the wrong times. People forgot their marks on the stage. We had taped off a stage in our rehearsal space, so we had the rough dimensions to work with, but those radically changed when suddenly there was more to worry about than empty space. In one scene, there was a table in a location no one expected, so we all had to figure out how to maneuver around the blasted thing. Sure, it looked good on the set, but it was a bit of a headache for those who had to work around the dumb thing.

One great part of the day was working with the stagehands backstage. After only seeing the actors and creative team, it was like a whole new world opened with many new faces. Personally, I had my eyes set on this rugged-looking redhead. He had short-cut red hair and a full red beard. I could almost imagine him as young Kris Kringle flying around in a sleigh. Instead of lifting a heavy bag of toys with his huge biceps, he worked on a lot of the rigging. Even though computers were essential to the modern theater, nothing beat a large backstage team to keep a show moving. It's live theater. Stuff happens. A computer is great, but stagehands still pull ropes and move set pieces.

I had a scene where I had to exit stage left, run backstage, head downstairs to an underground passage that ran the length of the stage, run back up the stairs on stage right and enter center stage right. I had approximately sixty seconds to get from one side to the other with a costume change in between. Lachtna MacGrory was assigned to help figure out the backstage logistics.

"And go," he said in an Irish brogue accent that made me weak in the knees.

I walked offstage, started a mad dash around the back, then scampered down the stairs, ran across the entire width of the stage underneath, and climbed back up the stairs to stage right.

I was almost out of breath when I got there. "One minute and ten seconds. We'll have to make it faster, Erika," Lachtna said. "Let's run it again. This time I'm going to be right behind ya."

We reset, and I took off. When I was up on stage right, he noticed a few things that could cut the time. So, he made the changes, and we reran it. The mad dashing reminded me of running sprints in high school. I was also thankful for all that time I spent on the treadmill.

"Fifty seconds," Lachtna said. "That should give you ten seconds for the wardrobe change."

"Does the costume designer know about this?" I asked.

"Probably not. I'll make sure the stage manager knows. They'll either re-choreograph or figure out how to make it work."

"Ten seconds isn't that long," I said.

"Maybe, but they pulled off a four second quick-change in a 2002 show in the West End. By that standard, we can do two quick-changes with a couple of seconds to spare."

I looked at him dubiously. I was also curious why he had that tidbit of history in his head. Apparently, he noticed the odd look on my face because he explained. "I'm a tad bit older than a look. I didn't work in the West End in the 2000s, but I've worked with many people who have."

"How'd you end up in the US?" I asked.

"I originally came over as the lead carpenter on a highly technical show from London. Ended up in New York, so I stayed. To work here, I had to get a work visa and permission to join the union, so when that contract was over, I got permanent workers status and have worked on several shows. Basically, a theater journeyman at this point."

"Lachtna," a voice called from another part of the stage.

"Duty calls. Talk to you soon, Erika," he walked away, and I admired that profile as much as I had the front one.

We got through the show twice before lunch and reran Act One after lunch to clean up a few things. By the end of the day, I'd gotten my run backstage down to 45 seconds, which should make the costume change more manageable. Of course, we still had to see what the costume designer came up with.

Those of us who were going to be performing at Macy's were sent back to the smaller theater, where we rehearsed that version of the opening number.

"*Attencion*," Divya Kappel, the choreographer, said as she clapped her hands. "Let's run the number with the recording."

I got to my starting position and we ran the number. Everything was going well when Kappel stopped the music and made a few adjustments. "Remember to find your camera. This is a televised performance, so you must look into the camera. Do not look to the mezzanine. Again!"

We got through it before breaking for dinner. We had to be back by 8:00 p.m., because the Macy's people were having rehearsal on Monday this year. That way, the parade people could figure out the timing and make any adjustments necessary. I ran home, ate, fed Bootsy, and returned to the theater by 8:00. We were all given sweatshirts and ballcaps with the show's logo for this trip. Honestly, beyond seeing it on a script binder, I hadn't seen the logo yet. It was colorful and cheerful looking. It had a classy look, while still looking appropriate for Christmas.

Only about twenty of the cast members were in this number. Of the main cast, only the elves were in the opening number, so none of the other principles were there. "Whoa," I said, stepping off the bus as a blast of frozen air barreled into me. In my parka, gloves, and face mask, the night air was freezing. A Macy's employee met the bus and took us to our staging area, where we were told to wait. The group huddled together for warmth. The vapor from our mouths intermixed in a fog. Even though it was crazy cold and late at night, there were still a bunch of tourists out to watch the rehearsal.

When it was our turn, a different Macy's employee came and got our group and led us to the famous green-painted rectangle in front of Macy's Herald Square entrance.

"Next up is the company of *The Naughty List*. Please listen to the assistant director. He will walk you through some basic instructions," some official-looking woman said before handing us off to a less official-looking guy.

"Hi, I'm Doug. I'm the assistant director in charge of the Broadway segments." He then ran through a series of explanations about where to focus and what to do. "Remember, this is live television. Once the music ends, you have seconds to get into a group in the middle and wave at the camera. We will then cut to a commercial break, and you will be directed to a staging location and taken to where your bus is located."

We then spent thirty minutes working with Doug as they planned out camera angles and how our two-minute and thirty-second version of the opening number was trimmed down from eight. Admittedly, the dialogue in the song's middle wasn't necessary for the parade. The shorter cut made the song more like a Christmas anthem, which could prove great for ticket sales. Nothing puts butts in seats like a good showing at the parade. Broadway shows get the Tony Awards in the summer and the Macy's Thanksgiving Parade in November to sell themselves and their shows to America and the world.

"In five, four, three..." there was a beat of silence, and the assistant director pointed at the group. We heard the music piped over the speakers, and we started mouthing along with the words. I missed one of my steps and almost ran over Katherine, but she saw me coming and got out of the way, preventing an elf pileup. One guy in the chorus usually slid across the stage, and he almost bit the dust because asphalt does not allow one's shoes to slide. Thankfully, he caught himself at the last second and didn't injure himself. Then our time was up, and the director yelled, "Reset!"

We went back to our places. The director conversed with the guys who were operating the cameras. The assistant director returned to his chair, got comfortable, and started his countdown again. This time, everything went as smoothly as could be expected. When we finished, we all raced together and waved at the camera that would be there Thursday morning.

"Okay, thanks cast of," the director peeked down at his clipboard before continuing, "*The Naughty List*. We'll see you Thursday morning."

We then piled back on the bus, which took us back to the theater. It was now a little after midnight, so I walked home and passed out on my bed before taking off my shoes.

That night, I slept like a baby. Unfortunately, my hamstrings were killing me the following day. *Maybe I needed to spend more time on a stair climber than on a treadmill.* I dragged my body out of bed. I'd forgone the gym. I figured between choreography and running up and down stairs, my body could take a day off from the treadmill. Instead, I got up, threw on a yoga video I owned, and stretched myself out. If the role continued to be this strenuous, yoga would quickly become my go-to exercise to ensure I didn't get too tight. I worked hard so my body was strong but flexible to endure an eight-show week once we opened.

The company was back on stage running the show at 9:00 a.m. I started the morning in a half-daze, which showed as soon as I started doing the Thanksgiving choreography instead of the show choreography. Thankfully, Peeter grabbed my arm and dragged me out of the way as a set piece moved on stage.

"That was close," I said when I exited stage right for a second.

"I was only watching out for you because I was afraid it would be me."

We then lined up for our next entrance. We entered stage right with this hobble, wobble dance move Kappel said looked cheerful. Katherine said it made us all look constipated. But we smiled and sold it to the mezzanine. Everything sailed along after that. The three elves got through our first book scene, followed by Peeter's big number, "Christmas, Nothing but a Merchants Holiday." Peeter is the cynical elf who thinks all of NYC should be placed permanently on Santa's naughty list. The song is funny, but it packs a punch with a political statement against consumerism, capitalism, and the demise of the Christmas spirit. That led to my character coming up with a grand idea to test how cynical people in NYC are today. Tinsel Hollicane—I still hated the name—comes up with the idea to leave three brand-new wallets in Times Square, each with $1000 in cash. I'm like, we'll include a business card. Let's see if people bring them back. But hey, we're elves, so we can watch what happens through the power of Christmas magic—no logic necessary. Of course, I have to explain all this in a horribly titled song, "Confusion to our Critics and Merry Christmas."

My wallet is picked up by Billy James, a Texas bloke and wannabe country singer, played by Caiden Wynter Jeanes. Jeanes had that wide-eyed innocent youthful look everyone associates with a fish out of water. And a kid from a ranch out in West Texas spending Christmas in the city was about as fish out of water as someone could get.

Katherine's wallet is picked up by Coleen Lawrence, a New York City schoolteacher who works with special needs children. The character worked with orphans in the movie, but special needs kids seemed a decent alternative for modern sensibilities. Tabatha Thomson played the role, and honestly, I didn't know anything about her. She was young, doe-eyed, and reminded me of myself when I first came to the city. Unlike me, she was lucky enough to land a role in a new musical right after she graduated college, so the 21-year-old matched the innocence of her leading man.

Lastly, Peeter's wallet is found by Kerrie Klark's character, Arlene Terry-Ball, who is supposed to be a jaded Tony Award-winning actor a bit past her prime. Klark, in reality, was in her early forties, but she pulled off looking at least five years older, giving herself the extra edginess of someone who has been there and seen it all. Anytime she came on stage, she demanded attention. Something in the intersectionality of her half-Puerto Rican, half-Black and 100 percent lesbian self, made her ridiculously gorgeous, charismatic and unattainable. She picked up the wallet, grabbed the cash, and tossed the billfold into the trashcan. If sold right, the audience would think what she did was wrong. But they'd also think they probably would have done the same thing. She pulled off this scene belting the comical number, "Heart of Gold with Other People's Money." Even as I watched her from the wings, I marveled at her comic timing and ability to milk the song of every laugh.

After this sequence, the three elves are in a New York high-rise, waiting to see if the wallets return. Admittedly, there was a bit of a logic gap here. Why exactly do elves own a high-rise in Manhattan? How could they afford it? And why did they all live together? These were pesky little questions that were never answered by the story. I was curious to see if a paying audience would go along with this and suspend belief. Heck, we were singing and dancing elves. What was a little more disbelief on top of that?

The penthouse set was gorgeous, even if it looked like no apartment I'd ever seen. Maybe Daddy Warbucks could afford this place, but the grand dame of this house was a retired elf (*who guessed they retired?*) named Madam Tanya Winterville, which was played by Maeve McKenna. Honestly, the way she descended the staircase reminded me of a cross between Glenn Close in *Sunset Boulevard* and Angela Lansbury in *Mame*. McKenna had a regalness to her that made me think she should be starring in a revival of *The Pirate Queen*.

Standing off stage left, Peeter joked, "She looks like Jack Frost's third wife. He got the North Pole, and she took Manhattan."

The orchestra played as she descended. Once she hit the bottom staircase, Josef the Butler, played by our only international cast member, Kishor Khatri, informed her that we, the elves, had called and were on our way up. Khatri quickly matched McKenna's poise and sense of regality. Heck, maybe he was Jack Frost's fourth spouse. Who knows? I learned to take things as they were written and avoid a bunch of unnecessary backstories. Some people want backstory for everything on stage, not me. Sometimes that extra information isn't necessary. Sometimes it's necessary to understand how a character got to a specific place in life. But most of the time, it was extraneous and didn't always help move the story along.

"Very well, Josef. Prepare the dining room. I have a feeling we'll be having company," McKenna's character says, which was our cue to enter from stage left.

There was some witty banter on stage, which we all delivered to get laughs. Then there was a doorbell. We didn't have the sound cues yet, so Serafina Porcher, the stage manager, yelled "Ding

Dong" from her seat next to San Nicolás in the house. I liked Serafina. By the time this show opened, she would know more about the show than any other person in the building. I always marveled at how stage managers kept everything going like clockwork. Talk about a masterclass in multitasking.

Peeter entered the stage door into the penthouse, followed by Katherine and me. I walked through the door and took an extra step before I remembered I needed to shut the door. I didn't want to make it look like I forgot, so I kicked backward and hoped for the best. It got a laugh, so I made a mental note to keep it.

"Come now, Icelyn, Blitz, and Tinsel," Madam Winterville started, "what mischief have you three been up to?"

Blitz explained his theory about the depravities of man, which was cut off mid-sentence.

"Ding Dong," Serafina yelled again.

Josef appeared, opened the door, and let in Billy James. We then hear Billy James' sorrowful tale of being in the big city and not knowing anyone or having any place to go on Christmas. The whole passage was cheesy beyond cheesy, but Caiden delivered the lines without making it seem too disingenuous.

"Ding Dong," Serafina yelled.

Josef appeared again and let in Coleen Lawrence. Her sweet disposition was enough to make any actual New Yorker gag, but I could see how she would sell to an out-of-town audience. She also has no plans for Christmas. She was going to read a book and head to bed early. Clearly, this character learned nothing about being a single gal in the city. I wanted to sit the character in front of *Sex in the City* and give her some lessons.

After both sad stories, McKenna gets to have her big moment on the stage. The song "Stay and Have a Good Cheer" was written primarily for McKenna's vocal range. She sort of half-sang, half-spoke the song. It reminded me of when I saw Elaine Stritch in her last role on Broadway as a teenager when she did *A Little Night Music* with Bernadette Peters.

"Take twenty," Serafina yelled from her spot as soon as McKenna finished the song.

I bent over at the waist and stretched out my back. After a while, standing on the wooden stage took a lot out of you, so I enjoyed a good deep stretch.

"Good morning, Ms. Saunders," a man's voice said.

I looked between my legs to catch Lachtna MacGrory staring down at me. I quickly stood up straight, causing the blood to rush out of my head, leaving me woozy for a second. Lachtna reached out to steady me as I asked, "How are you this morning?"

"I'm doing great. And yourself?" He dropped his supportive hand from my upper arm now that I was firmly planted on both feet.

"So far, so good. The first act was running smoothly. Any idea why they called a break?"

"Not a clue," he admitted. "Gives me a chance to double-check a few items in the meantime. Anyway, back to work."

He walked away, and I stared after him.

"Whatcha looking at?" Katherine asked.

I spun my head toward her, "Umm...nothing." The red flush on my face didn't fool her at all.

"You have the hots for everyone's favorite leprechaun!"

"Katherine..." I stammered out. "Isn't that like racist or something? You know, calling a guy from Ireland a leprechaun?"

"I don't think he would mind," Katherine looked past me. When I turned my head to see what she was looking at, Lachtna stared back at me and gave me a wink. "I'd slide down the rainbow into his pot of gold anytime."

"Katherine!" I chastised.

"Oh, come off it. I'm jealous that all the hot guys fall for you."

"That's not true," I said, but I could feel the flush in my cheeks.

I ran to the bathroom while I had a chance, then grabbed a new water bottle before walking back on stage. As I was getting back, Lachtna was walking my way. A smile lit his face. "Erika, some of my mates that work backstage are going to a pub tonight. Why don't you and the other girl elf join us?"

"Let me check with her, but I think that can be arranged."

"Places!" Serafina yelled. "We're going to pick up from where we stopped. I'll have notes about the first half of Act One before lunch."

I hurried to my mark on the stage.

"I saw you talking to the Irish hottie," Katherine said as she joined me back on stage. "Has he proposed and promised to take you back to Ireland with him?"

"No," I drew out, "but he invited us to a pub with some of the rest of the stagehands tonight."

"Did you say yes? Please tell me you said yes. I haven't had a night out with a group of strong, burly men in so long."

"I said I would check in with you."

"Then it's a total yes," Katherine exclaimed. "I don't know what I'm going to wear. What does one wear to a pub these days? Do we have pubs in NYC? We have a bit of everything here, so I'm sure there's an Irish pub around somewhere."

"Or he could mean any bar," I clarified. "I'll ask during our next break."

"Cue music," Serafina yelled. Eugene immediately played the last few bars of the song we were working on before we took our break.

The rest of Act One ran relatively smoothly. Once we finished Act One, the cast was asked to gather in a circle on the stage as Serafina went over the notes. I grabbed my binder from backstage and my requisite number two pencil. I sat on the floor, ready for anything Serafina had for me. Serafina had notes about everyone and everything. She clearly had a fantastic eye for detail. I took all kinds of notes about specific line issues and blocking things she'd noticed while we ran Act One that morning. It was nice to be working with such a consummate professional again.

"And on that note," Serafina said as she wrapped up, "I'll see everyone back here in forty-five minutes."

And just like that, we were off for lunch. The rest of the day flew by in pretty much the same way. We got through Act Two. At the end of the afternoon, Serafina promised to run the entire show without stopping in the morning.

After conferring with Lachtna and Katherine, I raced home. I took a brief nap before running through the shower. Once I was certain I smelled good, I threw on a pair of deep burgundy leather pants and a tight black top that showed all my curves in the right places. Before I left the apartment, I made sure Bootsy wouldn't kill me in my sleep by making sure he had food and water while I was gone.

I exited the elevator in a rush and almost smacked right into my new neighbor. "Oh, hey," I said, sidestepping to avoid running him down. "Sorry about that."

"No harm, no foul," Kirk said. "Where are you off to in such a hurry?"

"Meeting up with a girlfriend and some stagehands at a pub. You?"

"Getting back late from a series of parent-teacher conferences. Trying to get some administrative work out of the way before Thanksgiving."

"I can't imagine."

Kirk hesitated, but his face told me he wanted to say something to me. "So, Carissra and I are having a Friendsgiving on Thursday late afternoon or early evening. I wanted to see if you and maybe Johnny and Amani wanted to join us."

"By late afternoon, I should be free. I have the parade in the morning, but I should be home by noon."

"Oh, you're going to the parade?"

"Yep."

"Where do you like to see it from? Carissra wants to go, but I want to find a spot that would be good for her. Ya know?"

"Honestly, I don't know. I haven't gone to see the parade in years. I'm working the parade. Our show is performing the opening number."

"I forgot about that." Kirk's face flashed with disappointment as he said that. I guess he really needed some advice. "Well, I don't want to keep you from meeting up with your friends."

"I'll see you around," I said. I started to walk away when an idea struck me. I spun around and Kirk had one foot in the elevator. "Hold up," I yelled. He turned around, and the elevator dinged its angry dinging to let us know it was tired of being held open, so Kirk got out of the way and let the elevator close. "I have an idea.

I get two free VIP passes to bring anyone I want to the parade. I wasn't planning on using them, but this may be a perfect chance for you and Carissra to watch the parade. I know they have seating and wheelchair access there."

"Oh wow..." Kirk stammered. "That would be freaking amazing."

"You'd have to be up early and ready to go. We must get on the bus at the theater by 7:30. Technically, I could get you the passes, and you could meet us there. I don't know how easy it would be to get Carissra there. At least with our bus, we have a close drop-off and pickup point."

"That would work for us."

"Great. I'll come by tomorrow after work, and we can iron out plans."

"Thanks! I can't begin to thank you for this."

"What are neighbors for?" I smiled and left him standing in the lobby with his jaw slightly dropped.

I got outside and was glad to find my Uber waiting for me. Most of the time, Uber drivers would wait a few minutes, but a few got mad and took off. I made sure I tipped extra, so it kept my rider rating high.

In minutes, the driver pulled up to an Irish pub in the heart of Times Square. Honestly, if I had been wearing more clothes, I probably would have walked. But I wanted to look sexy and not like a puffy snowman the whole night.

"Score!" a loud yell of Irish men accompanied my entrance. They were all watching soccer on the television and not looking at me. I wormed my way through the group of mostly men up to the bar. I ordered a cranberry and vodka, and the bar matron gave me a look that practically screamed *American*!

"Hey there, sexy," a deep Irish voice said next to my ear.

"Hey there, back," I said, spinning around to find Lachtna decked out in a light blue soccer jersey and holding a glass of beer in his hand.

"Glad you found the place," Lachtna said.

"It's right in Times Square. We're practically at TKTS. I'm amazed I haven't been in here before."

"Yeah. Even though it's in the city's heart, it caters to an exclusive Irish clientele."

"Boy," the bar matron yelled. "Is this lass yours?"

"Nah, Saoirse. We work together," Lachtna responded as he threw down money on the bar for my drink without asking.

"Well, tell her next time to buy herself a drink for a grownup." The old woman let out a cackle as she placed my drink on the bar and turned away.

"What did you order?" Lachtna asked.

"Cranberry and vodka."

He burst out laughing, and I stood there, stupefied. I must have made some big Irish faux pas. "She's giving ya a hard time. To her, it's either whiskey or beer. Anything else is toilet bowl water."

"Well, that's a pleasant thought," I grumbled as I drank my delicious toilet bowl water.

"Come on over. We got a table and saved ya a seat. Katherine's already there."

Lachtna pushed his way through the crowd of men who were pretty much all wearing the same jersey as he did. On the far wall were a couple of high-tops pushed together. Katherine sat at one and was in deep conversation with a Puerto Rican guy who worked on the show. I recognized him but didn't know him at all. Lachtna pulled out a stool for me, and I sat down and was glad my seat was next to him.

"Don't worry, the game's almost over. Then things will quiet down a bit," Lachtna yelled into my ear over the roar of another goal.

"So, who's playing?" I asked, trying to pretend that I cared.

"It's Dublin versus Monaghan. It's the All-Ireland Senior Football Championship semifinals. This determines who plays against Wexford next week in the finals."

"What are they called?"

"In Gaelic, they're the *Áth Cliath*. But most call them The Dubs, as them being from Dublin and all."

"And I take it the guys in the light blue," I said, looking at one of the television monitors showing the game, "are The Dubs."

"That they are," he said with more pride in his voice than I expected. I smiled.

"Oh, come on! What the f—" the booing in the surrounding crowd drowned out a guy's voice.

"What happened?" I asked.

"Ref should have called a penalty, but he's apparently blind as a bat," Lachtna said, his attention diverted back to the game and away from me.

Well, this is going well. I turned my attention back to the screen and watched. I may not have known what was going on in the game, but I knew enough to know the game was coming to a climax by the way the rowdiness in the bar grew.

"Score!" The room erupted, and from the chest-bumping around the room, I put it together that Dublin had won. Inside I let out a weak, "yippee," but I kept it to myself and plastered on a smile.

"Need another drink, luv?" Lachtna asked.

His pint was already empty, and I had barely sipped mine. "Nah, I'm still fine," I said, holding up the mostly full glass as proof. Over the next half hour, the pub thinned out. It was still loud and rowdy, but it wasn't wall-to-wall men in jerseys.

"So, tell me about yourself, Erika," Lachtna said. He was already on another pint.

I told him about growing up in Iowa, then he told me about growing up in a little town called Nass, about thirty-two minutes outside Dublin. He'd gotten a degree in theater at The Lir Academy, Ireland's National Academy of Dramatic Art at Trinity College.

"After college, I went to London to become an actor in the West End. That didn't turn out quite as planned. Ended up taking a part-time job as a carpenter for a set designer. My father had been an actual carpenter, so I'd grown up helping him with woodworking projects. I moved up the ranks. I broadened my area of specialization from woodworking to theater rigging and special effects. Out of nowhere, I moved to New York." He looked at me and smiled. "Be right back. Gotta go to the jacks."

I smiled and nodded as he walked over to the restroom. Katherine scooted over to a stool next to mine. "How are things going?

You two have been talking nonstop. I haven't had a chance to say hello."

"Things are going well," I admitted. "He's a great guy. More intelligent than most people would probably predict. He has that tough guy, macho exterior, but he's a big melty marshmallow."

"And you want to make a s'more out of him?"

"Katherine! I'm not sure what's that supposed to mean, but...but get your head out of the gutter." Katherine laughed. "What about you? How are things down at your end of the table?"

"I'm enjoying myself. I could have my pick of the litter."

"Any specific puppy you want to take home with you?" I jested.

"Nah, I'm not in the mood to house train right now."

I roared out a laugh.

"Need another drink?" Lachtna asked, coming up behind me.

"No, I'm fine. Thanks, though."

And that's pretty much how the rest of the evening went. Lachtna and I talked and laughed, and he drank, and he drank. I swear, I've never seen a man put away more alcohol in my entire life. I almost wondered if his body would be pickled by the night's end. By midnight, I called an Uber.

Lachtna took time out of his drinking to walk me outside as I waited. The chill of the night hit me the second I stood outside.

"Brrr," I said as my body physically shook.

Lachtna wrapped his muscled arms around me and pulled me in. Immediately, his body heat against my back warmed me, melting away any sense of cold. His hot breath on the back of my neck as he leaned his lips down and lightly kissed the back of me. My body shivered, but not because of the cold this time.

"I know a way to make ya warmer," he whispered. "Come back to my place."

A part of me was intrigued, but another part of me knew it was a bad idea. I spun around in his arms to face him.

"I won't lie. Part of me would love to do that, but the adult part of me says it's a work night, and no good could come from that."

He stiffened as the words came out of my mouth. He pushed me away from his body. Not violently, just firmly, as he said, "Very well then. A guy can take a hint." He spun around and went back inside, leaving me once again to the elements. I stood there, dumbfounded. *What was that?* I hadn't really turned him down. Heck, if he had kissed my neck again, I might have gone with him.

I shivered as I pulled out my phone to see when the Uber would get there. Thankfully, the driver was a block away, so I didn't feel the need to go back inside. I swear I could hear the clanking of my teeth in my head as I waited. The Uber pulled up, and I practically jumped inside to get out of the cold.

I wondered what I had done wrong the whole drive home but figured it was all the beer in his system. The Uber dropped me off, and I was in bed almost as soon as I hit the front door.

The following day, I slept through my alarm. I finally got up because Bootsy was kneading me, clearly telling me it was food time. When I rolled over, the clock read 8:00 a.m.

I flew out of bed and rushed through the shower. I made it out of the apartment in a record 35 minutes. I had enough time to stop and get a hot tea and a banana on the way to the theater. I didn't feel the cold against my skin because I was in a hurry. I was even more in a hurry than a normal New York hurry, which is 'get out of my way, I have someplace to be' mode. If a tourist had gotten in my way that morning, I probably would have plowed right through them and not noticed.

I put my stuff down and made it to the stage right as San Nicolás entered the theater with his staff and the stage manager. They sat down at their table, and Serafina yelled, "Top of Act One. Places."

I looked over from stage right and saw a new guy sitting behind the piano. *Where's Eugene?*

"Oh, my!" Katherine exclaimed.

"What?"

"Do you know who that is?" Katherine squealed.

"Cut the theatrics and tell us," Peeter said through a yawn.

"That's Gerard Bartholomew," Katherine said, salivatingly looking at the old man.

"Should we know who he is?" Peeter asked.

"Well, duh!" Katherine said, giving Peeter a dressing down with her facial expression. "He was, well, I guess is, only one of the most celebrated music directors in Broadway history." She listed the litany of shows Mr. Bartholomew had run music for over the years. "He retired years ago. How did we get him?"

"I'm sure like everything else," Peeter said, "Rebekka Eldridge bought him. Let's face it, if the amount of money she is clearly throwing at this production could win a Tony, they'd be measuring me for my tux."

I hated to admit it, but as soon as Bartholomew started playing the piano, he elevated the experience of the show. Eugene had been an amazing pianist, but Bartholomew was on a whole other level. Even without having seen the show, Bartholomew directed us in a way that Eugene never could.

I got to my quick-change moment, and I dashed off stage right, down the stairs, and across the underground tunnel. To make sure I could make the run, the stage manager assigned stagehands to direct traffic and ensure no one would be in my way. Lachtna was always stationed at the base of the stairs on stage left. As I passed Lachtna, he didn't look at me, but I could still smell alcohol on him. I didn't have time to worry about him, so I dashed up the stairs. I was getting faster. I wish I knew how long this would take once we got the costume here.

During one scene, I had a few minutes of downtime with the elves as the happy couple sang a sappy love song. I motioned with my head for Katherine to join me.

"Have you noticed the cold shoulder Lachtna's giving me? I can't figure out what I did wrong."

"Oh, yeah, he was beyond pissed after you left. I don't know what you said or did—"

"I said I wouldn't go home with him last night because we had work today," I spat out. "What the elf!" Katherine's eyes grew as soon as I'd said it, but then she started laughing and had to throw a hand over her mouth to keep herself from being heard on stage.

I shook my head. Part of me was frustrated, and another part was thankful I'd dodged whatever bullet Lachtna was.

A large crashing sound and a scream from the stage jolted us out of our merriment. Without thinking, we raced to the stage to see what had happened.

Maeve McKenna was splayed across the stage.

I looked around and noticed Caiden and Tabatha standing there wide-eyed and shocked. "What happened?" Katherine asked.

"We were coming off—" Tabatha squeaked out.

"The set, it just..." Caiden tried to take over. "It came flying in when it wasn't supposed to. It lifted her off the ground and tossed her like a rag doll."

I didn't need to know anything else. I knew who oversaw that set piece. I'd watched him manage the piece every day.

The EMTs showed up and wheeled off a rather fragile-looking McKenna from the stage. Almost immediately, people from the union, along with safety inspectors, were in the theater, trying to find out what had happened. I needed to tell someone, but I didn't know who I should tell. I didn't know if what was running through my head was real. The group of newcomers had a face I recognized. Jeremy McCartan, from Equity, walked into the theater in a suit. He talked to the San Nicolás and Serafina. I needed to get his attention.

Wait! I know someone who knows McCartan. I pulled out my phone and shook my head as I texted Asher. I wasn't sure if he had the same number from when we were together, but I hoped he did.

Erika*: Do you have McCartan's number?*

I was on the other side of the auditorium, so I could see Asher as he leaned back against the chair so he could pull his phone out of his pocket. He looked at the message. Asher's fingers flew over the device.

Asher: *Who is this?*
Erika: *Wow, thanks. I totally feel the love.*
Asher: *Erika?*
Erika: *Who else? Anyway, I need McCartan's cell.*
Asher: *Why?*
Erika: *I have information he needs.*

Asher: *Then go tell him.*

Erika: *Asher, just give me the number.*

Asher: *Whatever.*

Erika: *It's important.*

Asher looked at the phone, then his fingers flew again, and the following message I got was a 914 area code cell phone number. I copied and pasted it before sending McCartan a text.

Erika: *Is this McCartan?*

Okay, so it's probably not the best way to send a text, but it worked because I got a message back almost immediately.

McCartan: *Yes. Who is this?*

Erika: *It's Erika Saunders. I'm going to step out into the lobby. There's a water fountain around the corner. Meet me there.*

McCartan: *What is this about?*

Erika: *I have information you need.*

I slipped out of my seat and headed outside.

"Where are you going?" Aarya asked, blocking the door I planned on using. "No one's supposed to leave."

"I'm going to the water fountain to refill my bottle," I said, holding up my now-empty bottle and jiggling it at her.

"Whatever," Aarya said, and they let me leave.

I went to the water fountain and started refilling my water bottle when I heard someone walk up behind me.

"What is this about, Erika? I don't have time for your nonsense."

I wanted to lash out, but I didn't. I paused and gathered my thoughts. "I didn't want to say anything in front of anyone else. But Lachtna MacGrory may have been operating equipment this morning inebriated." McCartan cocked his eyes and narrowed them at me. "I'm not joking. Last night, I hung out with him and some of his friends at a pub."

"Oh really?" McCartan said with a look that insinuated all kinds of things.

"It wasn't like that. Trust me on that one." I let out a huff. "Anyway, I passed him during a scene change this morning; I could still smell alcohol on him."

"If this is some kind of game you're play—"

"It's not a game. I may be way off base. But I'm almost positive MacGrory was responsible for the rigging. From what I can tell, it was a rigging problem that led to the accident. If that's the case…and if I'm right about Lachtna still being drunk…" I let the end of my sentence hang out there.

McCartan stood there for a second, reading my face. "If you're messing with me, I will make sure you can't get another job anywhere in this industry."

"I get it," I said, resigning myself to whatever happened next. "But I'm not messing with you."

As he walked away, he pulled out his cell phone. I couldn't hear much, but I heard the words *breathalyzer* and *police*.

I plastered on a smile and slipped back into the theater.

"Where were you?" Katherine said as I sat back down.

Before I had a chance to say anything, two uniformed cops entered the theater.

"You didn't?" Katherine asked.

"I had to," I said.

"But if you're wrong?" Katherine didn't need to end the sentence because I already knew what she was thinking.

I sat in my chair and nervously played with my fingernails. The police led Lachtna MacGrory from the theater in handcuffs about ten minutes later.

"Well," Peeter said, leaning over the seat between Katherine and me, "There's another one for the naughty list."

Chapter 18

The rest of Wednesday flew by in a flash. Serafina read McKenna's lines to keep the show moving forward. Even in a case when someone gets injured, show people don't have time to stop and take stock of anything. By the time I got home that evening, I was physically and emotionally exhausted. Before I went into my place, I walked next door and knocked on Kirk and Carissra's door. I heard shuffling inside before the door opened.

"Oh, hey, Erika," Kirk said. He was wearing a red apron with a cartoon turkey with a speech bubble that read, '*They stuff what where...Oh, hell no!*' I laughed when I read it. Kirk smiled knowingly.

"Love that," I said. "I needed a laugh today."

"Uh-oh, what happened?"

"I won't bore you with the details of my crazy life. I came by to talk logistics about tomorrow."

"From what I can tell, nothing about your life is ever boring. And right now, I'm getting ready for tomorrow. So, come on in and have a glass of wine."

"I don't want to bother—"

"Not a bother at all. It's boring cooking in here all by myself."

"Where's Carissra?"

"She's over in the other tower at a friend's house."

"I'm glad she's making friends in the building."

"Me too." Kirk opened the door a little wider and gestured for me to come inside. I hesitated for a second but took him up on his offer. I walked in, and he ushered me to the other side of the kitchen. There was a window with a ledge separating the kitchen from the dining room area. "Hope you don't mind red."

"Not at all. I'm pretty open with my wine preferences." He pulled a red wine glass from a cabinet before popping the cork off an already-opened bottle. He poured the glass and sat it in front of me.

"It's an Australian Shiraz," Kirk said. "Beyond that, I can't tell you anything else about it. I know if you swirl the glass, you can see if the wine has 'legs.'"

Just for the fun of it, I swirled the glass and watched as the residue of the wine clung to the top part of the glass as it slowly slid down. "Nice."

"So, tell me about your day. In the immortal words from Charlie Brown, 'Psychiatric Help, Five Cents.'"

"Wow, you're definitely cheaper than my therapist," I joked, making a mental note to call and schedule an appointment. I clearly had a lot to work through from the past few weeks. I spent the next forty minutes detailing the craziness that started on Monday and ran through this morning.

Kirk looked at me and patted me on the shoulder before saying, "Whoa...you've had a couple of...days, haven't you?"

"That's one way to put it," I said, nudging him with my shoulder. "At one point, my life wasn't this crazy or full of drama, but geez."

"Well, I guess drama does come with the whole theater thing. Doesn't it?" Kirk asked.

"Oh, theater people are definitely larger-than-life characters, but this has been crazy for even my regular drama-riddled life."

We sat there for a moment, just holding each other's gaze. *God, he has beautiful eyes.*

There was a sudden sound at the front door as it opened, and Carissra wheeled herself inside. "I'm home," she started to yell but then saw Kirk was in the kitchen.

"Oh hey, sorry I'm later than I said I would be. I got caught up in a video game I was playing."

"Not a problem. Honestly, I hadn't noticed." Kirk gestured toward me, but I doubted Carissra could see me from where she sat. "I've been catching up with Erika."

"Hi, Erika," Carissra said as she wheeled herself past the kitchen to where she could see me. She looked at the glass of wine in front of me and asked, "More drama at work or more man troubles?"

"Wow..." I said, squeezing my face together in shock. "You don't mince words."

"Hey, I calls them likes I sees them," she said with a smile. "From my vantage point, there's no reason to beat around the bush."

"Well, to answer your question, I guess it's a bit of both, but I won't bore you with the details. Kirk has already been my therapist for the night. Besides, I don't want to trouble a teenager with my drama."

"Whatever," Carissra said, rolling her eyes dramatically. "I may be a teenager, but I'm quite perceptive."

"That she is," Kirk said. "She never lets me get away with anything."

"So," I said, looking between them, "We should discuss tomorrow. Like I told your uncle, you can either take the bus or meet us there. I have your passes here." I reached into my purse and pulled out two laminated passes that hung on lanyards. "These will get you into the VIP area. I've been assured that once you're there, finding accommodating seating won't be a problem."

"Will you get to join us?" Kirk asked.

"Once my part is over, I will hang out with you. I'll warn you, though. Right after the parade ends, Midtown is crazy. In all honesty, it might be easier to walk home at that point. But again, let me know what's easiest for you."

"I think we'll stick with you...if you don't mind?" Kirk asked.

"I wouldn't offer if I minded. In that case, I'll knock on your door at 7:00 a.m. I know it's early—"

"Remember who you're talking to. I'm out of here at that time most mornings, and Carissra isn't usually far behind me."

"That's right. I forget you live on a non-show business schedule."

"Around this building, I know that's something unique," Kirk joked.

I hung out for a while longer and watched as Kirk worked around the kitchen. I finished my glass of wine. Once I was wined-up, I went back to my apartment and was greeted by a none-to-happy

Mr. Bootsy. I fed him and gave him lots of love and attention before crashing.

"Okay, cast of *The Naughty List*," our old friend Director Doug yelled at us from our staging area. Right after the cast of *The Hallow Men*, you'll get ready. The commercial break should be about 45 seconds, then the announcers will chit-chat for another minute. That gives you under two minutes to get into position." With that, Doug left the staging area and went back to a control tent where he was calling the shots for the Broadway performances.

"This thing itches," Katherine said next to me.

"Mine too," I admitted.

That morning, our costume designer surprised us with brand-new costumes for the parade. This was great, except that we'd never worn the costumes or rehearsed in them. I glanced around, and everyone looked uncomfortable.

"Just remember, scratching yourself on national television is not very elf-like," Peeter said. He was dressed like he was about to make a trek across Antarctica.

"You're going to freeze once you take off that parka," I said.

"I'm hoping the adrenaline of the performance will be enough to prevent me from turning into an elf-cicle."

The music for one of the few good songs in *The Hallow Men* started, so I turned my head to watch the cast perform. Honestly, their performance on the street looked better than it had during previews. I'd already heard rumors that the show was tanking at the box office, so this performance could boost their ticket sales and prevent the show from closing. Despite how much the show sucked, I didn't want to see anyone in their cast or crew out of work.

"*The Naughty List*," Doug, the director, yelled. "You're up."

The whole group ran out into the middle of the street in front of Macy's and got into our opening positions. We stood waiting forever before we heard the opening chords of music. Thankfully,

Peeter was right. Adrenaline took over, and our short performance went off without a hitch. When the song ended, we all raced to the center of the road to wave at the camera. I let out a sigh of relief.

We walked back to the staging area to pick up our coats, scarves, hats, and gloves. I bundled up. Some of the cast were already making their way back to the bus area to be taken back to the theater. A few of us planned on lingering and catching the bus after the parade.

"Are you actually staying?" Peeter asked. "My jingle bells have practically shrunken to the size of chestnuts."

"I'm from Iowa originally. This isn't cold."

"Whatever," Peter said dismissively. "You enjoy your cold. I'm going to go home where it's warm. See you tomorrow."

"What about you?" I asked Katherine.

"Me, I'm going to hang out for a while. Never seen the parade up close, so this should be fun."

"You can sit with my friends and me."

"I'm actually meeting someone here."

"Really?" I asked, with a flash of my eyebrow suggestively.

"Yes," she said with a smile. "I invited Rafael to be my plus one."

"Rafael, the Puerto Rican hottie stagehand?"

"That's the one," Katherine said. A flush ran to her cheeks despite the cold weather.

"Well, I won't keep you. Go get warm next to your Puerto Rican stud."

Katherine rolled her eyes and walked toward the VIP seating. I pulled out my cell phone to text Kirk to see where they were. There were already a couple of other texts.

It's your mother

As if I didn't recognize the number. The text also shows up as *Mom's Cell*, so that was also a dead giveaway.

Mom: *Saw you on the television. You looked so cute in our little outfit. Call us later. Love, Mom.*

Then another text appeared.

Asher: *Hey, Erika. Thought the cast looked great. See you tomorrow. Happy Thanksgiving.*

Well, that was an unexpected text.

Brice: *Overall, I thought the performance was good. Hopefully, the rest of the show doesn't suck.*

Ahh, Brice's superpower was his ability to compliment, but he did it backhandedly to remind you he's your agent.

I decided to respond to the texts later. I shot Kirk a text, and almost immediately, he texted back to let me know where he was sitting. After making my way through the crowd, I found Carissra and Kirk with ease.

"Welcome," Kirk said as he scooched over on the metal bench to let me sit between him and Carissra. "Thanks again for inviting us."

"I'm glad I could use my passes," I said. "So, what did you think?"

"Well, it was good."

Ahh, the joys of straight men and their ability to describe things.

"It was better than you made it out to be," Carissra said.

"Thanks...I think."

"Well, you know," Carissra said, "all we've really heard about the show are the problems."

She was right. "Sometimes, when you're in the middle of creating a show, you don't always realize what it looks like to an outsider. I know the history of the problems and how things have changed, so I don't always get to think about the show with a new pair of eyes."

"That makes—"

The first marching band of the day started playing right in front of us, so I couldn't hear what Carissra said. It gave me a chance to appreciate that I'd probably been harder on the show than I should have been.

The parade flew by in a dizzying flurry of Christmas colors, music, balloons, and floats. By the time Santa Claus's float rolled by, I was ready for the parade to be over. Don't get me wrong, I loved the sights and sounds. But, as much as I hated to admit it and would never dream of saying this to his face, Peeter was right; it was elf-ing cold.

We wormed our way through the crowd to where our bus was located. Only a handful of cast members had stuck around, so it was almost empty on the way back to the theater. Once there, we piled out. I went inside to return my costume. I'd told Kirk and

Carissra to go home, but they insisted on staying, so I changed as quickly as I could.

"The turkey should be done in about twenty minutes," Kirk said from the kitchen.

His friends-giving ended up being Amani, Johnny, another couple and their son from the building I didn't know, and one of Kirk's colleagues who didn't have anywhere else to be. I did a quick headcount, counted the number of chairs Kirk had, ran over to my place, and dragged over a few extra chairs. Thankfully, Kirk had a spare folding table, so we were all going to be at the table together.

"What can I do to help?" Amani asked, clearly not used to standing around and not helping.

"Absolutely nothing," Kirk said. "You brought sides, even though I told you not to."

Amani shrugged. "I can't help myself."

"That's my man," Johnny cut in. "He can't go to anyone's house without bringing at least two dishes."

"I'm not that bad."

"Keep telling yourself that, honey."

Kirk finally stared at the group huddled outside the kitchen in the cramped entry hallway. "Okay, all of you, go sit down."

"Aye, aye, captain," Johnny said with a mock salute. He grabbed Amani by his upper arm and dragged him into the living room.

I huddled on the other side of the opening that separated the kitchen and dining area, which was becoming my usual spot when I hung out with Kirk. "Now that all the chefs are out of the kitchen. Do you need anything?" I said it softly enough that only Kirk could hear me.

"Nah, I'm good... Why don't I pass you stuff, and you can put it on the table?"

"Sounds like a plan."

Kirk started unwrapping things and handing them to me. I then placed them on the table. Before long, the table was so full I wasn't sure if there would be enough room for everyone to have plates in front of them.

"The turkey is done," Kirk said. He pulled the turkey out of the oven. The little thermometer in the turkey had popped up. He lifted it out of the oven.

"I don't know where you're going to put that on the table," I warned him. "It's already pretty darn full."

Kirk leaned around to stare at the table and gave me a sideways smile. "I guess we have enough food to feed an army out there. I'll slice the turkey here and put it on a platter."

"Okay."

A few minutes later, Kirk came out of the kitchen with a giant platter of cut turkey and everyone oohed and awed. We ate and talked for the next two hours. When it was all said and done, I tried to get Kirk to let us help him clean up, but he wouldn't hear any of it. I promised to drop by the next day to pick up the chairs I'd hauled over.

"Thanks for an amazing Thanksgiving," Kirk said as I was leaving. He stood in the entryway, his hand gripping the top part of the door as he leaned against it.

"What? You cooked everything. I showed up with a couple of bottles of wine."

"Not that. You made this whole day special. Since the accident, I've not seen Carissra light up like she did at the parade. I didn't realize how much we needed that."

I reached out and gently patted him on the chest, letting my hand linger just a second longer than was just a friendly pat. "I'm glad I could do that for her. Being a semi-celebrity has its privileges." I looked at my hand and quickly removed it before saying, "Well, I have rehearsal tomorrow. Gotta get some sleep."

"I can't believe you don't get a day off," Kirk said, shaking his head.

"We start tech week on Monday, so we need to be clear on where things are with the show before we start with lights, special effects, the orchestra, and many other people flying about the theater to help us get ready for our first performance.

"When is that, by the way?"

"Not this Tuesday, but the following one."

"That fast? You just started rehearsing."

"In our world, things are often this fast or faster. But," I drew the word out before I finished my thought, "this is really fast for a new musical. As they say, that's show business."

With that, I turned and walked next door. When I pulled out my key to unlock the door, I glanced to my left. Kirk stared after me with a contented look on his face.

Chapter 19

I woke up the following morning early. I know my body. It runs like a machine. And anytime I put extra stress on that machine, it likes to rebel in subtle ways. Yesterday I stressed out my body twice. I performed outside in the cold. And while we were only lip-synching to the music, I think everyone on the ground was still singing. We just weren't full-on belting for the balcony singing.

Then there was Thanksgiving dinner. I enjoyed every bite, and I would do it again in a heartbeat. However, my body wasn't used to that much food in one sitting, so I was more sluggish than usual as my body was still processing what I ate. To help my body readjust, I needed to take a moment and support it. If I was going to survive eight shows a week, I needed to make sure my body was in peak performance.

So, off to the gym I went on an early Black Friday morning. The gym was pretty much empty. There was another guy lifting weights, but other than the two of us, I could have heard a pin drop. I guess most people don't need to be at work by 9:30 today. San Nicolás had given us a whole extra thirty minutes because it was Thanksgiving. Whoop-de-doo! And I guess those people who are up early are looking for shopping specials and not a quick warmup for the day.

After running, I went back to my apartment and dragged out my yoga mat. I didn't have time for an entire routine, but I needed to limber up before heading into a full day of rehearsal. After running through a traditional asana set, I took a child's pose for a few minutes. I enjoyed the cool mat against my forehead as I stretched my arms out in front of me while continuing to practice my ujjayi pranayama breathing.

A lump of fur pressed in next to me. I giggled. "Well, I guess someone else finally got up in this apartment." Bootsy purred in response. When Bootsy was a kitten, he had a bad habit of jumping on my back while was I in the middle of a pose. I was constantly shooing him away from the yoga mat. Over time, he learned that when momma was on the yoga mat, Bootsy needed to stay away from momma. I may have accidentally kicked him once or twice when transitioning into a one-legged downward-facing dog or when I was raising my leg for a bow pose. He's an intelligent cat. He figured out that I couldn't see where he was a good deal of the time when I was doing yoga, so he'd learn that he could approach me when I was in a handful of poses.

He trilled next to me. "Okay, okay. I get it. It's breakfast time." I put my feet beneath my body and rolled up to a standing position one last time. Then stretched toward the sky before swooping my arms into a prayer pose. "Namaste." I got off the mat and walked into the kitchen. I grabbed my water bottle and took a swig as I pulled out Bootsy's food, opened it, and spooned it out for him. I placed it on the ground, and he practically pounced on it like a tiger attacking a wild animal.

I sprayed off my yoga mat and rolled it up, then tucked it away under the couch where I kept all my home exercise equipment. "Okay," I said to the empty apartment. "Time to get to work."

Something inside me said, "check your email," so I picked my phone off the end table charger where I'd put it when I got back from running. I scrolled through. I could spend the entire day deleting emails about Black Friday deals. Thankfully, I was not in need of any big sales. I'd already done the bulk of my Christmas shopping throughout the year, so I needed to buy some wrapping paper, then ship everything to my family in Iowa. My parents may come to New York for my opening. "That reminds me, I need to but a bug in their butts about that. We'll need to get reservations made, and tickets reserved fast if they're coming." I tend to talk to myself when I'm in my apartment alone. I needed a few more cats, and I could be a full-on cat lady in the future.

Meeting Today – Nine AM! I read the subject line of the email from Asier_Zlota_SanNicolás, so I kind of guessed who it was from. *On behalf of the producer and myself, we are having a company meeting at 9:00 a.m. before our regularly scheduled rehearsal at 9:30. We hope you will all make it. – San Nicolás.*

"Son of a Scrooge, there goes that extra thirty minutes," I said. I looked over at the clock, which read 8:15.

I was in and out of the shower in record time. I breezed by Bootsy on my way out of the apartment with a quick "I love you" before dashing to the theater. With thirty seconds to spare, I walked into the theater. The escalators were working, so I traveled up the flight to the main theater entrance and found a few people standing outside the entrance.

I walked over to Peeter and asked, "Any idea what this is about?"

"Probably the bad publicity we're getting," Peeter said. "Seems like we have a mole in the company who's been spreading our dirty laundry."

"Whoa," I said. We all know that casts and crews are like sieves. The information seems to flow out of them. But airing the dirty laundry in the press is a bit of a no-no.

Aarya poked their head out of the theater. "They're about to get started. Please come in." They said it politely, but we all knew it meant 'get your butts inside,' so we did as our favorite intern commanded.

I walked down front and sat on the aisle, taking my coat off and setting it in the seat next to me with my purse on top. I'd take them back to my dressing room when I got a moment.

"Thank you for getting here so early even after we tried to give you a later start time today," San Nicolás said. "I hope you all had a good Thanksgiving and are now ready to buckle down and finish the work." Standing next to San Nicolás, Rebekka Eldridge cleared her throat. "Oh yes, our producer has called this meeting, so I will turn it over to her." He made a grand sweeping gesture toward the producer as he said, "Mrs. Eldridge."

"First, I appreciate what the group pulled off yesterday at the parade. Our ticket sales started at 8:00 a.m., and they are pouring in. It appears we pulled off a Christmas miracle. We've already opened seat blocks into mid-March. At this rate, we'll be opening seat blocks into early summer when we start our Cyber Monday sale." There was a round of applause at that good news. "Now for the less-than-pleasant part of why I'm here. It has come to my attention that someone here has been speaking to," she glanced down at her notes before saying, "TheBroadway411."

I heard a series of groans from around the room. TheBroadway411 was the Broadway equivalent of Page Six, TMZ, and Perez Hilton all rolled into one nasty little website. It thrived on all things Broadway gossip. After Asher and I broke up, I'd been something of a smash for about a month as every piece of my life had been dissected on that website. It's a truly trashy experience.

"Salacious rumors and gossip about the inner workings of this production should not be made public. You all signed nondisclosure clauses. It's one thing when you're talking to your family or friends, but talking to the media is strictly prohibited. This is a terminal offense."

Uncomfortable murmurs around the room started immediately. *Great, now everyone's going to be wondering who the mole is. Terrific way to build company unity*, I thought sarcastically.

"There are lines of communication within this company. You can talk to either Asier or Serafina if you have a problem with production. If you have HR questions, you can call my office. If you have union questions or concerns, you can talk to your Equity Deputy or reach out to Equity directly."

Who is our Equity Deputy now? I wondered. *We haven't voted on a new one since McKenna's accident.*

"That's enough of this unpleasantness," Eldridge continued. "I was waiting until Monday, but everyone needs a pick-me-up after this conversation. Today is going to be a busy. The logo merchandise has arrived, and everyone is getting a gift bag. It will have two different T-shirts, ball caps, pins, and other souvenirs we'll be selling in the lobby." Just then, some of Eldridge's minions rolled in a big cart with bags overflowing with stuff. As the cart rolled past, I read the cast names on each bag, which meant they had already put the right sizes in the bags. "Everyone will receive an embroidered polo and coat to wear for public appearances. Also, the final costumes will be here by noon today for everyone. So, we'll have costumed rehearsals starting this afternoon. All the dressers have been called and know to be here today." She looked around the room before asking, "Any questions?"

No one spoke, so she dismissed the group. San Nicolás told us to be in places by 9:30, so I had enough time to grab my swag bag, put all my stuff in my dressing room and make it back to the stage with a couple of minutes to spare. I found Katherine and Peeter whispering when I got there.

"What are you whispering about?" I asked as I approached.

"We're playing detective," Katherine said with a half-smile.

"I think it's one of the stagehands," Peeter said flatly. "They're ever-present in the background without making waves. They hear and see a lot. It would be elementary for one to learn things and spread it around." As if to prove his point, a stagehand climbed down the ladder right behind us, which caused my stomach to lurch into my throat as he dropped the last couple of feet to the ground with a thud.

"Excuse me," the guy said as he brushed past us and walked across the stage.

"See what I mean?" Peeter said. "They're like those creepy elf dolls that people keep in their houses that allegedly spy on children for Santa."

"Yeah," Katherine started, "those are just creepy as fu—"

"Places," Serafina's voice chimed over the intercom.

"We'll talk more later. I wish whoever went to the press understands how this adds to the pressure," I admitted. "I'm sure it's someone new who doesn't know the unwritten rules about airing one's laundry in public. It's amazing how quickly that can demoralize a company."

The sound of the orchestra starting the overture in the pit snapped me back to attention. It was time for my A game.

Thankfully, there was no more talk of spies as we headed into Monday and the beginning of tech week. Part of me couldn't believe we were getting closer and closer to opening the show.

"Okay, people," Serafina said into the intercom system. "This is going to be slow going. We may only get through a dozen scenes today. I know it's painstaking as the lighting people work around you. Stay out of their way. And keep the noise down."

I was in my position for the top of Act One. Gerard Bartholomew conducted the pit orchestra in the overture. The curtain rose and I opened my mouth to sing—

"Hold," Serafina's echoed throughout the theater.

I looked out on the stage to see what was wrong. I glanced at the assistant stage manager, who was sitting off to my right, and asked, "What's happening?"

"There's a spot out of alignment," he said. "It'll be a moment."

I stretched my neck and heard it pop when I leaned it to the right. I was trying to keep myself limber just in case we made it far enough to start any of the choreography.

"Places," Serafina's voice filled the theater. "Picking up at measure twenty-three."

"Can we back it up five measures to give the cast a lead-in?" Bartholomew asked from his bench in front of the piano.

"Whatever you think is best, maestro."

The overture started and we got an entire line and a half out of our mouths before we heard "hold" again over the speakers. And that's how it was for Monday, Tuesday, and Wednesday. We started and stopped so often I wondered if we could ever make it through the show with all the technical issues we were having.

On Wednesday afternoon, we had a short break as some flying mechanism wasn't working right.

"Take twenty," Serafina said over the system. By this point, I had dreams with Serafina popping up and yelling, "Hold!"

I slipped backstage and ran to the restroom in my dressing room. Outside my dressing room, I found Rebekka Eldridge waiting for me.

"I've been looking for you," she said. She eyed me like a Disney villain getting ready for one of their schemes. "You're the new representative for the company with Equity."

"I didn't volunteer."

"Of course not, dear. I just told you, you were."

"We didn't vote on it. The cast is supposed to vote."

She let out a huff and turned away. With a wave of her hand, she said, "We don't have time for that." She walked away, clearly deciding the conversation was over.

I stood there, mouth agape. "Well, I guess my first job as the Equity Deputy is to report myself." I opened the door to my dressing room. While I was on the toilet, I texted Jeremy McCartan at Equity.

McCartan: *We had the paperwork in our office on Monday. You didn't know?*

Erika: *The producer just stopped by my dressing room and told me.*

McCartan: *And there wasn't a vote?*

Erika: *No!*

I added the exclamation mark for emphasis.

McCartan: *Thanks. Until I can work this out, please stay in the position. I promise it's temporary.*

I walked back to the stage only to find Eldridge introducing the cast to the replacement for Maeve McKenna since she would not be returning to the show. The woman who stood with Eldridge was about as opposite from McKenna as possible. Where McKenna had been serious and eagle-eyed, this woman was cheerful. She looked like Mrs. Claus in the flesh. Where McKenna had been lanky, this woman was short and stout. I wouldn't call her heavy, but she was larger than McKenna had been.

"Well, I hope the costume designer has time to redo her wardrobe," Peeter said from behind me.

I turned and shot him a look.

"My bad, madam Equity Deputy." He gave me a small salute.

"How do you know about that?" I asked.

"There was a vote while you were gone."

"What?" I gasped.

"Eldridge walked in and said, 'Erika Saunders has volunteered to take over the Equity Deputy.' Then she made us vote on it just so it was 'above board.'"

"I was only gone for like fifteen minutes."

"It didn't take long," Peeter assured me.

I looked back to see Eldridge walking off the stage before the voice from God on high yelled, "Places. Picking up at Act Two, Scene Three."

We were back to starting and stopping. Thankfully, we had fewer and fewer stops, which was great. During one stop, I was close enough to the new actor who joined us, so I said hello.

"Hi, I'm Erika Saunders." I extended my hand in greeting.

"It's great to meet you, Erika. I've heard delightful things about you," the woman said.

"Oh, really?" I asked with a bit more leeriness in my voice than intended.

"Oh!" she exclaimed, clearly realizing the sound of my trepidation. "Nothing bad. I promise. Mrs. Eldridge told me you're our union rep. I'm glad to be here. I'm Jocelyn Michaels professionally, but my friends all call me Quinn, so please call me Quinn."

"Places!"

"We'll talk again soon," I said, rushing back to my last position. I heard Quinn yell "Toodles" after me as I turned my back.

"Did she say 'toodles?'" Peeter asked when I neared.

"Yep."

"Wow, a person who 'toodles' in New York. Isn't there a law against that?"

The piano started playing, and the show started and stopped repeatedly for the rest of the afternoon.

When I got back to the Manhattan Plaza after work, I was ready for a quiet night and a glass of wine—or two.

I pushed into the building and nodded at the security guard before heading to the elevator. With no one else in the car, I slunk against the back wall and sighed.

"Can you hold the door?" a voice called.

I pushed myself off the back wall and kicked out my foot to trigger the sensor that forced the door from closing.

"Thanks," the person said. "Oh, hey, Erika."

Until I heard Kirk say my name, I hadn't noticed him. "Oh, hi. Sorry," I said, shaking my head as if trying to get the cobwebs out. "I was kind of in my own world. How are you?"

"I'm great," Kirk said. "Just finished up at school a little later than usual. I started this new rocket club at school."

"You let kids play with rockets?" I looked at him, furrowing my forehead.

"They aren't allowed to do anything dangerous. It's more of a science and math club, but we use rockets to help them apply what they're learning. And it's fun for me because the kids in the club come from a range of backgrounds."

"So, they're not the kids you teach?"

"One of them is. The rest are other kids interested in science and math."

"Yeah, that wouldn't have been me," I admitted. "My dad tried to teach me how to balance my checkbook. I was like, 'Why? I just look on my bank's app.'"

Kirk laughed. "I was the same way until I was in college. I came to find out that I was good at math and science. I'd had a series of teachers who got me excited. But enough about me. How was your day?"

"It was a day at the office. We're in tech week. Which is the equivalent of...I have no idea what it's the equivalent of in the normal world."

"Well, why don't you join Carissra and me for dinner, and you can tell me all about it?"

I was about to say no but I had nothing in my house to eat anyway. "Sure, why not. I'll grab the wine and come on over." The elevator dinged and opened on our floor.

"Great, I'll see you in a few."

"What are you making?" I asked, then added, "So, I know whether to bring a white or red wine."

"Family lasagna recipe. Prepped it last night, so all I have to do is shove it in the oven. It'll take about 45 minutes to cook. We can talk while we wait."

"Be there in a minute. Let me check in with Bootsy first."

I unlocked and opened the door to my apartment. Bootsy was curled up in a ball on my bed. I slipped out of my clothes and put on something more comfortable. I ran my hands through my hair, then pulled it back into a ponytail with a band I had on my dresser. After walking into the kitchen, I pulled out a can of Bootsy's favorite food. I leaned down so he could get a good whiff, and to get back into his good graces for having been gone all day. I stood up with the can in hand. He looked at me before he pawed the air as if to say, "Where's the food going?"

"Just let me get a spoon," I said, looking at my favorite little furball. I grabbed a spoon from the drawer and spooned it out into his dish. He came over and immediately started eating it. I grabbed a bottle of red wine from the small wine rack I had on the kitchen counter before heading over to Carissra and Kirk's place. Bootsy was so enthralled with his meal that he didn't bother raising his head as I left.

I knocked lightly on the door, and Kirk immediately let me in. I handed him the bottle of wine, some generic something or other I'd picked up at the corner liquor store. He opened it and poured us each a glass before we headed into the living room to sit on a couch.

From my vantage point, I could see Carissra in her bedroom on a headset. "What's she doing?" I asked.

"Playing video games with some friends of hers from back in DC. They do this regularly. It's a good way for her to keep in contact with them. She was always a gamer nerd."

"I'm not a gamer nerd," Carissra yelled. "Hi, Erika."

"You can hear that?" I asked.

"I hear all. Muwahh!" she said, playing out the spooky villain vibe.

"In all seriousness, her microphone picks up a lot, I've found. But she has selective hearing when she has those things on." Kirk turned to me and said, "Watch this." He swiveled toward Carissra's bedroom and said loudly, "Carissra, have you finished your homework?"

She turned her head and gave him a quizzical look before fake yelling, "What? I can't hear you over the headphones."

I laughed and so did Kirk.

"So, tell me about this technology week."

"It's just tech week. It's usually the week before a show opens when all the technological elements of a show are implemented. For us, it's primarily a lot of lights and special effects that must be tested, retested, and tested some more."

"Okay, so that doesn't sound too bad."

"Oh really? Let me tell you about my morning." I explained the stop and start process of how things were going.

"You sung two words and they stopped you?"

"That's nothing. On Monday, we were stopped before we even opened our mouths," I laughed.

"Other than that, how's the show going?"

"At times, things are going smoothly, and other times I swear I'm living in a farce. If it can go wrong, it has gone wrong. And usually, when technology goes wrong, it goes wrong spectacularly."

"How so?"

"Take this afternoon, for instance. We have this poor new actor who joined us today."

"Really? Seems a bit late in the game, doesn't it?"

"She's replacing the woman who's head my drunk date almost took off."

"Your drunk date?"

"I thought I told you that story?"

"Maybe...?" Kirk questioned. "But I'm pretty sure I would have remembered someone almost losing a head on stage."

I told him all about my evening at the Irish pub and the aftermath. "But as for today. Poor Quinn must come up from below the stage on an elevator, but the thing had been calibrated for the previous actor's height and weight. Quinn was lifted up through the stage about boob height when the thing stuck."

"What did you do?"

"We 'hold,'" in my best imitation of Serafina. "Some of the crew ran out and helped her out. Basically, pulled her up through the stage."

"Why not lower her back down?"

"The motor burned out. Again, they calibrated it for a tall, thin woman. And Quinn is short and not as thin."

"That seems like a really bad mechanical design."

"It should have worked with a range of people and differing heights and weights. Someone above my pay grade made a decision, and now the mechanism is going to cost thousands of dollars to replace."

I went on to entertain Kirk with all the crazy antics flying around the stage. Tech week is always a comedy of errors, but this week was incredibly crazy.

The oven beeped. Forty-five minutes had flown by. Kirk pulled out the meal, and Carissra came out of her bedroom. She helped set the table, and we all sat down and ate. I continued telling them stories about the show.

"This is better than a comedy routine," Kirk noted.

"And it's my actual life," I said with a smirk. "Sometimes, you can't make this stuff up."

"Can I be excused?" Carissra asked, having finished her meal.

"More gaming?" Kirk asked.

"Just an hour more. Then I promise to get my reading done for school. I only have like two chapters tonight. And it's a book I read when I was in DC, so I already know it. Just need a quick refresh."

Kirk looked at her for a second before saying, "Tell your friends I said hello."

"Will do," she said, spinning around and wheeling herself back into her bedroom.

Kirk leaned back in his chair. "I'm lucky. She practically takes care of herself."

"She's very mature for her age."

"She grew up fast after her parents died. I wish she didn't have to grow up that quickly, but I'm glad she did. Makes my life easier, too." He let out a sigh before saying, "Well, I should get this cleaned up."

"Let me help you."

"No, you're a guest."

"I eat over here more than I do at my house these days. At least let me dry something."

"There's a new invention called a dishwasher...it dries for me."

I stuck my tongue out at him. He stood and started carrying stuff back into the kitchen. Against his wishes, I stood up and handed him stuff through the living room window into the kitchen.

When the dishes were all in the dishwasher, I looked at my watch. "Oh geez, it's already 9:30. The night flew by."

"I should get some grading done. Then I need to go to bed," Kirk said.

I headed to the door with Kirk right behind me. He reached around me and opened it. When the door swung inward, I stepped backward and found myself squished against Kirk as we let the door by.

I stayed for a second longer than necessary but then stepped out into the hall. Kirk leaned against the door as I turned and leaned against the door frame.

"I had a lot of fun tonight," I said. "You're so easy to talk to."

"I had fun, too. I'm glad Carissra and I have such an amazing neighbor."

We stood there for a second, gazing at each other. And kept staring at each other.

"What are you two doing?" Carissra asked as she rolled into the kitchen.

"Just saying goodbye," I said, shaking my head out of the fog. "It's been fun." I reached out my hand for a goodbye handshake.

Kirk looked crestfallen for an instant before he reached out and shook my hand. "Good night, Erika."

I moved entirely into the hallway, and Kirk shut the door to their apartment. I leaned forward and knocked my head against the wall. *A handshake! What was that?*

Chapter 20

The rest of the weekend flew by in a blur. We had several minor mishaps, but everything was gelling. On Monday, we successfully ran the show three times and planned on running it once on Tuesday before our first preview that night. First previews are always nerve-racking experiences. I invited Brice, Johnny, and Amani to the first preview. Brice and Johnny would be kind, but bluntly honest. Amani was going to be my cheerleader, who I also needed.

Since it was the first preview, and on a Tuesday, we started the show a half hour earlier than we normally would. I got to the theater at 6:00 p.m., and the cast met on the stage for a quick pep talk and warm up before we headed off to get into our costumes. At 6:30, I started on my makeup. The makeup designer had made a pretty easy-to-replicate makeup for my character.

"The house is now open," Serafina's voice said over the speaker in my dressing room.

There was a light knock on the door. "Come in," I said. The wig stylist came in to help me get my microphone fitted and the wig on. The microphone pack sat against the small of my back, and the wire was taped down against my back and neck. The microphone sat under the lace-front hairline at the front of my forehead. There was no way to see the hidden microphone unless you were close.

"Thanks," I said as the wig artist left. He opened the door and passed my dresser, Gladys Lapinski, who came in and helped me get into my costume. She was all mine. I had enough costume changes that I had a personal dresser who tracked me during the show. My quick change—when I ran from stage left to stage right in the middle of the show—would have been impossible without her.

I did one last look in the mirror in time for Serafina to say, "Five minutes to places, five minutes to places." I thanked Gladys and said I'd see her for my first costume change before heading out to stage right for my first entrance.

The backstage area was abuzz with movement. People were dashing to-and-fro, ensuring everything was where it needed to be. A chorus boy almost ran me over. He apologized but kept going. I'd had a brief conversation with him once, so I knew this was his first Broadway show after college. Quite a few of our cast members were making their Broadway debuts in this show. And while this technically wasn't their Broadway debut yet—that happened on opening night—I understood the anxiety and excitement. I couldn't help but think back to the first preview of *The Faith Healer*. I'd been so afraid I would forget my lines and blocking. But then the orchestrations started, and my body went into autopilot and navigated me through the show despite my nerves.

"Places." I heard Serafina's voice call as I got to the stage. I made my way to where my other elves were stationed.

"Break a leg," Peeter said. "Well, maybe not you, Erika," he laughed at his own joke. "Too soon?"

"It will always be too soon, goofball." He was trying to ease his nerves, so I didn't take the jab personally. "I would say break a leg to you, too, Peeter, but I don't have time to hire a hitman and train another elf," I said with a wink.

"Get a room," Katherine joked.

The lights dimmed, and a single spotlight shone at center stage. San Nicolás walked on stage and greeted the audience. "Good evening, and welcome to the first preview of *The Naughty List*." A roar of applause filled the theater. As the noise died down, San Nicolás continued, "As you know, this is a preview, and while we do not anticipate any problems, it's possible that there could be moments when things don't go exactly according to plan. Please bear with us. Now, sit back and enjoy the show."

As soon as he said this last line, I watched one of the backstage monitors as Gerard Bartholomew conducted the downbeat in the pit and the orchestra started the overture. I breathed deeply to calm my nerves and got ready to sing my first note.

"Hold!" Serafina's voice echoed in my ear.

"Are you elf-ing kidding me!" Peeter said.

I looked at the assistant stage manager sitting next to us in his cubby. "There's a problem with the Act Curtain. It's not opening. The automation rigging system isn't responding. They're sending a stagehand to do it manually."

My jaw dropped open. Sadly, that was the beginning of the night of a thousand problems. Our little two-and-half-hour musical took almost five hours. We hadn't had this many problems since our first day of tech. If it could go wrong, it went wrong. The proverbial cherry on the ice cream cone from hell was when we blew a fuse at the top of Act Two. The company electrician spent fifteen minutes diagnosing and fixing the problem. Thankfully, she had spares of everything sitting around in her workshop.

By the time we took our final bows, the entire company was exhausted. The audience, which had remained through the entire five hours, was supportive and still gave us a standing ovation. I doubted we deserved one that night. Maybe they gave us the ovation for simply finishing the show.

As the cast made its final bow and the curtain closed, Serafina, San Nicolás, and Eldridge walked on stage and gave us polite applause. From the thin-lipped smile on Eldridge's face, I could tell she was not a happy camper.

"Well, first previews are often rough," San Nicolás said, trying to reassure us. "We have a few kinks to iron out before we open."

"Kinks?" Peeter whispered next to me. "I've seen fewer kinks at the Folsom Street Fair."

I tried not to smile at his joke, so I let out a cough instead, covering my mouth.

"The artistic team needs time to process everything that happened tonight, so we'll wait until tomorrow morning to go over notes," San Nicolás informed the group. "Good night. And get some rest. We still have a lot of work in front of us."

"Okay, people," Serafina then said. "Call time for tomorrow morning is our usual 8:00 a.m. We'll rehearse until 3:00. Your call time for tomorrow evening will be 7:00 p.m. unless your hair and makeup require the extra half hour." She then nodded and added, "Get out of here."

I got back to my dressing room, and Gladys helped me out of my costume while the assistant hair supervisor did the same with my wig and microphone. While all this was going on, I texted Brice, Johnny, and Amani to let them know it would be a few minutes before I was free. I told them to head over to the restaurant, and I'd meet them there.

I showered as quickly as possible before throwing on the simple pair of jeans and sweater I'd worn to the theater that evening. The receiving line for autographs was out the back entrance to the building, near the loading dock, but I didn't feel like taking selfies with any adoring fans at 1:30 a.m. Instead, I walked through the theater and out the main entrance. I figured anyone looking for the cast would be out back, so slipping out the front would be quick and easy.

I was about to walk across the stage and up through the orchestra seats when I heard a loud argument on stage. I wasn't trying to eavesdrop, but I couldn't help myself. They were just simply too loud not to.

"This was a total sh—"

"Language," Eldridge barked. "How many times must I say this around here?"

"I'm sorry," Noam Weiss, the show's general manager, said. "But this was a disaster."

"What happens on my stage is none of your business," San Nicolás said with no emotion in his voice. "Keep to the things you know…go write a paycheck or something."

"Why, you little smarmy—"

"Silence!" Eldridge said with two claps. I couldn't see her, but I could imagine her well-manicured eyebrows arching simultaneously. "Yes, tonight was rougher around the edges than expected. But let's focus on the positives."

"No one given a free ticket asked for a refund," Weiss said.

"Weiss," Eldridge said, clearly warning the man not to continue.

"The positives were that the acting and music worked," San Nicolás said. "There are a few areas that need tweaking. And we need to redo the eleven o'clock number. It's not working."

"I hate admitting it," Eugene Moses said, "but there are about three songs that aren't working and at least two that are dragging the show. I don't want to cut anything, but we must. Mable, what are your thoughts?"

I hadn't heard Mable speak very often, so I was curious to listen to what she had to say.

"The book is working, mostly. I need to punch up some jokes. Some of the elf moments aren't getting the laughs we thought they would."

"Is it delivery or the jokes?" Eugene asked.

"Maybe a combination of both, but I think the jokes need help," Mable responded.

"I may know a dramaturg who did a stint at Second City in Chicago. I can call him tomorrow?" Serafina chimed in.

"How much will that cost us?" Weiss asked.

"I don't know," Serafina admitted.

"I don't care about the budget," Eldridge said. "I want the show to work. Call the dramaturg."

"Mrs. Eldridge," Weiss cut in, "as the general manager, I want to warn you that any changes to the budget can impact other parts of the show."

"Do I look like I'm concerned with budgets? I know that's your job, but I can always throw in another $100K or more if it makes the show a success. This show is my late husband's legacy. It. Must. Work." There was silence as no one said anything else. "That will be all. And Weiss, once we know how much the dramaturg will cost, send the expense report to my office, and we'll transfer funds into the show account."

A voice cleared behind me. I spun to see Vladislav Nicolai, the house manager, standing behind me in his usual three-piece suit. "It's not nice to listen in on others' conversations," he chided in his thick Russian accent.

"I wasn't...I didn't mean...Oh, son of a nutcracker!" He raised an arched eyebrow at my outburst. "It's not like I intended to spy. I was trying to walk through the theater, and they were there." I gestured toward the stage. "I couldn't get past them."

"And why didn't you exit by the rear stage door where your adoring fans were waiting?"

"After the show tonight, I wasn't in the mood to plaster on a smiling face and take selfies," I admitted.

"Mm-hmm... Let me show you a different route." I gestured for him to show me the way.

He walked me backstage, and we headed downstairs. There was a door about midway down the hall I ran through every night. He opened the door, which led to another hallway. "This is where the administrative offices are for the theater," he said as we walked through the brightly lit hallway. Sure enough, we passed several office suites with glass doors. The last one on the left had Nicolai's name on the door, so I made a mental note of where he lived when he wasn't running the theater. At the end of the hall was a metal door. Nicolai pushed open the door, which led into an alleyway.

"Go to the right. It brings you out in front of the theater."

"Thanks! This will make life easier if I need to leave the theater after a show quickly."

He nodded. "And Ms. Saunders, in the future, I would refrain from eavesdropping. Theater is a dangerous business. We wouldn't want you to break a leg again before opening night." He closed the door with a loud thud that reverberated off the alleyway.

Did he just threaten me? I mean...it was like a line right out of a Russian mob film. I walked down the alleyway, glancing over my shoulder a couple of times to make sure he hadn't followed me. Once on 47th Street, I let out a sigh of relief. I'd been holding my breath.

I walked the two blocks to the late-night restaurant where I was meeting Amani, Brice, and Johnny.

By the time I arrived at the restaurant, the boys had already had appetizers and were drinking without me. They said their polite congratulations as I sat down. I smiled and accepted them. They were being polite. They didn't need to tell me it was a disaster. We all knew it.

We chitchatted about everything but the show. I told them about my experience with Nicolai. They all raised their eyebrows at the broken leg comment.

"Geez," Johnny said. "He sounds like an extra out of a Russian mob film."

"That's exactly what I thought," I admitted. "I won't lie. I kept looking over my shoulder to make sure he wasn't coming after me with a tire iron and go all Nancy Kerrigan on me." Brice laughed, but Johnny looked dumbfounded. "Geeze, I forget how young you are. Basically, a figure skater hired someone to attack another figure skater."

"Oh, you mean the movie *I, Tonya*," Johnny said, nodding.

"You realize that movie was based on a true story?" Brice asked.

"It was?" Johnny asked. "Is that widely known?"

"Oh, it's a good thing you're pretty," Amani said. Brice snickered, and Johnny let out a little pout.

"You think I'm pretty?" Johnny asked Amani, as he tried to switch the topic to his favorite subject...himself.

"And that's what you take out of the conversation, dear," Amani said. "Everyone thinks you're pretty." Amani placed his hand on Johnny's shoulder before leaning in and kissing him on the side of the cheek.

"You two are so cute...it's disgusting," Brice remarked.

"Tell me about it," I said with an exaggerated roll of my eyes. "They're like this all the time. Makes you almost want to believe in love. Thankfully, the piece of coal that exists in the center of my chest isn't that easily persuaded."

"That's because you've had a string of bad dates," Johnny said. "Your prince in shining armor is out there."

"You've been dating again?" Brice asked.

"Though I may put an end to that soon." I ran down the list of dates I'd had recently. Brice chuckled at how each date was more absurd than the last.

When I was done talking, Brice looked at me and said, "I know you've had some bad dating luck, but there is a guy I work with. He's another lawyer."

"Another lawyer? I don't—"

"He's a great guy. I wouldn't set you up with him if I didn't believe you would hit it off. And he's not American."

"Oh really? I love a good international man of mystery."

"He's 35, gorgeous, tall, and Icelandic. Trust me, if he had one remotely gay bone in his body, I'd be throwing myself at him."

"I don't know...With the show and everything else—"

"Come on, Erika, what do you have to lose?" Johnny said, encouraging me.

"Oh, why the heck not!" I smiled to reassure Brice that I was on board. Inside my head, I wondered if I'd made another bad dating decision.

Chapter 21

We had a company meeting the following morning at 8:30 a.m., which was hard for us to drag ourselves out of bed for. I looked around the theater, and there were larger than usual cups of coffee. Most of them looked like they hadn't gotten more than a couple of hours of sleep. When you're in a show, it's hard to come down from the adrenaline high after the curtain goes down. Many theater types become natural night owls because we're amped up and take some time to go to bed. When I toured, I often exercised after the show to drain my body of my excess energy. It also meant I could sleep in later because I wouldn't have to get up early to hit the gym.

I spied Mr. Weiss and his Russian henchman, Nicolai, for a moment, but the two men didn't stay in the theater for very long. At 8:30 on the dot, Serafina and San Nicolás walked into the theater. "Good news," San Nicolás said. "We figured out the problem from last night. It was a computer issue." San Nicolás gestured to Serafina.

"Yesterday afternoon, between our rehearsal and the first preview, our computer system performed an automatic upgrade. I don't completely get the Internet, but apparently, our computers were still connected to it, which shouldn't have happened. We're not completely sure where the break in protocol happened." The look on Serafina's face told me she knew exactly who was to blame for this oversight. "The upgrade was incompatible with two different systems we use to run the show. Both vendors have promised software updates today. We will not be running the show with a lot of tech this morning or this afternoon. We are in a holding pattern until they fix it. Going forward, our system will be isolated and not connected to the Internet, so this shouldn't ever happen again."

"What happens if it doesn't get fixed today?" Asher asked from the other side of the theater.

"We'll postpone our second preview," Serafina said. The room immediately erupted into a set of murmured conversations. "I know, I know," Serafina roared over the group. She waited for the room to die down before she continued. "Many of you have friends or family that are coming tonight. If we reschedule, we will do our best to accommodate all the comp tickets through Weiss' office."

"This isn't what any of us wanted to hear this morning," San Nicolás cut in. "But for now, we must move on. This morning and maybe this afternoon, we will run the show with a rehearsal pianist. Our esteemed musical director is fixing some issues the orchestra had last night in a different rehearsal studio this morning. Hence, our composer is once again gracing us with his presence to help us run the show." San Nicolás looked around the room to ensure no other comments. A few people took this as notice to stand up. "But first," he said, looking at those who had stood. "But first, we have notes. Our stage manager has put together a comprehensive list."

I pulled out my notebook containing the book and score, along with my trusty number two pencil. I readied myself for whatever Serafina threw at me. She spent almost 45 minutes giving notes. Based on her feedback, I was practically amazed she had time to run the show last night. She went through a list and called off a name. She would then inform that actor of every problem she'd caught. She saw it all, from missed dance steps to going up on a lyric. I had forgotten about her eagle eye for detail.

"Erika Saunders," Serafina said and looked in my direction. All eyes looked at me as I sat up a little straighter. "I only have a couple of notes for you," she said, looking at her list. I admit I let out a little sigh of relief. "First, watch the foot you enter on at the top of Act One. We wanted the three of you to be walking in sync with each other. Last night, you were off. Second, on 'He'll Drink Too Much, and Laugh Too Much,' you went flat on the high note. I think it was a breath support issue. Try breathing before the refrain to make sure you have enough steam when building to that note. Last, the quick-change."

I let out a small, "Snowballs!"

"I know. The quick-change is the bane of your existence," Serafina acknowledged. "It was decided that the dress change didn't match the shoes. So, we're adding a shoe change as well. This means you'll have less time than we predicted. Two extra dressers will now be assigned to help with that change. We'll run the quick-change when we get the system up and running." She contemplated her list and said, "Peeter Gaspari." Serafina looked around the room and found him sitting over near Asher.

I stopped listening at that point. The first two notes made perfect sense. I knew I was going up on that high note, and I agreed that the breath placement may be the answer. The quick-change shoes made me want to crawl into a hole and go back to sleep. I wasn't sure how the new addition would work, but I wouldn't know until the costume designer got here with my new shoes.

The rest of the morning went according to plan. By early afternoon, the software company had patched their software, and everything was working as it should have. I texted Brice and Johnny to tell them the good news about what had happened the previous night. Both texted me back to let me know we weren't the only show with tech problems the previous evening. Apparently, this system update threw a lot of computers for a loop. On the positive, it meant the story about the computer software update was making waves and making news, so the rough patches of our first preview wouldn't make as much of a splash as we'd all feared.

That night's preview went off with no major glitches. The costumer didn't have my new shoes ready, so I was still wearing the unfortunately mismatched shoes. Honestly, the shoes were black. Black goes with everything, so I didn't see the big deal.

During intermission, I ran to my dressing room to use the restroom. I'd need to pee since the top of Act One. I knew better. When I was done, Gladys ensured my costume was back on me properly. I had a few minutes left, so I checked out my phone. I had a message from Brice.

"I talked to Benedikt Einar, and he's seeing *The Naughty List* tomorrow night. He would like to take you out for a late dinner afterward." Well, that was interesting. Brice's lawyer friend was already planning on coming to our show.

"What's wrong, Erika?" Gladys asked.

"My agent wants to set me up on a date. The guy's supposed to be at the show tomorrow night and wants to take me out afterward. I don't know if I want to deal with that. First dates are hard enough. And after a show, I don't exactly look like I'm ready for a night on the town."

Gladys looked at me and said, "If you decide to go on the date, I'm sure I can wrangle up a team to help you get ready. I'll ask Carlos in the wig and makeup department to help. You know he'll jump at the chance to turn you into Cinderella."

The image of watching Carlos do a little glee dance at being asked made me laugh. "I guess that's one of the true joys of working on Broadway. There's always a team that has your back." I texted Brice to tell Mr. Einar that dinner was a go.

***

Thursday flew by, and the evening show was our best run-through yet. I'm sure Serafina would have notes for us in the morning; she always did, but the notes helped people fine-tune the show. When the final curtain closed, I rushed back to my dressing room. Gladys helped me out of my costume while Carlos took off my wig and the microphone rigging. After a night of hoofing it on stage, I was a hot, sweaty mess, so I took a fast shower. From the front row, we may look like we're in a winter wonderland where it's all cold and icicles, but it can be oppressively hot under the heat of the lights. During the winter months, it's not that bad. But during the summer months, it can be miserable. And heaven forbid you have an air conditioning unit go out during a show. There's a reason most Broadway houses are cold enough to hang meat in during the summer—it's so the talent doesn't pass out on stage.

After my shower, I toweled off and dressed in my undergarments, brushed my teeth, and put on deodorant.

My amazing team was ready to go the second I entered the room. I planned on wearing something a little more casual, but decided to glam it up a bit. I wore a pair of thin-fit blue jeans with a rather tight forest green sweater dress over them. I finished the outfit with a pair of faux leather boots dyed the same color as the dress. In this outfit, I could look both upscale or scaled-down depending on where my date took me. That was one tiny piece of information Brice had not filled me in on. Once Gladys finished making sure my outfit looked perfect, Carlos moved in and quickly did my hair and makeup. Carlos was a wiz. He was fast and could accentuate a girl's features without making her look over the top. He went with a rose-colored eye shadow that set well against my dress. He wanted to use a nude illusion, so he outlined my lips in a salmon color, then filled them in using a lighter version of lipstick.

By the time he was done with me, I was smoking. I thanked both for their help.

"Any time, girl. You know where to find me," Carlos said as he left.

Gladys thanked Carlos, too, then bid me a good night. I looked down at my watch and realized only about thirty minutes had passed. I grabbed my coat and headed toward the stage door.

Nicolai was standing next to the stage door when I got there. Part of me was hesitant, but I marched right up to the door as if I owned the place. "Good job tonight," he said with a single head nod. "You might need this," and he handed me a marker before he opened the door. A line of fans stood out back, waiting to get autographs and pictures with the cast. I hadn't considered fans stagedooring when Brice had recommended Benedikt Einar pick me up here.

"Thanks," I said to Nicolai and exited into the cold. Security personnel stood on each side of the barrier wall to ensure the fans didn't get too close. I pulled the lid off the marker and turned to the first woman.

"I absolutely loved the show," the woman gushed. She handed me her *Playbill*, and I signed it. I then took a selfie with a teenage girl from Columbus, and I signed her *Playbill*. Down the line I went, talking to adoring fans of all genders and ages. Everyone was so amazingly polite and thanked me for taking the time to greet them. When I got to the end of the line, a *Playbill* was extended out to me. I accepted it and handed it back to the gloved hand without thinking. Only then did I look at the gloved hand and follow it up to a pair of azure-blue eyes.

"Benedikt!" I said with a surprised gasp.

"Ms. Saunders, it's a pleasure to meet you. Might I say that you look more beautiful up close than you did radiating from the stage tonight?"

The security guard eyed us for a second, but I nodded, and he let me out. Benedikt offered his arm. He was a tall drink of water. He had to be at least 6'5" and built like a fitness model. His blonde hair had a trendy cut that could have walked off the page of any fashion magazine. I smiled as I leaned into him as we walked down the street. As we crossed through Times Square, the holiday decorations were out in force. Everywhere I looked, there were snowmen and women, Santas, elves, Christmas trees, and a menorah or two.

"Where are we going for dinner?" I asked.

"I wanted to be a traditionalist on the first date, so I made a reservation at Sardi's." He peered down at me, and those blue eyes practically burrowed into my soul. "If you would prefer, we can always go somewhere else."

"I think Sardi's would be lovely. I haven't been there in years."

"Perfect."

We walked over to 44th, crossed Broadway, and walked up to Sardi's. The place was decently busy for a late Thursday night. We were seated quickly.

"Would you prefer the booth or chair side? I know the booth side makes you more visible to the room. I wasn't sure if you would prefer the chair, so your back was to the room, offering you a bit more anonymity," Benedikt said with his gorgeous Icelandic accent.

"I'll sit in the chair. That way, I can focus my attention on you," I said with a coy smile.

"Can I help you with your coat?" he asked. I turned my back and let him slip my coat off. *Wow, a real gentleman.* Then he pulled out my chair and helped me sit down. He took off his woolen overcoat and sat it down next to where he would sit on the booth seat before unbuttoning his suit jacket and sitting opposite me.

Brice had not done this man justice. If there was an entry for *Icelandic Deity* in the encyclopedia, Benedikt Einar's picture would be sitting next to it. I stared at the picture-perfect chin with the dimple. His skin looked flawless. I could tell he took good care of himself physically. His pectoral muscles were practically bulging underneath his tie and buttoned-up shirt. Even the black-rimmed glasses stressed his best facial features, forcing you to look deeper into those amazing eyes.

Once we'd ordered, he spent twenty minutes peppering me with questions. He knew what I did for a living, so we bypassed those questions. I told him about my life in New York. He wanted to know what it was like moving to the city after growing up in Des Moines. Unlike some dates where you feel like you're being interviewed for a newspaper, Benedikt made the conversation seem natural.

"So enough about me," I said after we'd finished with our salads, "tell me about you. How did you end up in New York?"

"Ahh…interesting story. As you probably know, I'm not exactly from around here. I grew up in Reykjavik, Iceland. I had a cousin who lived here. When I was in high school, I came and stayed with her for a week up in Boston. I fell in love with the US."

"In Boston?" I said, feigning shock. "I'm surprised you didn't go running back to Iceland."

"Ahh, yes. The famous Boston-New York rivalry."

"Hey, if it wasn't the Yankees and the Red Sox, I'm sure these two cities would find something else to fight over."

"You're probably right." He lifted the glass of red wine and took a sip. The wine tinged his lips slightly. "After visiting the US, I decided I wanted to come here for my undergraduate degree. Then I went to Yale Law School. I could have gone back to Iceland when I graduated, but several firms here courted me. I'd already fallen in love with the city. Friends and I would travel down from New Haven on the weekends, so making a move to the city was the next logical step in my life."

"How long have you lived here now?"

"Let me see, I moved here when I was 25, so that would be right at a decade in May."

The waiter arrived with our meals. I had the cannelloni au gratin. For Italian food, it was some of the lightest I've ever eaten. They didn't give you a ridiculously sized portion. And eating later at night, I wasn't looking for an enormous meal before bed. Benedikt had a grilled porkchop.

Conversation with Benedikt was effortless and natural. Time passed quickly. Before long, we'd been sitting at Sardi's for almost two hours, and we were the second to last couple there. I didn't want to be that couple who prevented the staff from cleaning up and clearing out for the night. I mentioned it to Benedikt, and he immediately paid for our tab. We left Sardi's and found that it had started to snow.

"I would like to walk you home, if you don't mind?" he asked.

I considered declining but said, "I think I would like that." He offered his arm, and we walked the two blocks to my apartment. Even though it was cold, Benedikt's warmth helped me stave off the cold as snow fell around us. Benedikt didn't seem to notice the snow as we strolled. But then, he *was* from Iceland.

We stood outside the building for a couple of minutes talking before I finally asked, "Would you like to come up for a nightcap?"

"I would, but I have an early morning meeting with a client. I'm going to have to decline. But I would like to do this again if you're amenable?"

"I'm definitely amenable," I said. I could only imagine how I must look to him as I stood there in the snowy morning hours practically radiating at him.

"May I kiss you?" he asked.

"I would very much like it if you kissed me."

He enveloped me in an embrace. He gently cupped my face before ever so lightly letting our lips connect. The world stopped as we stood there, connected by the thinnest of delicate tissue. When he pulled back, I fluttered a bit. Breaking off the kiss must be what it feels like for a fish yanked out of water. For a second, I couldn't imagine breathing on my own.

"Good night, Erika," He turned and started strolling down the street. As he left, he started whistling the overture to *The Naughty List*. I watched him walk away. I lost track of time. Suddenly, I felt so small and cold standing on the sidewalk, so I forced myself into the warmth of my building.

I nodded at the overnight guard and floated over to the elevator bank. I pushed the button and waited for it to get there. When the elevator opened, I looked up to see Kirk standing in front of me with a load of laundry in his hands.

"You're up late," I said, getting into the elevator.

"Whoa," he said. "You look amazing tonight."

"Why, thank you, I beamed. My agent, Brice—I don't think you've met him yet—set me up with this Icelandic giant who took me out for a late-night dinner."

Kirk's face fell slightly, but he quickly masked whatever he was feeling. "Well, from the way you're beaming, I'm guessing this one went better than the others?"

"Most definitely," I said, and let out a contented sigh. "What about you? Why are you up so late?" I asked again.

"I made the mistake of taking a nap when I got home. I slept till 11:00 p.m. I had gotten nothing done before the nap, so I decided to play catch up. And I figured the laundry facilities would be empty at this time of night."

"Were they?"

"Were they what?"

"Empty?"

"Oh, yeah...they were empty. Well, not completely empty. Someone else was in and out, but that was it."

The elevator opened on their floor, and I motioned for Kirk to leave first since he was carrying the clothes basket. All I had was my purse.

"Well, I hope you can get back to sleep," I told Kirk as I got to my door.

"Me too," he replied. I turned the key in my lock and was about to push the door open when Kirk added, "I'm thrilled this date worked out for you. You deserve a piece of happiness."

I turned to respond, but he was already in his apartment. I pushed open my door and found a slightly upset Bootsy waiting for me.

"I know. I'm late. Just let me get changed, and we can snuggle before bed. How does that sound?"

Apparently, it sounded fine to him because he turned around and headed right into the bedroom. I flipped on the lights and found him lying in the middle of the bed with his tail flopping, looking at me as he groomed one of his paws.

I got off my clothes and took one more look at myself in the mirror. I had to admit, Santa's little dressing, makeup, and hair helpers had done an amazing job with me tonight. I needed to get them a gift basket or something.

I washed my face and got into my pajamas. I grabbed my phone, which was on my dresser, and walked back into the living room to put it on its charger. Since I hadn't done that in a few hours, I looked at the texts.

Brice: *How was the date?*

Erika: *Benedikt is amazing. I think we'll be seeing more of each other.*

I had a text from a number I didn't recognize, so I opened it.

Unknown: *Erika, Rebekka Eldridge. I got your cell phone from your personnel file. We need to talk to you in the morning. I hope you can be in by 8:30.*

I rolled my eyes and looked at the clock. I could get about six hours of sleep. After plugging in the phone and setting the alarm clock, I crawled into bed to cuddle with Bootsy. I barely had Bootsy snuggled beside me before drifting into a pleasant sleep.

Chapter 22

When the alarm went off, I ran through a yoga series to wake up my body. Then I showered, dressed, fed Bootsy, and was out of the apartment by 8:10, so I had plenty of time to walk to the theater and grab a coffee at Hello, Coffee! on the way. I showed up at the theater and wasn't surprised that the facility was so quiet at this early hour.

I rode the escalator up to the orchestra level entrance. I was surprised to find Jeremy McCartan pacing the floor when I got there. He looked over at me as I stepped off the escalator.

"Erika," he said. "Do you know what this is about?"

"I haven't a clue. I received a text message from Rebekka Eldridge last night asking me to be here."

"Hmm…" McCartan said. "I received an email late last night letting me know they were meeting with you and that I should be here as well."

We tossed around a couple of possibilities but were interrupted when Vladislav Nicolai appeared and told us to follow him.

"What's this about?" McCartan asked.

"Not my place, sir," Nicolai said.

He led us through the same passage he'd previously taken me through to the alley exit. Only this time, he led us to a conference room. He opened the door. Eldridge, Weiss, and San Nicolás sat at one end of the conference table.

Eldridge gestured toward the end of the table. "I'm glad you're both here on time. This should make things easier." She gestured and said, "Please sit." We pulled out our chairs. I glanced at McCartan, who raised an eyebrow at me, but didn't question the odd setting for this meeting.

"For the purposes of this meeting, we are recording the proceedings," Noam Weiss informed us. "Technically, in New York, we don't have to tell you this, but we think it's a best practice."

"I'm not sure how comfortable I am with this," McCartan said. "You summon Erika and me, then inform us you're recording the meeting. I feel I must obje—"

The door opened behind us.

"I'm sorry I'm late," an Icelandic voice said behind me. "I thought this meeting was happening in Eldridge's office, not here."

My Icelandic giant walked into the room. Without glancing down to look at me, he took a seat at the other end of the table. *Did he know about this? He mentioned an early morning meeting last night.*

He opened his briefcase and pulled out a legal pad. He turned and looked toward me. His face flashed surprise at seeing McCartan and me. I doubted he was surprised to see McCartan, but he looked shocked to see me.

"This is my personal lawyer," Eldridge explained, "Benedikt Hannes Einar. He's a partner at Jonson, Einar, and Berkowitz."

McCartan nodded, and I did my best to shoot Benedikt a pleading look that screamed *what is this about?* Instead of getting an answer, his face was impassive and all business.

"For the record, I'm here to ensure this process is handled to the direct letter of the Actor's Equity contract," Benedikt informed the group. "I am serving as legal counsel for Rebekka Eldridge and not Naughty List Productions." Benedikt turned and nodded toward Weiss.

"I'm Noam Lavie Weiss, and I represent Naughty List Productions as the general manager," Weiss started.

"For the record, I'm Asier Zlota San Nicolás. I'm the director of *The Naughty List*."

"I'm Rebekka Eldridge, lead producer for Naughty List Productions." She looked at Ryan and me and added, "With us today are the executive director of Actor's Equity, Jeremy McCartan. We also have Erika Saunders."

"As the company general manager," Weiss then said. "The burden of terminating an actor's contract falls on my back." *Huh?* "It is with immense sadness that this meeting has been called to end Erika Lynsay Saunders' contract with Naughty List Productions."

"What?" I said in a voice higher and shriller than I intended. A flash of surprise crossed Benedikt's face, but he quickly masked it.

"This should come as no shock to Ms. Saunders," Weiss said, looking at McCartan and not me. "We've known for some time that a member of the cast was violating the nondisclosure agreement within their contract and speaking to the media about the company's proprietary information. From what we have pieced together, Ms. Saunders spoke with someone at TheBroadway411 about current backstage gossip, including personnel matters and technical issues. As such, the damage was done at the box office after—"

"I've done no such thing," I cut in. "I've never talked to the press. I haven't talked to the press in years."

"We were afraid you'd try to deny the allegations," Weiss said. He gave me a look that was two parts anger and one part pity. He placed a small tape recorder on the table. *Where does someone find a tape recorder these days?* For three minutes, I listened to a recording of myself talking about the incident with Lachtna MacGrory and Maeve McKenna. I had no idea how they got the recording or when it was made. Then it hit me, Carissra's gaming microphone. I remember Carissra and Kirk talking about how good it was at picking up voices. My mind raced a million miles a minute. How could something so innocuous as a conversation with my neighbor become public knowledge then be used to get myself canned?

"As you can see," Weiss said. "We have incontrovertible proof of Ms. Saunders' guilt."

"I see," McCartan said, not bothering to look at me.

"How did you get that recording?" I blurted out.

"So, you don't deny it was you on the recording?" Eldridge shifted her steely gaze to me.

"Yes, but—"

"For the record," Benedikt said without looking at me, "Ms. Saunders has admitted that the voice on the recording is hers."

That snake!

"What's the background noise?" McCartan asked.

"What do you mean?" Benedikt asked.

"When they played the audio, there was like fighting noises or something."

"The audio was enhanced to make it clearer before sending it to TheBraodway411," Eldridge said.

"Yes, but how did you get it?" McCartan asked.

"It was easy. I threatened the woman who runs the site. She sent me the recording." Eldridge met my eyes. "The young woman tried to stall, but once I had my lawyers," she nodded in Benedikt's direction, "threaten her a few times. She folded quickly." At that moment, I envisioned Eldridge scheming to get 101 Dalmatian puppies to make herself a nice fur coat. She relished watching me squirm.

"We expect Ms. Saunders to be paid for the work she did through last night and get credit in the *Playbill* for having created the character," McCartan said, turning the conversation back away from Eldridge.

"We thought that might be your reaction." Weiss played another recording clip of me discussing the show and its content. "This is an obvious violation of the NDA. If you push us, we'll take Ms. Saunders to court. I seriously doubt she has the funds in reserve to hire a lawyer to fight this case." McCartan nodded. "We will pay Ms. Saunders through last night, but we will omit her in any materials associated with Naughty List Productions going forward."

"This would include any mention of the show on her bio," Benedikt added. "This is a hard cut with the company. If these conditions are not met, the company reserves the right to sue Ms. Saunders for breach of contract."

I looked at McCartan. "Can they do this?"

"Yes," was all he said back to me. "All things considered, they're letting you off scot-free." He shook his head before adding, "You know better, Erika. I'm stunned."

"I did nothing wrong," I said for the first time, feeling some sense of my usual moxie rising.

"Please don't bother with any explanations," Benedikt said. "You were a valuable member of this company, but we simply cannot keep you on staff after the inherent violation of trust from your actions."

Well, at least he was living to his first name. My own Benedict Arnold was in the room. A few minutes later, Benedikt produced a stack of papers and had me sign them. Both McCartan and I looked at every sheet before I signed and moved on to the next.

When I finished signing, Vladislav Nicolai showed up and escorted McCartan and me to my dressing room. Someone had already gone through and boxed up the few personal items I had. I had been more focused on the show than on decorating. I kept hoping that I would have more time to decorate once the show opened. Sadly, my entire life fit into a single cardboard box.

"I can't believe this is happening," I said to McCartan.

"Why did you do it, Erika?" McCartan said, looking at me. "This is the type of error I expect from one of my younger clients...not a seasoned pro like yourself."

"Despite what you may have heard on the audio recording, I did not talk to the press."

"Oh, really?" McCartan said to me skeptically. "So, you're telling me that what I heard with my own two ears isn't real?"

"I don't—"

"Just don't, Erika." He looked at me, shook his head and sighed. "Be glad they aren't taking you to court." Tears welled in my eyes. I forced myself to breathe deeply because I would not cry in front of this man. "I don't know what will happen next. Equity will hold a disciplinary hearing at some point. I'm disappointed. As hard as you've worked to get back on Broadway, you threw it all away by talking to a gossip blogger."

He didn't wait for my response. He left my dressing room. With both boxes in hand, Nicolai escorted me out of the building. He at least took pity on me and led me to the alleyway entrance so I could avoid having to see anyone in the cast.

Once I was out in the cold air, the waterworks started. In all honesty, I'm amazed I got home with all the water streaming from my eyes. I made it to my apartment, set the boxes down inside the door, and bawled like I hadn't cried in years. After an hour of my personal pity party, I picked up my phone and texted Brice.

I was fired. I don't want to talk about it yet. I'll call tomorrow.

A string of texts was already coming in from my castmates, but I didn't want to deal with them. Instead, I put on my coat and went walking around the city. I walked around for an hour before finding myself on 5th Avenue, standing in front of Radio City Music Hall. There was an eleven o'clock showing of the Radio City Christmas Spectacular, so I bought a $90 ticket in the nosebleed section.

I sat in anticipation, reading the *Playbill* while waiting for the show. The audience was surprisingly packed for an 11:00 a.m. performance on a Friday. Tourists started pouring into the city at Christmas time to get their shopping done. For the past couple of years, I'd tried to avoid leaving the house on Fridays and Saturdays during the holidays to avoid the crowds.

I flipped through the program, waiting for the show to begin. I recognized a couple of people in the show and was genuinely glad to see they had work. When the lights dimmed, I cried again. Thankfully, I wasn't ugly crying this time. I had a waterfall traipsing down my cheek for ninety minutes.

When the show was over, I turned my phone back on. There were a ton of texts. A few of them had links to newspapers and bloggers' sites. Asher sent me a link to Michelle Bouvier's article in *The Post*. I wanted to ignore the link, but I wouldn't let myself get away with pretending it wasn't there.

"*Erika Saunders was fired today from* The Naughty List. *Cast members, who wish to remain anonymous, have confirmed that Saunders was fired under highly dubious circumstances. Saunders was fired for a breach of contract. She allegedly had contact with bloggers at Broadway411 who used the information to publish content on their website that was proprietary by the production. I'll update this story as more information becomes available.*"

I was about to text Asher but decided I didn't want to talk to anyone. Instead, I was going to have a full-on pity party. I stopped by John's of Times Square on 44th, grabbed a large Margherita pizza, and headed home to my apartment to eat until I could bust. It's not like I had to worry about fitting in my costume tonight. So, if I ended up a little bloated after all the pizza, I didn't have to give an elf.

Chapter 23

I took the pizza back to my apartment and I squirreled myself away. There were a million and one emails, voicemails, and text messages. So many people were trying to get a hold of me, I wondered if someone would try a carrier pigeon or singing telegram. I didn't want to talk to anyone, so I avoided looking at anything and refused to answer my phone or open my door. At the rate the messages were pouring in, I half expected my therapist to call to make sure I was okay.

I sat down on the floor with my back resting against the couch. The pizza lid was open, so I could more easily grab my next slice. I'd also opened a bottle of wine to wash it all down with. I didn't bother with a wineglass. Bootsy came and curled up next to me. He could tell that momma was not in a good mood and needed his comfort. I grabbed a slice of pizza and decided to find out how my life had ended so quickly.

I tried to find the audio for myself on the internet, but I quickly realized I didn't know how to do that beyond googling myself. I found the article from an anonymous user at TheBrodway411. The article was set up like an interview. It omitted the fact that it was pulled from a conversation without my knowledge.

My phone vibrated, and it was a call from my lawyer. Brice must have called him. I thought about not picking up, but I hit the call button.

"Hello?"

"Erika, Charles Pearson, your lawyer."

"Yes, Mr. Pearson, I remember."

"I heard about that unfortunate business that happened today. I wanted to let you know what we know so far. Apparently, the audio came from a streaming platform for gamers. Honestly, how anyone picked up on the fact that you were having a conversation with someone over all the fighting noises is beyond me."

"You've heard the audio, then?"

"One of my associates found it. It wasn't easy to find. Where were you when this was recorded?"

"I was at my neighbor's apartment. His teenage niece had been playing video games, and we were sitting on the couch talking."

"Hmm...That's good to know. And both would verify that?"

"I would assume so...since that's what happened."

"And you don't suspect either of them having done this on purpose?"

I hesitated for a microsecond before saying, "They're not the types who would do something like this on purpose."

"Not even for money. People do all kinds of things for money."

"No. Again, they're not the types." If it had been some of my other neighbors, I would have had some second thoughts. But Carissra and Kirk were about the most straightforward people I knew. There was a twinge of guilt in the back of my mind that I considered for a microsecond that they'd set me up.

"Well, this is good information to have. If anything changes, I'll let you know." And with that, my lawyer was off the phone. *Will I get billed for the five minutes or a full hour for that phone call?*

I picked up another slice of pizza and ate it. Then I picked up another, folded it in half and ate it too. I continued my way through half the box and the entire bottle of wine. I folded the lid on top of the pizza box, curled into a ball on the floor and cried myself to sleep.

Around 7:00 p.m., someone knocked on my door. I was still lying on the floor. I pulled a pillow from the couch and covered my head, hoping whoever it was would disappear.

"Erika, I know you're in there," Johnny's voice came from the door. He was loud enough to wake the whole building. Admittedly, I was still slightly inebriated. I hoped that Johnny would magically go away if I didn't answer the door.

"I'm coming in," he said. Only then did I remember that I'd given him a spare key for emergencies. Light streamed in from the hallway, lighting my body curled up in a ball. I twitched my head to the side to avoid looking in the light. "Oh, my!" Johnny said. "This is bad." He flipped on the hallway light switch and shut the door. "Oh, Erika, honey..." His voice trailed off.

He walked over and sat down on the ground next to me, picking up the bottle of discarded wine from the floor and putting it on the coffee table. "You want to talk about it?" he asked. I shook my head. "That's okay." He reached out and touched the side of my face, brushing hair from my eyes. He stroked his thumb over my cheek. For a long time, he said nothing, knowing that this was not a time to speak. He didn't try any stupid platitudes like "it gets better" or "this will work itself out." He sat there and caressed my face while I slipped back to sleep.

When I woke, I was on my bed with a pillow beneath my head. I stirred and tried to sit up, but I got lightheaded.

"Easy there," a voice reassured me. "You've been out for a few hours."

I rubbed my eyes and found Kirk sitting in a chair next to my bed reading.

A garbled sound tried to escape my throat.

"Let me get you some water." Kirk folded his book in half and walked out into the kitchen.

I heard him search through the cupboards before finding a glass, then the tap water turned on. I wanted to yell that there were water bottles in the fridge, but my mouth was dry as a desert, and words didn't want to form. Of course, I wasn't sure if this was because of my hangover or the mortification at having my neighbor see me like this. I didn't want to look in a mirror because I'm sure I looked like a royal hot mess.

He walked back in and handed me the glass of water. I started drinking. I wanted to guzzle all of it but that would be a bad idea, so I took sips. When my mouth was hydrated, I sat up in bed with my back against the headboard. I did my best to look presentable. Not that it mattered. He'd already seen me at my worst.

"So, you're probably wondering why I'm here," Kirk said. While I was drinking, he'd sat down again, and his book rested in his lap. I nodded. "Johnny had to go. But he didn't want to leave you alone, so he asked me to watch over you. Carissra's out of town this weekend, so I didn't have any other plans until this evening."

"What time is it?" I asked.

Kirk rolled over his wrist and looked at his watch. "It's a little after 9:00 a.m." He looked at me for another minute before asking, "Want to talk about it?"

"Not really."

"That's okay. Johnny filled me in on the basics. He told me to tell you that some guy named Asher dropped by last night. He also said don't freak out. Johnny handled it."

"Thank goodness for minor miracles," I muttered.

"You should probably call Johnny soon. He was very worried about you."

"Thanks."

"Do you need anything?" Kirk said, practically jumping out of the chair. "I could make you some coffee? Maybe a cup of soup? It may be a bit too early for soup. I could scramble you an egg?"

I held my hand for him to stop and I smiled up at him. "Thanks for watching over me. I think I have it from here."

He looked down at me with concerned eyes. "Are you sure? I can stay..."

I inhaled and let out the air before I said, "I'm sure. Yesterday was rough, and I didn't handle it very well."

"We all have those days," he replied, smiling at me. "Again, if you need anything, I'm next door."

"I'm fine. I officially release you from guardian angel duty."

He took a couple of steps toward my bedroom door before turning around and saying, "I'm next door. Pound on the wall if you need me."

"Thanks."

With that, he left. A couple of seconds later, I heard the door to the apartment open and shut. I let myself lay back down as Bootsy came over and nestled against me. He started kneading my leg. "I love you, too, Bootsy." I may have slept all night, but I was exhausted. After laying there for a few minutes, I forced myself out of bed. I walked into the living room and found it spotless. Someone had done a great job cleaning up after me. *Johnny? Yeah, that wouldn't happen. Kirk? Oh, I hope not.* The idea of Kirk seeing my apartment in the mess it must have been yesterday made me want to hide for the rest of the year. *Amani.* I imagined Johnny called Amani at some point and he came over. While Johnny watched over me, Amani set about cleaning.

I sat down on the couch and picked up my phone. I wasn't quite ready to face life, but I had to at least respond to a few people. First, I texted Johnny.

Erika: *I'm up and acting like a human. Thanks for last night. And thank Amani for cleaning my apartment.*

The little symbol letting me know he was writing me back appeared on my phone.

Johnny: *Sorry I wasn't there when you woke up. I had to enlist Kirk because I had a gig this morning.*

Then a second text came right after it.

Johnny: *How did you know Amani cleaned?*

I laughed at that one.

Erika: *Because I know you well enough to know it wasn't you. Deduction, my Dear Watson.*

I then thought for a second about what to type next.

Erika: *Thanks for last night.*

It was all I could come up with.

Johnny: *You're welcome. And don't worry, I didn't let Asher into your place. Though, he was genuinely worried. I'll come by and check on you later.*

Ahh, Asher. The absolute last person I wanted to deal with today. Despite his good intentions, he had inadvertently caused my last nervous breakdown, leaving me less than enthusiastic about catching up. Besides, he and the rest of the cast likely knew more details than I did at this point.

A quick message to Brice let him know I was alive but going silent for a couple of days, with instructions to text Johnny in case of emergency. My parents received a similar text assuring them of my well-being, though I couldn't bring myself to tell them to cancel their plane tickets for opening night. The topic had become too painful to discuss further.

Seeking solace, I drew a bath and added my favorite lavender-scented bath bomb. The long soak lasted until the water turned lukewarm and my skin pruned. Afterward, a quick shower and a change into old sweats preceded an evening in the living room, where AMC's classic movies provided a welcome escape. Nothing more recent than 1980 would do for my current mood. Thankfully, the 1944 movie of *Arsenic and Old Lace* was playing. I folded my legs to the side, and Bootsy nestled in front of me on the couch as we watched.

The credits were rolling when there was a knock on my front door. I wanted to ignore the knocks for fear it was someone coming to check on me. Bootsy eyed me, and I rolled my eyes and dragged myself to the door. I checked the peephole. Kirk stood on my doorstep. I opened the door. "Everything okay?"

"Yeah, just wanted to see if you had any milk. I'm in the midst of a cooking emergency. I'm supposed to be baking cookies for a party tonight. I haven't done this in years, so I'm freaking out a bit." He had a wide-eyed frazzled look of a man feeling out of place in the kitchen, which was surprising since he was a superb cook.

"Let me grab the milk, and I'll be right over."

"Thanks." He spun and hurried next door. If this was his attempt to get me out of my apartment today, it worked. I went over to the fridge and was about to leave with the milk, but left Bootsy a saucer full in case I didn't come back with any. I also needed to make sure it was still good.

Bootsy lapped it up, and I smelled it, so I headed next door to Kirk's cooking emergency. I knocked on the door, and he practically flung the door open.

"Oh, thank you!"

He reached out and grabbed the milk from my outstretched hand and flew back into his kitchen. I wasn't exactly invited in, but he hadn't shut the door.

The kitchen looked like a bomb had gone off. "Whoa," was all I got out.

"This is a disaster!" Kirk said, throwing his arms in the air.

"What's the problem?" I may not cook, but I know a little something about baking cookies.

"I'm supposed to be bringing two dozen of my grandmother's cookies, and something is just wrong. I've tried the recipe three times, and it's not right."

"Can I see the recipe?" I asked politely, in case it was some secret family formula that only three people in the world could ever see.

He handed me the index card, and I read it. Seemed perfectly logical to me. "Do you mind if I send it to Amani?"

"Sure."

I took a picture of the recipe and sent it to Amani's phone. He texted back immediately.

Amani: *Please don't tell me you're baking. I don't want the building to burn down.*

Erika: *Ha, Ha! It's not for me. Kirk's recipe is missing something.*

Amani: *The recipe doesn't mention toasting the anise seeds. This can impact the flavor profile.*

"Kirk, are you toasting the anise seeds first?" I asked.

"Should I be?" he responded.

"That's what Amani said. Apparently, toasting them can 'impact the flavor profile.'" I said in my best Amani imitation.

"Okay, let's give it a try."

I texted Amani back, thanking him for his help, and promised to let him know if the toasting was the magic culprit. In no time, Kirk had the anise seeds toasted and into the pizzelle maker on his kitchen counter. As soon as the first one was finished, he got it out and let it cool for a second before taking a bite.

Kirk's immediate look of satisfaction was all I needed to know about our success. He ripped it in half and gave me the other part. I relished each bite and watched as Kirk made pizzelle after pizzelle.

"You know, if you're not doing anything tonight, you could come with me to this party. Carissra was going to go but then went down to DC to spend time with an old friend. The hosts of the party are expecting me with a plus one."

"I wouldn't want to intrude. And I'm not sure I'm in the mood to be around people."

"They're not people, they're teachers," he joked. "It's my school-teacher holiday party. There will probably be 25 people there. They're a lot of fun and nice people. None of them work in entertainment, so there's that."

"I don't know what I would wear."

"Anything you wanted to. Technically, it's an ugly holiday sweater party, but I'm still debating."

I raised an eyebrow at the way he drew out the word *debating*. He gestured for me to look around the corner. Sitting on top of the dryer was a neon-colored Hawaiian-themed sweater with a pink flamingo wearing a Santa hat, fake beard and snow glasses. It read, *Alo-Ho Ho Ho* in pink letters across the bottom.

I walked back into the living room and stared at him in the kitchen. "Wow," was all I got out. "If there's a contest, you'll probably win."

"Hardy-har-har. It's not that bad."

"Oh, it's that bad." I chuckled and smiled for the first time in 24 hours. "It's so bad that it's almost perfect. I'm almost tempted to go with you just to watch people's expressions when they take it all in. Where does one find a monstrosity like that?"

"Amazon," Kirk said matter-of-factly. "I typed in *ugly Christmas sweater*, and there were many of them. That one was a little over the top, but it was more special when I took it out of the box."

"Well, if it doesn't win as an ugly sweater, you could wear it as a bicycle safety vest. There's no way a driver couldn't see you with that thing shining at them. Honestly, if I didn't know better, I swear it glows on its own."

"Oh, it actually has glow-in-the-dark threads."

"Wow...now I have to go to your party to cheer you on."

"Really?" he asked me.

"And pass up an opportunity like this? I'm there. What time do I need to be ready?"

"It starts at 7:00 p.m., so I'll pick you up at 6:45? We can walk over. It's only a couple of blocks."

"Sounds like a date," the words slipped out of my mouth so effortlessly. Thankfully, he wasn't looking at me when I said them. I blurted goodbye and walked next door to figure out what I would wear for the evening.

What am I going to wear? I tore through my closet like a crazy person. I didn't have many Christmasy outfits, so I went with a traditional color pattern. It wasn't until I was fully dressed that I realized it was the same outfit I'd worn to the audition for *The Naughty List*, which meant I had worn it on the day I met Kirk. *I can't believe that was only like six weeks ago...if that.* I sat there trying to do the mental math in my head but gave up.

"We'll say six weeks. It's faster," I told Bootsy. For some reason, he didn't feel the need to respond to my craziness. How rude!

I was ready by 6:30 and proceeded to pace around the apartment, unsure what else to do. Bootsy watched me from the couch as I walked to-and-fro, like some kind of crazy tennis match—only I was the ball. When the knock finally came at 6:40, I was like, *finally*. I walked over to the door and opened it.

"You're ear—"

"Hey there," Asher said. "You look amazing. Going somewhere?"

I crossed my arms in front of my chest. Bootsy made a dash for the door at that moment, but I swooped down and grabbed him at the last second.

"Who's this little guy?" Asher asked.

"His name is Bootsy. Best rebound man I've ever had." Once the words were out of my mouth, there was no taking them back. "At least I didn't name him Asher 2.0," I tried to joke.

Asher stared at Bootsy. "So, you're my replacement?" he questioned with a smile as he scratched Bootsy on the head.

"As to your first question, I am going somewhere. My neighbor invited me to a Christmas party. I needed to get out of the apartment, so I agreed to go."

"Good for you," Asher said.

"You might as well come in," I said, getting out of the door and gesturing with Bootsy to enter. Once Asher was inside and the door closed, I put Bootsy on the ground. Bootsy sauntered back to his place on the couch and warily eyed Asher. *Good Bootsy.* Part of me wished Bootsy had drawn blood when Asher pet him, but I suppressed that thought as soon as it entered my head. I'd been on Team Death to Asher for so many years, it was hard to see him as a guy or a colleague. Even if we had buried the hatchet—and it hadn't been in his back—I still wasn't his best friend.

"Why are you here, Asher?" He looked a bit taken aback by my bluntness. "I'm sorry. It's just...my neighbor will be here any minute, so I don't have time for a lot of small talk."

"That's fine. I get it. I just...I wanted to say what they did to you yesterday sucked. Frankly, the cast is in an uproar. Some were not exactly happy with what you said, but even they thought you had maligned no one or the show. Everything you said was fact."

"Thanks for letting me know. That means a lot."

"I volunteered to be the Equity Deputy immediately. I don't know how, but we're going to fight this."

I let out a sigh. "That's nice, but I can't put my hopes in you...not because it's you, but because there's an audio recording of me making the comments. Admittedly, I didn't know they were being recorded, but that apparently doesn't mean much."

"Wait...huh? Back up. I'm missing some details here. We were told that you were interviewed by someone on that trashy website, TheBroadway411. Is that not what happened?"

"Not exactly." There was a knock on my door. "Guess my date is here."

"Date?" Asher asked as he flashed me his matinee idol smile.

"Not like that...At least, I don't think it's like that. Honestly, I don't know what to think right now. My brain isn't firing on all cylinders today." I walked to the door and opened it. Asher walked up behind me and peered over my shoulder at Kirk.

"Oh, hey, Erika," Kirk said. "I didn't realize you had company."

"It was unexpected," I said. "He was just leaving."

Asher pushed around me and out into the hallway. "I wasn't joking, Erika. We'll figure out a way to fight this."

"Thanks," I said. "Well, let me grab my coat," I said, turning to Kirk. I shut the door and left the boys in the hall staring at each other while I grabbed my coat and purse. I forwent the purse and took my phone and my key. "Goodbye, Bootsy. Momma loves you. I won't be out too late." He looked at me from the couch and nestled into a blanket for a nap.

I walked back to the door and found Asher and Kirk still standing there. "Sorry about that," I said, cutting through some kind of invisible tension. "Did you two introduce yourselves?" From the expressions on their faces, I could tell the answer was no. "Asher Alexander, meet Kirk...Brewster." I totally forgot Kirk's last name at first. I rarely needed to say it, so it didn't pop off my tongue like Asher's had. The two men exchanged handshakes. "Well, as much as I wish we could all stay and talk, Kirk and I have a party to get to." I motioned to the elevator, saying, "Shall we?"

Kirk offered his arm, and I graciously accepted it, locking my arm in his as if it was the most normal thing. I caught the quick side gaze from Asher and did everything in my power not to roll my eyes. He had a way of getting under my skin. Even though it'd been over three years since the breakup, he could still push my buttons.

We rode the elevator down to the ground floor in awkward silence. When we got there, Asher said goodbye and went in one direction, and thankfully Kirk and I headed in the other. When Kirk and I were finally alone on the street, I said, "Well, that was awkward."

"Does he drop by unannounced often?"

"Oh, heavens no. That was a first. Apparently, he dropped by last night, too, but this was the first time he's done that. I didn't even know he knew where I was living until this morning. Not that it's much of a secret. For that matter, I don't know where he lives. I feel like I'm talking too much. Am I talking too much?"

Kirk chuckled. "We all have exes, and they all seem to have the ability to dredge up the past when we see them."

"Oh really? Tell me about your exes," I said with a quirk of my lips. I know he couldn't see it, but I hope he got the playful tone in my voice.

"As this is a holiday party, I'd rather not. You know, let's keep things festive. We can reminisce about our ghosts of dating pasts another day."

We walked arm in arm for a couple more blocks. We were on streets further from Broadway, so we didn't see the influx of tourist traffic around here on the weekends. We passed a giant bus loading people who had clearly spent the day shopping. It happened every December. Tourist buses filled with shoppers made their way into the city to see a matinee, have lunch, and shop to their little hearts were content. Unfortunately, they added a considerable amount of foot traffic to the already busy city. Thankfully, the bulk of the tourists huddled around the shops 5th Avenue or the ones around Times Square. Once you get a block or two away from the shopping epicenters, foot traffic drops off considerably.

"So, what did Asher drop by for?" Kirk asked.

"He was checking in on me. The cast thinks I purposefully gave an interview to TheBroadway411. I was about to explain that to Asher, but you showed up."

"I could have given you two a minute—"

"No need. I'm trying to stay positive tonight, so I didn't need to go back over all that again."

Before long, we found ourselves in SoHo at a cute brownstone. We walked up to the door, and there was a paper sign directing us to the third floor. The host had added *Not There Yet* and *One Flight to Go* posters printed in festive colors on each level. There was no need to knock, there was another sign that read *Come In. The Party's Here!* in blocky lettering with Santa waving.

Kirk reached down and twisted the door handle and pushed open the door. I could tell we were still on the earlier side. Only a handful of guests turned to look at us when we entered.

"Kirk," a voice yelled before a pleasant-looking woman came bounding over. "Welcome to our home." It was only then that I realized the entire house was decked out in blue and white for Hanukkah. All the signs that had guided us to the apartment had been decked out with menorahs, dreidels, gelt, and other signs of the Jewish holiday. I hadn't been paying attention. The cheerful looking woman wore a fuzzy blue and white sweater with a polar bear spinning a dreidel.

"Leslie, this is my neighbor, Erika. Erika, this is Leslie. She's an English teacher."

"It's grand to meet you, Erika," she said, reaching for my hand. I quickly offered it and she shook my hand firmly. "My wife is around here somewhere. She teaches high school science at the same school Kirk's niece attends." She looked around the room quickly before yelling, "Bethany! We have guests."

A thin woman decked out in a reindeer sweater complete with blinking lights came into the room. "Wow, Kirk. That sweater is...I don't know if my retinas will ever be the same."

"I know, right?" I said.

"Bethany, this is Kirk's neighbor, Erika."

"Nice to meet you, Bethany," I said, extending my hand this time.

"Likewise," Bethany said, shaking my hand.

"I'm glad to see that Kirk's move into the Manhattan Plaza landed him a good neighbor."

The door behind us opened, and another couple entered the apartment. Leslie's attention immediately went to the newly arrived couple.

"Please, come in and enjoy yourselves," Bethany said. "You can put your coats on the bed in the guest bedroom. It's down the hall. The door's open, so you can't miss it." With that, Bethany turned to greet the new couple.

Kirk said hello to a few more of his colleagues, constantly introducing me along the way. I smiled and shook more hands that evening than at most meet-and-greets. We finally deposited our coats and went back into the living room. Kirk found the dessert table and pulled out the pizzelles. Immediately, a couple of his colleagues *oohed* and *ahhed* at Kirk's baking handiwork.

The next hour was a whirlwind of meeting new people and shaking hands. For the first time in years, I wasn't "Erika Saunders–Broadway Star" or "Erika Saunders–Queen of the Cabaret." I was just Erika, Kirk's plus one. I hated to admit it, but it was nice to have a level of anonymity in a group of people. No one wanted an autograph. No one wanted to ask me if I knew "so and so" or if the gossip about "name your Broadway star" was true. We talked about completely different topics from the ones I'm used to discussing with industry types. We talked about the joys of dealing with kids and their parents.

Around 8:00, Leslie and Bethany broke out the main meal, which included matzo ball soup, Kosher beef brisket, latkes, challah bread, and sweet noodle kugel. I piled my plate high, and Kirk found a spot for us at a folding table with Damian, a colleague who taught art, and his boyfriend, Kevin, who was a doctor. Damian was a forty-something Black man dressed in a periwinkle sweater with a sloth dressed in a scarf and hat. Kevin wore a Darth Vader-Claus sweater. Immediately, their sweaters clearly differentiated their personalities. We talked about what we liked to do in the city. Kevin told us some highly entertaining stories about crazy cases that appeared in the emergency department. There was something amazingly nice about the sheer normalness of the evening. I don't think I'd had one of these since I moved to the city. In my world, everyone had a connection to the entertainment industry. I'd almost forgotten that not everyone's life revolved around auditions, openings, and closings. Most people in the city live perfectly normal lives.

"So, what do you do, Erika?" Damian asked between bites.

I'm very glad that I didn't have a glass of wine to my lips, or I probably would have done a spit take. "I'm uhh...What I'm trying to say is...I'm kind of well—"

"She's in between gigs at the moment," Kirk helped me as I tried to recover.

"Oh?" Damian asked with interest.

"She's a performer," Kirk said, which sounded ridiculously vague and could have covered anything from birthday clown to pole dancer.

"What Kirk means is that I'm a Broadway actor and cabaret singer," I said, using my usual tagline.

"Oh, really?" Damian said, putting his wine glass back down on the table. "Been anything I might have seen?"

First, I absolutely hate it when people ask me this question. How am I to know what the heck you've seen? Second, I never know how to answer this question. Do I start at the top of my resume and work my way down?

"I thought I recognized you," Kevin said. "I totally love your *I Hate Men Cabaret!* I caught all the highlights on YouTube. Don't you remember her, honey?" he said, turning to Damian. "She was the one who sang like every bitter, jaded song in the American songbook. She made Alanis Morissette look pleasantly even-tempered by comparison."

A look of recognition crossed over Damian's face. "That was you?"

"In the flesh," I said. It only took a moment before both looked from me to Kirk and back to me again. They didn't have to voice it. They were wondering if Kirk caused my man-hating. "In case you're wondering, I've only known Kirk for about six weeks."

"Ahh..." the gay duo said in unison.

Kirk looked at me with a "what was that about" look. Under the table, I patted his knee in my best reassuring way as I mouthed, "I'll tell you later."

Thankfully, that was the closest brush to having my secret identity exposed for the evening. But being around ordinary people made me wonder if I was missing out on life. I'd spent so much of my life trying to be on Broadway. What if Broadway was never meant to be? In the words of the theater goddess herself, Patti LuPone, "I'm an actor, and an actor acts." If I gave up acting, what would I be then? A washout? A has been that never was? Thousands of girls come to New York City every year with dreams of being on Broadway. I've made it farther in the business than most of them could ever dream. All things considered, I've made a decent run of things.

"What do you think, Erika?" Damian asked.

"Huh?" I said, trying to refocus on the conversation. My mind kept pondering the meaning of life.

"It's been a rough week for her," Kirk said. "I'm amazed she let me drag her out of the apartment tonight."

"Tough week in the cabaret business?" Damian asked with a hint of genuine interest.

"Something like that. But I don't want to talk about it. Sorry, if I'm a bit of a space cadet tonight, my mind is running in too many directions."

"Oh, honey," Kevin cut in as he reached out and grabbed my hand. "I've been there. Some days my little hamster wheel is running so fast, I can't keep up with all the crap running around inside my head. This one," he jerked his head at Damian, "said I should try meditating. Yeah, I don't think so. All that means is I'm going to sit in a lotus position while the little hamsters run. On those dreadful nights when the hamsters won't shut up, I have Special K."

"What!" I said in shock. "Isn't that some illegal club drug?"

"Not that kind of Special K. I'm talking Klonopin, not Ketamine or the cereal. Klonopin is the only thing my psychiatrist has found that helps me keep the anxiety down and hamsters quiet so I can get some sleep."

"I can attest to that," Damian said. "Before he got on Special K—it's our little nickname for it—he would stay up for 24 hours straight because his brain wouldn't shut up."

"I blame my parents. They raised me to be a neurotic New Yorker. This," he said with a wide motion to himself, "is the result of their neuroses combined with my own."

Kevin and Damian started laughing, so Kirk and I joined in, but I don't think Kirk and I got the joke. Not really.

"So, honey, if this keeps up, talk to your psychiatrist. Maybe Special K is right for you?"

"Yeah," Damian chimed in. "I'm a lightweight. I only take Wellbutrin for mild anxiety and depression. I wasn't sure it was working until one day Sarah, she works in the library. She's around here somewhere…" Damian looked around the party to see if he could find her. He finally pointed out a woman wearing a lime-green Christmas tree sweater. "Well, Sarah, she comes up to me and is like, 'Damian, has something changed? You've been so happy lately. You haven't gone off on anyone in days.' And I was like, you know what, it's true. That's when I knew it was working."

There was something so normal and yet so odd listening to two men discuss their therapists, psychiatrists, and which drugs they were taking. Kirk and I got an impromptu lecture on the benefits of modern psychopharmacology in between courses.

Once dinner was over, it was time for games. I wasn't much in the mood for games, but I got dragged into them. Of course, everyone wanted to play charades. I've been with too many theater companies who take charades way too seriously. Thankfully, this group didn't seem like the type that would critique your acting abilities if you couldn't figure out how to get everyone to guess *The Assassination of Jesse James by the Coward Robert Ford* in thirty seconds using no words.

All the topics were holiday songs, so they weren't too difficult. When it was my turn, I stepped up and took a slip of paper from the Santa hat. I unfolded it and silently read, "Rudolph the Red-Nosed Reindeer."

Bethany shouted, "Go!" as she flipped over the one-minute sand timer.

I pointed to my nose.

A half dozen people yelled out the answer. I took my bow and sat back on the couch.

"That wasn't fair," Kirk said as I nuzzled beside him. "You get Rudolph, and I got 'Children, Go Where I Send Thee.'"

"Quit your griping," Damian said from the other team. "I'm still surprised you don't know your good old Christmas spirituals."

Kevin was next. He drew a slip of paper, scrunched up his nose and he said, "This will be fun."

"No talking," Leslie barked, which garnered a laugh from the room.

"Go!" Bethany yelled again.

Kevin started doing something that looked vaguely like YMCA. People on his team shouted out song titles, and he got more and more confused and aggravated.

"Time!" Bethany yelled. "The other team gets a chance to guess for the point."

They looked to our team captain, a history teacher I honestly hadn't talked to. He looked to the rest of us before saying, "We have no idea."

Kevin stared at us and let out a slight huff. "Hanukkah, Oh Hanukkah!"

"Are you kidding me?" Damian said. "How was that Hanukkah?"

"I was trying to be a menorah," Kevin replied. The entire room busted out laughing. Thankfully, Kevin took it well and laughed along. Before long, the game was called a tie, and both sides won. It was a holiday party, after all. Everyone got small goodie bags to go for winning. Clearly, Leslie and Bethany had planned this outcome from the beginning.

We retrieved our coats, said our goodbyes, and headed back into the frosty night air. It was almost midnight. I shivered against the cold.

"Let's huddle together, conserve heat," Kirk suggested.

I snuggled close. I had to take three steps for every one of Kirk's. He was tall. You don't realize how tall someone is until you try to keep up with them. December had blown in, and the wind was howling through the streets. Whenever we came to one of the west-to-east cross streets, the wind would barrel down on us from the Hudson. We sped through intersections to get to the cover of buildings again along the sidewalks.

I pushed the door open to the Manhattan Plaza and held it for Kirk.

"*Brr*," I said with a shake as I stepped into the heated building. "It's elf-ing cold out there."

"I know," Kirk said. "I always forget how cold it can get when the winter winds wind their way through the city."

We headed to the elevator and made our way upstairs.

"Thanks for dragging me along tonight. I needed this."

"You're welcome. I'm glad you came. With your usual schedule, I wouldn't have even thought to ask you to come to a school party." As soon as the words left his mouth, he gasped at his perceived insensitivity. "I am so sorry. I shouldn't have said it like that."

"But it's true. In all reality, two days ago, I wouldn't have been available tonight. I would have had a show. I couldn't have gone with you." I turned and looked at him. "I'm glad I *could* go with you. And I'm glad I *did* go with you."

Kirk smiled at me. I leaned in toward him as the elevator doors opened on our floor.

"Where have you been?" Johnny's voice cut through the silence and through the moment.

"I was at a party," I said, stepping out of the elevator. "How long have you been waiting for me to get back?"

"I came to check in on you and you weren't around. You didn't leave a note or nothing."

"Oh geez, I totally forgot you said you'd come by and check on me."

"It's my fault," Kirk said, trying to deflect some of the blame. "I kind of distracted her with baking cookies and a school party."

"No, it's my fault. I planned on texting you, but then Asher showed up."

"Wait, step back," Johnny said, looking at me like I'd grown a third eye. "Asher was here."

"Yeah."

"And no one died?" Johnny said. He turned to Kirk and asked, "Or did you help her hide the body?"

"No," I said exasperatedly. "No one died. Asher and I are on speaking terms...of sorts. He wanted to check in on me."

"After the riot act I read him last night, I'm amazed he had the gall to show his face in this building again."

"Johnny, what did you do?"

"Nothing that didn't need to be done years ago," Johnny explained.

In that moment, if I had been Asher, I probably would have feared for my life. Johnny looked like he was ready to rumble and throw down. Of course, he wouldn't because that could cause his expensive leather boots to get scuffed.

I glanced at Kirk and mouthed, "I'm sorry."

"I'll see you tomorrow, Erika," he said. "See ya, Johnny. Erika is one lucky lady to have someone like you in her corner."

"Don't tell him that," I joked. "We don't want his ego to swell."

"Oh honey, you know my ego is large enough to fill this building. It can't swell any more than it already has." This caused all three of us to laugh. Kirk entered his apartment, then I entered mine and Johnny followed me inside. Part of me craved to tell him to go home, but I couldn't do that.

I took off my coat, hung it, and squatted down to pet the white furball weaving in and out of my legs.

"I'm sorry, Mr. Bootsy. Was I gone too long? Did you miss momma?"

"I will never understand people who talk to their animals. I'll call you Dr. Dolittle." He paused for a second before adding, "I was in *Doctor Dolittle* when I was in college. I played a llama."

"Do I want to know?" I asked.

"No," he admitted with a smile. "It was as weird as it sounds. So, changing topics. You and Kirk seem to be getting close?"

"We're just friends."

"Uh-huh. And you're telling me that if I hadn't been standing right outside that elevator when the doors opened, you wouldn't be doing the horizontal mambo right now?"

"Johnny!"

"Yes?"

"It's not...I don't...we're just...Argghh!" I finally let out.

"Uh-huh," Johnny responded. "I see how it is. It's too early to tell?"

"Exactly."

"Do you want it to go there? Because if not, you need to put on those breaks and fast. You know relationships with neighbors can be dicey."

"I know. Almost as bad as living with someone and a relationship goes belly up."

"True. Very true." He looked at me and guided me to sit down on the couch. "I won't tell you anything you don't already know. You're an adult. All I'll say is, be careful. And if you need me to whack him, I know some people."

I busted out laughing. "Being an extra in a mob movie isn't the same as knowing real people in the criminal underworld."

"Hey, you never know." But the way he said it made it clear he didn't.

"My hero," I said, bringing him in for a hug. "Now go. You've checked up on me. I'm doing fine."

"Really?" he asked, narrowing his eyes.

"Okay, maybe not *fine*, but I'm doing better. And for now, that's as good as it's going to get."

"Okay. But if you need me, call."

"I promise," I said. "Now go. You have a hot guy waiting for you downstairs. Just because you stopped me from having my fun tonight doesn't mean you can't have yours."

"I'm sure if you threw on something a little more see-through and knocked on his door..."

"Johnny!" I said, slapping him against his shoulder lightly.

"Ouch," he said, pulling back, overacting his pain.

"Yeah, I'll show you ouch. Now, get outta here," I said in my best mob accent.

"Wow, you're less gangsta than I am," he said as he stood up off the couch.

"Out, I say! Out damn spot. Out!"

"Sure thing, Lady McB." He walked toward the door. "Night, Erika. I'll talk to you tomorrow."

"Night, Johnny." I grabbed Bootsy and held onto him as Johnny opened the door. "And Johnny, thanks for being the most amazing friend a girl could ever ask for."

He smiled, shrugged and blew me a kiss before shutting the door.

Chapter 24

I spent most of Sunday finally responding to emails and texts from people I'd avoided the rest of the weekend. My lawyer wrote to say they were still inquiring.

"*Erika, the more we dig, the more convoluted this case becomes. Technically, you were in a private residence having a private conversation. Still, your conversation was being picked up by the microphone of the young girl in the private residence. That conversation would have been kept private, but she was engaged in a video game with other players in a more public space. To make things worse, one of the other players was streaming the video gameplay. As such, the young girl you know did not know anyone was streaming the video game. Someone who writes for TheBroadway411 was watching the stream, and recognized your conversation for what it was and captured the stream. As you can see, the conversation went through many mediated channels. Technically, we could argue that recording a minor's private video game time could be illegal, but the video game industry already alleges that it's a public space, so no laws were broken. It's a hard one. – Charles Pearson.*"

Upon finishing the email, my head felt ready to explode. "So much for technology," came the grumbled response. A simple 'thank-you' reply was all I could manage, along with a request to keep up the excellent work. Words failed beyond that point. Instead, I turned my attention to listing other potential life paths. Waiting tables? A brief stint during college came to mind, and that one came off my list. Then there was that fleeting moment as a barista. Unfortunately, that exhausted the list of usable job experience. Regional summer stock performances rounded out the resume, but playing Belle in *Beauty and the Beast* hardly qualified one as a librarian, just as touring Elphaba didn't make for a suitable flying monkey trainer.

I could always go back and get another degree. The idea of running back to college made me want to crawl into a hole. I was a good student, but I wasn't an exceptional student. Admittedly, I don't know if my grades from my undergraduate years would be good enough to get me into a decent master's program. And if they did, what would I study? I wrote a list. *Teacher...* and then I wrote *Playwright*. Both assumed I would be any good and could find a job. Thankfully, I could still be a cabaret singer for a while, but my savings were rapidly disappearing.

I needed to schedule a meeting with my accountant next week and really look at my financials. I didn't know what else to do. The more I pondered about my financial situation, the more worried I became. I had student loans, my apartment, electric, singing lessons, and a stack of other bills that had to get paid somehow.

The room spun around me, its edges blurring into a dizzying whirl. My chest tightened, each breath coming faster and shallower than the last. I lifted my hand to my forehead and found beads of sweat around my temple. *Was this a fever? I didn't have time to be sick.* I noticed my hands were shivering. My pulse was racing. "Is it me or is the room getting hot?" *I'm too young to have hot flashes.* I freaked out. It was as if my body suddenly rebelled against me. Then it hit me. "I'm having a panic attack." *What's wrong with me? I haven't had one of these since high school. Think! Think! What are you supposed to do?* I bent at the waist and put my head between my knees, and I took a series of deep breaths in through my nose and out through my mouth. I stayed in that position until my heartbeat stabilized. When I calmed down, I reminded myself that I was in this same financial position I had been in just six weeks ago, and I had been getting by.

I did the thing I most dreaded doing next. I called my parents.

"Hello?" my mom's voice said over the phone.

"Mom," I squeaked out.

"Erika, what's wrong? I can hear it in your voice."

"I...I was fired, Mom. I'm no longer on *The Naughty List*." Tears immediately flooded. I spent the next thirty minutes telling my mother everything.

"Oh, my Erika. I wish I was there to help make this right. I'd go have some words with this producer woman and give her a piece of my mind."

And I knew she would. My mother wouldn't care if that's not "how things are done" in New York. She'd stomp into Rebekka Eldridge's office and give her a verbal tongue lashing. Just the thought of that made me smile.

"I just feel...so...helpless."

"I'm sure you do, dear. But you're not. You are a strong, brilliant, talented, independent woman. I would never tell your sisters this, but I've always admired you the most. You had a dream as a child, and you went after it. When that nastiness happened with Asher, you had your dark moments, but you pulled yourself out and became a cabaret star. I have zero doubts that you'll be able to do the same thing again here."

I wasn't exactly a "star," but I loved that my mom always saw me that way. "I just don't know where to begin."

"As Lao Tzu said, 'the journey of life begins with one step.' Just take a step, Erika. Let your feet be your guide. For today, maybe do something you love. What brings you the most joy in life?"

"It's always been the theater," I said.

"Well, don't let these people take that away from you. Go, reconnect with your joy."

"You're right," I said. "I don't know how I'm going to do it, but I will. I love you, Mom. More than you can ever imagine."

"I love you more, Erika. And always know, you can always come home...even if it's just for a visit."

After we finished our conversation, I decided I needed to find my joy. I picked up my phone and called Johnny.

"What's up, Erika?"

"Do you still know the Phantom?" As soon as the words escaped my mouth, I realized how odd that sounded. "Err...I mean, do you still know the guy playing the Phantom?"

"I knew what you meant. And yes. Why?"

"Think you can get us tickets for the matinee?"

"He told me to call him any time, but it may be late. Why?"

"I need to find my joy!"

"I have no idea what that means, but I'll call you back in ten." With that, he hung up the phone.

I sat there on my couch waiting to hear back from him. Sure enough, my phone started vibrating nine minutes later.

"I have two orchestra tickets for the 2:00 p.m. matinee. I told them to leave them at the box office under your name. He's a huge fan of yours, by the way."

"Really?"

"Yep. He caught your 54 Below show and absolutely loved it."

"Ahh...that's so sweet of him. Please thank him for me."

"Nope, you can do it yourself. I had to promise you'd visit backstage after the show was over."

"I don't know if I'm ready for that, but that's hardly the worst thing I've done to get tickets to see a Broadway show."

"Who are you taking?"

"I was hoping to take you..." I said, almost a little too desperate sounding.

"No can do," he said. "I already have plans with Amani."

"Okay, I think I might just go next door..."

"Erika, you sly dog, you," Johnny joked.

"It's not like that," I said a little too quickly.

"Keep telling yourself that."

I hung up the phone, walked next door, and knocked on Kirk's door. He opened it wearing a pair of low-rise jeans and a T-shirt. He immediately rested his hand on top of the door and leaned against it, which caused the bottom of his T-shirt to rise high enough for me to see the muscles of his stomach. It took all my powers not to swoon.

"What are you doing this afternoon?" I asked.

"Grading, then picking up Carissra from the bus station at 7:00. Why?"

"I know this is last minute, but wanna come see *The Phantom of the Opera* with me?"

"Today?"

"I have two tickets. My mother told me I needed to find my joy. And *Phantom* was the first show I ever saw. It was a touring production my mother took me to. It's the show that made me fall in love with musical theater. Now, don't get me wrong, the show has faults—a ton of faults—but it will always be one of my favorites. It introduced me to this crazy world I now live in."

"I don't know..."

"Come on, how often do you get to go see *Phantom* as a guest of the Phantom himself?"

"I have nothing to wear," he said.

"Just wear what you would wear to teach."

"I'm usually in khakis and a sweater these days. Not exactly what one wears to the theater, is it?" he asked.

"Wow, you haven't been to the theater recently?"

"Not since like maybe grade school," he admitted.

"Trust me, you'll be dressed perfectly fine."

"Okay, if you're sure..."

"Trust me, I'm sure."

"Then why not? Like you said. I can honestly say the Phantom has never invited me to anything before."

"Amazeballs!"

"Did you really just say that?" he asked, wrinkling his face at me.

"I did, and I stand by it. Pick you up in an hour?"

"I'll be ready."

And like that, I had a date to the theater and the chance to reclaim my joy.

The show was terrific, as always. And Jerrod, the guy playing the Phantom, was absolutely a doll. He introduced us to everyone. Though he flirted with Kirk more than I would have liked. But what can I say, the Phantom has good taste. After the show, Kirk and I had sushi before heading to the Port Authority to pick up Carissra.

We walked back to the apartments as a group of giggling, crazy people. Carissra told us about her time in DC, and Kirk and I told her about the school party and seeing *Phantom*. Thankfully, we didn't tell her about any of the other nastiness of the weekend. By the time we returned home, I was ready for bed. I said goodnight and headed into my apartment.

There was a piece of white paper folded in half sitting inside my doorway. I figured it was a message from the building housing committee, so I unfolded it and read it. "Erika, the company of *The Naughty List* voted unanimously in favor of you returning to the show today. I think we may make this happen. Everyone is beyond upset at how Eldridge handled the situation...especially when they found out what actually happened. Oh, and watch the paper for an article tomorrow...should be interesting. Yours in equity, Asher."

I slept in on Monday and didn't wake until almost 9:30 a.m. Dragging myself out of bed, I headed down to the gym to get a good run before figuring out what I would do for the day. Halfway through my run, Johnny suddenly materialized in front of the treadmill, arms flailing like a madman desperately seeking my attention.

I pulled the AirPod out of my left ear. "What has you in such a tizzy this morning?"

"Where have you been?" Johnny gasped. Clearly, he'd been running around.

I regarded the treadmill. "I've been running," I said between breaths.

"You haven't answered your phone."

"I turned it off when I was running. Can it wait until I'm done?"

"No!" Johnny said, looking exasperated. "You're needed at the theater," he glanced at his watch, "like ten minutes ago."

"What theater?" I said, still feeling the moving tread beneath my feet as I jogged.

"Girl! You. Are. Not. Keeping. Up." He said with a clap in front of my face after each word.

"Okay, okay," I said, turning the treadmill off. "You have my full attention. What's the fuss?"

"Call Brice…Now!" He watched as I fiddled with my phone and searched for Brice's number. Thankfully, there wasn't anyone else in the gym at this mid-morning hour, so Johnny hadn't disturbed anyone with his brief outburst.

"I take it Johnny found you," Brice said.

"And good morning to you, too," I said. "I was jogging. Why? What's up?"

"Let's say your castmates pulled a coup this morning. They've demanded you're back in the show or they all walk. Surprisingly, this was backed by Equity. And the other unions came onboard."

"Wait…what? Why?" I said, trying to understand what was happening.

"There was an article in *The Post* this morning by Michelle Bouvier. Asher and several other company members went on record saying firing you set a horrible precedent about privacy in the digital age. Bouvier dug up all the known facts about what happened to you. You come off sounding like the actual victim in all this."

It took me a moment to process everything running through my head. Part of me was surprised that I was back in the show, and another part of me couldn't believe that my leading champion was the man I'd spent the last three years hating.

"So," Brice started again. "They wanted to see you at the theater at 10:00, but clearly, that isn't happening."

"Tell them I'll be there by 11:30. I need to get ready."

"I'm going to have them push the meeting back to one. I'm going to be there, Pearson is coming, and McCartan from Equity is planning to be there. We want to have a full-court press on your side of the table."

"I'll be there." I hung up the phone and threw my arms around Johnny.

"Eww… You're a hot, sweaty mess. I have girl-stank on me now."

"Get over it," I said, pulling him in for another hug.

"Go, get ready! And text me as soon as it's over."

His voice trailed as I rushed from the gym. Before leaving, I looked back at Johnny and said, "Will you please wipe off the treadmill for me? Thanks."

"If it was anyone else..."

I didn't hear the rest of the sentence because I was running to the elevator.

While I was in the shower, I got a follow up text.

Brice: *Your team is meeting at Hello, Coffee! at twelve-thirty. We want to present a unified front when we walk into the Maurer Theatre.*

I didn't think I'd ever had a "team" before. I finished getting ready and headed out into the cold December weather. There was a light snow falling, but it melted on contact, creating slick sidewalks. I took my time and headed to the theater. When I got to Hello, Coffee!, Asher and Jeremy were drinking coffee at the corner table.

"There's the girl of the hour," Asher said. "How are you doing?"

I sat down at the table and said, "My head is swimming. I haven't had time to process what's going on."

"That's okay," McCartan said. His face suddenly became serious as he added, "I'm sorry I didn't put up more of a fight the other day. I should have trusted you."

"Hey, I get it. The way the facts were laid out—along with the audio recording—made it look like I'd violated my contract."

"But I should have known that you wouldn't have been that sloppy as a professional. I truly am sorry."

"Water off a duck's back," I said.

"Wow," McCartan said. "I don't think I've ever heard anyone use that in an actual conversation before. I mean, I remember when Jinkx Monsoon said it repeatedly on RuPaul's Drag Race..."

"It's a Midwestern thing," Asher said. "We have all kinds of sayings you East Coasters never hear in conversations."

"Good afternoon," a voice said. I looked up to see Charles Pearson strolling over. He had his briefcase with him. As usual, he was dressed in a tailored suit that was probably more expensive than my entire wardrobe. *And that's where all my billable hours go.*

"We're waiting for Brice Stark," Asher said. "Then we can head next door."

"So, what exactly will happen when we get next door?" I asked.

"We have a game plan all mapped out," Pearson said. "This is going to be fun. Rebekka Eldridge needs to be knocked down a peg or two, and I'm looking forward to being the man to do it." I looked more shocked than I intended because he added, "Don't worry. We've got this."

Brice showed up a couple minutes later, and the entire group walked next door into the theater. Noam Weiss was pacing in the entryway when we got there.

He looked at my entourage and said, "It's good to see you again, Erika. Right this way."

My "team" followed him through a side door and into the theater's corporate offices. He navigated the group to the same conference room I'd been fired out of days earlier.

Rebekka Eldridge sat at the head of the table in a black pantsuit ensemble with a delicate strand of pearls hanging around her neck. The scowl on her face told me everything I needed to know. Along with Eldridge was San Nicolás, Benedikt Einar, and now Weiss.

Asher pulled out a chair for me, which was rather chivalrous. He was turning into my surprising knight in slightly soiled armor.

"Well," James Pearson started. "I'm glad everyone could make it on such short notice. We're here to discuss the wrongful termination of my client."

"What?" Rebekka exclaimed. "She broke her contract."

"Did she?" Pearson asked. "Mr. Einar, please explain to your client how privacy laws work in the State of New York."

"Pearson," Einar started, "You know as well as I do that this area of law is far from exact. We do not know how the courts would rule in a case like this."

"Maybe, but do you want to take this to court and let a jury decide? Who do you think they'll side with? Mrs. Eldridge or Ms. Saunders?"

Eldridge started to say something, but Einar held up a hand, then whispered something in her ear. A disgusted look washed over her face. Whatever Einar had said, Eldridge was not happy.

"You're right," Einar said. "We don't want there to be any more bad press, and litigation would drag this show through the mud."

"So, what do you propose we do now?" Pearson said.

"We're willing to bring Ms. Saunders back into the production," Einar said.

"And…?" Pearson asked.

"And what?" Eldridge asked. "What else could she possibly want?"

"An apology," Asher cut in, "in front of the cast and crew."

"I have nothing to apologize for," Eldridge said, crossing her arms.

"Oh, and back pay, of course," Pearson added.

"She didn't work," Eldridge proclaimed. "Why should she be paid?"

"She missed three workdays because of you," Pearson said. "I think back pay is the least you can do."

"I would also like to amend all the original cast members' contracts to earn them one percent of the show's net profits and 0.25 percent of the net profits from all future commercial productions," McCartan said.

"Preposterous," Weis said. "No one gets a deal like that."

"That's where you're wrong," McCartan said. "Producers always seem to forget about *Hamilton*. So, there is precedent."

Einar conferred with Eldridge before speaking. "I've conferred with my client. She's willing to accept Ms. Saunders back into the company and apologize. She will not agree to the financial conditions you stipulated."

"Then I won't come back," I blurted. I was probably the person who was the most surprised by my sudden outburst. "I'm with Mr. McCartan. The cast deserves a small stake in the production. Making this investment in the cast furthers our commitment to the project and its success."

"She speaks," Eldridge said.

"Keep that up," Pearson said, glaring at Eldridge, "and we'll make it two percent of the show's net profits." He narrowed his eyes on Eldridge, who huffed.

"Oh, and one more thing," Pearson said. "Mrs. Eldridge will not communicate directly with my client. If she needs to say something to my client, she can have her lawyer pass it on to me, and I'll convey the message to Ms. Saunders."

"That's preposterous," Eldridge burst out. "I'm the producer. I have rights."

"Maybe so," Pearson acknowledged, "but you're losing those rights each time you open your mouth."

Eldridge let out a high-pitched whine and pouted, but she said nothing.

"Can you give us a few minutes to confer?" Einar asked.

"Of course," Pearson said. "We'll be in the hallway when you're ready to accept our offer." He said it so confidently. I was glad he was on my side.

Pearson stood, and the rest of us followed as we exited the conference room. We walked as far away from the door as possible before my group started conferring. The meeting had gone better than planned. I hadn't been privy to any of the plan's specifics, so I had been as shocked as Eldridge was with the demands. The demands were genius, but. I was surprised how far my team took them.

The door opened, and Benedikt Einar walked into the hallway and walked over to us. "We're willing to accept everything, but we'd like to negotiate 0.8 percent on net profits and 0.20 percent on future earnings."

"Done," Pearson said as he extended his hand.

Benedikt turned to me. "For what it's worth, I'm glad this worked out the way it did. I think the show is better with you in it." With that, he turned around and headed into the conference room.

San Nicolás walked out and said, "Thank Santa that mess is over with." He turned to me and said, "Welcome back, my dear. You've been truly missed. Are you ready to get back to rehearsals?"

I looked at Pearson, who nodded.

"I'm ready when you are."

"Then let's go. There's no time like the present," San Nicolás said enthusiastically. "I'll give you a minute to say goodbye. We'll start the afternoon rehearsal in fifteen minutes."

"I'll be there," I said.

San Nicolás turned around and left the group.

"I don't know where to begin," I said. "Thank you! Thank all of you." The waterworks started, and I did my best to squelch them to avoid ruining my makeup.

"No need to thank me," Pearson said. "That's what I'm here for."

"Now go," Brice said. "Rehearse and make this show a sellout."

"And, Erika," McCartan said, "now that you're back with the company, I hope you'll return to being the Equity Deputy. Asher is good, but he's not you."

"I'm not quite sure how I'm supposed to take that," Asher said, putting his hands on his hips. We all laughed.

We said our goodbyes, and I walked with Asher up the stairs and into the theater. As soon as I walked on stage, the cast and crew burst into applause. Katherine ran over and flung her arms around me.

"It's about Frosty time you got back here. It hasn't been the same without you."

"I missed you, too."

"Well, I guess you're better than having poor Serafina read your lines over the speaker," Peeter said as he patted me on the shoulder.

"She didn't?"

"Yep. It was a bit of a *snow* show, if you know what I mean," Peeter replied.

"Speech," someone yelled. And more people said the same thing. I finally gave in.

"I'm glad to be back on *The Naughty List*. I missed all of you. Now, we don't have much time before we open, so let's get this elf-ing show moving."

Chapter 25

The rest of the week was a whirlwind of rehearsing, tweaking the show, new songs, new dialogue, and evening performances. I didn't know if I was coming or going. Beyond the cast and crew, I saw no one else. I sent thank you cards to everyone who had helped me get my job back.

After the Saturday evening performance, a group of cast members went out to a restaurant near the Manhattan Plaza. The show had run smoothly, and I thought we'd hit our opening night with no major problems. The restaurant was nice enough to stay open late for us. We pulled together several tables and sat and enjoyed each other's company.

I ended up sitting next to Asher. We were now talking and texting almost every day. It reminded me of the good old days—before we started dating. I hadn't realized how much I'd missed my *friend* Asher over the past few years. He'd matured more than I could imagine.

"Toast!" Asher said, clinking his glass. "To all of us on *The Naughty List*. May we stay forever humble and make Santa proud!"

There were a bunch of "hear, hear!'s" around the room.

I took a quick breath and stood. "I'm not one for giving speeches, but I want to thank you for what you did this week. You'll never know how much this meant to me. Here's to a long run." I lifted my glass, and everyone around the table did the same.

Asher put his arm around me when I sat down, and he leaned in to whisper in my ear. "You'll never know how glad I am that you're back with the company. I can't imagine working on this show without you."

"Likewise. If you had asked me three months ago if we'd be sitting next to each other having dinner, I would have told you, you were out of your mind."

"I know. After the way we ended things, I didn't think you would ever talk to me again. I can't reiterate enough how sorry I am about all that."

"Water under the bridge," I said, raising my glass to him. "Here's to us, looking forward, not backward."

He clinked my glass, and we both drank.

The rest of the meal was relatively uneventful. I learned about some of the craziness that happened while I was gone that no one had told me about yet. I told them about playing charades with "normal" people.

The only slight downside to the night was that we all had a lot to drink. Instead of throwing Asher in a cab, I dragged him back to my apartment. I promised him he could sleep on my couch.

The elevator door opened on my floor, and Asher collapsed against the floor and started laughing loudly. "Shh..." I said. "You're going to wake the neighbors."

"Let them hear me," he belted, breaking into a semblance of *Ragtime*.

"Shh..." I tried again.

A door down the hall opened. I turned to see who it was. Kirk stood in his doorway wearing only his boxers. His hair was disheveled.

"Hey, look, it's the hot neighbor," Asher yelled. "Howdy there, neighbor."

"Sorry," I said. "We were celebrating."

"I can see that," Kirk said flatly. "Please, keep your boyfriend quiet. Some of us are trying to sleep."

"He's not—"

Kirk shut his door before I could finish the sentence. Before the door shut, I caught a glimmer of emotion on Kirk's face, but I wasn't sure what it was. Annoyance? Regret?

"Uh-oh," Asher said. "I think your hottie neighbor is mad. He doesn't like me."

"I can't imagine why," I responded as I dragged Asher down the hall into my apartment and dropped him on the couch. He was heavier than he looked.

I changed and got into bed. Bootsy, the little traitor, slept on top of Asher rather than with me. I didn't have long to complain because I was asleep before I hit the pillow.

I awoke with a splitting headache. I apparently had drunk more than I had intended to. There was snoring coming from the living room. I poked my head out the door and was surprised to find Asher sawing logs on my couch. I didn't remember bringing him home last night. For a split second, I was afraid something may have happened between Asher and me, but the memories of the previous evening came back to me.

I grabbed my phone off the charger next to the couch. I had one message from a number I didn't recognize, so I pushed play.

"Hey Erika, Eugene Moses here. I'm *The Naughty List*'s composer, in case you've forgotten my name. Anyway, I know this is your day off, but I had an idea for a new eleven o'clock number for the show. I wanted to see if you could come by my apartment today and help me iron it out. If all things go smoothly, and San Nicolás likes it, we may put it in the show as soon as tomorrow night. Anyway, call me back when you get this."

Eugene lived in an apartment above a bakery in Chelsea. I walked up the four flights and knocked on his door. "Coming!" a muffled voice called from inside. A second later, a young woman opened the door.

"You must be Erika. I'm Jackie." She opened the door wide, and I walked into the apartment. "Eugene stepped out for a minute.

He promised he'd be right back." I looked down. Jackie was quite obviously pregnant. "I'm having a craving for Mountain Dew and Funyuns."

"Together?" I said without thinking.

"I know. Tell me about it. Normally, I don't like either, but I've been craving them today. Eugene has been a godsend during all this."

"So, he's not—"

"No. He was my high school sweetheart. But that was eons ago. No, the baby's father is in the military and currently overseas on deployment. Eugene has known both of us for years, so he opened his home for me and the little one," Jackie said, pointing to her belly.

"When's the baby due?"

"She was supposed to be here three days ago. If she doesn't hurry up and come out on her own, the doctors will induce labor this week. I was hoping to have her out and in the world before your show opens, but she isn't cooperating."

"I'm home," Eugene yelled as he opened the door. He saw me and said, "Oh hey, Erika. Glad you found the place." He then glanced between Jackie and me and asked, "I take it you have introduced yourselves?"

"All three of us have been introduced," Jackie joked. "Anyway, you two have fun. I'm going to go lay down."

Eugene handed her the bag from the corner bodega. He pulled out a couple of bottles of water and handed me one. "I figured you'd want water."

"It's nice that you're taking care of Jackie and her unborn daughter."

"Jackie and I were high school sweethearts a long time ago."

"That's what she told me," I said.

"And with Brian overseas, I knew she needed someone close to lean on." There was a wistful look in Eugene's eyes as he looked in the direction she walked. Part of me wondered if he still had feelings for her. I guess adolescent love doesn't always die. "Well, let me play the new song."

"You said it's a new eleven o'clock number?"

"That's the goal. Right now, we have the long speech from Madam Tanya. Honestly, it's an old holdout from the source material. I don't think it works in the show. Instead, there's the moment when Billy James is shot and Madam Tanya asks for the elves to save him. I don't know what magical Christmas power elves have over life and death. But apparently, audiences don't care."

"Tell me about it. That part of the show was always awkward, but then a lot of the producer's changes have been strange to me."

"Don't even get me started on Eldridge. You see what she changes. You can only imagine the crazy stuff coming out of her that the artistic team has put their feet down about."

"Really?" I asked. I had assumed the artistic team had caved to Eldridge's every whim.

"Oh yeah. I know there is some crazy stuff now, but you didn't see her desire for a big number with show elves."

"What?"

"Oh yeah, Eldridge wanted a big number like one she saw at a Las Vegas review. She wanted tall headpieces and practically nude elves doing high kicks or some nonsense. She thought it would add to the pizzazz."

"Oh, thank the stars you saved us from that one."

"San Nicolás convinced her it would take away from the family show feel and drive away potential customers. She throws out money left and right, but I think she has a lot more riding on the show's financial success than she lets on. Sure, she says it's all about her dead husband's legacy, but we—the artistic team—all think she needs this show to run and the new theater to be a success."

"Well, let's hope we can give them one heck of an eleven o'clock number."

Eugene walked over to an upright piano sitting in the corner of the apartment. He pulled out a couple of stacks of printed pages. He handed one to me and laid the other one out on the piano. "Tyreek's sorry he couldn't be here. He has something else going on this afternoon."

On top of the page were the words "Give Him a Chance to Live. Music by Eugenius Moses. Lyrics by Tyreek MacQueen."

"Why don't I play the number first, then I can walk you through it?"

"Works for me," I said. I put the water bottle on the ground and read through the song while Eugene played it on the piano. It absolutely captured the moment in the show. And vocally, it fit me perfectly. Eugene knew my voice and what it could do, and he captured everything I had in me within this one song. By the time he stopped playing, I was crying. "Holy elf balls! This is amazing. It's perfect."

"And I wrote it for you. I wanted you to have a moment to shine. It's like I told you the very first time I met you. I've been a fan for years. I can't imagine doing this show without you. I want young singers to look up to you and try to match your talent as they attempt to belt this song for years to come."

"I hope I'm up to the challenge," I admitted.

"I have no doubts. Trust me, I wouldn't have written it like this if I didn't have full faith in your talent and that amazing tool you have. Let's get to it."

We spent the next four hours working on the number. We changed a few things here and there to figure out where I could breathe to ensure I hit the sustained high note at the end of the song. I'd never had a song written for me like this. Eugene sensed what my instrument could do in a way that I hadn't even known. He truly was a genius.

Chapter 26

Eugene and I introduced everyone to the new eleven o'clock number on Monday during rehearsal. The cast and creative team were bowled over by how perfect the song was and how amazing I sounded singing it.

"Yes, but can you sing it eight times a week?" San Nicolás asked me.

"I can do it," I told him. Admittedly, there was a voice in the back of my mind screaming, "No. No, you can't." But I wasn't about to show fear.

"You'll need to write a modified version for the understudy," San Nicolás told Eugene and Tyreek. "And for Erika, if she's ever not up for it." He then turned to me. "I know you think you can do this song every performance, but it's a stretch. I don't think it will break you. Like Eugene, I have faith in you, but I want to have a backup plan—just in case."

I nodded. "It makes sense to me. And if I get sick or have a head cold, it's smart to have a variation."

"What if we dropped it a key?" Eugene asked. "You could still belt it, but you wouldn't have to worry about the high notes."

"That could work," San Nicolás said. "Work on it, and we can rehearse it later. We'll alternate the versions during rehearsals to get you used to both. Sound good, Erika?"

"Sounds perfect!"

Eugene and I spent the next couple of hours working on the alternative version with Tyreek. "We'll come up with some visual cue you can give the musical director at the beginning if you ever need the alternative," Eugene said after we'd been rehearsing for a while. "Maybe you could pull on your ear like Carol Burnett used to do?"

I narrowed my eyes and said, "Maybe not," with a snort. "But I'm sure we can come up with something. But between you, me, and the piano, never expect me to sing this version. I'll do the original every show. I'm a professional. I wouldn't commit to doing something if I didn't think I could pull it off well."

"That's what I figured," he said with a wink.

With both versions in the can, we started rehearsing the staging late Monday morning and continued into the early afternoon. San Nicolás didn't want to put it in the show that night, but Eugene convinced him we had to see how it fit if we would have it ready for opening night.

After rehearsal, I went home for a short nap, had a quick bite, and some cuddle time with Bootsy before the show. We had a 6:30 call time, so I was leaving the apartment at about 5:45 to give myself plenty of time to walk there and get a hot tea on the way.

"Bye, Bootsy," I said, calling over my shoulder before leaving the apartment. I opened the door and exited, and Kirk walked right past me, saying nothing. He didn't stop and say hi or anything. I almost called out to him but figured he had something else on his mind.

I hurried downstairs and ran into Carissra in the lobby. "Hey, I just saw Kirk."

"Oh?" she questioned with an odd look on her face.

"What?" I asked. "I feel like I missed something."

Carissra looked around to see if anyone was listening and motioned for me to lean down. She quietly said, "He saw you with Asher the other night. Are you and the gay guy back together?"

"Me and Asher?" I asked with a jolt. "Oh, heck no. I've been down that path. We're just friends. Like you said...he's gay. Very gay. I won't go down that road again. My days of being an actor's beard are over."

"Well, from what you've told me, that didn't exactly stop you the first time..." Carissra let the implication of her statement fall in the air.

"Oh," I said as it dawned on me. "Kirk thinks I'm back with Asher. So, he's what...jealous?"

"Pretty much... Well, that's my theory anyway," Carissra said. "He moped all day yesterday. And even today, he's still in a foul mood. The only reason I could come up with was you dragging a drunk Asher back to your apartment the other night."

"How did you hear about that?" I asked.

"The walls in our apartment are not that thick. I think the whole floor heard Asher when you two came off the elevator. Plus, my uncle may have been muttering to himself about different things he would like to do with your ex."

"But why would that matter? Even if I got back together with Asher, which will happen when Frosty vacations in hell, that wouldn't impact my friendship with Kirk."

Carissra narrowed her eyes. And even though Carissra was like half my age, I felt like I was the child being looked down upon by a parent.

"What?" I asked.

"Are you that dense?" she asked bluntly.

"Hey, that's not very nice," I said, defending myself.

"When it comes to my uncle, I won't play nice. You know he likes you, right?"

And there it was, the unspoken was finally spoken and by his niece. I stammered but couldn't form any words. Finally, I said, "I have to go to the theater." I left Carissra looking after me as I walked into the falling snow as I walked to work. In the back of my head, I'd known that Kirk was into me. And if I was completely honest with myself, I was into Kirk. But neither of us made a move, so I figured it was all in my head. And now, here was Kirk's niece stating it so plainly. I wasn't ready to deal.

Before heading into the Maurer, I stopped at Hello, Coffee! I walked in and ordered an herbal tea. As much as I love my coffee, I didn't want to drink anything that would dehydrate me before a show. While the barista steeped the tea, I pulled out my phone and texted Johnny.

Erika: *I think Kirk's into me.*

Johnny: *Well, duh!*

Johnny: *Did you not know that already?*

I got my tea and headed into the theater. Before heading to my dressing room, I signed in on the callboard. Once in my private little space, I set my tea down and scrutinized my phone again.

I stared at the screen, not knowing who I should text. I realized I didn't have Kirk's cell phone number.

Erika: *Do you have Kirk's cell phone number?*

Johnny: *Are you telling me you don't? What am I going to do with you?*
A couple of seconds later, a 914 area code number appeared from Johnny.

"*Hey Kirk.*" I typed. Then deleted it. I tried, *It's Erika. Got your number from Johnny.* Then I deleted that one too. I typed, *It's Erika. Would love to talk tomorrow when you get home from school.*

I then put the phone down and stared at it. Part of me wondered if I stared at it long enough, would that magically make him text me back faster? Finally, it buzzed, and I snatched up the phone immediately.

Kirk: *That works for me. See you tomorrow.*

I relaxed slightly. I hadn't realized the amount of tension that had settled in my shoulders.

That night was the family and friends dress rehearsal. My parents weren't flying in until early tomorrow morning, so they would miss this dress rehearsal but would be here for opening night.

When I finished belting out the eleven o'clock number with all my might, the crowd jumped to their feet. In the wings, Eugene embraced Tyreek. If they were happy and the crowd was ecstatic, we'd done it. Even Peeter, who was slightly upstage from me, gave me an enthusiastic thumbs up. I took three steps back as the flat lowered for the last scene, the big wedding.

"Girl, you did it!" Katherine said as we exited stage right into the hands of our waiting dressers, who were there to get us ready for the quick costume change into the last scene. We had almost ninety seconds for this quick-change, which seemed completely relaxed and laid back compared to the one I had earlier in the show.

"I'll be honest," I said as Gladys zipped up the back of my costume before handing me off to Carlos, who inspected my wig to make sure it hadn't shifted during the song. "I wasn't sure how people would react. The cast and crew thought it was good—"

"You were amazing," Katherine said. "I couldn't sing that song if I had a year to rehearse and all the vocal lessons to go with it."

Carlos tapped me on the shoulder, letting me know I was good to go, before turning his attention to Katherine and double-checking her wig. He pulled out a can of hair spray and touched up the back part of the wig to make sure it would stick in place through the final number.

We then made our way to where we entered for the grand finale, "A Christmas Wedding." The set looked like it was the top of a wedding cake and there would be snow on stage. A set of snow blowers created thousands of realistic-looking snowflakes, but the flakes were really a water-based foam that evaporated on contact. The snowflakes looked pretty when they fell to the ground, but the cast didn't have to worry about someone slipping or gagging.

"Cue elves," I heard the assistant stage manager say. Katherine and I immediately entered from our side as we met up with Peeter and Jocelyn. We became the wedding observers while Jocelyn climbed to the top and acted as the officiant. It was fitting that our Madam Tanya reigned over this affair.

We sang, we danced, and when the show was over, we held for almost five minutes as the audience applauded. We were finally given the cue to leave the stage before we lined up to go on stage to take our bows. The four elves were second to last as groups. We bowed once as a group, then we each got individual bows. The applause was deafening. We parted ways. Katherine and I went stage left, and Peeter and Jocelyn stage right as Caiden and Colleen took their final bows. Then Caiden and Colleen led the company in one last bow as the orchestra played the show's end.

Right after our bow, a couple of confetti cannons burst over the crowd, raining down a sprinkle of confetti snow on the first couple of rows. There was more applause as the curtain lowered.

We congratulated each other backstage on a job well done. I patted a few people on their backs, but I quickly scurried off to my dressing room. Gladys and Carlos were there. Gladys helped me out of the dress, and Carlos helped me out of my wig and grabbed the mic pack. While we were getting me undressed, Serafina's voice came over the system and said, "Congratulations cast. There's a reception in the lobby. We will have notes tomorrow at 9:30 a.m. Enjoy the night."

Only one more day of early mornings. After tomorrow's opening, the show would be frozen. No more early morning rehearsals. No more new songs getting placed in at the eleventh hour. In all honesty, except for including the new eleven o'clock number, most of the show had been frozen for a week. Now, we were refining things, and Serafina ensured we weren't changing things as we went along. The longer someone is in a show, the greater the likelihood that they'll alter things because they're bored or not paying attention. Sometimes the producers and artistic team look the other way. Occasionally, they get mad at you if you change too much. And most important, don't start riffing on songs and trying new runs after a year into the run. That's the fastest way to get called in by the stage manager for some quick rehabilitation.

Once Gladys and Carlos finished, I ran through the shower before I went outside and greeted family and friends. I didn't have any family at this performance, but I knew many people who had been invited. Unlike a regular night where we walk the line of fans out back, this night, they had a small reception in the theater lobby. I walked out front and said hello to several people from other shows that had come to see the show on their night off. It was one of those things we all liked to do for each other in the small theater community. When us theater people have time to support another show, we do it. And since most of us work all the time, we see each other's shows the second we get the opportunity.

I picked up a glass of champagne as a woman I'd toured with came rushing over to tell me what a fantastic job I did. I thanked her and told her I was glad that she was still kicking it after three years in *Chicago*. She was determined to be Roxie one day. And I didn't doubt that she would get there. She was that good.

Chapter 27

After saying hello to a lot of people and even posing for a handful of selfies, I went back to my dressing room, grabbed my purse and coat, then headed out the side alley door. I wasn't in the mood to get stopped by anyone else in the lobby who was still having a grand time. There would be no one out back, so I went with the best option. The downstairs office's lights were out. Thankfully, the hallway lights had motion detectors, so I walked through the hallway, found my door, and exited into about a half inch of snow on the ground. Nothing much by New York standards, but since it was after midnight, no one was going to be coming along to shovel the sidewalks.

"Why am I wearing heels?" I asked myself as I regarded my heeled boots. Sure, they looked terrific, but they weren't the most practical to trudge around the snow in. I made my way home slowly, watching each step to avoid a super-slick stretch of sidewalk or a patch of black ice.

When I crossed Broadway, the buzzing from my pocket let me know I'd received a text. I reached in and grabbed my phone.

Eugene: *Sorry I missed the reception tonight. Jackie just delivered a healthy baby girl. She wanted to make sure I told you. See you tomorrow.*

Erika: *Tell her I said mazel tov!*

I then scrolled through my other texts. There was a message from my parents letting me know the flight plans...again. I don't know how often they've emailed or texted me their flight and hotel information. They were staying at the Marriott Marquis, which was a half block from the Mauer Theatre, so it was the perfect place. They had complete access to Times Square and were close to the theater. And they were far enough from my apartment that they wouldn't drop by unannounced. At their age, which was on in their early sixties, they were more likely to take a cab than hoof it a few blocks in the snow. Which admittedly is strange since they live in Iowa. One would think they were used to dealing with snow.

The next text on my phone was from Johnny.

Johnny: *Call me!!!*

He wasn't one to use emojis, so seeing a happy face let me know he had good news, so I hit the call button.

The phone had barely rung when he picked up. "Where are you? I've been looking everywhere for you?"

"We had the family and friends rehearsal tonight. Followed by a small reception. I had to show up, smile, and take a few pictures. Why?"

"I have news."

"I could use some good news," I said.

I must have sounded grumpier than I intended because Johnny was immediately like, "What's wrong?"

"Nothing's wrong...What's your news?"

"I want to tell you in person. How long till you get home?"

"Ten minutes...max."

"I'll be there waiting for you."

He hung up the phone, and I slipped the phone back into my coat pocket. I picked up my pace, but I still watched where I stepped. The last thing I wanted was to twist my ankle or break a leg the night before the show opened. Admittedly, that would be just my luck.

I got back to the Manhattan Plaza and waved at the night guard.

"Your show still opening tomorrow?" she asked.

I sadly couldn't remember her name, but the guards were knowledgeable about the people in the building and all our projects. Heck, I found out more about what's happening around New York by chatting up the guards than I do from reading Page Six in *The Post* some days.

"It is."

"You excited?"

"That and a bit terrified."

She chuckled. "Break a leg. My parents, cousins, and I are all coming to see it next week with the kids."

"Great. I hope the kids enjoy the show. We like to think we have something for audience members of all ages."

"My niece is a sophomore at LaGuardia High, so we try to see as many shows as possible."

"LaGuardia, that's the High School of Music & Art and Performing Arts?" I asked. I think I had it right, but it's not like I pay that much attention to public schools since I don't have children.

"Yep. That's the one."

"Well, let me know when you attend. I'd be happy to show her around backstage."

"That would be amazing," the guard said, clearly surprised I would offer. "I'll let you know what night it is we're going to be there. Are you planning on taking any vacation days before the first of the year?"

I barked out a laugh. "I won't see vacation days until after the Tony's in June—if I'm lucky. We're in it for the long haul…fingers crossed."

"Great. Have a good evening."

"You too," then I started walking away. I turned around and said, "And I'm not joking. Let me know when you're coming. I'll give you the backstage tour. Merry Christmas."

"Merry Christmas, Ms. Saunders."

I turned around, parting of me wondering what Christmas bee had landed in my festive bonnet as I hit the elevator button. It dinged open immediately. I got on, hit the button for my floor, slunk against the car's back wall, and enjoyed the ride up.

The elevator door dinged open. The popping sound of a cork interrupted my thoughts. Johnny stood in the hall with two champagne flutes and an uncorked bottle that he immediately poured. I was barely out of the elevator when he thrust a flute in my hand.

"Don't get me wrong, I love the gesture, but what exactly are we celebrating?"

"I got a job."

"What?"

"Yep. They're reviving *Passion,* and I'm playing Giorgio Bachetti."

"Oh wow! I didn't know *Passion* was being revived this season."

"It's a quasi-British import from the Donmar Warehouse in London. You know the director who loves to have the actors play instruments on stage. The entire ensemble is only six people. I landed the job because I was a flutist in marching band in high school. Never knew that would land me a job on Broadway."

"How long has it been since you picked up a flute?" I asked as I let us into my apartment. I flipped on the light switch in the entry hall.

"I've secretly always played. It's been a tool I've used to calm myself. I'm no Lizzo, but I got some mad skills."

"Look at that. I'm still learning new and interesting secrets about my best friend."

"I just look like an open book, honey. I gotta keep a few surprises to make your life interesting."

"Where's Amani?" I asked, before setting the glass of champagne on the kitchen table. A furball snaked around my legs, so I bent down and gave Bootsy some love and attention. "I know. You must have felt abandoned all evening."

"I was abandoned. You were at work. Amani was at work."

"I was talking to Bootsy, goofball." I looked up at Johnny's little pout and burst into laughter. "Do you want me to pet you, too?"

"Only if you rub my belly," he joked back.

"When do rehearsals begin?"

"First week of February. I'm getting the score next week. The director wants everyone off book by the first day of rehearsal."

"Oh, wow! But then, when you have the genius material of a Sondheim show, you know there won't be changes to the master's work."

"All hail Sondheim."

"To Sondheim," I said as I grabbed the champagne flute from the table and clinked it with Johnny's glass. I sat the champagne on the table and said, "I'm going to make some hot chocolate to warm me up. Interested?"

"With or without marshmallows?"

"With, of course. Why bother if you aren't going to have the marshmallows?"

"Then, by all means, I will partake in both hot chocolate and champagne. I swear that sounds like a song on a Rufus Wainwright album."

"It probably is," I said as I pulled out the teapot. I added some water to the kettle, set it on the stove, and turned on the stovetop burner.

Johnny sat down at the table and kept Bootsy company while I prepped the mugs for their chocolaty goodness. Even though it was only instant hot chocolate, I'd at least splurged on a high-end brand that came with the tiny baby marshmallows already in the powdered mix.

"How was the show tonight?" Johnny asked as I leaned back against the kitchen counter, waiting for the teakettle to boil.

"A few minor bumps, but nothing problematic. The new eleven o'clock number will blow your socks off. I've never been lucky enough to have a show-stopping number before, so it's kind of fun."

"Didn't you have the eleven o'clock number in *The Faith Healer*?"

"I did, but it was a powerful, yet depressing song," I said. The tea kettle whistled, so I grabbed the kettle and poured the water into the mugs. I put a silver spoon in each mug and handed it to Johnny. "Gotta stir it yourself," I said. I sat down at the table and leaned back, relaxing for the first time. "What were we talking about?" I asked.

"Your new number."

"That's right. This is the number Eugene had me run over to his apartment on Sunday to learn. He's a talented composer. I've had more direct interaction with him than either Tyreek or Mable, but the three seem to work well together. I know they have other projects lined up, so I'll be interested in seeing what they do next."

I decided I needed something to nibble on while I double-fisted my cocoa and champagne. There was a package of pizzelles on the counter. I reached over from my chair and tried to grab them, but I was about six inches too short.

"What are you doing?" Johnny asked.

"Getting cookies," I said.

"Do you want me to get those for you?" he asked from his seat on the opposite side of the table, which was even further away from the package.

"I can manage." I stood up and grabbed the cookies, unwrapped them, and set them between us.

Johnny reached over, grabbed one, and immediately took a bite. "Whoa, these are fantastic. What bakery did you buy these from?" Johnny asked.

"The one next door," I joked. Johnny gave me a befuddled look, so I added, "Kirk made them."

"Oh really? And how are things with Mr. Tall, Gorgeous and Plays Well with Kids and Animals?"

I let out a deep sigh. I leaned forward and hit my head against the kitchen table. "I've been such an idiot."

"I figured that out from your texts before the show. What happened?"

"I've been on all these dates trying to find someone for opening night, and I didn't see the amazing man in the apartment next door. I totally friend-zoned him. And now, I think I hurt him because he thinks I'm back with Asher."

"Whoa, how the heck did that happen? And please tell me you're not back with Asher."

"Why does everyone keep thinking I would ever get back with Asher?" Johnny didn't say anything, but the look he shot me had sarcasm written all over it. "I'm most definitely not with Asher. He's finally realized he's 100 percent gay. He's a Kinsey 6.0; 5.5 at the lowest." I sipped from my champagne flute and followed it up with a swig of hot cocoa.

"What happened? I can tell when you're stalling. And you are totally stalling."

I let out an overly exaggerated sigh and told Johnny the story. "So, I'm meeting with Kirk tomorrow afternoon to 'talk about things.'" I looked up at Johnny, and he reached out and grabbed my hand. "I'm worried I friend-zoned him too long."

"Well, all you can do is put it out there and see what he says." A tear was coming on, so I moved my other hand to wipe it away. "Oh no, girl! There will be no crying over men tonight. We've been through this. In the words of my grand pappy, two tears in the bucket, mother f—"

"Elf it?" I offered, and we both laughed.

Before long, Amani called Johnny to let him know he was off from work and was bringing him home a celebratory dessert he'd made at the restaurant. I walked Johnny to the front door and said goodnight before heading off to bed. Once Johnny was gone, Bootsy jumped up on the bed and made it clear that he was ready for both of us to be asleep.

I got up the next morning, showered, and dashed around Midtown to get my errands finished. I had to go back to the shop and pick up the dress I was wearing for the afterparty that evening. The designer wanted to do one more fitting. Once he was happy, he promised to have it at the theater before 7:00 p.m.

I then had lunch plans with Brice and my parents at Juniors across the street. I had taken my parents to Juniors for cheesecake after a show once, and they'd fallen in love with the place. Anytime they talked about coming to the city, getting Junior's split pea soup was right at the top of the agenda. Since Juniors was right across the street from my parents' hotel, I texted them I'd meet them there at eleven, then ensured Brice knew where we were meeting them.

I showed up at 10:59 and found my parents were already seated at a table with Brice...and my sisters.

"Surprise!" my sisters said in unison.

"No one told me you were coming," I said, still shocked that my sisters had shown up for an opening. They'd never made it out to see me in a show here. They'd seen me back home, but they'd never seen me perform professionally. I looked at my mother. "This has your handwriting all over it."

"Of course, it does, dear," my mother said. "Your sisters were so sorry they never saw that last show before your little...accident." *And my mental breakdown*, my mother was kind enough to not add.

"But I don't have tickets for them tonight," I spat out and dropped into my chair.

"Not to worry," my mother said, patting me on the knee. "We already had everything taken care of."

I thought about it for a second and turned my head to look at Brice. "You knew," I said, squinting my eyes and making an overly dramatic angry face, "didn't you?"

Brice laughed. "Of course, I did. Once I realized tickets would be hard to get through the new year, I called your mother and warned her. She then convinced your sisters to come out for a few days and fly back to be with their families late tomorrow night. They'll miss most of Christmas Eve with their husbands and children, but they'll be there for Christmas Day."

"I can't believe you pulled this off," I admitted.

"What she's not saying," my father added, looking at Brice, "is that we tried to throw her a surprise birthday party two or three times, and she always figured it out weeks before it happened."

"I was a slightly nosy child," I said with a shrug.

The waiter came by and interrupted us as we all ordered. I had a small salad. My youngest sister, Teresa, listened to me and said, "That's all you're going to eat? Don't you need something more...substantial to get you ready for a show?"

I smiled and explained that I didn't like eating heavy on show days because it would drag me down. I then explained my basic diet, which was practically foreign to them. I'm not one of those granola cruncher types, but I don't want to put anything in my body that would prevent me from performing at 110 percent.

"Oh, that's right," my older sister Kimber said. "You have reporters in the audience tonight."

"Actually," Brice interjected. "Most of the major theater critics have already seen the show. A couple may still be there tonight, but most are probably writing their stories right now or have them sitting on a hard drive waiting to print as soon as the show has officially opened. The days of the critics showing up for opening night, then running to *The Times* to write a story to make sure it made it into the morning edition, are days gone by."

"Well, that takes some of the drama out of it," Kimber said.

"Today, most people know everything going on with a show before a critic has even seen the show," Brice admitted. "As your sister's agent, I work with the show's publicist to ensure Erica is seen in the best light possible."

"Does this mean you already know the reviews?" my mom asked, clearly interested in the conversation.

"No," Brice said flatly. "But I have a pretty good sense about how shows will be reviewed. Occasionally, a critic surprises me, but rarely."

"So, what do you think they will write about Erica?" Teresa asked. Ahh, my little sister, she always enjoys any chance to stir up a little drama. I'm almost amazed she's not the one who went into acting.

"Well, I'll keep my opinions to myself, but I've seen the show, and it's in good shape. Some of it depends on which critic writes the article. I know both critics from *The Times* have seen it, and those two have radically different tastes."

"Okay, so let's officially change topics," I said. "It's bad luck to talk about reviews before publication." It wasn't a true theater superstition, but it was one I made up on the spot.

"Oh, I know," Teresa said with a mischievous glint in her eye. She got this look on her face that said, "I'm about to stir the pot." She turned to look at me and asked, "Seeing anyone?"

"Teresa! You know better," my mother chastised.

I blanched and stammered for a second. Without thinking, I said, "You'll see my boyfriend tonight at the theater. He's a schoolteacher and looks amazing in his tux." As soon as the words had flown out of my mouth, I wished I could physically grab them and shove them back in. That little piece of news had gone over great with the family. Brice shot me a look that said, "What are you talking about?" And I sat there and smiled, thinking to myself, *What the elf was I thinking?*

As soon as lunch was over, I said I had errands to run and would see my family at the theater that night. I walked a couple of blocks with Brice. He never asked about the boyfriend issue, but I knew he wanted to. I didn't have any errands to run. I wanted to go home, hide in my apartment and rest before that evening's performance.

And, of course, prepare myself mentally for the conversation I planned to have with Kirk.

I was running lines one last time when there was a knock at my door. I glanced at my watch and was surprised to see that it was already 3:00 p.m. I looked at Bootsy, who hadn't stirred with the knock. I took my notebook and sat it on the coffee table next to the tea I was drinking. I reminded myself to breathe, stood, and walked to the door. I checked through the peephole to make sure it was Kirk.

I opened the door with a friendly, "Hey there."

He tilted his head and furrowed his forehead before saying, "Hello." His affect was flat.

I gestured for him to come inside. "Can I get you something? I made tea a bit ago, but I can make coffee, tea, hot cocoa…"

"I'm fine," he said, lifting a water bottle he had in his right hand. I shut the door and followed him into the apartment. Instead of sitting on the couch, he sat down at the kitchen table in the same chair Johnny had been in last night.

Before joining him, I walked over to the coffee table, picked up my tea, brought it back into the kitchen area and sat down.

"What are we doing, Erika?"

"What do you mean?" I asked, a little taken aback by Kirk's briskness.

"Sometimes, I think you like me. Then there are times when I feel that you're completely unavailable. I want to know which one is right."

"Okay, then," I started. "First, for the record, Asher was drunk the other night, and I didn't trust he'd get home on his own. We are not in any kind of relationship beyond a friendship. Sure, he's my past, which is where I plan on keeping him. If you had asked me two months ago if I would ever be friends with Asher Alexander, I wouldn't have said yes in a million years."

"What changed?"

"He's changed. He's not the same man I dated three years ago."

"So, you're friends now?"

"I wouldn't exactly say that we're friends. In all honesty, I don't know what we are. I know what we aren't. Before he was my boyfriend, he was my best friend. And I won't lie, I've missed my best friend. I found Jonny after Asher. Unlike Asher, Johnny knew who he was from the moment I met him, which was refreshing. Asher was a scared little gay boy who didn't know how to come out. Johnny was out and proud."

"Wait, so Asher's full-on gay now?" Kirk asked.

"Yep. Took him a while to realize it, but he's unambiguously gay now."

"Oh..." Kirk said. By the look on his face, I could tell that he was reprocessing the scene from the other night with this new information. "Wow, from what I saw the other night, I thought..." he let the words hang in the air.

"It's okay," I said, reaching out one of my hands hesitantly to grasp one of Kirk's. "You knew about my history with Asher, so seeing us like that..." I didn't feel the need to finish the sentence. "If I hadn't been so concerned with getting Asher to bed safely... I should have realized what it looked like."

"I shouldn't have jumped to conclusions. It's like my father always used to say, 'when you assume things, you make an ass out of you and me,'" Kirk said in a gruff voice.

"As for us," I started. "I like you. It took me a while to realize that. And I won't lie, I'm scared to death of dating a neighbor because good neighbors are so hard to find. I don't want to ruin that."

Kirk laughed. "I get it. But nothing ventured, nothing gained."

"You are full of wisdom today," I said with a smile.

"Yet another of my father's axioms of life...he had many."

"I know it's last minute, but I have a pair of tickets waiting for you at the box office tonight." Kirk started to say something, but I waved him off, saying, "You don't need to commit. And I don't know what Carissra and your plans are. I know this close to Christmas...it's entirely possible you already have a busy night ahead."

"We'll—"

"I'm freaked out enough about tonight," I started. It took me a second to realize I'd interrupted him. "Sorry about that. I didn't mean to cut you off. I'm a bit of a flake right now. And I don't want you to feel the need to commit one way or the other. I'd be ecstatic if you were there, and I'll completely understand if you have plans and can't be there. If you can't come tonight, I'll be happy to get you tickets for any show." I heard my cell phone go off playing the ringtone I use for my mother from across the room. "What now?" I groused. "Sorry, my family is in town. That's my mother calling. Give me a second." I stood and walked over to the charger next to the couch and lifted the phone. "Hey, Mom, now's not a great—"

"Your sisters somehow made it out to Staten Island and do not know how to get back."

"You've got to be kidding," I let out a quick huff. "Give me a second." I turned to Kirk and told him the situation. "I'm so sorry," I told him.

"No worries. I totally get family." He stood up from the table and came closer. "As for tonight—"

"They hopped on a train," my mother said into my ear, "but they're not sure where it's taking them. No, wait. They're on a bus now. Your father's talking to them on his cell." I could hear my father in the background. "Okay, I'll tell her. The bus is supposed to take them to Penn Station where they can catch the Ronkonkoma...what kind of word is that?"

"That's the Long Island Railroad!"

Kirk grimaced when he heard my side of the conversation. "I'll let you deal with this. About tonight—"

"So, they want to take the railroad?" Mom asked.

"No!" I said emphatically. "When they get back to Penn Station, they'll be in Manhattan. Have them go outside and get a cab back to the Marriott Marquis."

Kirk smiled and mouthed, "Good luck," as he motioned to the apartment's front door.

I mouthed back, "thanks." I was about to say something else when Mom cut me off again. Kirk left the apartment while I handled the crisis.

"How the heck did they end up on Staten Island?" I finally said. "It's not like it's that easy to absently end up there."

"Don't get all snippy with me. I'm not the one who needs a chaperone. I swear...I can't take your sisters anywhere."

I looked down at my watch and thought to myself, *I don't have time to deal with all this drama today.*

Chapter 28

By miracle of miracles, we got my sisters back to the hotel before I had to leave for the theater. To say that I had opening night jitters was an understatement of magnanimous proportions. Part of me was like, *it's just another opening. You've got this.* Another part of me was like, *it's the most critical opening of your career. Don't elf it up!* I got to the theater two hours early to give myself a respite from all the craziness. It also gave me an excuse to turn off my cell phone and let the chips fall where they would fall when it came to my family. They're adults. I had to trust they'd somehow get to the theater on time.

At six-thirty, there was a knock on my dressing room door. I got up and walked over and found the delivery woman with my dress. I thanked and tipped her before hanging it behind the door. To make sure everything was in there, I took a quick peek inside the garment bag. My dress was as amazing as it had been when I'd picked it out.

I threw down my yoga mat in my dressing room and ran through a quick sequence to get my body limbered up and to help center myself for the rest of the evening. I finished my last pose when there was another knock on my door.

"Come in," I said as I stood up.

Gladys walked into the room. "Just letting you know I'm here. Need anything?"

"Not now. Give me about twenty minutes, and I'll be ready to put my costume on. I need to apply makeup first."

"Sounds good. I'll be back in twenty. When I see Carlos, I'll let him know."

"Thanks."

After taking a quick shower, I applied my stage makeup. I'd finished the last touches when Gladys knocked on the door and entered with Carlos. They helped me get into my costume.

"The house is open," Serafina's voice said over the speaker system in my dressing room. "That's thirty minutes to the top of Act One."

Carlos helped me fix the microphone on the top of my head before placing the wig and ensuring it was secure.

"Fifteen minutes. This is your fifteen-minute call," Serafina said over the intercom.

"You've got this," Gladys said. "Break a leg."

Internally, I grimaced at the thought of breaking a leg on opening night…again. I had to remind myself that it was a theater trope, and she didn't want me to break a bone literally.

I did a quick touch-up of my makeup and made my way to stage right for the top of Act One. I was in the hallway when I heard Serafina call places, so I hurried and got to stage right as the auditorium lights flickered on and off, telling the audience to find their seats.

The auditorium lights dimmed, and San Nicolás walked onstage to thunderous applause. "Good evening, ladies and gentlemen and welcome to *The Naughty List*," San Nicolás' voice boomed throughout the auditorium. "We hope you enjoy our little production as much as we enjoy performing it." San Nicolás then read the standard list of things not to do at the theater, including don't record the show, don't take flash photography, and "unwrap those infernal candy wrappers before the show or you will get an elfin piece of coal in your stocking." As San Nicolás finished his curtain speech and walked off the stage, the lights dimmed one last time before the orchestra started the overture.

"For the love of Rudolph, let's do this!" Peeter said behind me.

"And for Santa's sake, don't elf it up!" Katherine added.

"Holy fudge! We've got this," I added right before it was time for us to enter stage right.

The show ran like clockwork. There were a few moments when the clapping at the ends of songs was longer than we were used to, but we got through Act One with zero problems. By the time we started the top of Act Two, the show was entirely in the swing of things, and I wasn't worried about anything. Muscle memory took over, and we sailed through the show. I was both fully present and watched the musical unfold around me like a specter watching from a distance.

As we headed into the eleven o'clock number, I was ready to go. When the music started, I took my place, and I sang like I'd never sung before. I put every ounce of anxiety, fear, depression, hope, excitement, and joy into those three minutes and thirty-three seconds of the song. When I hit that last high note, it was as effortless in my throat as breathing. When the downbeat hit, I watched the audience as my chest heaved up and down. I was surprised when one pocket of audience members jumped to their feet, followed by the other pockets. Before I knew it, the entire theater was standing and applauding. We'd had a great crowd all night long, but this was a first. I stood there smiling, doing my best to stay in character so we could move on to the next scene.

When the audience finally sat down, I exited stage left for my last quick-change into the wedding scene.

"That was amazing," Katherine said in the wings. "You're always good, but that was at a completely different level."

"I don't enjoy tooting my own horn, but I transcended there for a moment. At that moment, I was not Erika. I wasn't Tinsel Hollicane. I was love. I was Christmas. I was every hope and desire people have during the holiday season."

"Save it for your first press interview," Katherine joked. She looked at me seriously and added, "You were brilliant. Absolutely brilliant."

I didn't have time to respond because it was already time to head back on stage for the finale. The song went off without a hitch, and by the time we took our bows. I knew…I just sensed we honestly had a hit on our hands.

After the applause, the creative team and Rebekka Eldridge came on stage and said a few words. Then we sang the last refrain from "Christmas Wedding" one last time, the curtain closed, and we all broke out in hoots and hollers on stage. We'd opened a new Broadway musical.

"Okay, people," Eldridge said. "I know we've had our trials and tribulations getting this show put up. But I want all of you to know how proud I am of this company. I think my late husband is sitting in heaven smiling tonight as his dream has been fulfilled. I look forward to seeing everyone at the opening night party at Sardi's."

With that, we were summarily dismissed. I rushed back to my dressing room and found Gladys and Carlos ready to help me out of my costume, wig and microphone. Once they finished, I ran through the shower. Carlos promised to be back in to help me with my hair and makeup. True to his word, he was there in thirty minutes.

"What are you wearing?" he asked. "I want to make sure your makeup matches."

I unzipped the garment bag. The rainforest night green dress was made of crushed velvet with a twisted ruched high slit and matching full-length gloves. I had six-inch red stilettos dyed to match the ruby necklace and earrings I would wear.

"Wow," he said. "That's absolutely gorgeous. I will paint you to match the accessories without being overkill."

I sat down in the chair, and he went to work. I closed my eyes and let myself take a respite while he performed his magic.

"You can open your eyes now," Carlos whispered.

I did as told and was utterly shocked by the image staring back at me in the mirror. Now, I know I'm an attractive woman. You don't get to star in several Broadway musicals if you're not beautiful. But I was absolutely shocked by the beauty that stared back at me through the mirror. I teared up. I couldn't help myself. I had never looked more amazing in my entire life.

"No," Carlos demanded. "You will not cry. You are perfection. I am not doing your makeup again. So, put on a stiff upper lip and be gorgeous."

I centered myself and said, "Yes, sir."

I slipped on the heels, then put on the dress. Carlos helped me zip it up in the back. I hadn't brought a coat to wear over it because

I would not be spending much time outside. I would go from the theater to the car waiting for me. And after the party, a car would take me home.

I walked toward the back door where the cars were supposed to be waiting for us. I ran into Vladislav Nicolai in the hall. "Just the woman I was looking for," he said as I approached. I still was weary around the man, but I threw on my best smile. "We had your car taken around to the front entrance."

"Why?" I said with a bit of hesitation.

He threw a dismissive hand and said, "It was too crowded in the back, so we split it up at the last minute. I've been catching people and redirecting them."

"Thanks for letting me know." I headed to the lobby to take the escalator down to the first floor. The house staff were finishing the post-show cleaning. A few of them congratulated me as I walked through the lobby. I got to the top of the escalator and rode it down.

I looked down at the bottom of the escalator. The most gorgeous man I'd ever seen wear a black tux. He stood there holding a bouquet of white roses.

"Whoa, you look absolutely amazing," Kirk said as I took the step off the escalator.

"You clean up pretty nicely yourself there, Mr. Brewster."

He stood there for a moment, gawking at me. *I guess the dress is doing the trick.* He finally snapped out of it and handed me the roses. "These are for you."

"Thank you." I held them up to my nose and inhaled deeply. "I love the aroma of freshly cut roses."

"That's what Johnny told me," Kirk admitted with a smile.

I threw my arms around Kirk's neck and leaned in. I craved to feel his lips against mine. Kirk's arm slipped behind my lower back and pulled me closer until our lips touched. The kiss was tender and passionate. My right foot tried to pop, but my dress was too tight to fully pop. It didn't matter. In my heart of hearts, I was having what everyone longs for...the first kiss with their true love. I don't know how I knew Kirk was my soulmate, but in the deepest crevasse of my soul, I knew he was the man for me. There was a taste of peppermint on his breath. We stood like that for an eternity. The theater melted away and it was just the two of us. I opened my eyes for just a second. Kirk was leaning into me. And I swear his right leg was kicked back, putting his weight on his toe. So, one of us had a foot-popping experience.

I broke away from Kirk. "Whoa," he said, still a little breathless. "That was amazing." He leaned for another kiss, but a voice clearing beside us forced us to break away faster this time. I turned my head and was surprised to see Carlos and Vladislav Nicolai standing there.

"I'm here because a little birdie told me you may need a makeup touch-up," Carlos said, glancing at Nicolai.

"And I'm here because your car is waiting," Nicolai said with no emotion. *I guess he's a big softy after all.*

Carlos swooped in and retouched my makeup. I reached up and rubbed a lipstick smudge from Kirk's lips. When I was presentable by Carlos' standards, Nicolai opened the front door of the building and ushered Kirk and me out into the waiting town car.

"I'll be there soon," Carlos said. "Please, no hanky-panky in the car. I will not be there to fix your makeup when you exit the vehicle."

"Yes, Dad," I yelled to Carlos as Nicolai shut the car door behind us. When we were finally alone in the car, I looked down to find that we were holding hands. I hadn't realized what we'd done until we entered the car. It was different and yet so normal.

"Did Carissra come?" I asked. "In the shock of seeing you in your tux, I forgot to ask about her."

"She apologizes for not being here now, but she was beat. Johnny promised to see her back to our apartment before he and Amani join us at Sardi's."

I nestled in beside Kirk and let out a contented sigh. "I'm so sorry it took me so long to realize how much I liked you," I told Kirk, looking into his brown eyes.

"You don't know how long I've wanted to kiss you, Erika Saunders," Kirk admitted. "I was attracted to you the minute I met you."

"Really?" I said, gasping. "Why didn't you make a move?" I asked with a playful shove.

"I kind of thought you were out of my league. You're a big hotshot star. I'm a normal, average Joe schoolteacher."

"Kirk, I don't know if you stared at yourself in the mirror after putting on that tux, but you are anything but average. In fact, you will probably be the hottest guy at the party tonight, so don't even think about going home with someone else." Even with the streetlights that filled the car as we drove, I could see Kirk blush.

"Are you ready for this?" I asked.

"For what?"

"The spotlight."

"What do you mean?"

I took a second to gather my thoughts and gave him a brief rundown of what it would be like when we stepped out of the car at Sardi's. "There will be reporters. There will be lots of cameras and flashes. Just plaster on a smile."

"Oh geez," Kirk said. "I guess I hadn't thought about that part."

"No worries," I said, squeezing his hand. "I'm going to be right there by your side."

Chapter 29

The car slowed, and I saw the red carpet running from the street into the building. The snow fell lightly, but not enough to keep the paparazzi away. Thankfully, the length of red carpet we had to walk wasn't very long, so we wouldn't be standing outside long. "Are you ready for this?" I asked Kirk again right before the doorman opened our car door.

Kirk didn't have time to respond. He lifted one leg out of the car and onto the carpet before pulling out all six feet and two inches of himself from the car. I could hear the flashing lightbulbs from inside the vehicle. I scooched myself over on the leather interior and offered Kirk my hand. With his hand firmly grasped, I slowly slid one of my legs out, placing the heel firmly on the carpet. I pulled my weight forward as Kirk gently helped me out of the vehicle. Without skipping a beat, I smiled brightly for the cameras. Kirk stood there holding my hand, unsure what he was supposed to do next. I slipped my hand from his, slid it behind his back and drew him closer to me. He was my arm candy for the night, and I wanted the world to see.

"Ms. Saunders, who's your new man?" a young woman yelled from the other side of the red velvet rope, which was held up by a series of polished brass stanchion posts.

I turned and looked at the woman, smiled and said, "You don't recognize Kirk Brewster?" I shot the woman a look of mocked shock before I turned away.

"Why did you do that?" Kirk whispered in my ear. "You know they don't know who I am."

"True, but it will keep them busy for a while trying to figure it out." I grinned mischievously.

"I don't know if that's a good thing or a bad thing," Kirk admitted.

"It's like peeling off a Band-Aid. Being with me will put you in the spotlight. This will get you a burst of attention, then they'll be bored before Christmas is over," I told him. "It's a trick my old publicist taught me."

"Ms. Saunders and Mr. Brewster, over here," another reporter yelled.

I gently swerved Kirk in their direction and smiled. Kirk turned and gave them a startled look. We stood there for a couple more shots.

"Can I get a kiss for the camera?" another paparazzo yelled.

I turned and looked at the young man. "Now, look who's trying to land himself on the naughty list?" I asked playfully. Before the man could respond, I dragged Kirk the last couple of steps as the second doorman opened the door and we slipped inside.

Kirk immediately loosened up. I hadn't realized how much he'd tensed up during his first walk on a red carpet.

"You know, I totally would have kissed you out there," Kirk leaned down and whispered. "I'd kiss you anywhere."

"In the immortal words of the first showman, P. T. Barnum, 'always leave them wanting more,'" Johnny said from behind us. I spun to see him and Amani wearing matching red velvet tux jackets with black satin lining and black tux pants. Amani wore a black cummerbund and tie, while Johnny was wearing a dark green set.

"You two look amazing," I gushed.

"I know," Johnny said. "But not nearly as gorgeous as that tall drink of water you have hanging on your arm."

"Good evening to you, too, Johnny," Kirk said as his lip turned up slightly at the compliment.

"It's not fair," Johnny said. "Your man looks better in a black tux than I do. Oh, look, my director for *Passion* is here. I'm going to go schmooze," Johnny said, pulling Amani away.

Amani turned his head back to me and mouthed, "I'm sorry." I smiled.

"Erika," Ralph Seegers said, approaching me.

I put on my fake smile and said, "Ralph, good to see you. Is your wife here?"

"Umm...no...well, she...wasn't able to come tonight."

"Well, I hope she comes to see the show with your children," I said with the biggest smile. I loved the flustered look that crossed his face. "Maybe you can bring them backstage for a tour and an autograph."

The flash of fear crossed his face was quickly replaced with a smile as fake as mine. "That would be great," he lied. "Anyway, if you and Mr...."

"Brewster. Kirk Brewster," I said, turning and giving Kirk a peck on the cheek.

"If you and Mr. Brewster could follow me for some publicity shots," he stammered out.

We followed from a close distance. Kirk leaned down and asked, "What was that about?"

"Remember the married guy I went on a date with?" Kirk's eyes turned into round O's as he remembered the story.

"That's him?"

I nodded and kept smiling.

There was a *The Naughty List* logo banner backdrop put together in the restaurant's corner with the show's photographer. I walked over, and the photographer took a series of shots with Kirk and me.

"Can I get a few shots by yourself, Ms. Saunders?"

Kirk almost looked relieved not to be in the camera's lens for a few moments. Without waiting to be asked, Peeter and Katherine bounded up on either side of me and started posing. The photographs we took ranged from the deranged to the crazy, but they all fit our characters perfectly. I stood there and took pictures with a ton of people.

Kirk got himself a drink and found a high-top table nearby where he could watch the comings and goings of people. Johnny and Amani had their pictures taken with me. I then took photos with my parents, then pictures with my sisters. Then, the whole family got a group photo. I thought my fake smile wouldn't hold up long enough to get through them all.

When I was done taking photos, I turned and found the entire Saunders clan had surrounded Kirk at the table.

"This must be the young man you were telling us about," Mom said as I joined the group.

It took me a second to realize what she was talking about. *Oh geez, I totally forgot that I'd hinted I had a man at lunch.* I played it off smoothly and nodded before saying, "Kirk, I guess you've already met my parents and sisters."

"Yes, we were getting to know each other. They were telling me stories about you."

"Well, I hope they only told you about the good things," I joked.

Kirk shot one of his amazing smiles and nodded.

"Wow, it's the entire Saunders family," Asher said, suddenly coming up next to me.

"Well, if it isn't Asher Alexander...the heartbreaker," my mother said.

"Ouch," Asher said. "I can't say I don't deserve that."

"You deserve that and a lot more," Kimber said plainly, looking down her nose at Asher.

"Well, it was good to see you all," Asher lied before turning around and walking in a different direction.

"Well, that was fun," Kimber said when Asher was out of earshot.

"Wasn't it, though?" my mom asked. "I've wanted to give that boy a piece of my mind for years."

"Mother," I said the word, drawing it out. "Believe it or not, Asher and I are in a *good-ish* place right now. I don't think we'll ever be friends, but we've carved out a good working relationship." I looked from side to side before adding, "But it was fun watching him squirm...if only for a moment."

"It's nice to know I'm not the only one who doesn't like that guy," Kirk said, giving my mother a conspiratorial wink.

"Welcome to the team," my mother replied with her own wink.

There was suddenly a clinking of metal on crystal flute. I turned my head to find Rebekka Eldridge standing in the middle of the room.

"Thank you all for your attention. I know I already said everything I need to say earlier today, but I want to reiterate how proud I am of this company. I hope you all enjoy yourself this evening. But not too much...we have another show tomorrow!" There were a handful of laughs and polite applause. "Now, I know you are all wondering how the review roundup looks. Let's find out." Out of nowhere, Aarya was next to Eldridge with a stack of papers. Eldridge took a second and looked through the pile. She made a couple of *tsk*-ing sounds.

"You're killing us," Peeter yelled. Nervous laughter filled the restaurant.

"Well...I guess I won't prolong the suspense for too long," Eldridge said, looking up from the stack. From the look on her face, I didn't think it would be good news. Admittedly, with all the Botox floating around in the woman's face, it wasn't exactly easy to figure out what her emotions were. "We're a bona fide hit."

The room erupted into applause. I hugged Kirk with abandon and planted another kiss on his lips without worrying about my makeup.

Eldridge spent the next few minutes reading reviews from *The Times*, *The Post*, *Variety*, and a whole slew of other major publications. All the articles were absolutely glowing. Several of them referred to me and the eleven o'clock number. Kirk squeezed my hand every time my name was said in a review.

Once Rebekka finished reading the stellar reviews, we partied with abandon. The champagne was broken out, and we toasted the creative team, the cast, our family and friends, and the media for giving us a chance.

"Before I sit down," Rebekka finally said. "I want to toast the man who is not with us tonight, my dearly departed husband, Bernie. For those of you who don't know, The Maurer Theatre and *The Naughty List* were his dream and are now his legacy. Here's to you Bernie, may you rest in theater heaven." She lifted her champagne flute toward the sky as reverent cheers of "to Bernie" were heard around the room.

When the party finally wound down, I bid farewell to my parents and sisters. I made sure they had an Uber back to the hotel, though it was only a few blocks away. My town car was out front, and Kirk and I hurried from the building into the waiting vehicle.

"Well, that was a lot of fun," Kirk said as we snuggled against the leather backseat.

"I'm glad you enjoyed yourself. I never know how someone will react the first time they attend one of these events. They're a bit high-profile for many people."

"I think I can get used to this."

"Do you want to be a star, Mr. Brewster?"

"Oh gosh, no. But I don't mind being your plus one." He leaned over and kissed me on my cheek.

When the driver pulled up in front of the Manhattan Plaza, we dashed from the car into the building. The night guard on duty nodded, but didn't look up from the book he was reading.

The elevator ride to our floor was filled with flirtatious glances and a few stolen kisses. Kirk paused outside my door as I unlocked it.

"I wish this night didn't have to end," Kirk said.

"Me neither. This was totally my Cinderella fantasy. I look gorgeous, and a handsome prince came dressed in a tux fit for the gods." Kirk smiled. "Where did you get that tux?"

"I borrowed it from Johnny. He had one that was a bit too big on him, sitting in the back of his closet for years. Lucky me, it was the perfect fit. Well, it's tighter than I normally wear clothes."

"The fit is impeccable. It practically looks like you were sewn into it."

"It feels like I was sewn into it, too."

"I know that feeling," I admitted. "Trust me, if my makeup and hairstylist hadn't helped zipped me up, I don't know if I would have made it to the party."

"Oh, really?" Kirk said with a mischievous smile creeping across his face. "Need help unzipping your dress?"

"Why, Mr. Brewster," I started in my best Southern *Gone with the Wind* accent. "I do declare. Are you trying to see my back?"

"Of course not, Ms. Saunders," he replied in a pretty pathetic Brett Butler impersonation. "I want you to know my services are available should you need them."

"Well, I think I need your services," I said as I opened the door to my apartment.

I didn't bother closing the door because Kirk would, and he was right behind me.

Chapter 30

First Sunday in June

I sat in the chair in my dressing room as Carlos did his magic. We'd finished a matinee, and I had two hours before I had to be walking the red carpet at the Tony Awards. I opened an eye to see how things were progressing. I'd spent a lot of time staring at myself in a mirror, amazed by what Carlos could pull off. He had a way of taking this Iowa girl and making her look like a Broadway star, which I guess I was now.

"Calm down," Gladys said, crocheting on the couch. In February, she'd taken up crocheting as a hobby during her downtime. Gladys' hooks move quickly as yarn came together in a knot pattern while Carlos worked his magic on me. "I know you're a bundle of nerves. But you're fidgeting, which will make Carlos' job harder." I looked down at my right hand. I hadn't even realized how twitchy I'd been. I took a deep breath and forced my hand to relax.

There was a knock on my door. Without waiting for someone to say, "come in," Serafina poked her head into my dressing room. "I just got off the phone with the award show's director. We'd hoped they'd reconsider, but your Tony Award category is immediately after our number. The director said you'll have maybe ninety seconds, but probably more like eighty."

"That's longer than most of my quick-changes in the show," I joked.

Carlos tilted his head to the side and raised his eyebrows while looking at me in the mirror. I didn't need him to say anything to know what was running through his head at that moment. I looked at myself now and wondered how the team could take me out of my costume and get me looking like this again in a little over a minute.

"Don't worry, Serafina," Gladys said from her seat on the couch, "we'll have her ready when they call her name."

"If," I said suddenly, "If they call my name."

Sure, the pundits thought I was a shoo-in for the award. But never accept a Tony Award until your name is called. In all honesty, it was easier to tell myself repeatedly that it was not likely to happen. I was in the category with three other fantastic actors. As far as I was concerned, all of us deserved it. The nominees in my category had a private brunch last weekend to get to know one another. I'd seen some of them around the community, but I hadn't had a chance to get to know them as people.

"I know you're protecting your ego," Gladys said, "but you're going to win. I have a nose for these things."

"Although I thank you for your confidence," I said, "I don't want to put the cart before the horse. The last thing I want is to assume I'm going to win, then be shocked on national television when I lose. If, and when, I hear my name, I'll be surprised."

"Okay," Serafina said, clearly letting us know that this was a conversation she hadn't planned on being in the middle of. "I need to check in with the rest of the cast. Your car will be here at six-thirty on the nose. Please make sure you're at the backstage door. The pickup window to get you to Radio City is tight, so don't be late."

"Aye, aye, captain," I said. Serafina shook her head and closed the door.

"Now, stop talking. I need to work on your lips," Carlos instructed me. I did as commanded.

There was another knock on the door. "What now?" grumbled Carlos.

"Come in," Gladys yelled since I followed Carlos' instructions not to move my lips.

Kirk walked in wearing a tux. After returning the tux he'd worn to the opening party, I'd surprised him and bought him one of his own. He hated it when I bought him presents. I convinced him it was as much a present for me because I wanted him to be able to tux up at a moment's notice.

"How's the lady of the hour?" Kirk asked. With Carlos' permission, he came in and gave me a quick peck on the cheek.

"Good," Carlos said, raising an eyebrow. "You didn't mess up her makeup this time. You're learning."

"I had a skilled teacher. And I've been practicing as much as possible at home," Kirk said to Carlos with a conspiratorial wink.

"Eww... I don't want to hear about that," Gladys piped up, "My poor ears. They're innocent."

"Whatever, Momma," Carlos started. "You're the dirtiest elf in this place."

"And don't you forget it." Carlos and Gladys both cracked up at some inside joke. I shot Kirk a look through the mirror and shrugged.

A few minutes later, Carlos was finished with my hair and makeup. Gladys then helped me into my ink-blue dress embellished with sequins and crystals. It was an off-the-shoulder, floor-length evening dress. I had a maroon pair of Manolo Blahnik six-inch stiletto pumps. I had a small hand clutch with a few essentials that had been hand-dyed to match my pumps.

"Would you like to do the honors?" Gladys asked Kirk, gesturing to the zipper.

"I would love to," he said, standing behind me. I could feel his breath on the lower part of my neck as he reached down and gently caressed my skin for a second before he grabbed the zipper and lifted it. The dress fit me like a glove, a very tight glove. A glove that would not allow me to eat, drink, or breathe for the next couple of hours. I looked at myself in the mirror, and I looked like every Disney princess fantasy I had growing up.

"You look...stunning," Kirk said. "I am the luckiest man in New York City."

"You're the luckiest man in America," Gladys said. "Now, go. Have fun. I'll see you on stage."

"On stage?" Kirk asked.

"Yep," I said with a slight exhale. "My category is right after our musical number, so Carlos, Gladys, and a team of dressers will help get me out of my costume and back to looking like this." I gestured to the complete outfit. "And they'll do it all in less than sixty seconds."

"How is that possible?" Kirk asked.

"The power of theater," I said with a wink.

With that, I moved toward the door, and Kirk followed me. We wormed our way backstage, then down to the first level and out the back to find our limo waiting for us. The driver had the door opened when we exited the building, and we were whisked away to Radio City Music Hall. Then we waited in traffic. And waited a little longer. There was a spot for limos in front of the venue dropping off their cargo before walking the red carpet. When it was finally our turn, I turned to Kirk and said, "You ready for this?"

"I don't think I'll ever be ready for this, but I'm always ready to be there for you."

The car stopped, and an usher opened the door and helped Kirk out, who then turned and helped me out of the limo. My dress had an immediate effect on the crowd gathered. The combination of professional and fan cameras turned in our direction and we immediately began hearing people yelling our names. Kirk and I would pose, letting the professional and amateur photographers take our pictures, before we moved down the red carpet a little farther and did it again. I'd coached Kirk on how to walk a red carpet so he wouldn't be surprised by the many stops and starts as we walked.

We got inside Radio City, and an usher showed us to our seats. I had to sit on the aisle as a nominee and Kirk sat next to me. We stood in the aisle for a few minutes and talked with people in our general area.

"Ten minutes," a voice over the theater intercom suddenly said, "Please, find your seats." Immediately, an usher came running down the aisle to get everyone in the right seats.

The overture to the show started as a female announcer said, "Welcome to the Tony Awards. With special appearances by..." I tuned out the list of celebrities that would hand out awards. I squeezed Kirk's hand and leaned over. "This is all surreal. I've always dreamed of making it to the Tony's ever since I saw my first one on TV."

"I'm glad I can share this special occasion with you. Just remember, take it in...take it all in. No matter what happens tonight, enjoy every second."

I smiled as the host of the night came on stage singing and dancing. He performed a medley of songs that parodied previous Tony winners. The lyrics were inventive, but I wasn't surprised. Eugene Moses and Tyreek MacQueen had been asked to write the opening number, and they have been working on it for six weeks. They'd run a few of the more cerebral lyric ideas past the cast to see if they made sense.

The show flew by. Before I knew it, I was ushered away from Kirk and rushed backstage to change into my costume. The company was performing a medley that ended with my high note in the eleven o'clock number. The Tony medley wouldn't tell anyone anything about the show, but it would showcase enough of the show to drive up the box office on Monday. We'd been doing well with ticket sales, but not winning a Tony could lead to a summer slump, which could lead to the show closing. Like every show nominated, our performance at the Tony Awards was our one shot at getting butts in seats.

Gladys and Carlos made sure my costume, mic, and wig were put together before grabbing my evening wear and shoes and heading to their position off stage right, where I would meet them once the number was over. Only Gladys and Carlos had known that the dress they'd be putting me into was not the one I was already wearing. Not even Kirk had been told about the second ballgown I would wear after *The Naughty List*'s performance. Gladys, Carlos, and I had conspired to do something spectacular, in case my name was called. If I stepped back on that stage to accept my Tony Award, we wanted to shock and awe the audience.

"Are my elfin peeps ready for this?" Katherine said as we got to stage left for our entry.

"As I'm ever going to be," I said. "How bout you, Peeter?"

"I could do this medley in my sleep," he said, which caused all three of us to snicker since he'd tripped over the stage during our rehearsal.

"And we're back from commercial in three, two..." a voice called over the intercom system.

"Please welcome, two-time Tony Award winner Maeve McKenna."

What? My head spun to the backstage monitor since I couldn't see that part of the stage from the wings. The camera panned to the other side of the stage where an older, elegant woman walked out in a long black dress that hugged her in all the right places. I hadn't seen Maeve since the accident on stage, so how they managed to get her back to introduce the show was a surprise. In rehearsals earlier that day, we'd been told that some Hollywood starlet who was looking to make her Broadway debut in the fall would introduce the show.

"*The Naughty List* is a brand-new American Musical based loosely on the 1940 movie *Beyond Tomorrow*. Three elves concoct a game to see if the people of New York City should be exiled to Santa's naughty list...permanently. If you didn't know, I was cast in the show and had to bow out because of a little...accident." There were laughs in the auditorium. Maeve's *accident* was widely known in the theater community. "Here to perform a medley from the show are Tony nominees Caiden Wynter Jeanes, Tabatha Sharlene Thomson, Erika Lynsay Saunders, and the incomparable company of *The Naughty List*."

The downbeat hit, and my feet moved. For the next three and a half minutes, we danced, we sang, and we delivered. By the time I belted my high note, I could tell the audience was eating out of our hands. I hoped the audience at home enjoyed the performance as much. As the song ended, there were three seconds before the director motioned for the cast to move off stage as two Hollywood actors—who had gotten their starts on Broadway—entered the other side.

"The featured actress in a musical..."

I didn't have time to hear anything because I dashed off stage. The cast had been repeatedly told that I was to exit first, then they'd come off and go around the team of dressers and me.

Before I stopped walking, I discarded my shoes and my hands over my head. Two dressers removed the costume while Carlos made quick work of my wig, microphone and battery pack.

With the wig off, Carlos yanked the clips he'd used to pin my hair. He ran a brush through my natural hair as he styled it. "Lift your left foot," someone said. I complied. "Lift your right foot." I complied again. I didn't know who'd asked me to do that, but I was back in high heels.

"Step in." I glimpsed Gladys among the folds of fabric as she helped me into the gown. This dress was a green A-line V-neck floor-length silk dress with layers and layers of lace cut to look like tree branches. Around the middle was a red sash that highlighted my narrow waist, causing the bottom part of the dress to flare out like a Christmas tree with me as the angel sitting on top. Red crystal ornaments hung around the skirt, completing the festive look. On my head, Carlos placed a diamond-encrusted tiara with a single ruby that was on loan from a private collection. The tiara came with three security guards, who had watched Carlos take it from the case and place it on my head. He hadn't told me the cost, but I'd looked it up online. I was only wearing a half-million dollars in jewels on my head. The other half-million was around my neck in a gorgeous diamond necklace with a five-carat ruby pendant.

"You're ready," I heard Gladys say. "You got this."

I took three steps forward to the side of the stage and waited on the mark I was told to stand on.

"The nominees for Best Performance by an Actress in a Featured Role in a Musical are. Julia Hardy, *The Hallow Men*." A polite round of applause was heard. "Carolyn Klimonski, *Passion*." More applause. "Winnie Matherson, *Gamer's Revenge*." Applause. "And Erica Lynsay Saunders, *The Naughty List*."

The television producers would display my headshot for the television audience. We weren't sure how long the quick-change would take, so the producers had scrapped the idea of zooming in on me for a closeup backstage in case we weren't ready yet.

"And the American Theatre Wing's Tony Award goes to..."

It may sound cliché, but my entire career flashed before my eyes. I saw myself as a young girl performing in school plays, then high school musicals. Then I started performing in college, then in regional theater productions. As soon as I'd finished college, I got my first Equity tour and saw half the country belting an E6 nightly in *Wicked*. Then I took a leap of faith, quit the tour, and returned to New York. I thought of the opening night of *The Faith Healer* and everything that happened over the next three years. I remembered bumping into Kirk right outside my door as I rushed to an audition, and he moved in next door. That singular moment in time would define my life more than I ever could have predicted. I found the Broadway show that would change my life forever. And I found my passion again.

"...Erika Lynsay Saunders."

I stood there. The cameraman waved his finger in my direction to let me know we were live. It took my brain a second to catch up. I'm sure it was only seconds, but I felt like I stood there for a day, lost in a haze of memories, as my brain finally registered my name.

My knees buckled slightly as my hand moved to cover my mouth. Tears started escaping. Somewhere from my left, I heard a stage manager yell, "Move!" My feet started walking before my brain could catch up.

I left the side curtain and walked toward the couple announcing the award. One held the envelope with my name, and the other held the Tony Award. The starlet gave me a quick hug and said congratulations. The guy hugged me too before I stood before Radio City Music Hall looking up and over the entire crowd.

"Wow, this place looks enormous from up here," were the first words to come out of my mouth. The room erupted in laughter. "That was so not in my acceptance speech," I followed up, which was greeted by more laughter. I paused and took in the entire theater. "I want to thank the American Theater Wing and the Tony voters... Wow, I just said that. It's like I'm in a dream right now." I looked over to where Kirk was standing on his feet still. Even from the stage, with the bright lights in my eyes, I could make out his beautiful face. "I love you, Kirk Brewster. And I love you Carissra, who is watching this at home. I want to thank my family. I love them, too. I want to thank my best friend, Johnny, who you saw earlier this evening in the number from *Passion*. I want to thank *The Naughty List's* amazing cast and crew, who help me remember the joy of musical theater each and every night. I thank my agent, Brice Stark, for making me go on this audition when I wasn't sure I wanted to." The orchestra started again, and I could tell that I was being told to wrap it up, so I just said, "I'm sure I'm missing people, and I'm sorry. I really am. I thank everyone I know and have ever known. All of you have helped me get to this place tonight. Without everyone, I would not be standing here today." The music continued to swell as I loudly said, "Go out and do something to put yourself on *The Naughty List*!" I hefted the Tony Award over my head as I was shuffled off stage left, and the next pair of presenters walked from the wings on stage right and started speaking.

The cast huddled backstage, waiting to greet me. I laid eyes on Gladys and burst into tears.

Katherine hugged me first. "I knew you'd win. I told ya, girl!"

Next, it was Peeter. "And to think, I didn't even like you at first."

Then Carlos and Gladys were there, and both were crying, making me cry more.

"I totally forgot to thank you," I blurted out. "How did I forget to thank you?"

"Seeing you get that award was all the thanks I'd ever need," Gladys said.

"I could have used a shout-out," Carlos joked, "but you had other things on your mind." He gave me a quick hug. "Now stop crying. I used waterproof makeup, but it can only live up to a minor flood."

Then Asher hugged me, followed by a parade of Eugene, Tyreek, and Mable. I didn't know where they'd come from. San Nicolás embraced me and said something in Spanish. I probably could have translated if my brain had been working properly, but I had no idea what he said. I then saw Rebekka Eldridge. She looked at me and said, "Good job. I was right. I hired the right woman." I wanted to make a smart-alecky comment, but then I saw Kirk being escorted backstage.

I ran to him and threw my arms around him. He spun me around, my feet leaving the ground as we twirled, which wasn't an easy feat because of my giant ballgown.

"I love you, Erika Saunders," he whispered. "Or is that now *Tony Award winner*, Erika Saunders?" He cracked a smile as he put me down.

Are the television cameras catching all this? I didn't care. It would make great TV.

He kept holding my hand. He then dropped to one knee.

"Erika Lynsay Saunders, I know this may not be the best time, but I think it's the right time." I saw him produce a Tiffany blue box before he opened it. It was the exact dream engagement ring I'd told Johnny about a couple of years earlier. "Will you marry me?"

"Yes," I practically screamed. I couldn't get the word out of my mouth fast enough.

Kirk slid the ring out of the box and onto my finger. I lifted him off the ground, brought his face toward mine and got lost in a momentary kiss. There was applause around us. Only then did I realize that Asher, Katherine, and Peeter were holding out their cell phones. I looked at the phones. My parents, sisters, Carissra, and Johnny watched the proposal as it was live-streamed.

I looked into Kirk's beautiful brown eyes. "I love you. I love you so much. I can't wait to be your wife."

"I love you, too. I can't wait to be Mr. Kirk Saunders or maybe Brewster-Saunders."

I kissed him again.

Everything else faded around us. I held a Tony Award in one hand, an engagement ring on the other, and one-million-dollars in jewels that were eyed by three guards who looked very nervous about everything.

The End

Drama Bill

DRAMA BILL

MAURER THEATRE

The NAUGHTY List

THE MAURER THEATRE

47th & Broadway
An Eldridge Organization
Rebekka Eldridge, *Chairman & CEO*

Noam Lavie Weiss, *General Manager*   Vladislav Nicolai, *House Manager*

BERNIE ELDRIDGE
PRESENTS

The NAUGHTY List

BOOK BY
MABEL WÄGNER

MUSIC BY
EUGENIUS MOSES

LYRICS BY
TYREEK MACQUEEN

STARING

ASHER FRASER ALEXANDER   PEETER ESTEBAN GASPARI
CAIDEN WYNTER JEANES   KISHOR KHATRI
KERRIE PATIENCE KLARK   KATHRINE KLOETEN
JOCELYN QUINN MICHAELS   MACY PARNEL QUEEN
ERIKA LYNSAY SAUNDERS   TABATHA SHARLENE THOMSON

INSPIRED BY ADELE COMANDINI'S SCREENPLAY
BEYOND TOMORROW

DIRECTION BY
ASIER ZLOTA SAN NICOLÁS

MUSIC DIRECTION BY
GERARD BARTHOLOMEW

CHOREOGRAPHY BY
DIVYA PHILOMENA KAPPEL

COSTUME DESIGN BY
LUCINDA GAYLE

STAGE MANAGEMENT BY
SERAFINA PORCHER

CAST

Arlene Terry-Ball	Kerrie Patience Klark
Billy James	Caiden Wynter Jeanes
Blitz Nightwish	Peeter Esteban Gaspari
Coleen Lawrence	Tabatha Sharlene Thomson
Icelyn Candywine	Kathrine Kloeten
Josef the Butler	Kishor Khatri
Madam Tanya	Jocelyn Quinn Michaels
Phil Hubert	Asher Fraser Alexander
Tabby Terry-Ball	Macy Parnel Queen
Tinsel Hollicane	Erika Lynsay Saunders

ACT I

"**Christmas in New York**" Engineers Icelyn Candywine and Blitz Nightwish work furiously to finish toy designs for Santa, even though it is already December. Tinsel Hollicane, a third elf, arrives with presents for all. "**Christmas, Nothing but a Merchants Holiday.**" The three elves go home to their house where Madame Tanya, a retired elf, is preparing for dinner.

When the guests cancel at the last minute, Tinsel comes up with an idea to obtain new guests for dinner. "**Confusion to our Critics and Merry Christmas**" Each elf throws out a wallet containing one-thousand dollars and his business card for a townhouse in Manhattan, where they stay when not in the North Pole. Icelyn's is found by Arlene Terry, who merely gives the money to her driver and discards the wallet. "**Heart of Gold with Other People's Money**" However, the other two are returned by more considerate people, Texas cowboy Billy James and teacher Coleen Lawrence. They stay for dinner and soon become good friends with the three men and Madame Tanya. "**Stay and Have a Good Cheer**" Through an open window, they hear carolers. The group goes over and listens.
"**Christmas Carolers**" Everyone is in good cheer and the spark of love starts between Billy and Coleen as they leave the townhouse and venture back into the winter weather. "**Goodnight Texas, Goodnight Teacher**"

The elves have to leave and go to work, but leave Madame Tanya to watch over them and report back to them on Billy and Collen's love affair. Madame Tanya invites Billy to stay with her while the elves are away. **"Stay with Me"** Madame Tanya spies on them as they date. One day Coleen and Billy are walking through the park when me mentions marriage. **"You Just Proposed to Me"**

Billy goes on an open audition where he runs into the leading actor, Arlene Terry. Arlene is immediately smitten and tells her manager, Phil, that she just must have that boy. Phil makes some comment about her being bad. She responds, if that's bad **"Put me on the Naughty List."**

Billy runs home to tell Coleen and Madam Tanya the good news. He jumps into rehearsals with Arlene, but ends up spending a little too much time with her.

Billy starts rehearsals with Arlene and he becomes a bit out of his element and starts to neglect Jean. The elves are a bit worried. **"He'll Drink Too Much, and Laugh Too Much"**

ACT II

"He's a Hit" The show has open and doing very well. Billy blows of dinner with Coleen again. **"Another Message from Billy"** Arlene makes the moves on Billy. **"Someone Who Really Loves Me"** The elves are watching from a distance and are not too happy with Arlene who has clearly bamboozled Billy. **"Smooths as Silk"** Arlene's ex-wife, Tabby, comes by Arlene's house and bangs on the door before Billy and Arlene can be compromised. Billy leaves by the back door, but not before Coleen persuades him to meet her later for dinner.

When Billy gets home, he finds Coleen, the Elves, and Madam Tanya there. Billy says he promised Arlene he'd go with her to Sardi's. Coleen sings **"Success, It's What I Wanted for You."**

At Arlene's, she's let in Tabby. The two fight and Tabby sings **"There's Always Been Someone Else"** Tabby leaves and slams the door. Walking down the street she sees Billy walking her way. Billy who is clearly contemplating not going to dinner with Arlene. **"On the Trail I'd Turn Back"**

Billy meets Arlene for dinner at a face restaurant. They're asked to sing a song. **"Give Us a Song"** During the middle of the song, Tabby races inside, draws a gun and shoots them both.

Billy is rushed to the hospital and not expected to live. Madam Tanya begs the elves to let help Billy. Tinsel Hollicane sings **"Give Him a Chance to Live."** The elves you're their magic to keep him from Dying. He wakes up, re-proposes to Coleen and the two get married. **"Christmas Wedding"**

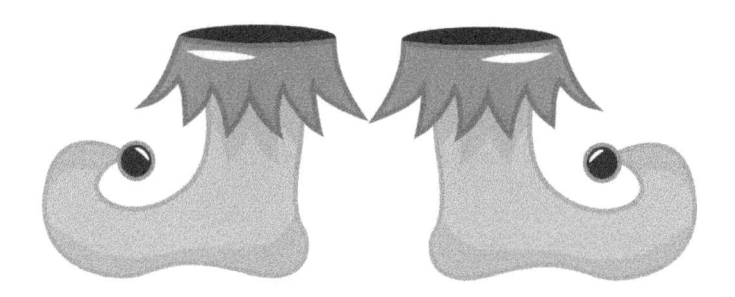

Trademarks Acknowledgment

The author acknowledges the trademarked status and trademark owners of the following wordmarks mentioned in this work of fiction:

Feinstein's/54 Below: 54 Below LLC
9-5 (musical), Dolly Parton, Patricia Resnick
A Christmas Carol: Charles Dickens
A Little Night Music: Stephen Sondheim, Hugh Wheeler
Actor's Equity: The Actors' Equity Association
Áth Cliath (The Dubs): Gaelic Athletic Association
Al Hirschfeld Theater: Jujamcyn Theaters
Alice, Warner Bros. Television
All-Ireland Senior Football Championship: Gaelic Athletic Association
Amazon: Amazon Inc.
Annie: Charles Strouse, Martin Charnin, and Thomas Meehan
AirPods: Apple Inc.
Avenue Q, Jeff Whitty, Robert Lopez, and Jeff Marx
Band-Aid: Johnson & Johnson Corporation
Barnum, Cy Coleman, Michael Stewart, and Mark Bramble
Beauty and the Beast: Alan Menken, Howard Ashman, Tim Rice, and Linda Woolverton
Boston Red Sox: Boston Red Sox Baseball Club Limited Partnership
Botox: Allergan, Inc.
Broadway Dance Center:
Bye, Bye Birdie: Charles Strouse, Lee Adams, and Michael Stewart
Cabaret: John Kander, Fred Ebb, and Joe Masteroff

Calamity Jane: Sammy Fain, Paul Francis Webster, Ronald Hanmer, and Phil Park
Carrie (book), Stephen King
Carrie (musical): Lawrence D. Cohen, Dean Pitchford, and Michael Gore
Château des Rontets,
Chicago, John Kander, Fred Ebb, and Bob Fosse
Children, Go Where I Send Thee: Original Composer Unknown
Cinderella: Giambattista Basile
Circle in the Square: The Paramount Group
Company: Stephen Sondheim, George Furth
Coney Island Polar Bear Club
Court of Master Sommeliers
Culinary Institute of America
Deck the Halls: John Ceiriog Hughes, Thomas Oliphan
Discovery Channel: Warner Brothers Discovery
Disney: The Walt Disney Company
Doctor Dolittle: 20th Century Fox
Donmar Warehouse: Donmar Warehouse Productions Ltd.
Dr. Seuss' How the Grinch Stole Christmas! The Musical: Timothy Mason
Duane Reade: Walgreens Boots Alliance
Elias Howe: New York City Public Schools
Facebook: Meta Platforms, Inc.
FaceTime: Apple Inc.
Fiorello H. LaGuardia High: New York City Public Schools
Follies: Stephen Sondheim, James Goldman
Folsom Street Fair: Folsom Street
Forbidden Broadway: Gerard Alessandrini
Funyuns: Frito-Lay North America, Inc.
Gentleman's Quarterly (*GQ*): Condé Nast
Gershwin Theatre: Nederlander Organization
Girl Scout: Girl Scouts of the United States of America
Godspell: Stephen Schwartz, John-Michael Tebelak
Gone with the Wind: Metro-Goldwyn-Mayer
Grinch: Dr. Seuss Enterprises, L.P. Geisel-Seuss Enterprises, Inc.
Gypsy: Jule Styne, Stephen Sondheim, and Arthur Laurents

Hallmark Channel: Hallmark Licensing LLC
Hamilton: Lin-Manuel Miranda
Hanukkah, Oh Hanukkah: Mordkhe (Mark) Rivesman
Havana Central: Havana Central LLC
Hello, Dolly!: Jerry Herman, Michael Stewart
How the Grinch Stole Christmas: Dr. Seuss
il Buco Alimentari & Vineria,
Into the Light: Lee Holdridge, John Forster, Jeff Tambornino
iPad: AVC Group LLC
iPhone: Cisco Technology Inc.
I, Tonya: Universal Pictures Home Entertainment
JFK International Airport: Port Authority of New York and New Jersey
John's of Times Square: John's Pizzeria
Juniors: Junior's Cheesecake
Kiss Me Kate, Cole Porter, Bella and Samuel Spewack
Klonopin: Hoffman La Roche Company
Law and Order: Universal Television
Light in the Piazza, Adam Guettel, Craig Lucas
Long Island Rail Road: Metropolitan Transportation Authority
Mack and Mabel, Jerry Herman, Michael Stewart
Macy's: R.H. Macy & Company
Mame: Jerry Herman, Jerome Lawrence, and Robert Edwin Lee
Manhattan Plaza: Related Companies
Manolo Blahnik: Manolo Blahnik International Limited
MetroCard: Metropolitan Transportation Authority
Merrily We Roll Along, Stephen Sondheim, George Furth
Marriott Marquis, Marriott International, Inc.
Mountain Dew: PepsiCo, Inc.
National Broadcasting Company: NBCUniversal
New World Stages: The Shubert Organization
New York Yankees: Yankee Global Enterprises, LLC
Netflix: Netflix, Inc.
New International Version, Biblica
Oklahoma, Richard Rodgers, Oscar Hammerstein II
Parade, Jason Robert Brown, Alfred Uhry
Passion: Stephen Sondheim, James Lapine

Peanuts, Charles Schultz
Playbill: Playbill, Inc.
Port Authority Midtown Bus Terminal: The Port Authority of New York and New Jersey
Perez Hilton: Mario Armando Lavandeira, Jr.
Pussycat Dolls: Universal Music Group
Radio City Christmas Spectacular: Mark Waldrop
Radio City Music Hall: Tishman Speyer Properties
Ragtime: Stephen Flaherty, Lynn Ahrens, and Terrence McNally
Rolling Stone: Penske Media Corporation, Wenner Media LLC
Royal Jordanian Airlines:
Rudolph the Red-Nosed Reindeer: Robert L. May
RuPaul's Drag Race: World of Wonder Productions
Sardi's:
Second City: The Second City, Inc.
Sex in the City: Darren Star Productions
South Pacific: Richard Rodgers, Oscar Hammerstein II, and Joshua Logan
Speedo: Speedo International Limited
Spiderman: Turn off the Dark: Bono, The Edge, Julie Taymor, Glen Berger, and Roberto Aguirre-Sacasa
Starbucks: Starbucks Coffee Company Corporation
Star Wars: George Lucas, Disney Enterprises Inc.
Sunset Boulevard: Andrew Lloyd Webber, Don Black, and Christopher Hampton
The Addams Family: Charles Addams
The Assassination of Jesse James by the Coward Robert Ford: Warner Brothers Pictures
The Audience: Peter Morgan
The Book of Mormon: Trey Parker, Robert Lopez, and Matt Stone
The Drama Book Shop: Drama Book Shop II, LLC
The Grudge: Columbia Pictures
The Last Five Years, Jason Robert Brown
The New York Post: NYP Holdings Inc.
The New York Times: The New York Times Company
The Phantom of the Opera: Andrew Lloyd Webber
The Pirate Queen: Claude-Michel Schönberg, Alain Boublil

The Producers: Mel Brooks, Thomas Meehan
The Smurfs: Peyo Productions
The Sopranos: HBO Entertainment
The Time New York: Dream Hotel Group
The Tony Awards: American Theater Wing, The Broadway League
The Washington Post: Nash Holdings
Thoroughly Modern Millie: Jeanine Tesori, Dick Scanlan, and Richard Morris
Tiffany's: Tiffany & Co.
TKTS: Theatre Development Fund
TMZ: Fox Corporation
Trinity College:
Tuck Everlasting: Chris Miller, Nathan Tysen, Claudia Shear, and Tim Federle
The Twelve Days of Christmas: Traditional with additions by Frederic Austin
Uber: Uber Technologies Inc.
Variety: Penske Media Corporation
Wellbutrin: GlaxoSmithKline
Wicked: Stephen Schwartz, Winnie Holzman
W;t, Margaret Edson
Wonderful Town: Leonard Bernstein, Betty Comden, Adolph Green, Joseph A. Fields, and Jerome Chodorov
Yale University:
YMCA: Jacques Morali, Victor Willis
YouTube: Google Inc.
Zoom: Zoom Video Communications Inc.

The author gratefully acknowledges any trademarks or registered trademarks that may have been inadvertently omitted from this list.

About the author

Jason Wrench is the author of *12 Days of Murder* (November 2021) and *Till Death Do Us Wed* (February 2022); the Up on the Farm series: *Finding a Farmer* (August, 2022), *Bewitched by the Barista* (September, 2022), *Sanctuary for the Surgeon* (January, 2023), and *Catching the Composer* (May 2023); *Wolf Island* (October, 2022); and the Love and Liquidation Series: *Boy Bands and Bullets* (November 2023), *A Choreographed Coup* (April 2024), and *Rhythmic Reclamation* (June 2024) all with Pride Publishing. He's also the author of *The Veil* and *Jekyll/Hyde*. And translated *Manor: A Novella by Karl Heinrich Ulrichs* (August 2024). And he's the man behind the cozy mystery pen name, J. J. Justice.

When he's not writing novels, he's a college professor at SUNY New Paltz in the Department of Communication. In that capacity, he's authored or edited twenty academic books, thirty-five plus research articles, and numerous chapters in other books.

In his downtime, he loves reading/writing, Broadway, coffee, and his puggle, Max (7-year-old) and Branch (6-year-old).

He's a member of the Romance Writers of America and the Textbook and Academic Author Association.

You can find his other works on his website: https://jasonwrench.com/

Milton Keynes UK
Ingram Content Group UK Ltd.
UKHW042006281024
450365UK00003B/203